Way Shower:

Light and Shadow

KUDOS FOR WAY SHOWER: LIGHT AND SHADOW

Janice Dietert presents another fast paced journey with many well written twists and turns in *Way Shower: Light and Shadow*. By blending multiple worlds and powerful insights, Janice Dietert provides an entertaining as well as profound reading experience. Join a feisty protagonist on a perilous quest to free her powerful, dare I say 'hunky', guardian angel and step into her own growing alignment with all that is good. The battle between the dark and the light becomes personal as those she loves are threatened. The connections between here and there, this world and that, are blurred in such an intriguing manner that the reader is caught up in the desires of the characters and carried along to a very satisfying conclusion.

- K. Hauger

Light and Shadow is the third book in the Way Shower trilogy... This time Ellen is able to pass through the veil while she is dreaming.

Ellen is definitely a feisty heroine, but one whose curiosity enables her to ask questions and think of possibilities that break her out of her box of limitations. She reminds us to get out of our head and start listening and feeling with our heart.

Ellen has another physical crises which requires surgery. While she is under the anesthetic, she goes deeper into her capabilities to learn more about reading light and shadows. She learns that to truly understand the light she must also understand... the shadows and how the meaning of light includes this understanding.

At the end, she understands that some of those life lessons were particularly hard in order to get her attention. Old beliefs and ways of doing things have to be scattered for the new way to be born, put into practice and then accepted as a new level of understanding.

I loved this book as much as I did the other two. Janice captivated my interest with this story and I would not be surprised if there were more books to follow... This book makes my heart feel good!

- J. Shaw

Also by Janice Dietert

Way Shower: Redemption
Way Shower
Shadows of the Anunnaki: Earthbound
Shadows of the Anunnaki: Origins on Nibiru
Between Two Worlds
Son of the Star

Coauthored with Rodney R Dietert, PhD

Science Sifting
Strategies for Protecting Your Child's Immune System
The Edinburgh Goldsmiths I: Training, Marks, Output, and Demographics
II
Compendium of Scottish Silver II
Scotland's Families and the Edinburgh Goldsmiths

Cover Art by: Kip Ayers
        www.kipayersillustration.com

Way Shower: Light and Shadow/

ISBN 978-0-578-13832-9

Dietert Publications
Lansing, NY

Way Shower:

Light and Shadow

CHAPTER 1

Ellen Pompea, a petite, young looking woman in her early 40's with inquisitive blue eyes and red blonde hair, stood observing her Guardian Angel, Daniel, as he paced through her dining room. She hadn't always been able to see him, however, surviving an accident-induced coma then near fatal pneumonia had left her always on the brink of two worlds. She had visited his reality each time she had been near death. The first time had brought the revelation that she was a Way Shower, a special human who was the product of a human female and a male angel, specifically an Archangel. The second visit had shown her the abilities she possessed that had been latent till then.

As she watched Daniel pace, Ellen's mind drifted back. For one, her Guardian Angel was also an Archangel. Over 6 1/2 feet tall and with a solid, muscular build, his finely chiseled features and crystal blue eyes hid a heart whose depths had yet to be plumbed. They had been through so much together, both here in her reality when he had protected her from an invader in the night and in his own world. When she tried to review it all, the sheer scope of the challenges they had faced together overwhelmed her, and Ellen pushed the thoughts aside.

For now, she stood in the kitchen focusing on his pacing and watching his great wings brush against the walls in her hallway. Finally, she shook her head, put the knife on the chopping board and wiped her hands on her apron. She stepped into the dining room placing herself in front of him blocking his forward movement.

"Daniel, you're making me weary just watching you," Ellen

protested.

He put his hands on his hips and blew his breath out in a snort. "Then stop watching!"

"Yeah, wish I could," she retorted. "But it's pretty impossible. What's bothering you? I don't think I've ever seen you this agitated before."

He smiled tensely. "You didn't see me before that guy broke into your house."

Ellen drew in a sharp breath. "True. Then...you knew the attack was coming?" she asked frowning.

He shook his head, his long blond hair flowing over his shoulders. "I knew something was coming and that it was big."

She studied him pensively. "Well, since the Embodied One promised I wouldn't have to nearly die in order to cross into your world again, and we built the Bridge of Dreams, I take it it's nothing death defying."

Ellen spoke of a bridge she had helped the Way Showers who lived in Daniel's reality create. Up till its construction, the only way a Way Shower could enter the angelic realm was by coming close to death in the human realm. Frequently, they had the choice of whether to stay in the angelic realm or return to their human body. But often, returning had not been an option given the severity of their injuries or illness, yet their lifespan had not been fully lived. So, they remained in the angelic realm. Now that the Bridge of Dreams was in place, no one had to come near to death in order to make the crossing, including Ellen.

Daniel looked up and studied her for a while. Finally, he shook his head in frustration. "I cannot see what is coming," he admitted. "I cannot even get an inkling. All I can see is darkness."

"And that doesn't bode well," she surmised.

He shook his head.

"Is there any way we can find out?" Ellen wondered.

"I need to see the Embodied One," Daniel replied.

"You can't just go see him while I'm asleep?" she asked.

Daniel shook his head. "The way this feels, I don't dare leave you."

Ellen glanced at the calendar. "Well, Robert is in Frankfurt for that conference this week. Now would be a good time for me to cross the Bridge of Dreams."

She spoke of her scientist husband who was also a Way Shower.

Daniel considered this. "I could ask Michael to station a guard on

2

the house."

"Seems like that would be safe enough," Ellen replied.

"You don't mind?" he pressed.

Ellen shook her head and smiled. "While you have your meeting, I can go see how the brothers are doing. For fraternal twins who took separate paths...."

"Priesthood and wizardry," Daniel remarked chuckling.

"They have the capacity to get themselves into trouble."

Daniel smiled. The brothers had taken on Ellen as if she were a younger sister and had saved her life once before.

"I agree," he said with a sigh of relief. "They probably need a visit for a good sorting out."

"And you can have your serious pow wow," Ellen added.

"Then, it's settled," Daniel said with finality. "We'll go tonight."

That evening, after a cheery Skype session with Robert, Ellen got ready for bed and turned down the covers. Before climbing in, she watched Daniel send a mental message to Michael. Within moments, four large, battle angels appeared. Daniel quickly assigned them to posts outside the house. Satisfied that her body would be well-protected, he watched her climb into bed then sat beside her holding her hand.

"I will hum your song," he told her, "and help you transition from here to the Between Worlds. I'll meet you there and help you cross over."

Ellen smiled up at him and squeezed his hand.

Daniel laid his free hand on her chest over her heart. He began a low, melodic hum, and Ellen felt warmth seep into her chest spreading throughout her body. Her eyelids fluttered then closed. One moment, she was listening to Daniel's warm voice; the next she was standing on a stone path that led to a round room with glass doors set in the midst of a cavern wall. Daniel stood at her side.

Ellen smiled brightly. "It will be so good to see Nathan again," she said hurrying forward.

Daniel shared her smile and followed.

Twice before they had been given permission by the Embodied One to have children. Hope, their daughter, had fulfilled Daniel's secret desire to be a birth parent and had been the means by which they had healed Ellen's comatose body. Nathan had been conceived in another dimension and was now the warden between the human world and the Bridge of Dreams.

Ellen jogged up to the clear door waiting while it whooshed open. She stepped inside and paused a moment quietly observing her

3

son. Though human in shape with an enormously powerful build, he also possessed feline qualities. His skin was striped between gray-blue and silver, lightly under the surface. His shoulder length hair was silver. When he turned and trained his amber cat's eyes on her, he smiled and the whiskers at the corners of his mouth turned up. Ellen hurried to him for a warm hug, and he purred softly in her ear. Daniel was next, though his hug was less warm and practiced.

"Aren't you getting lonely and bored being here all by yourself?" Ellen asked.

Nathan shook his head. "You forget. Cat's are solitary. But I've not been alone. Someone passed through just a couple of days ago."

Ellen's eyebrows peaked, and she glanced to Daniel for his reaction.

"They were clean?" Daniel immediately wanted to know. "No Minions?"

The amber eyes blinked slowly and Nathan nodded. "Perhaps you will meet up with him," he suggested.

"I may have to make it a point," Ellen replied.

"Well, until then, I have some business to take care of with the Embodied One," Daniel reminded her.

Ellen nodded absent-mindedly, reached up to kiss Nathan's cheek then allowed Daniel to lead her out the back door, down the tunnel to the chasm and across the Bridge of Dreams. She looked up at the four enormous Dolphins who hovered beside the Bridge. Their eyes glowed bright red as they scanned the pair then returned to normal allowing Daniel and Ellen to cross to the other side.

Once there, Daniel put his arms around her, Ellen set her obsidian pendulum swinging, and they were suddenly sucked backward into the Facility that Raphael had previously built and that his technical healers now ran. The Facility itself was a Dome of green glass that had been placed together like sections of an orange. In the center close to Daniel and Ellen was an emerald green crystal column. Holders spread out from the central column like the spokes of a wheel, and each holder contained an exquisitely carved, clear crystal chamber. Just beyond each chamber stood a hollow crystal column. Each chamber had once held a single Way Shower to which it was attuned, while the columns had held the corresponding Guardian. Using tones and harmonic resonance, Raphael had attuned the individual Way Showers to one another thereby allowing them to work together to create the Bridge of Dreams.

When Daniel and Ellen appeared in the Facility, heads turned. One

4

healer, Nariel, a tall slender woman with dark blond hair, crystal blue eyes and short hawk-like wings, grew a big smile and hurried to greet them. She had once considered Daniel's potential as a birth partner before he realized his life guarding Ellen was paramount. Unable to find a suitable partner, she had left the parenting program, met Daniel's older brother, Oriel, and had trained to be a healer. While non-birth parents did not form partnerships or share living arrangements, they often would develop a deep bond and would exchange personal tokens. Such had been the case with Nariel and Oriel.

She reached their side and gave Ellen a hug. "So good to see you! It's wonderful to welcome you back in this manner."

Ellen returned the hug and smiled broadly. "It's amazing to be here without having to nearly die."

Nariel let Ellen go and walked them through the domed Facility. "I must tell you, another Way Shower has made his appearance recently."

Ellen nodded. "That's what Nathan told us."

"Is he still here?" Daniel wondered.

Nariel shook her head. "His Guardian took him to the Lands Below, but he passed back over the Bridge a little while ago."

Ellen frowned. "Now why didn't Nathan mention that?"

"Time/space," Daniel reminded her.

She blew out a frustrated breath. Learning to comprehend and navigate time/space had been such a challenge on her last two trips to the this world. Where she was used to traveling a distance in a certain amount of time in the human world, here in the angelic realm, you navigated a certain amount of time at a particular location. She could feel the familiar consternation headache coming on and rubbed her temples.

"Where did he go in the Lands Below?" Daniel asked giving Ellen's shoulder a sympathetic squeeze.

"Oh, I'm sure he visited the Priest and the Wizard," Nariel replied. "Since then they've been talking about developing a University for new Way Showers passing through."

Ellen raised an eyebrow. "Really? Those two think they can work together on this?"

Nariel chuckled. "No one said anything about cooperation between those two, but their enthusiasm is running high."

Ellen laughed.

"Perhaps you should go 'sort them out'," Daniel suggested.

"Well, it would give me something to do while you see the Embodied One," she agreed.

They reached the door, which whooshed open wide to give an angel's wings plenty of space. Nariel waved as they stepped outside and returned to her work. Daniel held his arms open wide for her, and Ellen stretched her arms up around his neck. He held her close, unfurled his great wings and leapt skywards with one swift downbeat.

Ellen watched the landscape pass by below them. Even when Daniel dove over the cliffs of the Great Above and swept through the clouds obscuring the Lands Below, her heart felt a thrill like no other. She might be terrified of heights in her own reality, but in Daniel's arms with his great wings to carry them, she always felt perfectly safe. They zipped out from under the cloud cover and soared over the dry desert where she had landed during her first sojourn.

"Should we head for the Desert City or for the Wastelands?" Daniel asked.

Ellen put one hand on his self-created chest shield and used the various segments like a stationary pendulum. She frowned. "Apparently neither."

Daniel pulled up and hovered in mid-air. "Then where to?"

Ellen pulled out her obsidian pendulum and continued to dowse. "If I didn't know better, I'd say they're on an adventure." She glanced up at him in amazement. "They're having an adventure!"

"That's not helping things," Daniel muttered.

Ellen pointed in different directions and watched the pendulum swing. "I think they may be near the mountain just beyond Hunter's cabin," she replied at last.

The first journey Ellen took in the Lands Below had seen she and Daniel captured by the Marauders and thrown into the Fight Ring on the Volcanic Mountain that separated the desert from the lush valley beyond. When Ellen had refused to fight, the Marauders had beaten Daniel to a pulp. He had been in danger of dying because of voluntarily giving up his immortality and with it his great strength. Out of desperation, Ellen had discovered her ability to heal and had brought Daniel back to life. They escaped the Marauder's dungeon and wandered into the valley where they met the Hunter who helped them on their way.

Daniel nodded. "I'll head in that direction. If we don't spot them, we can always drop in on Hunter and ask if he's seen them."

"Sounds good," Ellen agreed.

He banked to the left and soon swept over the Volcanic Mountain. He followed the clear stream that tumbled out of the dungeon caves and followed the silver ribbon of water downstream.

Suddenly, she pointed. "That's an old campfire."

"Someone's been here," he agreed.

Swooping into the valley, Daniel used his keen eyesight to sweep the landscape. They flew over Hunter's house and headed straight for the mountain at the far end. Finally, as they neared the foothills, Daniel spotted a group just setting up camp. He slowed and glided to the ground nearby.

The Wizard, a younger, vital Gandalf sort of figure, glanced up, spotted Ellen, and leapt to his feet. "Look who's here!" he whooped scrambling over packs and people to welcome her.

He gave Ellen a great big hug literally picking her up and swinging her around.

"Did you really think I wouldn't come back?" she asked as he set her down.

He ducked his head sheepishly.

The Priest, in his long crimson robes and low cap that covered his graying hair, welcomed her next. Then the others lined up. There was Toby, an older sailor wearing a blue and white, horizontally striped shirt, red kerchief about his neck, captain's hat upon his head and a pipe propped between his teeth, and Betsy, his short, pleasantly plump, round-faced wife, who lived in the Seaside Town far to the west. The Tavern Owner, a bear of a man with slicked-back, black hair and an earring in one ear, who hailed from the Desert City, was with them as well and gave her a wave of his hand.

Betsy took Ellen's hand and led her toward their tent. "I have extra, dear. You can stay with us."

"Thanks," Ellen replied, "but why are you all on the road?"

"We decided it was high time we honor those Way Showers who died in the Ice Queen's tunnels," the Priest said.

"Doesn't feel right to move forward till we close out that chapter," the Wizard agreed.

Ellen nodded. "I like the idea of a memorial. Could I come, too?" She asked this as much of Daniel as of the party.

"We'd love ta hav' ya," Toby said with a puff on his pipe.

Ellen glanced up at Daniel, who gave a slight nod.

"I'll look for you around the gap," he told her quietly.

"Ok." She gave his arm a squeeze.

When he leapt into the air to return to the Great Above, the Wizard frowned. "He's not staying with us?" he asked.

Ellen shook her head. "We actually crossed over to give him time to meet with the Embodied One. He's been sensing something he needs guidance on."

"Concerning you?" the Priest asked furrowing his brow.

"Apparently. But look...tell me more about this memorial," Ellen encouraged as she changed the subject.

The brothers sat near the campfire, and Ellen wrapped herself in one of Betsy's quilts as she listened to the heartwarming ideas her friends had devised to remember those the Ice Queen had trapped and who never made it out alive.

CHAPTER 2

Daniel loved transit in his world. In less than the speed of thought, he winked out in the Lands Below and appeared on the walk in the gardens before the Great Halls in the Great Above. He immediately directed his footsteps toward the broad stairs and columned portico that led to the Throne Room. The wardens parted allowing him through.

He stood for a moment just inside the doors and took in the grandeur of the vaulted ceilings and giant columns all in brilliant white marble. Because of the Light of the One, he could see every nook and cranny as if a search beam were trained upon it. Nothing could hide from the Light.

With nervous butterflies in his stomach, Daniel marched forward toward the Throne where the brilliance was magnified exponentially. He reached the stairs before the Dais and dropped to one knee with his head bowed. He waited in silence.

"Daniel, rise!" came the thunderous voice he had known since birth.

Daniel rose continuing to keep his head bowed in order to protect his eyes from the penetrating light. He heard soft footsteps approaching him, and a tall, broad shadow filtered the light. He looked up into the eyes of the Embodied One.

"You have a heavy heart," the Embodied One observed.

Daniel nodded.

"Yet, I sense that Ellen's health is well, her outlook optimistic," the Embodied One noted.

"I sense this, too, yet...."

"You are filled with foreboding," the Embodied One said.

Daniel nodded. "It is almost what I felt before she and Robert were attacked, but not quite. The signature is somewhat different."

The Embodied One frowned. "And when you trace her timeline?"

"Darkness," Daniel replied. "I see nothing but darkness."

"Hmmm," the Embodied One said tilting his head to one side. "How...perplexing."

"We crossed the Bridge of Dreams this evening so I could seek your advice and gain clarity," Daniel told him.

"And where is Ellen?"

"Michael sent a guard for her house, and she is with other Way Showers who are preparing a memorial for those who died under the Ice Queen's captivity," Daniel replied.

The Embodied One shook his head slowly. "How curious...these humans. Always memorializing and writing things down."

Daniel nodded his agreement. "It is to help themselves remember and to provide a reference marker for future generations."

"They do not understand the nature of time," the Embodied One mused.

"Their world conspires to keep time locked in an alien structure," Daniel remarked.

"Ah well. Such musings will not answer your questions, nor clear your vision," the Embodied One said.

"No, Sire. They won't."

"I don't supposed you have looked at Ellen's purpose lately and checked her progress towards it?" the Embodied One asked.

Daniel shook his head. "Not lately."

"Then let's begin there," the Embodied One said waving one hand through the air to create a screen of Mist.

A moment later scenes of Ellen's life came into view, some overlapping while others were playing out separately.

"Now, let's see what this tells us," the Embodied One said concentrating on the portrayals before them.

On the mountainside in the Lands Below, Ellen listened as Toby and Betsy talked about their idea.

"It seemed like such a shame they should just rot to dust in that hole, poor dears," Betsy mourned.

"Aye. Even scurvy scum get a burial a' sea," Toby agreed.

"We can't bury them all, of course," Betsy remarked.

"They're a'ready far underground," Toby pointed out, taking a draw on his pipe.

"So, how do you plan to memorialize them?" Ellen wondered.

"A rock carving," the Priest suggested.

"Like Mt. Rushmore?" Ellen asked.

"Yes, but one thing hasn't felt right to me," the Wizard remarked.

"Here we go again," the Priest muttered and rolled his eyes.

"Whose head?" the Wizard asked ignoring his brother.

"What do you mean?" Ellen asked with a perplexed frown.

"Well, surely not the Ice Queen's," Betsy sniffed.

"Or her as Amanda," Toby added.

"Someone who escaped perhaps?" Betsy asked looking meaningfully at Ellen.

Ellen emphatically shook her head. She had escaped the Ice Queen's clutches in the Ice Palace twice. She had no desire to immortalize those memories. The first time Daniel had been frozen in a block of sub-zero ice, and she'd barely managed to get free and rescue him. The second time, she herself nearly succumbed, and Daniel could only help her from a distance. As it was, when Ellen and the Ice Queen had fought, they'd fallen over the edge of the gorge and had plummeted toward the rapids below. Ellen had been whisked to safety by a deranged dragon, all because she had snatched the magical Star Pendant that it responded to. The wild ride on the dragon's back had only been tamed when Daniel joined her and set the dragon on a course for home. Ellen shivered; they had been two very near misses.

"Too bad there wasn't a way to capture each person's face and display it," Ellen said wistfully.

The Tavern Owner, who had sat listening in silence, spoke up. "There is."

Everyone turned toward him.

"How?" Betsy asked.

"Well, there are a few of us missin'," he pointed out.

"We would need someone who could envision each person's face," the Priest mused.

"Why, the Visionary can do that," Betsy said.

"And someone to create the pattern of the image on the cliff face," the Wizard added.

"The Weaver?" Ellen wondered.

The Tavern Owner nodded.

"So how do we get them here?" Ellen asked.

The Priest stood and stretched his limbs. "I'll go," he said. "I think I still remember their coordinates." He brought out his pendulum.

"I'll come, too," the Wizard interjected hauling himself off the ground with the aid of his staff.

"Better hurry," the Priest admonished as the wind kicked up around him.

A moment later the Vortex of Power from the Temple rose up from the ground around them. While the others in the party threw their hands up before their faces to protect themselves from the leaves and twigs the whirlwind kicked up, the Priest set his pendulum in motion. A few moments later, the Vortex lifted off the ground and headed for the treetops. Ellen watched till it was out of view.

"Better get some sleep," the Tavern Owner suggested crawling into a one person tent.

Betsy motioned to Ellen, who crept over to join her, and the two women crawled into the tent. Toby sat on the ground with a blanket around him and leaned back against a log. For a while he puffed on his pipe sending smoke rings dancing between the trees. Now and then, he stirred the fire to keep the embers glowing bright. However, once his pipe went out, it wasn't long before his chin touched his chest and loud snores disturbed the crickets' song.

In the Great Above, Daniel and the Embodied One studied the scenes of Ellen's life and purpose with keen interest.

"When she is completely aware and open," the Embodied One said, "Ellen will merely need to step into a room and the tenor of the activity there will change. A glance or the wave of her hand will renew health and vitality."

"She is well on her way to accomplishing this," Daniel pointed out. "She has performed healings in her world and this. I'm a product of her ability."

The Embodied One somberly studied the scenes Daniel brought up with but a "Hmm."

"And Ellen has developed ways to send aspects of herself with Robert when he lectures. When she does, rigid personal dogmas amongst his fellow scientists have been known to ease and fall away."

The Embodied One merely nodded.

"And Ellen exerts quite a field effect where she goes, particularly if Robert is with her. Parallel universes have a way of mingling, and people
12

around her experience very interesting effects," Daniel noted. "Plus, don't forget the way she brought back not just the Temple from ruins, but the entire Desert City when she needed to take on the Vortex challenge."

The Embodied One remained silent for a while as he observed the scenes. Finally, he banished the Mist with a wave of his hand.

"What?" Daniel asked, bewildered. "Is there something wrong with Ellen's progress?"

"I will admit that Ellen has made much progress since learning she is a Way Shower," the Embodied One said after a time.

"Whenever she comes to this realm, she can do whatever she intends," Daniel added hastily.

"She can," the Embodied One acknowledged.

"That isn't enough?" Daniel pressed.

"I would feel better if she were more consistent with her abilities in the human reality," the Embodied One stated.

Daniel considered this observation for a moment then sighed. "I encourage Ellen at every opportunity," he confessed. "But imprints from past experiences have a way of blocking humans and locking them up inside."

"Even Way Showers?" the Embodied One asked. "Products of both human and angelic parents?"

"I think even moreso for Way Showers," Daniel replied. "They seem to endure harsher lives than their plain human counterparts. They have as much to unlearn as they have to learn."

The Embodied One considered this news for a while.

"I am always with her," Daniel said at last. "I do my best to anchor her in the most useful reality. And I open the doors for her future self to call to her and pull her forward. It just isn't always enough when the harshness of the past has the strongest pull."

"So, she can achieve things with you and with Robert?" the Embodied One mused.

"Yes," Daniel replied, a zing of electricity zipping up his spine.

"And when she's alone?"

"It's harder for her," Daniel admitted.

"Perhaps you're too often with her," the Embodied One said absent-mindedly.

"I'm her Guardian Angel," Daniel reminded him. "It's my job to be with her always."

"But as close as you are," The Embodied One almost whispered to himself. "I wonder...."

13

Daniel frowned and took a step back. "What are you saying?"

The Embodied One turned to look at him. "Hm? Oh, that this is a puzzle I must ponder for a Time," he replied.

"You think I should pull away from Ellen? Not be as close?"

The Embodied One shook his head as he headed back to the steps leading to the Dais. "I do not know what I think...yet. Change nothing, Daniel, till my Father and I have thoroughly considered the matter."

Daniel bowed his head, the Light momentarily brightened then dimmed. At this he considered himself to be dismissed. He walked back through the Throne Room, across the portico, down the broad steps to the gardens below. For a moment he considered returning to Ellen's side but, after checking time in Ellen's world and her progress in this world, he opted to wander the meditation gardens, instead.

Taking a right and then another, he ambled along the Cloister Walk until one garden to his left seemed to tug at him. Allowing his footsteps to be guided, he meandered into a lush, walled garden with a spreading oak whose branches stretched out over an oval pond. An acorn on the end of a branch fell off and landed in the water creating circles that rippled out toward the edges. Daniel sank onto a stone bench and focused on the pond to the exclusion of all else.

Around daybreak the sound of branches snapping and the brothers' raised voices roused the camp on the mountainside. Toby was up in a flash ducking out of the way. A branch narrowly missed the Tavern Owner, and he thrashed his way out of his tent with some choice words hurled about. Betsy and Ellen poked their heads out to see what all the commotion was about. Moments later, the Vortex set down and disappeared. Its occupants tumbled to the ground.

Muttering under his breath, the Wizard crawled to his feet and stalked off. The Priest scrambled up hurrying over to give the Visionary, a tall, lithe woman in a shimmery silver dress, a hand as she got up. The Weaver, a tall, dark-haired, goateed man in seventeenth century attire, was left to his own devices and rose slowly as he gazed in awe at the forest about them.

"I had no idea there was such variety here in the Lands Below," he murmured.

Ellen, who had crawled out of the only standing tent, meandered over. "When I first awoke in the Lands Below, I was in the middle of an arid desert," she told him. "But from there I've been through Waste Lands, inside lava tubes, walked across broad plains, sailed on an ocean,

14

landed on an ocean island...it's not a lot different from home. Just a whole lot less populated."

The Weaver stared at her with his mouth agape.

Meanwhile, Toby had stoked the fire and Betsy was starting breakfast. The Tavern Owner, who had disappeared into the woods, came crashing back out through the underbrush and dumped a load of firewood beside the fire. The Priest made a comfortable spot near the fire and helped the Visionary over to it. Once the food was ready, they ate in silence for a while. Finally, the Visionary put down her bowl.

"What is this place like where we are going?" she asked. "Tell me its story."

"It's not a very pleasant place," the Wizard said, and the Priest shuddered.

"It was a place of great beauty," Ellen began, "great cruelty and entrapment."

The Visionary turned toward her. "Go on."

"You remember what the Ice Queen looked like when Michael brought her into the council?" Ellen asked.

The Visionary nodded.

"All that green ice made her into a fairy tale," Ellen continued. "She built a bridge of it spanning a deep gorge in the mountain pass, and created a castle from it in the caverns deep underground. Those tunnels ran from that gorge clear to the center of this mountain."

Toby whistled appreciatively.

"But...where did she get the energy to create and sustain the illusion?" the Weaver asked.

"Angels...." Ellen replied. "Lots and lots of angels. She lured in the Way Showers, trapped them and encased their Guardians in green ice."

At that moment, they heard the flap of great wings and looked up. Daniel neatly lowered himself to the ground at Ellen's side.

"He was nearly one of them," Ellen said patting his shoulder.

Daniel raised an eyebrow as he glanced at her.

"The Ice Queen had started encasing him in that green ice," she continued.

Recognition lit Daniel's face. "If Ellen hadn't called the Temple Flames to her hands and melted the ice, my life force would have been drained to sustain the illusion."

The others murmured.

"She did it again in the Minion's Lair," Ellen added, "only that time she added a Way Shower, Henry, to the mix."

"So what did the illusion really do?" the Weaver wondered.

"First, it lured Way Showers who were tired of trying to find a way home," the Wizard said, his face dark with memories.

"But once you entered her cavern, this dullness took over," the Priest said.

"I have no idea how long we sat there," the Wizard murmured. "Days? Weeks?"

"Hours," the Priest answered. "Any longer and we would not have broken free."

"But how did you break free?" Betsy wanted to know.

"The Ice Queen had to attend to a couple more new Way Showers," the Priest replied.

"While her attention was focused on them, it was just enough of a break in the illusion to allow us to find a way out," the Wizard explained.

"Then how many were ultimately left inside?" the Visionary wondered.

"At least one hundred," Ellen replied. "Maybe more."

The Visionary and the Weaver blanched.

"I think the idea here is to discover their images," Ellen interjected, "then time travel to a happier moment and let that be the pattern that gets imprinted on the cliff face."

The others nodded in agreement.

"A memorial really should be about them at their best," Betsy affirmed.

"Now, that that's settled, I say we strike camp," the Tavern Owner suggested.

"Sounds right 'ere," Toby replied heading for his tent.

Ellen looked up at Daniel. "Is it time for me to cross back? Or have you just finished talking with the Embodied One?"

Daniel mentally checked the time in her reality. "It's close to when you need to go," he told her. "We can always come back tonight."

She nodded then went over to Betsy. "Morning's coming on fast back home. I'm going to need to go."

The Wizard lifted his head. "Will you come back next night?" he asked.

Ellen nodded. "That's my plan. Daniel can find you wherever you are, or we can just plan to meet up in the gap."

"Meet us in the cavern," the Priest said.

Ellen nodded and turned to Daniel. "Ok, I'm ready."

He gathered her up and spun out. The return seemed unusually swift. Before she knew it, they were through the Facility and crossing the Bridge of Dreams. In the middle, Ellen stopped and restrained Daniel with a hand on his arm.

"What happened when you talked to the Embodied One? Did you find out what's making you feel so anxious for me?" Ellen asked.

Daniel shook his head and glanced away. "Not exactly. But we don't have the time to talk about it here."

"Tonight when we come back?" Ellen pressed.

Daniel nodded half-heartedly.

"Promise?"

He raised his head and held her gaze. "I swear."

CHAPTER 3

Ellen didn't remember the rest of the crossing. The next thing she knew, the sun was up, and the dog was rummaging around in the crate beside her bed. With a glance back at the clock, Ellen got up, slid on her clogs and quietly made her way upstairs. She pushed the button on the coffee maker, put kibbles in a bowl with some water, and headed for the bathroom. When she came out, coffee was ready. Ellen poured herself a cup, ambled back downstairs and let her Bichon out of the crate. The white, bouncy ball of fur gave her a squeaky, yippy greeting then scrambled upstairs to eat. Ellen sat on the couch gazing out the patio door until excited paws scrambling down the stairs grabbed her attention. She let Boodles out and watched her check all the spots in the backyard frequented by the neighborhood fox. Boodles came back inside and danced on her hind legs for a treat.

With the dog at her feet, Ellen headed back to the kitchen for breakfast. She watched the birds fly in to the deck feeder.

"They're going to want a refill soon," Daniel said fading into view.

Ellen nodded. "Once I'm showered and dressed, I'll fill up the feeder."

"Nothing on your calendar?" he asked.

She shook her head. "Not beyond working out at the gym."

"Ever think of actually working on your abilities while you're here in your reality?" Daniel asked following her up the hall to the home office.

Ellen slid into her chair and woke up her computer. She started AOL then looked up.

"I do think about it, but it's frustrating. A lot of times, like today, I only have myself to 'practice' on."

"Yes, and you end up getting entangled in every nuance of your problems," Daniel noted.

"I'm definitely not my best subject," Ellen admitted clicking open her mailbox.

"Email from Robert?" Daniel asked.

"Mm-hm," she murmured while reading it. "Great. Another night of bad sleep."

"So, why not 'practice' on Robert?" Daniel suggested.

"I do," Ellen replied. "But it either doesn't work well or doesn't stick."

"Unless it's an emergency," Daniel remarked recalling when Robert had broken his fingers a few years ago and Ellen had healed them overnight, and the time he'd given his thigh a second degree burn and Ellen had watched the burn disappear in 30 minutes. "I just don't understand why you could do those two things...."

"Big things, major things," Ellen pointed out.

"Miraculous things in your world," Daniel agreed, "but the mundane eludes you."

Ellen took a moment to reply to Robert's email then exited AOL and returned to the kitchen. She put her coffee cup in the sink and shut off the coffee maker. Turning around, she leaned against the counter wearing a pensive frown.

"I've always thought a good surge of adrenalin was part of the difference," she said at last.

"That can't be all of it," Daniel protested.

Ellen shook her head. "No, I don't think it is. With some of the more mundane issues, like Robert's sleep challenges, there are all these other patterns that seem to hold it in place."

Daniel frowned and tilted his head.

"Well, there's definitely a stress pattern," Ellen pointed out. "And we both know he's either in front of a computer screen or the TV till the moment he turns off the light."

"So are the patterns a problem for him or for you?" Daniel wondered.

"Probably both. The patterns sort of lock the sleep challenge into place, but I also have a tendency to go straight at the problem," Ellen admitted.

"So you shift the problem, but the other patterns pull it right back

19

into place," Daniel surmised.

"That's my guess," she said. "When it comes to emergencies, they're in the now. No additional patterns have had time to build up around them."

Daniel nodded and watched her head for the stairs.

After a quick shower, Ellen headed to the gym then ran errands before returning home. A quick walk with Boodles in the nearby park, and she was in for the day. She put a bowl of popcorn in the microwave partly just to watch her canine companion go nuts. First, the dog whined while glancing back and forth between the microwave and Ellen. Then Boodles danced on her hind legs, started pawing at the range and finally jumped up and down in front of the stove as the popping overhead got louder and faster.

Ellen was laughing so hard, she could barely hold her cell phone still while she got a video of the dog's antics. When the timer rang, Ellen stopped recording and posted the video to Facebook so Robert and friends could get a chuckle. Then she got up, took the bowl downstairs to the couch with her white "shadow" following at her heels.

Ellen enjoyed Ghost Hunters on SyFy while the dog watched every morsel of popcorn she took from the bowl. Periodically, Ellen tossed a fluffy kernel to the dog, who greedily caught it in mid-air and gulped it down.

Daniel, who sat on the arm of the couch beside her with his arms folded, eyed the television skeptically. "I don't know what you find interesting about this show," he grumbled.

"We'll begin with 'my daughter got me hooked'," Ellen replied, "and end with 'it's far more objective and way less melodramatic than other ghost hunting shows'."

"But why ghosts?" Daniel complained.

"I saw one once or twice...my dad after he died, for one," she replied. "Makes me feel like I'm a little less crazy."

"But every week?"

"Goes back to 'and my daughter got me hooked'," Ellen retorted glancing up at him. "It's that 'hooked' bit you don't get."

He nodded.

Ellen checked her watch, shut off the TV and bolted upstairs. In minutes she had Skype up and running. Robert soon came on, and they spent the next 20 minutes with him describing his interactions at the conference and Ellen listening.

"Just don't forget to run the shower a bit to humidify the room," she reminded him.

"Good idea," Robert replied. "I forgot last night, and the room was really dry."

"See you tomorrow. Love you," Ellen called, and the connection ended.

She turned out the office light, set up coffee for the next day and put Boodles to bed.

"Heading to bed yourself?" Daniel asked as she crawled in with a Woman's World magazine.

"In a bit," Ellen replied. "Just some light reading till my eyelids start to close."

Daniel paced until she finally dropped the magazine onto the floor beside her bed, pulled on her sleep mask and shut off the light. Then he sat beside her and ushered her across the Bridge of Dreams like he had the night before.

The next thing Ellen knew, they were standing near the stone staircase that led up into the cavern. She glanced to her left noticing that the huge, carved, green ice bridge had finally melted. She frowned and turned around to see Daniel a few steps up and shielding his eyes against the morning sun. He jumped, spread his wings and glided to the ground beside her.

"They just made it into the pass," he announced.

Ellen frowned and put her hands on her hips. "How did I get here?"

Daniel raised his eyebrows. "The Bridge of Dreams."

"I don't even recall falling asleep," she charged.

"Well, I sped things up a bit," he admitted.

Ellen slowly scanned her environment swinging her eyes upwards when an eagle cried overhead. She watched its graceful flight path for a while before turning back to Daniel.

"Don't," she said. "I want to know for certain what is this world and what is a dream."

"And this doesn't feel like my world?" he asked.

She shook her head. "Too abrupt. It gives everything a surreal quality...and I miss getting to see Nathan. I like the transition where I remember the Bridge and getting to where I'm going."

"Well, if you were more used to time/space travel...." Daniel began.

"But I'm not. That's not how humans are designed," she remarked. "Just accept it."

His shoulders slumped but he nodded.

Before long, they could hear voices echoing off the cliff walls as the other Way Showers made their way toward them. Finally, they were all reunited.

Daniel took Ellen aside. "Would you mind if I left you till right before it's time to go back?"

She studied him darkly. "I thought you promised to tell me what's wrong this time."

Daniel rubbed his fingertips across his forehead. "You're right. I did. Ok, sooner than that."

Ellen's frown turned worried. "What's wrong, Daniel?"

"I-I just want to question others with more experience," he replied. "My Mentor for one and...maybe Raphael."

She nodded. "That's probably a good idea." She reached up and gave him a kiss on the cheek.

Daniel glanced about nervously.

"Go on," she said making a shooing motion with her hand.

He waved to the other Way Showers then leapt into the air.

"Where's he going?" the Wizard asked shielding his eyes with his hand.

"To do some research," Ellen replied joining them.

"So, how do you want to do this?" the Tavern Owner asked.

"What do you need to do in order to view the patterns?" Ellen asked turning to the Visionary.

"I would need to be within the same walls as those who died," the woman replied.

"Anybody have a light?" Ellen asked.

"Right 'ere," Toby replied hauling a lantern out of his knapsack.

"Good," Ellen replied. "If we're lucky we might find a torch or two inside."

The group headed for the steps and started climbing upward.

"What do you think we'll find?" the Wizard asked.

Ellen paused, waiting as Toby helped Betsy climb upwards. "Don't know," she said shaking her head. "Last time I was in the cavern, there were skeletons scattered all over, but with this whole time/space thing...."

"It's anybody's guess," the Wizard agreed.

"One thing's for sure," called the Priest from behind his brother.

"What's that?" Ellen puffed as she began climbing again.

"There still won't be anybody found alive."

22

A hush fell over the group and all that could be heard were the scrape of footsteps on stone.

"Thanks for that cheery reminder," the Wizard retorted.

His brother looked up. "Well, it's the truth."

"Which you had to broadcast as loudly as possible," the Wizard grumbled.

"Guys, some other time," Ellen hushed as she stepped into the main gallery of the cavern.

Toby lit the lantern and held it aloft.

The Wizard and the Priest gazed about them in keen interest.

"So this was what was under all that ice," the Wizard said with a whistle.

"She sure did imagine her surroundings as beautiful," the Priest added almost wistfully.

Ellen nodded. "She created her own twisted fairytale."

"I can feel the essence of lost souls," the Visionary murmured.

"Where do our brethren lie?" the Weaver asked.

Ellen moved to Toby's side and directed him down the tunnel to their right. The Wizard spotted a torch in a hanger on the wall, brought fire to his fingertips and lit it. He took it from the holder and followed.

"I'm just going to stay near the entrance," Betsy called to them.

"I'll stay with her," the Tavern Owner added.

Toby waved his lantern to signal he'd heard her, then followed Ellen as she turned left and carefully made her way down a narrow set of stairs. The others joined them as quickly as possible. At the bottom of the stairs, an empty door frame led into a mammoth chamber where the bones of the Way Showers they'd lost lay. The Visionary gasped at the onslaught of the sheer numbers but soon calmed herself. She, Toby and the Weaver set off to find and access the signature pattern for each person. The Wizard, the Priest and Ellen carefully picked their way out into the hated chamber.

"We kept falling asleep near the door," the Wizard remarked.

"Daniel kept urging me telepathically to wake up," Ellen said.

"We didn't have anyone but each other," the Priest said.

"Yeah, I'd kick him; he'd give me a shove," the Wizard added.

"Kept us awake," the Priest conceded.

"Finally, a use for sibling rivalry," Ellen muttered under her breath.

The trio continued on the narrow path till they reached the now dry streambed. The brothers stopped and stared.

"We nearly lost it here," the Priest recalled.

"I started wrestling with him," the Wizard added.

"We fought the whole way across the bridge," the Priest said.

"Daniel had to actually yell at me to keep me from drinking," Ellen told them.

The Wizard patted her back and they continued on. When they reached a long pile of bones, he held his torch aloft and they beheld a slick, calcite wall.

"Wow!" Ellen exclaimed. "Daniel wasn't kidding when he said the notched wall was an illusion."

"Bet those climbing cleats and gecko gloves came in handy," the Wizard cried gleefully.

"And how! I knew you'd put them in the back pockets for me," Ellen said gratefully.

"We couldn't get the pendant out of the stalactite," the Priest said.

"Made the best replica we could and got out of here," the Wizard said.

"I made mini-vortexes act like stepping stones out to the stalactite then melted some of the ice on it with Temple Flames," Ellen recalled.

"Well played," the Priest commended.

They turned toward the long tunnel to the exit. Off to their left, Toby's lantern light bounced along, periodically stopped and swung in place. The hushed voices of the Visionary and the Weaver reached their ears as they worked over the skeletons.

"Want to head out?" the Wizard asked with a nod toward the tunnel.

Ellen nodded. "I could do with a long walk."

Together, the trio turned down the long, dark tunnel and progressed deeper into the mountain. They had a lot of time. It would take the Visionary a while to collect the personal pattern of every Way Shower who had died.

CHAPTER 4

Daniel exited the group quickly and focused his sole intent on his Mentor. All sorts of questions churned through his mind. *"Is there something I didn't understand in my training as a Guardian? Did I somehow miss some segments of training completely? I did come in a little late to the program because of the Archangel training. Or is this because Ellen and I are charting such a new course that no one can actually guide us?"*

He hoped, he prayed for answers and clarity. After all he had done in her service, even briefly giving up his immortality, to help her discover who and what she was and was capable of, he didn't know what was left for him to do.

Daniel snapped his wings out and abruptly appeared in the Great Above. He had materialized near a white, turreted, stucco building set on a hillside and banked toward a broad, wooden balcony with low railings and wide, double doors set to accommodate wings. He landed on the balcony and peered in the door. Since the room beyond was empty, he eased the doors open and quietly stepped inside.

The polished oak floors felt so familiar to his feet as he walked across the room to the floor-to-ceiling book shelves. Daniel stood with his hands on his hips staring up at the great volumes lining the shelves. They belonged to his Mentor, a trainer of Guardian Angels.

"Perhaps one of these has some useful information," he thought.

Daniel spotted a bound volume high over his head, leapt into the air, plucked the book off the shelf and soon glided back to the floor with the weighty, green leather tome in his hand.

"Guiding Humans on Their Life Path," Daniel read aloud. "Sounds perfect."

He took the book to a nearby stand, set it down and carefully opened it. There inside was a Table of Contents written in a strongly flourished script.

"Not my Mentor's writing," he noted.

Since he had come into the program a little late, Daniel decided he might have missed something from those early lessons and began reading the book from the beginning. He was over half-way through when he heard the thud of booted feet landing on the balcony. He didn't look up. The double doors opened with an authoritative air.

"My dear, Daniel," a warm, older male voice said. "How good to see you!"

Daniel raised one finger on his right hand while his left hand followed closely under a line of text. Reaching the end of the section, he gave an exasperated sigh.

"Dear boy, what are you studying so intently?" Mentor asked swiftly crossing the room and raising the corner of the book to see its title.

"I'm stuck...or Ellen is...and I don't know what to do for her," Daniel admitted finally turning towards his elder.

The older angel gently closed the book, put his hand on Daniel's shoulder and walked him into a bright, airy solarium off to their left. He took him to a bench overlooking a fish pond and gestured for him to sit. Daniel sank onto the stone bench, clasped his hands between his knees, leaned his elbows on his thighs and watched the brightly colored fish swim below them.

"What knowledge are you seeking that I haven't already imparted to you?" Mentor asked.

Daniel sighed. "The Embodied One and I reviewed Ellen's progress toward her life purpose and, in spite of the huge steps she's taken, he seems to feel there's more she could be doing."

"Such as?" Mentor prompted.

"He feels she should be able to do the miraculous in her world as consistently as she does it here," Daniel replied. "But she has really good explanations as to why it's genuinely harder. I don't know if the Embodied One just isn't aware of them, or if I'm somehow failing her."

Mentor was silent for a little while. Finally, he lay his hand on Daniel's shoulder. "Developing toward their full potential as humans isn't always easy or a straight line," he began. "There always seems to be a point humans reach, a point of no return, after which they either shut down completely out of fear or step into their personal fullness."

Daniel considered this a moment. "Do you think that here, Ellen has no fear but in her reality she hits a wall of fear?"

"I think that here, she believes she is so protected that she can do whatever she is called on to do. I think her lack of fear is based in her total faith in you," Mentor told him.

"Then that's a bad thing!" Daniel exclaimed.

The older angel shook his head. "No, Daniel. That trust she has in you is a necessity. Ellen can stretch, grow and develop her strengths because she knows you'll always catch her. This environment in our reality is a training ground that supports her creativity and allows her to take monumental risks."

"So, why doesn't that carry over into her world?" Daniel wanted to know.

"Because, as you very well know, in the human realm, the rules change. There you have have to stand back and allow certain things to occur in her life in order for her to build inner strength and be able to recognize her true self."

Daniel nodded glumly. "Some of those things have been pretty awful at times. They've about broken my heart."

"But...?" Mentor encouraged.

"When I know the possible outcome, know where the experience will take her...." Daniel swallowed hard, "it's more bearable to witness."

"It is a delicate balancing act, Daniel, by far. Yet, I've observed you in your task. You do your job well," Mentor commended.

Daniel nodded silently. "Then how do I help Ellen stretch and grow in her world?" he asked glancing up.

Mentor gave his question careful consideration. "Just ideas, mind you," he prefaced. "Nothing hard and fast. But she may either need to follow a path on her own to its completion, or she may need an experience here that's so all-encompassing that the shock wave reverberates into her world, never to be undone."

"She and I haven't had enough of those experiences in this reality already?" Daniel cried in frustration. "What more is left?"

Mentor thought for a moment then rose and ambled into the center of the Solarium. Daniel followed, curious as to Mentor's next move. The older angel stopped in front of an island rock garden where beautiful flowers trailed between the rocks. He gazed at them, and as he did so, their inner radiance began to brighten.

"What do you notice about these flowers, even the rocks?" Mentor asked.

Daniel knit his brow. "They're glowing?"

"Am I sending them energy?"

Daniel tested the frequencies then shook his head. "No."

"Yet, they change in response to my presence," Mentor pointed out. "The Light within me prompts a surge of light within them."

Daniel tilted his head to one side.

"Ellen needs to find that light within herself and learn when it has touched another. When it has done so, she will know she can impact her world without trying," Mentor explained.

"How do I guide her towards that?" Daniel asked.

Mentor shook his head. "You don't. You allow her to discover this light and its effects on her own."

"Stay hands off?" Daniel queried.

"Maybe, maybe not," Mentor replied. "You are the one who will best know. Don't force the issue. When the time is right, you will know the correct action to take and will have the courage to undertake it."

Daniel sighed deeply. "I have a feeling the most intense phase of Ellen's life has just opened."

"Yes...." Mentor said staring off into space, "and beyond it...I see sparkles."

Daniel chuckled. That had been a code word between them for ages. He nodded. "Ok. I'll look for sparkles."

They turned and walked back into Mentor's study. Daniel headed toward the balcony but stopped and turned.

"Thank you," he said sincerely.

Mentor smiled warmly and bowed his head.

Daniel leapt skyward then spun up and out heading back to the Lands Below to collect Ellen.

In the mountain pass, Ellen stood with her hands on her hips as she gazed up at the cliff face. The Visionary, Weaver and the Tavern Owner had been working most of the day, and the result was nothing short of miraculous. The Visionary had gathered the energetic signatures of each Way Shower who had died in the cavern. The Weaver had taken each pattern, molded it into a 3-Dimensional image on the face of the cliff, and the Tavern Owner had solidified the pattern into the rock. They had started on the bottom and worked their way up, with Ellen and the Priest bringing in the Vortex and using it as platforms. The Visionary had finished her work and was resting on a boulder. The Priest was just lowering the Tavern Owner back to the ground. The rays from the setting sun caught the cliff face, and Ellen gasped.

"It's almost as if they're alive!" she exclaimed.

The others crowded near her and gazed at the memorial in awe. Where the sun's rays caressed an image, the face took on a holographic quality and came alive with the expression and personality of its former bearer.

"A true work of art," the Wizard praised with a nod to the Visionary and Weaver.

The Visionary gazed at the wall herself, tears coming to her eyes. "I could feel each individual," she admitted, "and sought their best qualities to bring forth."

"Well, you and Weaver did it, "Ellen said.

At that moment, they heard the rush of wings then the crunch of booted feet on gravel. Ellen turned and stretched out her hand to Daniel.

"What do you think?" she asked excitedly. "Isn't it amazing?"

Daniel looked up and gazed at the faces that were turning and smiling. They seemed to breathe life into the solid rock wall. He nodded. "Quite an achievement," he acknowledged.

"Guess this means it's time to go back," the Wizard said.

Ellen nodded. "Pretty soon."

"We should bed down in the cavern," the Tavern Owner suggested. "At this altitude, it will get windy and cold at night."

The others agreed and began collecting their gear to haul up the stone stairs.

"Don't be a stranger," the Wizard told her, leaning close to Ellen's ear.

"Oh, I won't. I've been hearing rumors of a University and this I have to check out," she replied slyly.

He smiled and gave her a wink, then grabbed his knapsack and began the climb up to the sheltering chambers.

Ellen turned to Daniel. "Guess it's almost morning back home."

"Not quite," he replied. "I promised to come back early and tell you about my meeting with the Embodied One."

She nodded. "Thank you for remembering."

He opened his arms to her, she slid her arms up around his neck, and he grasped her firmly before spiraling up and out.

The Priest and the Wizard stood on the steps having watched till Ellen disappeared.

"Is it just me," the Priest began, "or is there something off?"

"No, not just you," the Wizard replied. "I get that, too. He's not himself."

The Priest shook his head. "Something weighs heavily on him. A darkness my inner sight cannot penetrate."

The Wizard muttered under his breath as they turned to finish the ascent. "This doesn't bode well. Not well at all."

Meanwhile, Daniel brought them out onto the lawn outside the Facility. He stretched out his hand and, as if he were unzipping the air from top to bottom, a tall thin sheen of silver appeared as his hand moved. He took Ellen's hand and they pushed through into the dimension the Embodied One had created just for them.

Now, they stepped out onto the dirt road, the silver door disappearing behind them, and followed the stone fence on their left till they came to where a rutted, dirt lane turned off. Just a little ways down the lane was a stone path that led to a slate house with a broad porch and a drying balcony above it for Daniel's wings. They made their way up the walk, mounted the steps to the porch and opened the door. Ellen stepped inside and breathed deeply.

Wide oak planks stretched from the door through the dining room to the kitchen in back. To her right was the oval archway built to accommodate Daniel's wings, and the plank stairs leading to the bedroom above. A large sitting area stretched beyond the stairs. Sunlight shining through the windows dappled the floor with light.

Ellen headed for the kitchen and made herself a sandwich. She came back out with it in hand and studied Daniel's face.

"Ok, whatever this is, it must be serious," she remarked. "You look like the weight of the world is on your shoulders. Where do you want to go to talk?"

Daniel stood with his feet braced, left hand on his hip, and ran his right hand through his hair. He shook his head. "I don't know."

Ellen finished off her sandwich, wiped her hands on her jeans and moved closer. "Want to take a walk around the pond?"

Daniel glanced out the window toward where tall, broad weeping willows swept the placid water with their long, slender arms. He shook his head.

"Bedroom?"

"No," he said immediately.

"Balcony?"

30

He closed his eyes and thought for a moment then shook his head again.

Ellen took his hand. "Ok. Let's go somewhere we've never spent time before."

Daniel allowed himself to be led back out the door and onto the porch. Ellen headed toward the broad porch swing with the wing notch in the back.

"There," she declared pointing.

After a moment, he nodded, turned, slotted his wings into place and sat down. Ellen slid onto the swing beside him tucking a leg up under her.

"Ok, what did the Embodied One say?" she asked. "What has you so upset?"

Daniel took a deep breath and blew it out hard. "It's still just this... this feeling, this...sense of foreboding," he admitted.

Ellen frowned. "The Embodied One couldn't give you any insights?"

"He did," Daniel said nodding. "We looked at your Life Plan, where you are now...."

"And...?" Ellen prodded.

"And where he feels you should be," Daniel replied quietly.

"And that would be...?" Ellen demanded leaning back and crossing her arms in front of her.

Daniel glanced at her and one corner of his mouth briefly upturned. He knew that stance. That was Ellen's "no nonsense, I'll verbally shred him" look. He snorted.

"You can't take him on, you know," he pointed out.

"We'll see. Now, what did he say?"

Daniel sighed. "That it was good you could perform about any 'miracle' in this reality you chose to, but that you weren't sufficiently consistent when it came to what you can do in the human reality."

"So, I'm just supposed to jump from not knowing there was anything special about me to being some kind of Messiah?" Ellen said in measured tones as she left the swing and stomped down the length of the porch. She spun around and headed back. "Really? He created this space/time thing, but apparently he doesn't comprehend his own freakin' creation!" Her voice rose at the end.

Daniel's eyebrows raised. She could have a point.

Ellen blew her breath out and sat back down. "So, what did he suggest was a 'fix' for my 'problem'," she asked using exaggerated air quotes.

"Heh!" Daniel snorted and shook his head. "The common suggestion seems to be I do too much for you, I'm too close to you. I almost feel as if I should leave you alone and let you flounder, and then maybe we'll hit the mark."

Ellen frowned with concern. "Did he really say that?"

Daniel shrugged. "Not so much...well not in the past. Both he and Mentor said you couldn't have come this far if I hadn't taken the actions I did."

"But in the future?" Ellen wanted to know.

"It's almost as if they were suggesting I step back and let you find your own way forward."

Ellen sank back in the swing. "And what do you think?" she asked quietly.

Daniel sank his elbows into his knees and covered his face with his hands. Ellen reached out, touched his shoulder and rubbed it soothingly. A shudder ran though his body. He looked back up.

"I've done so much, none of which I regret for one second," he hastily added.

Ellen smiled gently.

"I gave up my immortality so you could discover that you're a Way Shower," he said.

"Took my place in the Lava Pit with the Sultan," she reminded him.

"Became a Minion...."

"Let me go with a bunch of mere Way Showers when I was nearly ready to deliver Nathan," Ellen recalled.

"But I could still see you, still intervene," he pointed out.

Ellen nodded and leaned her head against his shoulder.

"But give up this," he whispered, "this closeness, this...this intimacy where I know your thoughts, sense your feelings, feel your presence."

"Are you sure that's what the Embodied One was talking about?" Ellen queried.

Daniel shrugged. "I don't know. He was vague. So was Mentor... said I'd know what to do and would have the courage to do it when the time came."

"You feel like something's coming, don't you?" Ellen said pensively. "You feel a dread in your heart because of what you sense, even though you don't know what it is."

Daniel looked down at his boots and nodded.

"I do know that feeling," she told him quietly. "That's when you're future is calling back to your past. You tell me that all the time."

"But, I don't live in space/time," Daniel protested.

"Maybe not," Ellen mused, "but you are far more intimately connected with me than other Guardian/charge pairs."

"True," he said lifting his head.

"Think there might be crossover?"

"You mean...me experiencing some aspect of your life?"

Ellen nodded.

"Hmm. Could be."

Ellen took his hand and brought it into her lap. "Let me tell you what I know."

Daniel nodded and gazed at her expectantly.

She took a deep breath. "When I first found you all battered from the Marauders in the desert, that was the best way a man could approach me. You were vulnerable, which meant I had no reason to fear you, distrust you or feel intimidated by you."

He nodded.

"You never told me who I was. You merely provided the backdrop against which I could discover it for myself," she continued. "You let me take the lead through the desert, about got beaten to death again in the Marauder's fight ring so I could make my own choices. And this pattern of your providing the backdrop against which I could make my own personal choices and learn my own nature on my own just continued from there. If being available to me means you're too much in the way, then I don't have any answers either."

"So...you don't think I did too much for you?" Daniel asked hesitantly.

"Yeah, you got beat up about ten times too often," Ellen joked then hugged his shoulders. "No, Daniel. I feel like I found my own way. If you're guilty of anything, it might be of leading me where to go next. But you always let go once I got there."

Daniel stiffened at these words. "What if I'm not even supposed to lead you?"

"Then just make sure you're cheering from the sidelines," she replied kissing his cheek.

CHAPTER 5

Daniel and Ellen stayed at their slate home, in a dimension out of the time stream, for a little while longer. They sat on the porch swing, his arm around her shoulders; her head on his chest. When her breathing evened out and her head grew heavy, Daniel knew it was time to leave. Part of him desperately wanted to carry her upstairs to their bedroom so he could curl up with Ellen in his arms and forget about doom. Instead, he scooped her up in his arms and opened the silver door whisking her back to her home. He lay beside her on top of the covers trying to just let go of his foreboding and allow the future to open as it would.

He turned his head to watch her sleep. All he could think was, "*I'm going to miss her.*" He didn't know why he thought that, why those words.

"*Is this about now?*" he wondered. "*Or is this about when I'll walk her into the Light at the end of her life?*"

He shook his head. He couldn't fathom the when. All he knew was that someday...someday there would be a hole in his life where her warmth and vitality had been.

When Ellen awoke an hour later, Daniel was now sitting on the edge of her bed. He stood and went upstairs into the dining room while she went through her morning routine. He reflected on her dashing about without any interaction with him at all.

"*Really,*" he thought. "*Most days I'm just a background presence in her life.*"

As Daniel considered this, he realized how often they went for days here before she suddenly interacted with him. Other days, it was as if he didn't exist. When Robert was home, the interludes lasted even longer; sometimes a week or two.

He shook his head. *"How can I be having too much influence on Ellen's life,"* he wondered, *"when I often have so little contact with her?"*

The thought certainly didn't appear rational on the surface. Yet, Daniel knew that the ways of the One of Light often weren't.

"I'm becoming too accustomed to the human need for logic and rational explanations," he chastised himself with a frown. *"Could it be due to crossover?"*

Daniel heard the front door close, realized Ellen was headed for an appointment and immediately shifted his location from the dining room to the car. He settled into the backseat of her RAV4 where his wings fit better and noticed Boodles in the front seat.

"Groomers?" he asked audibly.

Ellen glanced up at him in the rear view mirror. "That and grocery shopping. Robert will be home in a couple of days. Would be nice to have something to feed him."

Daniel nodded and tagged along on her errands. That afternoon, Robert sent Ellen the draft of a paper his conference team was preparing. She spent a couple of hours suggesting edits and sent it back so he'd have time to make corrections before the evening's session.

"It does make me wonder what he did before he had an editor-on-call," Daniel remarked.

Ellen chuckled. "Hey. It's been a good deal. I don't have to work outside the home, I get to write my novels; I just have to be available when he needs help. This is not an onerous lifestyle."

He shook his head. "No, this is true. Your life with Robert, minus some unforeseen external bumps, has been the best your life has ever been."

Ellen nodded. "And I'm grateful every day."

"You certainly deserve this life," Daniel affirmed.

She nodded and headed toward the kitchen. "I definitely feel like I've paid my dues."

"So, have plans tonight?" he asked while she cooked supper.

Ellen shut off the stove and scooped her own version of Turkey Burger Helper onto her plate. "Oh, I'm quite interested in this University the Priest and the Wizard are planning. I'd love to hear their thoughts. All right with you?"

He nodded and stood nearby while she ate.

After finishing her meal and feeding the ever-starved Boodles, she wandered out into the backyard pulling weeds from the gardens as she went. Daniel sat on the marble bench by the bird feeder and watched her. She glanced over, never ceasing to be amazed at how the Mourning Doves knew Daniel was there and arranged themselves around him. They even knew to fly over his head.

With the sun beginning to set, she went out to their former standing stone that had toppled one winter due to freezing ground water and heaving. She sat on the rock facing the sun, kicked off her shoes to put her bare feet on the ground and maintained soft focus on the setting sun till it dipped below the treeline across the field.

It was moments like this that Ellen missed her old cat, Buster. He'd died recently of a severely enlarged heart. She'd done her best to keep him healthy enough to make it through the summer, his favorite season, and for a while the medications seemed to help. But toward the end, no amount of drugs were making things better. The last straw was when her calm, loving, docile cat began to attack Boodles, who had known her feline friend from the moment Ellen brought her home at 3 months old. That was when she had known it was time to let her old feline go. Of all the cats she'd ever had, this one she missed the most. He was her ever-present white shadow with the body-soothing purr. She could use that marvelous purr right now.

Sighing, Ellen slipped her socks and shoes back on and headed into the house, Boodles racing ahead and waiting inside the house for a treat. Once around on her hind legs for "Dance, dance," and a "Walk, walk" forward to keep her hind quarters strong, then Ellen headed upstairs to the office to turn on Skype and wait for Robert.

"So did I get the draft back to you in time?" she asked when he came on.

"Yes, thank you. I had the corrections before the session, and the others didn't have much to add," he replied.

"So, you won't have much to rework before submission," she commented.

"If I'm lucky, I'll get all the changes made before I leave and that will be less for me to do when I get home," Robert replied.

"It will be nice to have you back."

"Well, I have a late flight on Saturday, and I still have to drive an hour. Don't wait up for me," he admonished.

"We'll see," she replied. "Love you."

The connection ended.

Ellen shut the computer down then left the office. After a round of *The Big Bang Theory*, *Castle* and *Bones*, she finally got tired enough for bed. When she crawled in, Daniel was waiting nearby.

"Ready?"

She nodded and turned off the light. "Just at least let me remember seeing Nathan," Ellen requested.

Daniel smiled as he sat on the edge of the bed. "Of course."

And with that, he started humming. Ellen drifted off to sleep and soon slipped into his reality. The next thing she knew, she was approaching the guard room, the door was swooshing back and she was in the arms of a young man with whiskers who purred. While it often seemed strange, she also found it incredibly soothing. Maybe it was because she had recently buried her cat. Maybe it was just that Nathan's purr seemed to carry the sense of his love all throughout her being. It was a unique experience that she savored.

"Simon has returned," he told her.

"Simon?" Ellen asked confused.

"That new Way Shower I told you about before," Nathan replied patiently.

"Right! Must be I didn't catch his name," she said.

Daniel waited by the back door watching mother and son. When Ellen had conceived him, no one could detect the pregnancy; not even her. He had had to shift her vibratory frequency to match Nathan's, and then she could experience the pregnancy. Ellen had been so afraid she would never see her son after he was born, but the Embodied One assigned him to be warden of the gates between the human world and the angelic realm, and now Ellen got the chance to interact with him as often as she chose to cross the Bridge of Dreams.

Now, Ellen kissed Nathan's cheek and headed toward Daniel and the door.

"Exactly where are we going this time?" Daniel asked.

"Wherever the Priest and the Wizard are having their pow wow over their new University," Ellen replied.

They strolled over the Bridge stopping for the Dolphins to scan them then moved on. In no time they had transferred to the Facility. Once outside, Ellen started dowsing.

"I get that they're at the Wizard's Tower, or at least Wizard is," Ellen finally announced.

"Good. That's a quick flight," Daniel replied opening his arms to her.

She clasped her fingers behind his neck, he held her close and they were off gliding through the air down to the Lands Below. They soared over the Desert where they'd been harassed then captured by the Marauders. Few landmarks still existed to show where they had ever been. After a while, Daniel banked to the right over the Wastelands and headed toward the Wizard's tower. They landed in the gravel strewn yard in front and hurried to knock on the door.

When the Wizard finally opened the top half of his door and spotted Ellen, he was quick to usher the two of them into the kitchen.

"Am I ever glad to see you!" he exclaimed grabbing Ellen's arm and heading for the trap door under the tower stairs that led to the basement.

"What's wrong?" she asked trying to keep up.

"New guy," the Wizard puffed. "Been at the machinery. Says he's 'upgrading' it."

A worried frown crossed Ellen's face, and she hurried down the ladder after the Wizard with Daniel following. What she saw looked like utter chaos. Over a mound of contraptions and books, she spotted the curly brown hair and plastic-rimmed glasses of....

"Simon?" she queried tip-toeing forward.

"That would be me," the young man answered without looking up.

"What **are** you doing?" she demanded taking in the chaotic arrangement.

"I updated this antiquated computer to something that uses quantum technology," he replied matter-of-factly.

"And what do you plan to do with the old computer?" Ellen asked warily.

"Scrap it," came the off-handed reply.

"NO!" Ellen and the Wizard chorused immediately.

Simon jumped knocking over a pile of books. He raised his head and pushed his glasses back onto his nose.

"It will be worthless when I'm done," he replied.

Ellen shook her head while the Wizard sputtered. "In a realm of time/space, it would be very possible for me to need to use the old model before your new model was ever thought of. Without access to the old model in time/space, I might have already died."

Simon blinked at her logic.

"You just make certain that old one works," the Wizard insisted.

"But it makes the new one redundant," Simon whined.

"Yes...here...now. But the new computer would be perfect in the new University," Ellen suggested.

She could tell from the scowl on Wizard's face this might take some convincing, but that was a battle she was ready to take on.

"Don't need any confounded gadgets at the University," he grumbled.

"Let's just remember that without that 'confounded gadget'," Ellen said gesturing toward the old, cobbled piece of equipment that sprawled throughout the basement, "I would neither be here, nor alive."

Wizard muttered something under his breath but said nothing intelligible.

"But with the quantum computer, you can ditch that pile of junk," Simon protested.

Ellen grabbed a chair, carried it over, set it down next to him and sat facing him. In a low, distinct voice, she told him, "This world works on the inverse principles of our human reality at the macro level. Didn't it even cross your mind to question why successive generations of computers were cobbled together instead of the previous model being scrapped?"

He blinked and shook his head.

"Where we operate configuring the amount of space over time, this world lets you get to a location at different times. I can come to this tower now, 5 years ago and a million years from now. In other words...."

"I understand quantum theory and the hypothesis of time travel," Simons sniffed.

"In the human reality, time travel is a hypothesis," Ellen replied. "It's something for science fiction authors to write stories about. Here," she said pointing at the floor, "in this reality...time travel is all you do."

"But I traveled over the desert," he protested.

"So did I...probably 100 years ago. That desert," she said gesturing up and out, "used to contain a Marauders camp. The next time I went through it, the Marauder's were a thing of the past, Daniel and I were legends and only the tops of the tents were sticking up out of the sand. This time when we flew over it...there was no trace of Marauders, nothing to say they'd ever existed. But if I used Wizard's Universe, I could easily go back to when they were there and face them all over again. Or tomorrow, I could land here and find myself confronting their chief."

Simon swallowed hard.

"Knowing this, describe for me the implications of traveling to this location, finding a life-saving clue via the old beast in one time, only to have the old beast decommissioned and destroyed in another time. Do we now have an antiquated computer stuck in a box like Schrodinger's cat?" Ellen asked. "Maybe it's still there in the previous time/space. Or maybe it's not because the future sent an echo back. If someone's life depends upon its truly having been there, like mine does, can you predict with 100% accuracy that destroying it now will allow for its physical presence then?"

Simon blinked a few times. "Based on the uncertainty principle...."

"No!" Ellen stated firmly. "No, you can't. And since my existence here and in the human reality depends upon its having always existed, you will treat that beastie with kid gloves."

She stood up and prepared to stalk away.

"So what would you have me do?" Simon asked haughtily.

"Get down off your arrogant, high horse and save that for the children back 'home' whom you've alienated," Ellen replied marching away. "And build a quantum coupler between the old and the new computer so they're entangled for future use."

Simon's eyebrows shot up but Ellen was already out of ear shot. The Wizard smirked as she rejoined them.

"Yes, I think that University is going to be a necessity," she remarked hotly as she headed towards the ladder up. "Apparently, it's possible to land in this reality and continue on as if you're never left your human life behind."

Ellen's voice faded as she climbed higher and neared the ceiling.

The Wizard gave a throaty chuckle and leaned towards Daniel. "Students at the University will be in for quite the ride if I can ever convince her to be one of our professors."

Daniel snorted, the corners of his lips upturned. "Did I ever mention she had two brothers whom she kept in line single handedly?"

The Wizard laughed gleefully. "No wonder I like her so well."

Simon sat listening as their voices echoed in the distance. "Even here I get laughed at," he grumbled. "Nothing new. Everyone laughs at me," he muttered turning back to the monitor. "They just don't understand me... nobody does."

He sighed heavily and turned his attention to the screen. As much as he hated to admit it, he had to agree with Ellen's logic. It was either that, or face her down, which he wouldn't do. He began clicking the keys, coding new programming, delving into work. He could always count on it for solace.

When Ellen, the Wizard and Daniel got back upstairs, they sat around the table in the rustic kitchen to talk.

"So tell me about this University," she prompted.

"Well, once Simon came through, my brother and I realized there really could be more...a lot more," he began. "He's all for doing things up neat, and for once I agree. Maybe if there had been someone to guide us, guide them, those Way Showers wouldn't have ended up in the Ice Queen's cavern."

"And they wouldn't be dead now," Ellen added.

The Wizard looked down at his robes and nodded silently. Ellen reached across the table and squeezed his hand sympathetically.

"We thought if we could give them the basics, help orient them...." he continued huskily.

Ellen shook her head slowly. "It can't be all books and classes," she told him. "This world is for experiencing. It's the only way you really learn here. Nobody telling you you're a Way Shower can give you the feeling that consumes you when you step into the Flames of Truth."

"But they need to know what's out there," the Wizard protested. "They need to know what they're up against."

"A class in the major challenges will not make it possible for them to even get close to the Vortex of Power much less stand inside it," she countered.

"Their Guardians lead them," Daniel muttered too low to be heard.

As Ellen and Wizard continued their argument about pedagogy, images from his journeys in the Lands Below with Ellen flashed through Daniel's mind. At the same time, he heard Mentor suggesting he shouldn't lead her anymore.

"*But she never would have made it this far through the trials if I hadn't,*" he thought.

The Wizard's and Ellen's voices filled his ears temporarily blocking his thoughts.

"*Could she be due to face some ultimate test?*" he wondered. "*Or is she coming to a point where she won't need me?*"

Daniel clutched his head, squeezed his eyes shut and gritted his teeth together as the argument raged around him - one without, one within.

"No!" he finally shouted jumping up from the table.

Ellen gave a small cry, and both she and the Wizard looked up at him ashen-faced.

"No. They-have-to-find-their-own-way," Daniel told them through clenched teeth, his face red with effort.

"Daniel," Ellen cried reaching her hand toward him. "Are you ok? What's wrong?"

"Nothing," he replied curtly, turning toward the door. "Nothing. I-I just need some time alone."

He wrenched the door open and slammed it shut behind him. Moments later, Ellen and the Wizard heard the downbeat of his wings then silence. The two friends sat for a while staring mutely. At last, Ellen got up and looked out the window. Finally, she ducked her head and folded her arms across her middle.

"Something's not right," the Wizard said quietly. "He's not doing well."

Ellen shook her head but didn't look up.

Neither of them heard the footsteps on the ladder and both jumped when Simon appeared in the kitchen doorway.

"I rigged that quantum coupler," he announced.

Ellen glanced up, her eyes red with unshed tears. "Good," she whispered. "Thanks." She tried a tight smile.

"Um...did I do something wrong?" he asked.

She shook her head, covered her mouth with her hands then dashed into Wizard's bedroom and shut the door with a hard bang. Seconds later, the men heard stifled weeping.

"I-I don't always come across well," Simon admitted. "But... people don't usually cry."

The Wizard shook his head and rose to his feet. "This had nothing to do with you."

"Then...what?"

The Wizard shuffled over, put a hand on Simon's shoulders, spun him around and headed him toward the spiral tower staircase.

"Let me show you my Universe," he suggested as they began climbing the stone stairs. "This will help you grasp time/space better."

Their voices faded as they ascended and all that could be seen of them were their elongated shadows on the tower wall flickering in the light from a torch.

Meanwhile, Daniel had spun straight up to the Great Above. He found the most secluded meditation garden available and fisted his hands at his sides while he paced.

"She wastes her time arguing the fine points of training others, but there's something big coming into her life, and she's so unconcerned, so easily distracted," Daniel fumed. "I want to say something to her, but Mentor suggested maybe I should stop leading her and let her figure it out. But is telling her the same as leading her? Or is it just 'providing the background' like she said?" he wondered miserably.

He suddenly felt the bright, electric sensation that heralded the arrival of the Embodied One. Only he wasn't ready to face him just yet. In a split second, Daniel slipped out of reach, and the Embodied One appeared in the empty garden, glanced about and frowned.

CHAPTER 6

Daniel didn't even set an intentional location. He took off trusting he would land where he most needed to. In this case, it was Raphael's Healing Chambers. He materialized in the middle of the curved hallway upsetting a cart. Reeling, he staggered back and collapsed against the wall. As if out of nowhere, healers rushed to his side, got him up, slung his arms over their shoulders and dragged him to a nearby room. A third healer became a blur of light as she rushed to find Raphael. The healers carrying Daniel just managed to get him onto a bed and swung his booted feet up. A second later Raphael appeared and rushed to Daniel's side.

"Daniel," he called urgently. "Can you hear me? What happened? Where's Ellen?"

For a moment Daniel batted his hands about his face. Then he found Raphael's tunic, grabbed it by the lapel and hauled him closer. "Send the others away," he rasped.

Nodding, Raphael waved his hands and his assistants turned and left. "Now tell me what's going on," Raphael insisted.

Daniel blinked his eyes open, stared at his hands clutching Raphael's tunic then let him go abruptly. He tried to sit up, but Raphael firmly held him in place.

"Where's Ellen?" Raphael asked again.

"Wizard's," Daniel slurred.

"Were you attacked?" Raphael asked.

Daniel shook his head. "Slipped sideways in the travel stream," he said with effort.

Raphael's mouth opened and closed. "Whatever for?"

"Side stepped the Embodied One," Daniel confessed in a low tone.

Raphael stepped back, his eyes wide, and his body tense. "What have you done, Daniel? You have to go back before he thinks I aided you."

Daniel shook his head and began to sit up again. "Can't...yet, Raph," he said with effort.

"Why?" his friend wanted to know.

"He-he wants to talk about Ellen, but I'm too jumbled up inside. About going crazy."

Raphael frowned. "What's going wrong with Ellen?"

"That's the thing," Daniel gasped out, now finally sitting fully upright. "I don't know. I can't see. All I see when I look at her path is darkness."

Concern clouded Raphael's face. "I will help you," he said touching Daniel's head at several points. "But you must go to the Embodied One as soon as I'm done."

"No worries, Raph. I promise," Daniel assured him. "And I'll make him understand that I sought you out."

But Raphael was no longer listening. Instead, his brow was furrowed with concentration as he focused on the darkness he saw swirling in Daniel's mind.

"Yes," he murmured. "I see it. I fear that by focusing on it, you have released the darkness and caused it to grow."

"Do you know what it is, Raph?" Daniel asked, his head tilted backward and his eyelids fluttering wildly.

Raphael shook his head slightly. "I cannot identify it, but I can contain it."

He continued to work for a while longer until Daniel's eyelids ceased fluttering. Daniel took a deep breath and sighed with relief.

"How is it now?" Raphael asked taking his hands away.

Daniel searched inwardly along Ellen's path. "I still can't see what's coming."

"But is the darkness still blocking you?" Raphael wanted to know.

Daniel shook his head and a slow smile spread across his face. "No. Now all I see is light."

Raphael let out a breath of relief. "Good. Now go!"

A split second later, Daniel reappeared in the Meditation Garden. The Embodied One looked up from where he sat on the bench. Daniel dropped to one knee before him.

"I am sorry, Sire," he apologized.

"You avoided me," the Embodied One stated evenly. "Why?"

Daniel took a deep breath to steady his nerves. "I have been conflicted about my roll in Ellen's life, wondering if I have or am presently doing right by her. But the darkness crept in until I could see nothing else. I-I was unprepared to talk. I sought out Raphael."

The Embodied One nodded. "And did he help?"

"Yes, Sire. And sent me straight back to you."

"And what do you see now, Daniel?" the Embodied One asked.

"Light, Sire. I only see light."

"Rise, my son."

Daniel lifted his head and pushed to his feet. The Embodied One patted the bench beside him and Daniel sat.

"I have been giving the matters you brought to me great attention," the Embodied One began. "I do sense a challenge coming for Ellen, a culmination of training perhaps."

"Then, should I be involved? Or should I allow her to find her own way?" Daniel asked.

"You are her Guardian, Daniel. You cannot help but be involved in some way," the Embodied One replied. "But be that actively or passively, I am not yet certain."

"Then what do I do?" Daniel asked, perplexed.

"For now, continue on as you have. What concerns me more is the darkness you have seen," The Embodied One revealed.

Daniel frowned. "How so?"

"I have tested it, tasted it, tried it," the Embodied One shared. "And while I know it does not represent evil, it resides entirely within you."

"Me?" Daniel asked, surprised.

The Embodied One nodded slowly. "The next time you feel it clouding your vision, come to me, Daniel."

Daniel ducked his head and nodded.

"Do not worry," the Embodied One said rising. "We will find the darkness's origins, and then we will deal with it. As long as its intent is not evil, there is nothing to fear."

Daniel swallowed hard as he watched the Embodied One leave. Something was inside him; something that would not allow him to see into Ellen's future. He sat on the bench still as stone for a long while wondering what this could all possibly mean.

At the Wizard's place, Ellen pulled herself together, went out into the kitchen and splashed cold water onto her face. Seeing the light from Wizard's open lab door, she climbed the spiral staircase and entered. She stood just inside watching the Wizard bustle about pointing out aspects of the Universe. Simon was bright, but this was too much, even for him.

"I just cannot believe this hodge podge takes you all over in time," Simon sputtered. "You need power equivalent to that of a black hole...."

"Black hole?" Wizard asked.

"Space phenomenon thought to be at the center of most galaxies," Ellen explained entering the room further.

"And," Simon continued, "stationary wormholes, which are only theoretical."

"My dear boy, that's patently absurd," the Wizard sputtered.

"And what you're suggesting is impossible," Simon replied.

"Show him," Ellen suggested.

"You don't mean, send him through the Universe?" Wizard asked.

"I do," Ellen replied, "with me."

She held out her hand and the Wizard went to the control stand, got his remote key and placed it into her palm.

"Where to?" the Wizard asked placing his hand over a sphere on the control panel in readiness.

Ellen mounted the steps to the wooden walkway that encircled the perimeter of the Universe. "Let's try the Desert City."

"Thought you were banned," the Wizard protested.

"I am now," she conceded, "but it wasn't always so."

"Why are you banned?" Simon wondered.

"Let's show him," Ellen said firmly. "Looking for the Temple."

Simon watched as the Wizard manipulated the ball. A location on the Universe lit up and slices of images stacked up on top of that location. The Wizard pulled down a lever and the slices became a steady column. The gadget in Ellen's hand beeped and a red light blinked on. She tucked it into her pocket.

"What now?" Simon asked.

Ellen spun around, headed straight for him and linked arms with him. "We're going out the Wizard's back door," she announced dragging him with her toward the wall on the other side of the Universe. She stood expectantly before the blank wall.

"And do what?" Simon cried.

"This!" the Wizard laughed and pull a lever.

In the next instant, the wall slid back, Ellen gave Simon a tug and they were sucked into a vortex. Though she managed to stabilize them with her pendulum, the ride was still bumpy and the landing rough. They fell beside palm trees at the Oasis outside the Desert City.

Ellen jumped up and dusted herself off. Simon slowly crawled to his feet as he gawked at the caravaners and camels.

"C'mon," she urged taking his arm. "We've got a whole city to see again, and again, and again."

They entered through the gate and Ellen made straight for the Temple. They climbed the steps to the portico, and she tugged the door open. In the light of the Flames of Truth, Simon spotted a Priest. When he came over to greet them, Ellen noted how young he looked in spite of the airs of maturity he put on.

"Do I know you?" he asked Ellen.

"You will...in a while," she replied and turned Simon back out onto the portico.

"What do you mean, he'll know you in a while?" he demanded.

"You'll see," she replied.

Ellen stepped down off the portico with Simon, walked around the corner, came back and went back up to the Temple door.

"Why did we just do that?" Simon demanded.

"Had to cover enough ground for the time to change," she replied and opened the door.

Shaking his head, Simon followed her inside where they were greeted by an elderly gentleman in faded robes.

"Oh, there you are!" he exclaimed. "My brother contacted me ages ago about this demonstration."

"Just a couple more times," Ellen assured him and dragged Simon back outside with her.

"A costume," he sputtered.

"And that explains the loss of two inches off his height, his severely arthritic hands and age spots on his skin," she refuted.

"Make up," Simon snorted.

"He was a Priest not a special effects artist," Ellen pointed out as she dragged him straight off the portico and crossed the bustling street.

As they turned to make their way back, the bustle slowed to a stop, people began disappearing and everything turned to dust and wind. By the time they got to the top of the steps, the Temple was in ruins. Ellen dragged Simon inside where they tip-toed around debris and found the center where the golden dome had collapsed to the floor.

"What happened?" Simon asked slowly rotating on his personal axis to take in the ruin.

"Another time period," Ellen replied. "But I brought it all back."

"Huh?"

She put her fingers to her lips and dragged him back into the shadows to hide behind a piece of wall. As they watched, she walked into the ruins with Daniel, who was without shield or sword. He relit the Flames of Truth, and Simon gasped when she stepped into the wall of fire. Ellen clamped her hand over his mouth.

"That's the first test of a Way Shower," she whispered into his ear.

They watched as she exited the Flames, and she and Daniel made their way toward the Dome. At first they couldn't make out what was being said. Then Daniel began marching in a circle around Ellen.

"Bring it back!" he chanted over and over again.

And as he did, Ellen began to vibrate. Before they knew it, the Vortex of Power began rising up out of the ground. It continued to climb upwards, eventually obscuring her from view, as it continued up to where the ceiling had been. As the Vortex maintained its spin, the Temple slowly began to rebuild itself around them. As brick and stones flew from the floor toward the ceiling, Ellen grabbed Simon's arm, took out the Wizard's gadget and held it in front of them.

"Gotta go," she announced and hit the red button.

Seconds later, they were flying backwards like bugs sucked up in a vacuum hose. In moments, they were hurled through the Wizard's back door landing hard on his lab floor. Simon lay with the wind knocked out of him while Ellen rolled over and gingerly got to her feet. She stood over Simon staring at his ashen face and wild eyes.

"And that, Simon, is why you may not dismantle the old computer. Because you never know where you are on the timeline," she said and stepped over him.

"But...you brought it back!" he protested finally able to sit up.

Ellen stopped and glanced back. "Because I had already visited the Temple previously. You just got here."

"And you know what time it is?" Simon yelled scrambling to his feet.

"Yes," Ellen replied. "I do. C'mon. Look lively. You have one more trip to take."

The Wizard shut down the Universe and ushered Simon out of the lab ahead of him. They made their way to his study at the top of the Tower. Ellen was already there clearing a space on the floor. As they watched, she grabbed a piece of chalk off Wizard's desk and drew a large circle on the floor.

She stepped inside and motioned for them to join her. "C'mon. I promise this will be a much less bumpy ride."

The Wizard grabbed his staff and ushered Simon inside. Ellen set her pendulum in motion, the Vortex drew up around them and they were off to the Temple in the Desert City. This time the ride was smooth, Ellen navigated directly into the Temple, and when she released the Vortex, they were standing just inside the front door. Simon's jaw gaped.

The Priest spotted them and hurried over. "I was wondering if you'd ever get here."

"This is our fourth time here," Simon protested.

"Or first," Wizard said with a wink at Ellen.

She took Simon's hand and led him toward the Flames.

"I saw you go into these," he marveled quietly.

She nodded with a smile. "Now, it's your turn."

"I-I don't know about this," Simon stammered.

"You're a Way Shower," Ellen told him. "It's all part of the learning experience."

"Who says I'm a Way Shower?" he demanded.

"Your very presence in the Lands Below declares it."

"Oh," he replied teetering on the edge of the Flames.

Ellen gave him a little nudge and he toppled in.

CHAPTER 7

Ellen and the brothers waited patiently in the Temple on the other side of the Flames. At last they saw a hand jut out and wave back and forth. Simon appeared behind it exiting the Flames with a look of wonder and astonishment on his face. He turned his hands and arms over checking for burns.

"How?" he asked looking up at last.

Ellen shrugged. "That's a question I never asked. I just allowed myself to be amazed."

Simon took a deep breath and sighed.

"Peaceful within the Flames of Truth, isn't it?" the Priest asked.

Simon nodded then glanced at the Vortex. He took a couple of steps toward it then glanced back. "You all get into that?"

Ellen and the Priest nodded while the Wizard remained motionless.

"Can I try?" Simon wanted to know.

The Priest gestured toward the Vortex. "Be my guest."

Simon cautiously approached the edge of the Vortex. Under his breath he tried to calculate angles of assault on the swirling mass of air. Shaking his head, he finally opted to step toward the edge. He felt himself be lifted off the floor and slung backwards like a pebble from a slingshot. He landed on the floor with the wind knocked out of him. The Wizard bent forward, grasped his hand and helped him to his feet.

"I found I needed more experience in the Lands Below before I could stand in the Vortex," Ellen said as Simon dusted himself off. "It's a measurement of how much you've embraced your personal power."

Simon shuffled around the Vortex studying it from different perspectives.

"One clue," Ellen added, "is that your ability to assail the Vortex comes from the heart," she said pointing to her sternum, "not your head."

Simon narrowed his eyes. "What about you, Wizard? Do you think your heart is stronger than your brain?"

The Wizard shuffled his feet and looked down studying his robes.

"You need to do this," Ellen whispered near his ear. "You're ready. I know you are."

He glanced up at her and his face reddened. But her kind, honest gaze gave him hope. He cleared his throat, squared his shoulders and handed his staff to his brother.

The Wizard took a step forward holding Simon's gaze. "Years ago when we entered this realm, I was a lot like you," he replied. "I was full of ideas from books, and theories and energy for building gadgets. I tried to enter the Vortex using all my smart mathematics and ended up exactly like you. And I never tried again. I found 'intelligent' ways around that issue. But...not anymore."

With that, the Wizard approached the edge of the Vortex. He closed his eyes and his face softened. Taking a deep, calming breath, he stepped through the whirling wall of wind and entered the Vortex.

"Yes!" the Priest exclaimed jubilantly.

Ellen beamed with pride.

Simon hurried over to the spot where the Wizard had disappeared, gingerly held his hand up only to have his arm flung back. "No way," he breathed.

"It's not magic, Simon," Ellen said. "You just have to let go of what you think you know and open a space for all possibilities."

He glanced over at her.

"Be Schrödinger's cat," she challenged.

Simon gave the Vortex one more look, snorted and walked away.

"Not ready," the Priest whispered leaning toward her.

"Nope and unwilling to admit it," Ellen replied.

A few minutes later, the Wizard appeared and stepped out of the edge of the Vortex. He wore a look of amazement and wonder.

"Not the same calm as in the Flames," he said, "but there is a stillness there."

"The calm at the center of the storm," the Priest replied handing the Wizard back his staff.

The Wizard gave Ellen a smile of gratitude then glanced about and frowned. "He's not back yet?"

Ellen shook her head.

"Do you know when you need to return?" the Priest asked, suddenly alert with concern.

"Not without Daniel," she replied. "Would your gazing pool let me see my bedroom back home?"

The Priest shrugged. "It should."

She and the Wizard followed the Priest past the heavy, scarlet, floor-to-ceiling curtain into his private chambers then out the side door into a walled garden. Nearby was a clear, shallow pool. Ellen approached it and knelt. The Priest handed her a bowl filled with flower petals. She took a handful and scattered them over the surface of the pool.

Ellen stared at the pool as the water shimmered, and the reflection changed to an image of her lying in her darkened bedroom.

"*If I could only see the clock clearly,*" she thought.

As if on cue, the image rotated to the left. She leaned forward squinting to see the clock face more clearly.

The Priest touched her shoulder and held her back. "Do not touch the water," he warned quietly.

Ellen nodded and pulled back. Finally, she got a clear glimpse of the LED readout.

"Five a.m.," she breathed.

"How much time does that give you there?" the Wizard asked from nearby.

"Thankfully, I'm not an early riser," Ellen replied shaking her head to clear the image and rising to her feet.

"So how much longer?" The Priest asked.

"About three to four more hours in the human reality," she replied.

The brothers sighed with relief.

"So are we just going to hang out here all day?" Simon called from the doorway.

"Bring your Xbox next time," Ellen teased.

Simon scowled and disappeared inside the Temple.

"No electronic toys," she explained to the brothers. "Better go check your tools on the shelves."

The Priest's eyes opened wide and he all but dashed inside. Ellen and the Wizard heard "Put-that-down!" and a crash and winced.

"**That** doesn't sound safe," Ellen remarked.

"Knowing him, it's not," the Wizard chuckled. "So what do you want to do until Daniel comes back for you?"

Ellen was staring down the walkway toward the wrought iron gate at the far end of the wall. "How old were you when you came here?"

The Wizard blinked. "Seventeen...eighteen, I suppose."

Ellen nodded slowly then turned toward him. "And do you remember your real names? Who you were?"

The Wizard's mouth opened and closed. He hummed a tune and studied the sky. Then he scratched the back of his neck and watched a caterpillar cross the walk. Finally, he had to shake his head in defeat.

"We forgot long ago," he admitted.

Ellen gently laid her hand on his arm. "It's important that you remember, Wizard. You are more than a title. You must remember who you are."

At that moment, Simon came flying out the door followed by the Priest swinging a broom at his backside. He stood in the doorway red-faced from exertion and breathing hard.

"Until you learn respect for other peoples' things, this Temple is off-limits to you," he roared and disappeared inside.

"What did you do?" Ellen cried.

"Nothing," Simon replied scowling.

The Wizard stalked over the him and squared off. "My brother has **never** flown in that kind of rage. Now, what-did-you-do?"

Simon backed up. "Dude, chillax. It was just a stupid glass ball."

Ellen's hand flew to her mouth. The Wizard's face went pale and he staggered backwards.

"What?" Simon asked, annoyed.

"That 'glass ball'," Ellen began, "was a finely tuned sphere of crystal that has been the brothers' only link while here in the Lands Below. No cell towers, dimwit."

Simon glanced up before slinking deeper into the garden. Ellen hurried inside and just caught the Priest as he was about to discard the precious shards.

"No! Don't!" she cried, and he stopped with his hand poised in mid-air. "Save them," she urged. "Maybe Weaver can do something to restore it."

The Priest looked down at the fragments in his dust pan and sighed with relief. "I didn't think of that."

"It's a possibility," Ellen pointed out. "Always look for possibilities."

He nodded glancing about for something to put the shards into. Ellen spotted the silk covering that had once draped the sphere, grabbed it and laid it out carefully on the floor. The Priest gently dumped the shards onto the silk then hurried into an outer chamber. He returned a moment later with a large basket. Together, he and Ellen picked up the silk and laid it in the basket.

"Think it can be fixed?" the Wizard asked from the doorway.

"I'm hoping so," the Priest replied pulling out his pendulum.

A moment later, the Vortex came up around him and the basket. Ellen stepped back and watched as he left.

Ellen glanced into the garden eyeing the sullen Simon. "Sure you want to create a University?"

The Wizard studied the young man for a while and nodded. "He comes from a world where he has never fit in."

"And doesn't fit in here, either," she pointed out.

"He stands a better chance of creating a way to fit in here," the Wizard replied.

At that moment a large set of wings obscured their view as an angel landed in the garden. Ellen's heart beat faster until he turned around and she saw that it clearly wasn't Daniel.

"You still need Simon?" he asked.

"No!" Ellen and the Wizard chorused immediately.

The angel frowned and turned toward Simon. "In trouble even here?" he asked quietly with great gentleness.

Simon hung his head. "I don't fit in anywhere. Just let me die already and get this over with."

A chill tricked down Ellen's spine. "You tried to commit suicide."

"You would too if everyone hated you," Simon retorted.

"The attempt was unsuccessful and he's been recovering," the angel explained.

Ellen went up to Simon's Guardian and pulled him a little ways away. "You need to stick with him while he's here. Leaving him by himself just makes him feel alone and abandoned. Then he gets defensive. You need to help him acclimate. We can't do that, particularly me. I'm not a permanent denizen."

The angel's eyebrows raised. "You're Ellen?"

"And I'm famous," she quipped sarcastically.

"A bit," the angel confirmed. "I'd hoped he'd be all right with you. I needed to review his life plan."

"Seems to be the season for reviews," she noted wryly. "Look, if you get a chance, take him to visit the Visionary. She has a life story that might put things into perspective for him."

The angel nodded and turned to Simon. "Ready to go?"

"Whatever," he replied.

"Wait!" Ellen called. "Did you happen to see Daniel?"

The angel turned and shook his head.

"If you should see him, would you tell him I'll need to return in a bit?" Ellen implored.

He nodded firmly and turned back to his charge. "Now, let's go."

The angel wrapped Simon in his arms, took off and disappeared in mid-flight.

The Wizard and Ellen turned away from the sky and looked around the garden.

"Looks like we're on our own," she said.

"What d'ya fancy?" he asked comically.

"Hm," Ellen replied pensively. "Do you and your brother have an idea where you might want to locate the University?"

He nodded. "We've given it some thought."

"And...?"

"There's a spot on the coast north of the Sea Town," the Wizard replied. "Nice rocky promontory rising out of the sea. Close to an old wood forest. On a direct sight line to the Dragon's cave."

Ellen had her eyes closed. "I think I know the area."

"Haven't checked it out yet," he told her.

"Then sounds like it's high time," Ellen replied hauling out the pendulum

She brought up the Vortex around them before the Wizard could protest. Before he knew it, they were rising above the City and heading out over the Desert. Ellen followed the Caravan Road till it turned then she kept on through the Wastelands. The Wizard spotted his snug cottage and tower below them and waved wistfully as it passed by.

"What direction from here?" she asked.

The Wizard pointed 45 degrees to the right. Ellen immediately shifted the Vortex and let it pick up speed. Before long, they whisked over a broad plain with tall grass waving in the wind. Soon, they approached a rocky mountain chain and the air about them grew chilly.

On the other side of the mountains, Wizard waved her toward the left. Before long, they caught the sparkle of sun off waves. They set down on the cliff near the rocky promontory. Ellen let the Vortex subside and slip back into the ground.

"So," the Wizard said putting his hands on his hips and gazing about. "What do you think? Has the right atmosphere."

Ellen stood on the cliff letting the sea breeze toss her hair. The salt tang filled her nostrils as seagulls called overhead or dove into the ocean for fish. She took a couple of steps and looked over the edge.

"There are stone steps cut into the cliff face," she announced, "and a large cave with a sea entrance below."

The Wizard came up behind her and peered over her shoulder. "Wonder who made the staircase?"

"Well, there is evidence in the Knight's crypt of other Way Showers who lived in these lands and died some time ago," Ellen replied.

The Wizard scratched his chin. "There's also stories about the Way Shower who turned to light and never died. He was supposed to have lived somewhere out this way."

"Turned to light?" Ellen asked glancing at him over her shoulder.

The Wizard nodded. "Ran across references to him a couple of times in my books."

"Was he in any of Henry's notes?" she asked.

Ellen spoke of the Way Shower Specialist who had lived in the Great Above and kept notes on all the Way Showers who had passed through this realm and their histories. He died after the Ice Queen encased him in ice to tap him as an energy source when she'd created the illusions in the Minion's Lair.

"Haven't had a chance to go through them like I'd like to," the Wizard replied.

"Would be good to do so at some point," Ellen replied absently as she rotated around to take in the whole scene. "I do like the looks of that forest," she remarked enthusiastically and headed towards the towering trees about a quarter mile off.

The Wizard followed her over the bushy ground. When they got to the forest eaves, they were both surprised to find a path leading into the woods. Though somewhat overgrown at the present, it was sufficiently rutted to suggest it was well-used at some point in the past.

"Curiouser and curiouser," Ellen murmured and took a step onto the path entering the woods.

Inside, under the forest canopy, the light was dimmer, more green and brown with periodic shafts of bright sunlight piercing the dense foliage. Trees with trunks as big around as a house stretched plumbline straight towards the sky. A deep bed of fragrant needles muffled their footsteps and led to a softening of even their voices.

"Didn't I tell you this was perfect?" the Wizard asked, eyes sparkling with delight.

Ellen nodded. "This wood is magical. It requires long, careful exploration in deep reverence."

She walked up to a big tree and put her hand against its bark. Before long, she turned and leaned her back against its trunk.

"About lulls you to sleep," the Wizard slurred from nearby where he, too, leaned against the trunk.

"Mm-hm," Ellen replied.

With effort she pushed away from the tree, grabbed the Wizard and tugged him away, too.

"C'mon," she said pulling him toward the eaves of the forest. "We have a promontory to check out."

They stumbled out of the forest into the open and tumbled to the ground.

"Now I know what to do for my insomnia," the Wizard said sitting on a tuft of grass and shaking his head.

Ellen nodded. "Would be good for meditation, too, but only in small doses. You'd need large quantities of caffeine to keep awake for any length of time in there."

The pair hauled themselves to their feet and retraced their steps to the sea cliff. They were about to pick their way out onto the promontory when Ellen caught sight of a Vortex headed toward them. She turned and pointed toward it, and the Wizard shielded his eyes with his hand as they watched it draw closer. Before long, it landed, dissipated and the Priest stepped toward them.

"So? Can he fix it?" the Wizard fired immediately.

"It will take Visionary, Weaver, and Auditor, but they think the sphere can be repaired, " the Priest replied.

The Wizard sighed with relief.

Ellen quickly filled the Priest in on the rock cut stairway, ocean level cave, old growth forest and its effects. Together, the trio headed out onto the promontory. The waves thudded against the rocks below creating a deep, resonant boom that throbbed in Ellen's sternum. The sea air was crisp and the tang enlivening.

"This really would be a good place to study," Ellen affirmed. "Amazing power and energy out here."

"Would have to be mighty strong walls, though," the Priest commented studying the waves as they hurled themselves upon the rock.

The Wizard nodded. "Granite."

Ellen turned to look at them, her eyes shining. "I can feel it...in my bones. This place was meant to harbor your dream. Do it boys! Don't let your dream die."

The Wizard and the Priest looked at her then at each other.

"Guess we're really doing it!" the Wizard exclaimed in awe.

"We were...kind of waiting for your blessing," the Priest told Ellen.

"Well, you've got it," Ellen responded leading the way back to the cliff.

She sat down and leaned back against a rock. The brothers studied her with concern.

"Are you all right?" the Priest asked kneeling beside her.

She took a deep breath and shook her head. "I'm starting to get tired," she admitted. "I think it's close to time for me to go back."

"But where's Daniel?" the Wizard asked scanning the sky.

"That I don't know," Ellen said, "but I think it's time I tried to connect with him."

The brothers stood a little ways off watching with increasing concern while Ellen sank into herself and tried to raise Daniel via their telepathic link. As she rubbed her temples before taking another stab at communication, the Wizard shook his head.

"Something is really wrong," he muttered.

The Priest nodded. "I definitely concur."

CHAPTER 8

Daniel left the Meditation Gardens and headed out to the formal gardens in front of the Great Halls. He spotted an empty alcove on the wall that ran along the edge of the cliffs overlooking the Lands Below and went over to sit down. He stared out over the edge at the cloud formations, the eagles and the Lands Below just like he had as a child. The sudden beat of wings close by startled him and Daniel glanced up. Oriel, his brother, headed toward him from the sky. Though older, the resemblance between the two was strong; the biggest differences were in size, with Oriel being larger from his days spent in Michael's army, and their shields were unique to them. Oriel sat beside Daniel and studied his face.

"There's rumors," he began.

"Like?" Daniel wondered.

"That you're having a 'challenge'," Oriel replied leaning close and speaking softly.

Daniel sighed heavily. "Maybe."

"You're too intense," Oriel observed. "Relax a little."

"She's my charge, Oriel," Daniel replied. "I have to maintain my focus."

Oriel glanced up gazing at the vista of cloud and sky. He pursed his lips and nodded. "You know...when I'm in battle...it's pretty serious there, too. But I don't brood on it."

Daniel sat back and threw up his hands. "You don't understand. This isn't battle. It's someone's life...their purpose...th-their growth."

Oriel nodded. "I get it. You have responsibility for more than just yourself. I don't know what that's like, Daniel. I don't," he admitted. "But this is what I do understand." He sought and held his brother's gaze. "You wouldn't be half the man you are now but for Ellen, and she wouldn't be the amazing, complex, brave woman she has become but for you. It's a mutual thing. You just don't get the one without the other."

"I know...I mean, that's what it feels like to me," Daniel confided. "I just don't understand why the Embodied One and Mentor have both hinted I should back off. Be less involved."

Oriel considered this. "Maybe that's all that comes to them at this point," he suggested. "Is that ALL they had to offer?"

"Well," Daniel said hesitantly. "When Mentor looked at Ellen's life line, he said he saw...."

Oriel waited expectantly. When Daniel hesitated, Oriel looked at him out of the corner of his eye. "Saw...what?"

"Sparkles," Daniel whispered sheepishly.

Oriel's eyebrows peaked. "Sparkles?"

Daniel colored and nodded.

"Is that some kind of Guardian code?" Oriel wanted to know.

"Well, kind of," Daniel admitted. "It's what he's always says when he knows everything will work out well in the end."

Oriel sat up and smiled. "Well, there you are!" he said slapping Daniel on the back. "He's seen sparkles. Everything turns out all right in the end!"

"Shh," Daniel hushed as others walking and flying by turned toward them.

Oriel glanced about then ducked his head. "Sorry. But...doesn't that make it ok for you?'

Daniel shook his head and put his hands over his face. "Ori...you have no idea."

Oriel frowned. "What do you mean?"

"Some of the things Ellen has had to go through that 'turned out all right in the end'," Daniel said.

"Like what?" Oriel asked with genuine concern.

Daniel swallowed hard. "It's almost too much to say. Two husbands who were abusive. Bullies all through school. We both thought she'd finally made it to 'safety' when she and Robert got married and her health finally improved," he said. "Then a few years ago, a guy kicked in their back door, attacked them, nearly beat them to death and left them for dead."

Oriel whistled low. "Wow! Sorry. I had no idea. To look at Ellen, you'd never know."

Daniel nodded and gave his brother a tight smile.

"So, that's why you're so intense now?" Oriel asked.

Daniel nodded. "It's so hard, Ori...to see the things she goes through...even when I know it will turn out all right in the end."

Oriel put his hand on his brother's shoulder then pulled him close for a hug. "I'm sorry, Daniel. I thought you just had to buck up. I didn't know."

Daniel squeezed his eyes tight to hold back tears. "It's ok, Ori. I volunteered for this."

"Yes, you did, brother. Yes, you did," Oriel replied. "But I don't think you knew you'd have your heart ripped out and rearranged in the process."

Daniel shook his head.

"So, isn't there something else those sparkles could be useful for?" Oriel prodded.

Daniel took a deep breath. "I've been trying to sort it all out. When I first visited Raphael, all I could see was darkness and it was eating me alive."

"Darkness?" Oriel asked, immediately concerned. "Is that bad?"

"The Embodied One says he can't detect any evil in the darkness, so he's certain it's not harmful," Daniel replied.

Oriel nodded.

"After Raph worked on me, all I could see was light," Daniel continued.

"Light's better if you ask me," Oriel commented.

Daniel nodded. "But it doesn't give me any better distinctions by which to view Ellen's life."

"Are there ever any sparkles in the light?" Oriel wondered.

Daniel thought about it for a moment. "You know...now that you ask and I look, there are."

"Then maybe that's the answer, Dani," Oriel said hopefully. "Maybe you don't look at the darkness or even at the light. Maybe you go for those sparkles."

Daniel considered this for a moment. "I think you're onto something, Ori. I think you're right. Those sparkles may be Mentor's breadcrumbs along the path of her life pointing out the steps she needs to take, even when they aren't otherwise obvious."

"So that's what you look for. If you follow those, you'll be all right in the end," Oriel said.

Daniel nodded. "Yeah. I think you're right. Thanks."

"Any time," Oriel said rising. "You need to talk, you come to me." And with that, he was off.

With Oriel's suggestion fresh in his mind, hope crept back into Daniel's heart. He sat in the alcove staring straight ahead and reviewed the moments in Ellen's past looking for evidence of sparkles. When he finally started seeing them and was certain he'd grasped their pattern and signature, he waved his hands in front of his face to dispel the history. With his brow knit in concentration, Daniel began to trace Ellen's life forward. With studious intent, he looked for sparkles and rejoiced inwardly as they started showing up.

"*Ori was right,*" he breathed inwardly. "*It's my way forward.*"

Meanwhile, in the Lands Below near the promontory, Ellen all but screamed in her head, and still she couldn't raise Daniel. The brothers stood helplessly by and periodically tried to either share their energy with her or amplify her mental signature. But Ellen had gotten nowhere, and she was beginning to feel light-headed and dizzy. No one had to tell her; she needed to head home fast.

Out of sheer desperation, she scrambled to her feet, searched the ground until she found a small stone then stood facing out to sea. She grasped the stone in her hand, closed her eyes and concentrated with all the strength she had left.

"*Daniel!*" she called mentally. "*Hear me! Now! I've-got-to-go-home.*"

With that, she threw the stone over the cliff. The brothers watched gasping when it suddenly disappeared. Too late, they saw Ellen's knees buckle, and she toppled off the cliff. Screaming for her, they dashed to the edge trying to grab her. They missed and lay staring in horror over the edge.

In the Great Above where Daniel sat in supreme meditation, a sharp sting hit his right cheek making him jump. His eyes flew open and he glanced about, startled. At his feet lay a small stone. He picked it up, furrowed his brow then suddenly leapt straight into the air.

Thought had nothing to do with his speed; sheer instinct guided his wings. He came out in the Lands Below, spotted Ellen toppling off the cliff and became a streak of white as he plummeted toward her. Daniel stopped just below her, held out his arms and allowed himself to sink

63

a little lower as he caught her in mid-air. They dipped down gradually coming to a halt near the tops of the waves with Ellen safely cradled in his arms.

He hugged her to himself and flew back up so the brothers would know she was safe. They waved to him then hugged each other for joy. Meanwhile, Daniel slowly spun away taking Ellen back across the Bridge of Dreams and returning her to her world.

It was the rare occasion when he chose to become solid flesh in the human reality, but in this case, a certain Bichon was pretty desperate and it was his fault. While Ellen continued to sleep until she could come around naturally, Daniel opened the dog's crate and went through the pet care routine he had watched Ellen perform every day.

Once the dog was fed and walked several times over, Daniel returned to Ellen's bedside and gently called to her. Gradually, she rose up through the layers of sleep until she finally opened her eyes. She glanced at the clock that registered noon and suddenly sat bolt upright in bed.

"Oh my God, Boodles!"

Daniel pressed his hand against her shoulder holding her back. "I fed her," he said. "Least I could do given the circumstances."

Ellen breathed a sigh of relief and leaned back against the pillows. "You don't serve coffee, too, do you?"

Daniel shook his head. "Sorry."

Ellen studied him. "What happened? I kept trying and trying to reach you. I was getting desperate, and I almost thought you weren't going to come."

Daniel hung his head. "I know. I-I kept trying to find your future line...some markers so I could see where you're heading."

Ellen sighed. "And...?"

He nodded. "I did at last, but then I got lost following the breadcrumbs."

"Um, Daniel?"

"Hm?" he asked, his eyebrows raising.

"Breadcrumbs are supposed to help you find your way home," Ellen informed him.

He gave a light chuckle. "Well, in this case, they led me to when it 'all comes out all right in the end'."

"That's good?" Right?" Ellen asked sitting up.

Daniel nodded. "I think so," he murmured. "I think so."

A couple of days later, Ellen awoke to the feel of the bed moving a little. She pulled up her eye mask, rolled part way over, then lunged for Robert who had just climbed in.

"You made it home!" she whispered whipping her mask all the way off and tucking it under her pillow.

He set her coffee mug down on a stand and turned toward her. "Mm-hm," he murmured kissing her. "Long layover at Newark, and it took a while to get my bags, but I made it home."

"Flight ok?" she asked wrapping her arms around his neck.

"Mostly. Drive home was a little tricky with the fog, but once I got close to home, visibility improved," he said pulling her closer.

"I tried to wait up," Ellen whispered crawling close to his body," but I got too sleepy."

Robert gave her little kisses all over her face and neck the way he had since they were dating. She smiled in the dark.

"Mm, you feel good," he whispered.

"I've missed you," she responded pressing tight to him.

"I missed you, too. Had this great, big, beautiful room in Frankfurt and nobody to share it with," he told her.

"Isn't that always the way when you travel and I'm not with you?" Ellen asked.

Robert nodded and cuddled with her, both of them drifting back to sleep until Boodles started "talking."

"Guess it's time to get up," he said though not entirely convinced.

He crawled out, picked up Ellen's mug and took it to the other side of the bed. After setting it down, he opened the crate and a bundle of happy, hungry fur lunged out, licked his hands then dashed upstairs. They heard her scramble into the kitchen and, minutes later, reverse back down the stairs and start clawing at the back door. Robert let her out, turned on the TV to watch soccer and waited for her to come back to the door. Once she was inside, he climbed back into bed with Boodles in tow and the "pack" had a festive snuggle till breakfast time.

Robert stayed home for a day or two to sleep off jet lag, but meetings at the University called so he finally headed off for work mid-week. Ellen saw him off with the hot cooked breakfast she always prepared then headed up to the office to go through her email and Facebook. Instead of working or going outside, she started playing a computer game. She continued this pattern religiously for a couple of days until Daniel realized she was purposely ignoring him.

Daniel stood in the doorway of the office and leaned against the jamb. "Are you going to keep this up long?"

"I always play a game in the morning," she reminded him.

"You've been playing all day long for the past two days," he pointed out. "What are you trying to distract yourself from."

"Who says I am?"

"You lose yourself in a game when there's something in your life too scary or upsetting to face," he observed.

Ellen nodded. "Ok, I'll admit it. I do." She peered harder at the hidden object scene on the screen.

"Is it me?" Daniel asked.

Ellen found the last hidden object, opened the main menu to save and exited the game. She still didn't look at him.

Daniel moved closer. "Is it because of what happened the last time we journeyed over the Bridge of Dreams?"

Ellen sat mutely for a moment then nodded. "What happens when someone's asleep here and they can't get back to their body?"

He knelt beside her. "I'm not sure."

"Would I have died?" she finally asked turning toward him.

He shook his head slowly. "I don't know for certain, but I don't think so."

"Then what would have happened?" Ellen pressed.

"Most likely I would have had to take you to the Facility, and Raphael would have had to use the crystal capsule to bring you around and send you home," Daniel explained. "I'm sure he's prepared for all sorts of contingencies. But if it would make you feel better, we could go talk with him and you could ask him that question."

Ellen nodded. "I would like to do that. When I couldn't get a hold of you, I was scared to death. I'd like some reassurance, that's for sure."

Daniel hung his head. "I'm sorry. That was my fault."

"But what happened, Daniel?" Ellen asked. "You've never not responded to my call before. I've always been able to trust you implicitly. After this, how do I know I can trust you again? How do I know it's safe to go back?"

He rocked back on his heels, a pained expression on his face. "I-I could always ask someone to back me up," he offered, though his face was pale at the thought. "Avner is your angelic father. He'd have your signature. He's probably the only other person who could home in on you like I can."

Ellen sighed heavily. "I don't want it to have to be like this. I want you, only I don't want the you who came so late to the game I fell off a cliff."

66

"I'm sorry, Ellen. I'm sorry," he reiterated. "I was just so relieved to have finally picked up the trace on your lifeline...I-I was intent on finding the event that gives me such foreboding."

Ellen reached out and squeezed his hand. "Yeah, I'd like to know about that, too. Too bad you couldn't set an alarm."

"Actually, if I do it ahead of time, I can set an alarm," Daniel admitted.

"If you promise to set that alarm, I promise to go back," she said at last.

Daniel sighed with relief. "That's good...good. The brothers have been frantic to know you're all right."

Ellen nodded and smiled. "Yeah. I guess we gave them quite a scare, too."

He nodded. "Tonight?"

Ellen smiled and nodded in agreement.

CHAPTER 9

That evening, Ellen let Daniel ease her off to sleep and into his world. They stopped in the circular guard room. Nathan's face went pale and his hands shook when he saw Ellen enter. He hurried to her with a growl, ran his hands over her then finally smoothed her hair down as tears glistened on his eyelashes.

Ellen furrowed her brow with concern. "Nathan, honey, what's wrong?" She reached up to wipe a tear from his face as it slid down his cheek.

A low, gurgling growl rumbled from his throat. "There were rumors. Something happened...an accident. He said you were dead."

"Dead! Who told you that?" Ellen demanded.

"The other one," he replied quietly.

"Simon?" Daniel asked.

Nathan nodded. "I thought a Minion had taken your body. But the shock of seeing you when I was grieving your loss...." His voice trailed off.

Ellen wrapped her arms around him as far as they would stretch. "Aw, honey. I'm so sorry you were told something so awful. You poor thing. I'm so sorry. I'm very much alive and I promise," she said pulling back to give him a smile. "I'm all me; no hijackers."

Nathan took several heavy breaths then smothered her in his arms. He wept from relief that his mother still lived. She pulled his head down closer and pushed her cheek next to his. They rocked back and forth like that for a while until finally Nathan released her.

"My heart is happy now," he said smiling. "My mother lives."

Ellen sighed heavily. "Looks like I need to have an extended talk with Mr. Simon."

Daniel cleared his throat. "It should be sooner rather than later," he told her. "He must have overheard something at Wizard's and drew his own conclusions."

Ellen nodded but still lingered beside Nathan. "Are you all right if I go across?" she asked quietly.

"Oh yes, mother," he replied beginning a quiet purr. "I have seen and held you. I have verified my mother yet lives."

She patted his cheek then turned and joined Daniel at the back door. Once they were through it and headed down the tunnel for the Bridge, she couldn't help but rant. "What is wrong with Simon?"

"He doesn't know Nathan is our son and would be devastated by hearing you were dead," Daniel reminded her.

"It's not his news to spread around," she fumed.

"He doesn't seem to understand human interaction," Daniel noted. "Yet, he's fully human. I'm confused."

"I suspect he's highly intelligent, which his peers found off-putting, so he hasn't had much social interaction. But I can see why he's always been in trouble if he always acts like this."

Daniel shook his head. "It's so hard to believe he's even out of place here."

"There is space for him here," Ellen replied as the Dolphins scanned them mid-bridge, "but some ground rules for how he treats people and interacts with them need to be established. He's a bull in a social china shop."

"Well, let's worry about cheering the brothers first," Daniel suggested.

"Yes, let's do," she agreed.

Daniel took her in his arms, they were sucked back into the Facility, and Daniel made short work of flying her to the Lands Below. They both sensed the brothers were together at the Wizard's Tower and headed there. When Ellen knocked on the door and the Wizard answered by opening the top half, he nearly ripped the lock off the bottom half so he could swing wide the door. He took one look at Ellen, engulfed her in his arms and swung her about. She spun out of his arms into the Priest's embrace. He, in turn, gave her a long hug and dragged her to a chair. Ellen sat and the brothers just stared. Finally, they also sank into chairs and started firing off questions.

"We thought you were dead," the Wizard said.

"We saw Daniel catch you, but it didn't seem possible you could have sustained the fall," the Priest added.

"I'm fine," Ellen assured them. "I passed out and fell. Daniel caught me and slowed my descent till we could stop. I'm all in one piece. I promise."

The brothers each went limp with relief and put their chins on their chests.

"We still need you, Ellen," the Wizard said at last.

"We can't create this University without you. We missed the opportunity to go to University, but you've been to one. You know what it's like...what's needed," the Priest added.

"And I wouldn't miss helping you set this up for anything in the world. But tell me, why did you think I died?" Ellen pressed.

The Wizard hung his head. "I guess we were too loud and Simon overheard us talking."

"He convinced us that it was physically impossible for Daniel to have caught you in mid-air without breaking your back," the Priest added.

They heard a muted gasp from the Tower doorway. Ellen's eyes narrowed as she turned to spot Simon looking like a deer caught in car headlights. She pushed back from the table and stood.

"Mr. Simon," she said coolly. "You and I are going to have a chat right now. You act like you haven't got a clue how to interact with another human being, in spite of the fact you are one. However, we need to set up some rules for how you will interact with others here because the crap you've been pulling has literally shattered several peoples' lives. And that, sir, is unacceptable."

Ellen motioned for him to head towards the basement. He stiffened his shoulders and turned. Together, they went into the basement and Ellen had him sit at the big, solid oak table in the middle. For a while, she merely observed him in silence.

"You brought me down here," he said sullenly. "I know you're going to yell at me."

She continued to study him. "What's your IQ?"

He blinked. "180."

She nodded. "How many friends do you have back home?"

Simon snorted. "A dog."

She nodded again. "Do you understand how other people feel?" she asked.

He narrowed his eyes and stared at her. "I don't care how other people feel. They always hurt me. Why should I?"

"But do you have a grasp of how other people feel?" she pressed.

He shook his head and stared at the table.

"Has anybody ever tried to teach you?" Ellen asked.

"Yeah, a few teachers and a psychiatrist," he replied derisively.

Ellen took a deep breath and let it out hard. "Simon, you are an exceptionally intelligent, gifted individual. That's wonderful and great. But you weren't born into isolation. You were born into society, into a culture. By not having a grasp of human emotions and being able to empathize with others, you constantly wound others and that's why they lash out at you."

"They hurt me!" he said forcefully.

Ellen nodded. "Yes, they do...but only after you've all but trampled their feelings to death."

He grunted. "I don't care."

"Well, my dear sir, you'd better start," Ellen told him evenly. "You know that young man in the gate Between Worlds?"

Simon looked up without expression.

"That young man is MY son," she continued.

His eyes widened.

"Are you capable of imagining what he felt when you told him I was dead?" she pressed.

Simon swallowed hard and clearly struggled.

"How would you feel if your mother were dead?" she asked.

"She is," he replied flatly.

"I'm sorry," she breathed quietly.

He shrugged. "I got the house and a trust fund. I can live by myself and build my computers."

Ellen sat back. "And you really don't feel any grief at your mother's passing?"

Simon sat quietly for a minute. "I miss her sandwiches."

Ellen tilted her head. "But not her company?"

"I don't need anybody's company," he told her evenly.

Ellen tapped her fingernails on the table a few times. "Ok. Since you don't have any understanding of how to act with others, I'm going to give you some rule sets. These you are to follow when you are here in this reality. Quite frankly, if you followed them in the human reality, you would have an easier time dealing with other people."

"Whatever," Simon quipped.

"Not 'whatever,' Simon," Ellen asserted. "This is the only way you are going to survive here. If you alienate people to the point they can't tolerate having you around here, you will be on your own against Marauders, Minions and others whose idea of fun is to beat the living crap out of you, keep you alive and do it all over again. Ask me how I know?" she said leaning forward and holding his gaze.

He stared at her until he couldn't anymore then he looked away.

"Rule one - ask before doing anything to or with anything you see in someone's space in this world. What seem like toys and wouldn't do a thing in the human reality are actually very powerful, necessary tools here in this world. Got that?"

He nodded.

"Rule two - whereas you know a lot in the human world, you haven't a clue how things really are or operate in this world. Spend more time observing and asking questions. Do not presume to know how anything works here. This world has its own rules."

He smirked.

"Rule three - treat others with respect here. Be polite. Do not repeat what you hear. Do not tell others what to do unless it's life and death and you're pretty certain you can prevent death."

"You're asking me to play stupid," he grumbled.

"Tell me, Simon. How is it possible, given natural laws in the human reality, to step into a wall of flames and come out unsinged?" Ellen asked.

He stopped short and blinked a few times.

"Ah," she breathed. "It's not...not in our regular world. But here," Ellen said gesturing around them, "things that would be considered impossible or miraculous are the mundane, everyday reality. Assume you know nothing here."

He swallowed hard.

"Now, let's begin this all over again and this time...play nice with the people you've met. You might find that if you do, not everyone is out to get you," Ellen concluded rising from her chair and heading back upstairs to the kitchen.

Ellen slid into her seat at the table and blew out her breath.

"Didn't hear any yelling," the Wizard sniffed with a measure of disappointment.

"Don't think I didn't want to," she replied, "but it wouldn't have accomplished my goal."

"Which was...?" the Priest asked.

"Give him a rudimentary assessment," Ellen told him.

"What for?" the Wizard scoffed. "He's entirely self-centered."

Ellen nodded. "Yes, and it could be he's just been so intelligent and socially awkward all his life that he stopped caring how others feel. Or he could be functionally incapable of knowing how others feel and how to act without being give a set of rules."

The brothers frowned.

"Is that even possible?" the Priest wondered.

She nodded. "It's the whole reason I left the University profession I was in. Too many like Simon getting accepted and only one of me to deal with them."

"So what do we do with him?" the Wizard asked in a huff.

"Make every statement a thought-based, concrete statement," Ellen replied. "Make personal boundaries clear. If he acts disrespectful, tell him. If he eavesdrops on personal conversations, call him on it. He is a gifted individual with the emotional life of a three year old. Now," she said putting her hands on the table, "about this University. You still up for it?"

The brothers nodded enthusiastically.

"Ok then. Where do you want to start?" Ellen asked.

"What courses should we teach?" the Priest asked.

"How can we make sure new Way Showers find it?" the Wizard asked.

"I want to know how you're going to build it," Ellen said.

Daniel watched as the three of them put their heads together. The discussion was long and often rowdy. At times, he smiled to himself.

"*But is this what she's supposed to be doing?*" he wondered inwardly as he watched. "*Maybe.*"

He had to admit that Ellen was the most animated he had seen her in months, if not years.

"*That can't be bad,*" he thought.

He closed his eyes and traced her timeline. Daniel smiled broadly and relaxed when he noted the signature sparkles hovering in the air over the three friends. She was on track. That's all he needed to know.

Daniel brought Ellen back several nights in a row. He stayed glued to her side until one evening she finally said something.

"Aren't you getting bored with all this chatter about the University?" she asked one evening as they crossed the Bridge.

"You're on your path," he replied smiling. "That's all that matters."

"But you don't have to stay right with me," she pointed out.

Daniel sighed. "I want you to relax and trust me again."

"So if I can always see you, I won't have misgivings?" she surmised.

He nodded.

Ellen put her hand on his arm. "I trust you, Daniel. Set that alarm thingy and come get me when it goes off."

"You're sure?" he prodded.

She nodded and smiled.

He pursed his lips in thought then nodded as well. "All right. I'll leave you to the brothers tonight."

Ellen reached up to put her arms around his neck for the flight to the Lands Below and gave his cheek a kiss.

CHAPTER 10

That evening Daniel brought Ellen to the Wizard's house. He stepped inside and stayed a while, but when it was obvious that Ellen, the Wizard and the Priest were deep into planning mode, Daniel put his hand on her shoulder. She reached up to squeeze it in acknowledgment. With that, he left the house and headed up to the Great Above. On arriving, he found the space inside himself that would warn him of her need to leave and activated it. Then he went about seeking out friends he had not seen since taking on his Guardian assignment and spent time with his parents. Always, as soon as that internal alert was initiated, he headed back to the Wizard's house and promptly retrieved Ellen.

Daniel repeated this routine for several days. Having exhausted those he desired to catch up with, he decided to fly over the Lands Below. As he glided over the territory, it struck him that there was far more to this realm than he had supposed. Before him were tall, imposing, snow capped mountains. But with just a slight turn, he swooped low over vast canyons meandering through dry land with sparkling rivers at the bottom.

"*Ellen would love to see this*," he thought remembering her reaction to seeing the Grand Canyon in her reality from a plane.

One day, as he swooped low over some foothills and rode the thermals up their grade, he came over the rise and stopped abruptly, hovering in mid-air. There, stretched before him endlessly, lay a narrow valley, very nearly a canyon. But what took his breath away were the innumerable caves that riddled the walls on all sides like so many gaping mouths or sightless eyes.

"The Valley of a Thousand Caves!" he breathed in awe. "Who told me about that?"

Daniel knit his brow as a voice sounded in his head as if it were reading a story. Daniel blinked and realized that Mentor had read a fable to him from one of the books in his library way back when he had first joined the guardian class.

"*Mentor said it was a myth*," Daniel thought. "*It's not supposed to exist, yet...here it is.*"

When he looked again, Daniel noticed a sparkle at the mouth of a cave. He closed his eyes and opened them. The sparkle remained. As if being drawn forward by unseen hands, Daniel moved quietly toward the cave landing just inside its opening. The sparkle bobbed along a little ways in and, much like a sleep walker, he followed.

It wound through that cave out to the exit and through a series of caves until it brought him to one with no exit. Instead, Daniel stepped into a glistening chamber, increased his radiance a little and threw his hands up to shield his eyes from the sudden brilliance of his light being reflected off of countless crystals that grew in and embedded every surface of the chamber.

"*Ellen would be so amazed*," he thought and, before he could stop himself, breathed "Wow!" out loud.

In spite of the glare of the light, he caught the dance of sparkles in his peripheral vision. Turning, he made his way toward them more aware and alert this time. There, emerging from a large round boulder, was a peach colored, spherical crystal with long, faceted points growing out from it at all angles. Curious, he frowned and stretched out his hand. When he touched a point, a zap zipped up his arm, and he felt something leave his body.

Alarmed, Daniel leapt backward. With a measure of distrust, he crept catlike around the crystal. Taking a deep breath, he crawled closer and peered at it without touching it. He gasped in horror. There, deep inside, was a small version of himself.

"What happened?" he asked, alarmed. "That thing yanked a piece of myself into it." He narrowed his eyes and frowned. "That's a piece of my light!"

Suddenly, he felt his inner alarm go off and sighed with relief. "Time to get Ellen."

Daniel stood up, set an internal GPS marker for the cave, then hurried outside. He sought Ellen's signature and took off landing outside the Wizard's house relieved to be on familiar, "safe" ground again.

76

Ellen turned toward the door when it opened and smiled up at him. She excitedly motioned him over. "What do you think?" she asked gesturing to a set of drawings on the parchment they had spread on the table.

"Is this the University?" he asked.

The Priest nodded. "We've started really nailing down what colleges we'll need."

"I'll get a tower that overlooks the sea," the Wizard said happily.

"And we hope to be able to bring the Flames and Vortex from the Temple in Desert City to a new chapel to be built on the grounds," Ellen added. "Plus, we have plans for the Old Forest, and we've talked to Toby about building a harbor below from which ships could take Way Showers for the Water Challenge when they're ready."

"And books...libraries...floor to ceiling shelves of them," the Wizard said dreamily. "We're in talks with the Great Red Dragon now to see if his grandson would be willing to oversee the 'horde'."

"Just don't forget, the quantum computer gets a basement lab space where it can be climate-controlled," Ellen said firmly.

"Who's going to run it?" Simon asked from the shadows of the tower doorway.

Four heads turned toward him.

"It's very obvious that this is your area of gift," Ellen replied. "Once you've at least managed to step into the Vortex of Power and have learned to use a pendulum for dowsing, I couldn't see anyone else in that position."

"Good. I don't want anyone else touching it," Simon retorted.

"That isn't up to you," the Priest said.

Simon made a face.

"Here's the truth," Ellen said staring straight at Simon. "If you're going to continue going between worlds, like I do, you will not be in that lab all the time. There will be times when others by necessity have to access that computer. Then there is the issue of time/space. Way Showers do die in this reality just as they die in the human world. That computer must be capable of being accessed across expanses of time past the point where you no longer exist. My suggestion for you is to build a computer in the human world that is only accessible by you. But here....? All must be able to work with it. Keep this in mind as you build it. I will be testing it for accessibility from time to time."

Simon growled under his breath, turned and slunk away.

"Has he gotten any easier to deal with?" Daniel asked.

"Some," the Priest replied.

"He stays away for longer periods now, though," the Wizard replied.

"Do you think that's because his body is recovering?" Ellen wondered.

The brothers shrugged.

"Don't know," the Wizard replied.

"Can't say," the Priest said.

"Well, I do know it's time for Ellen to return," Daniel interjected.

She rose and gave each brother a hug then readily went with Daniel. As they left the Facility and approached the Bridge, Ellen got curious.

"So, where have you been going while we've been planning," she asked.

"Mmm, here and there," he replied evasively.

She raised an eyebrow and glanced at him out of the corner of her eye. "So where might 'here and there' be?" she pressed as they started over the Bridge.

"Oh, a bit of time in the Great Above catching up with friends and my parents," Daniel replied. "And some time off exploring."

"Exploring?" Ellen asked, immediately intrigued. "Where?"

"Oh, places in the Lands Below," he told her. "There's actually a lot more to it than I realized."

"Cool! Find anything interesting?" Ellen wanted to know.

"Maybe. Got to find a book Mentor read to me once," Daniel said. "I think I found a place that's only been fabled to exist."

"Really?" Ellen exclaimed, her eyes sparkling with excitement. "Now I'm torn."

"About what?" he asked as they stopped for the Dolphins to scan them.

"Well, helping the brothers with their University or going off with you and exploring your new find," Ellen said eagerly.

Something tugged uncomfortably at his heart. "I'd love to have you with me," he said quietly, "but you know the brothers really need you. You're helping them make a dream come true. We can always explore together."

Ellen sighed. "Good point. I guess you're right. But you've got me so curious."

Daniel laughed out loud. "What doesn't have you curious?"

"Not much," she had to agree as he whisked her home.

The next evening, Daniel could hardly wait to leave Ellen with the brothers. He took off immediately for the Great Above. He left even as she was opening the door to the house. As she stepped into the Wizard's kitchen, her eyes swept toward the Tower stairs and looked past them to the basement entrance.

"Not here," the Wizard said coming down the spiral stone staircase.

Ellen jumped.

"Sorry, didn't mean to startle you," he said ambling into the kitchen.

"Where's your brother?" Ellen asked.

"I just saw him off," the Wizard replied. "We're definitely going to need everyone's gifts if we're going to build the University."

Ellen smiled broadly. "Good for you! If the University is for Way Showers, having every Way Shower involved is a wonderful, collaborative effort. Now, speaking of every Way Shower," she said narrowing her eyes, "let's see how accessible this computer is."

She headed for the basement hatch with the Wizard following. When they got to the bottom of the ladder, lights automatically flicked on. He jumped and glanced about expecting something to leap out at him.

"It's ok," Ellen assured him. "Must be Simon installed a motion sensor. As soon as it detects motion, the lights come on."

The Wizard grunted but said nothing.

They looked throughout the basement and finally found a laptop-sized computer.

"What use is that dinky thing?" the Wizard wanted to know.

"In my time, you could fit all of the data on the old computers and the books and scrolls that you, the Priest and Henry collected onto something this size or smaller," she explained.

"Impossible!" the Wizard fumed.

Ellen just smiled.

"C'mon, let's see what a quantum computer can do," she suggested.

Ellen approached the computer and reached out to touch it. An arc of electricity leapt out at her hand and she got zapped. Yanking her arm back, she shook her hand.

"Ouch!"

"What is it?" the Wizard asked peering distrustfully at the machine.

Ellen put her fingers in her mouth for a moment then took them out and shook her hand again. "He put a forcefield around it. Nobody but he can touch it."

The Wizard hastily pulled back. "I thought you told him to make it accessible to everyone?"

"I did," Ellen replied heading for the ladder.

"What are you going to do?" the Wizard asked following her.

"Take a little trip through your Universe," she replied, her voice muffled as she climbed out of the hatch.

"This ought to be good," the Wizard laughed gleefully as he followed her up to his lab.

In another part of the Lands Below, Daniel faded into view at the mouth of the Crystal Cave. Thinking that perhaps he'd dreamed the whole episode from the day before, he entered the cave, found the chamber and increased his radiance enough to see clearly.

He stood with his hands on his hips and shook his head. "It was real all right."

Daniel carefully sought out the unique crystal and accidentally touched a longer crystal spire in his efforts to get a closer view. Like the day before, he felt a shock run up his arm and something leave him for the crystal. Shaken, he sat back hard on the floor.

"*This can't be good*," he thought, his heart pounding as he breathed hard.

He blew out a lungful of air then carefully slowed his respiration. When he felt calmer, he looked closer at the sphere on the rock and shook his head.

"There's still a piece of me in there," he muttered. "And it seems to be a little brighter."

Backing away quickly, Daniel retreated to the cave entrance and took off immediately for the Great Above. He came out on Mentor's balcony. As he stood scanning the room beyond, he heard Mentor's warm voice coming from the garden below. Glancing to his left, Daniel spotted him leading a group of Guardian trainees in a lesson.

"*Good, I won't be interrupting anything*," Daniel thought and pushed the balcony doors open.

He strode purposefully across the hard wood floor, scanned the floor-to-ceiling bookshelves, found the section on myths and fables and quickly skimmed the titles on the book bindings. A sudden spark caught his attention out of the corner of his eye. He turned and noticed sparkles. He leapt into the air, a chill trickling down his spine as he reached for the book they illuminated. He grasped it firmly, glided to the floor and set the book on Mentor's stand.

Daniel paused a moment with his hand over the book. The cover was vaguely familiar to him, though now it seemed to be from another time and place. He curled his fingers under almost drawing his hand away. At the last moment, he went for it and opened the book.

As he pulled the heavy cover back, a blast of wind hit him in the face sending his long blond hair streaming out behind him and ruffling his wing feathers. The pages turned themselves flipping in rapid succession. Suddenly, a bright light shined straight up in his face. When it dimmed, the pages lay flat. Cautiously, Daniel leaned forward and stared at the page. He gasped. With almost photographic quality, the Valley of a Thousand Caves lay before him on the page.

Daniel swallowed hard and his mouth went dry. He tried to read the words on the page. He knew the words but it was as if they filtered into his mind and hid in the dark recesses. He frowned, shook his head and tried again. With great effort and concentration, he made the words remain in his presence, and what he read chilled him to the bone.

"Once the crystals begin to claim your light, you cannot undo the process," he whispered.

A sinking feeling hit his stomach. *"What do I do?"* he wondered feeling entirely foolish.

Daniel turned the page but the words on that page seemed to be at war with themselves. He got little out of the text except the phrase "one of pure light." Frustrated and embarrassed at his folly, he turned toward the door to see if Mentor were coming.

At that moment, he sensed the alert to reclaim Ellen and see her home. Forgetting all about the book, he hurried to the balcony and took off for the Lands Below.

Back in Mentor's study, the book trembled slightly on the stand. Suddenly, light and a shower of sparkles shot from the pages. Just as quickly, the light went dark, and the book snapped shut. It lay on the stand perfectly still. A sudden burp of sparkles spewed from the pages then all went dark and silent.

CHAPTER 11

The Wizard sprang up the tower stairs after Ellen. He drew his lab key from a cloak pocket with a flourish and bowed to let her enter first. As soon as she was inside, he brushed past her and made straight for the control panel to his Universe. Ellen watched him with interest.

"What are you all giddy about?" she asked.

The Wizard looked up. "Today I'm coming with you."

Her eyebrows raised sharply. "Oh really? Who's going to monitor things here?"

He waved her question aside. "What little you know," he snorted. "Whilst you gamble about through my back door, I twiddle my thumbs and nap."

Ellen thought back to when the Wizard had split Daniel and her into multiple selves on a previous visit. While three teams had exited through his back door, hers and Daniel's originals had sat within a large chalk circle. It had been monotonously boring while they'd waited.

"Ok, then sir," she said. "Do we need more than one of your gadgets?"

The Wizard peered at the dials on his control then out over the Universe. "No. One should be sufficient."

He locked down his destination and return coordinates and unplugged the tracer from its niche.

"You ready?" he asked standing and rubbing his hands together with glee.

Ellen held out her hand for the gadget, and he neatly dropped it into her palm. She linked arms with him and they headed for the blank panel on the backside of the room.

"Ready?" she asked.

"And how!" he exclaimed.

Together, they watched the panel slide open then jumped into the swirling vortex. Moments later, they were deposited unceremoniously in the basement lab. Ellen held the Wizard down by his shoulder and put her fingers to her lips. Slowly, they rose up and peered over the unwieldy machinery of the antiquated computer. Simon sat at a work bench putting components for the new computer together. He talked to himself as he worked, and they quietly listened.

"She thinks she knows so much and she makes the rules," he grumbled. "I'm not making this for them. I'm making this for me. Nobody's ever going to touch it."

The Wizard and Ellen glanced at each other.

"What are you going to do with him?" the Wizard whispered.

Ellen silently rose and began working. "This is not the only parallel universe and dimension in which Simon resides," she murmured. "Let's find a more useful parallel, particularly one in which he feels more amenable to working with us."

"Sounds good to me."

Ellen stretched her left hand out toward Simon. Dropping into her heart space, she softened her focus till she could see an arch appear on a plane beside her. Mentally she entered the arch and parallels of the present moment stretched out as far as she could see.

The Wizard watched her work, frowning with intense focus as he followed her actions.

Seeing his concentration, she whispered. "The key is in the intent. I intend to have more access and openness around here. If that doesn't become a possibility soon, I see a date with the Embodied One in Simon's near future."

The Wizard shuddered.

With that, Ellen said, "I need the most useful parallel to light up, one in which access to the quantum computer is open to all."

A bright image lit the field before her and she maneuvered the shining parallel into place. As if turning large mirrors, she took the edge of the present parallel universe, turned it so it no longer reflected into the room then grasped the edge of the new parallel universe and pulled it into place. Both she and the Wizard felt a snap in the air and she let the image go.

"Think that will do anything?" the Wizard whispered.

"Won't know till we return," Ellen hissed hauling out the gadget. "Ready?"

The Wizard linked his arms with her. "Ready," he whispered.

Ellen hit the red button, and they were instantly sucked back into the vortex only to be deposited on his lab floor moments later.

"Now, let's see what changes we can notice," Ellen said picking herself up off the ground, dusting herself off and heading back to the basement.

This time when they approached the laptop, no security zapped Ellen as she touched the computer. They heard a shuffle behind them and turned. Simon watched from near the table.

"When did you get here?" Ellen asked frowning.

"When did you get here?" Simon responded. "I went upstairs for a sandwich and saw nobody. Came back downstairs and here you are."

"We had a little...adventure," the Wizard told him.

"Thanks for taking the forcefield off it," Ellen commended.

Simon frowned. "I didn't put a forcefield on it."

The Wizard looked surprised.

"Ok, the parallel's in place," Ellen said with a sigh of relief. "Can you show us a bit of how this works?"

Simon nodded and came forward. "It operates on biometrics instead of pass codes," he told them bringing out a small plate attached to the computer. "Put your pointer finger here, the scan inputs an image of your fingerprint here," he said pointing to the screen where Ellen's print showed up, "and I save that as your authorization."

He repeated the process with the Wizard.

"I'm working on a retina scanner and a blood drop scanner that will process your unique genome."

The Wizard was lost but Ellen was impressed.

"Is there some way to override the system in case someone needs to access it who is less tech savvy or travels in when no one's here?"

"Uh-huh," he admitted begrudgingly. "It's...."

Ellen waited.

"Susannah," Simon replied quietly.

"Was that your mother?" Ellen asked.

Simon shook his head. "It's a girl at the tech lab I work at part time. I like her."

"Does she like you, too?" Ellen queried.

"Doesn't know I exist," he replied.

"Bet she does," the Wizard said. "The ones you like but think they don't know you from Adam? They're the ones checking you out at every opportunity when you're not looking."

"And if you're so focused at work...that could be a whole mess of time," Ellen concluded.

Simon paled.

"Thank you for making it possible to access the computer," she said rising. "You'll have to show me more another time."

Upstairs, they heard the kitchen door open and close. Seconds later, Daniel appeared in the basement.

"Time to go," he announced.

Ellen smiled up at him.

"You'll have to teach me that parallel trick sometime," the Wizard said.

"You saw what I did," Ellen replied. "Just play with it and set out the intent for the most useful parallel to show up. You can't go wrong that way."

The next evening Ellen just wanted a full night's sleep, but Daniel seemed impatient to go.

"Daniel, I've been going every night for a week," Ellen reminded him. "It feels like I'm working all night and all day, especially since I've been working on the new novel. I'd like a breather."

Daniel took a deep breath, ran his hand through his hair and nodded. But Ellen couldn't miss the tense set of his jaw nor the shadow that crossed his face. She observed him intently.

"Something's up," she said quietly. "What's wrong?"

"Hm?" he asked glancing up.

She moved toward him. "You can't fool me, Daniel. I can feel your tension in the pit of my stomach. What's wrong?"

He sighed heavily. "I'm not sure yet but I need to do some more research."

Ellen knit her brow and tilted her head to one side. "Is this about me...or you?"

Daniel winced. "I-I can't say...yet."

She shook her head. "You don't have to. It's written all over your face. No secrets, Daniel. You know the rules."

"Not a secret, Ellen," he assured her. "I honestly wouldn't know how to tell you."

"But you will when it makes sense to you?" she pressed.

Daniel nodded.

"Ok, afternoon naps it is," she replied and got ready for bed.

After they crossed the Bridge and Daniel left her at the Wizard's house, he went straight to Mentor's school. This time when he landed on the balcony, Mentor was inside pouring over a scroll. Daniel knocked before pushing the balcony door open. Mentor looked up from under his bushy eyebrows then raised his head, a smile lighting his face.

"Daniel! Come in!" he welcomed.

Daniel strode across the floor mentally trying to devise an innocuous conversation. He cleared his throat.

"Do you remember back when I first started with you, you read a story to me from the Book of Lore?" he began.

Mentor pursed his lips and nodded.

"Do you remember the story?" Daniel pressed.

"I believe it was about the Valley of a Thousand Caves," Mentor replied.

Daniel nodded. "Well, while Ellen has been helping get the University started, I've been exploring the Lands Below."

Mentor studied his face. "You found the Valley?"

Daniel nodded. "I think so."

"So it was you who had the Book out to read!" Mentor exclaimed.

"Sorry, my alert indicated it was time to take Ellen back," Daniel apologized. "I was wondering if you could tell me more about the Valley and the caves. That Book is difficult to read."

Mentor stretched his hand up. The Book wiggled on the shelf and slid out dropping neatly into his hand. "It is indeed a difficult text," he agreed. "It is written in the First Language. I can read it with difficulty but even I have not mastered it."

"Have you ever gotten beyond the first page?" Daniel pressed. "All I could pick up was one phrase, 'one of pure light'."

Mentor set the Book on the stand, and they stood back while it opened itself to the page in question. He peered at it intensely for a moment.

"It's about the Crystal Cave," Mentor said at last.

"And, out of a thousand caves, why is this one important enough to write about?" Daniel wondered.

"There are special crystals within the cave that, when touched, draw light in any form into themselves," Mentor explained reading further.

"Is this just visible light or-or soul light or what?" Daniel asked, his hands beginning to sweat.

Mentor frowned as he read. "Apparently, any light. This text was written to warn our kind to avoid the Crystal Cave."

"Does that mean someone once entered that cave and got sucked into a crystal?" Daniel asked, both alarmed and hopeful.

Mentor strained to read. "Yes...yes it would seem that someone did."

"Did he ever get back out?"

Mentor flipped the page, looked at the swirling mess of words then pinched his nose. "I get the suggestion the person was retrieved."

"But not the how," Daniel surmised.

Mentor shook his head and closed the book. "To read that page would take someone fluent in the First Language."

"Who?" Daniel wondered.

"Try Avner," Mentor replied. "He was the first one the Embodied One taught."

"He probably even helped create the language," Daniel said relief flooding him.

As he headed toward the balcony, Mentor called after him. "Why the sudden interest in the Crystal Cave and the Valley?"

Daniel paused a moment before turning. "When I came upon the Valley and beheld it, I heard your voice in my mind reading from the Book of Lore. It seemed hard to digest that I'd found a myth come to life. But everything in that book confirms that I've found the real thing."

With that he waved, went to the balcony and took off. In the Between Space, Daniel sought Avner's signature and headed straight there. In a flash, he appeared in the Meditation Gardens by the Great Hall. He turned his head and spotted Avner sitting on a bench overshadowed by a large tree. His head was upturned as he serenely observed birds in its branches.

Avner was the first Archangel the Embodied One ever created and was the perfect specimen of strength, endurance and light. Head and shoulders above the rest, his long blond hair hung well below his shoulders and his chest shield was unique even to his kind. His wings were a full yard greater in span. He knew no equal. And yet, he was the first to turn toward the Darkness. He turned all but the youngest of his brethren as well. Michael remained loyal to the Embodied One. But after Ellen helped Michael free the angels, including Daniel and Oriel, who had been changed into Minions against their will, Avner had been discovered with the ten Archangels he had turned, and they had all been taken to the

Prison of Light.

Unbeknown to most, Ellen was one of the Way Showers Avner begot and, therefore, an inherited connection existed between them. He used it to contact her and through it, she was instrumental in returning him to the Light. The moment she found his heart and returned it to his chest, he transformed from a Minion back into his angelic self.

Daniel cleared his throat before disrupting his elder.

Avner glanced up and smiled. "Come, join me."

Daniel entered the walled garden and stood near the elder Archangel.

"Please, sit," Avner insisted. "I was just watching those birds building a nest. After all the time I spent in the wretched darkness, it is pure pleasure to be free in these gardens again."

Daniel sat beside him and watched the birds for a moment. "Mentor says you know the First Language."

Avner nodded. "The Embodied One and I worked it out together."

"Are you familiar with the Book of Lore?" Daniel asked.

"Familiar! I wrote it in the First Ages," Avner replied.

"Then...you can read it," Daniel breathed.

"Aye, though I must say I wish I'd had a better sense then as to how to control the words. Why do you ask about the book?"

"Because, I think I found the Valley of a Thousand Caves, and I'm trying to learn all I can about it," Daniel replied. "I can read the first page, and Mentor can read the second page, but the last page eludes us."

Avner frowned. "I'd forgotten about the Valley till you mentioned it."

"Would you come read the third page to me?" Daniel asked.

Avner nodded. "Yes, I'd like to see what I had to say about that Valley myself."

On cue, they rose simultaneously and took off for Mentor's school. Upon arriving on the balcony, the door swung open wide for them and they entered side-by-side. Mentor looked up at them then hurried to greet Avner.

"I suppose he's told you about the Book and finding the Valley," Mentor said.

"Yes, I'd forgotten about it, but now Daniel has me curious," Avner replied.

He spotted the Book on the stand, strode toward it and watched as it opened itself. He read the first page and shook his head. "Interesting, I describe the Valley in detail."

88

"Yes," Daniel said eagerly. "It made recognizing it simple."

"Yet, I don't include its location," Avner muttered with a frown.

He turned the page, his eyebrows rising as he read. "Yes, I remember the Crystal Cave. One of my brothers got a portion of his light sucked into one of those crystals. Interesting that I give no directions to the cave."

"Did he ever get his light back out of the crystal?" Daniel asked and held his breath.

"Maybe that information is on the third page," Avner murmured. However, as he read a dark cloud descended over his face. "Ah, now I know why I hid the Valley's location."

"Why?" Daniel and Mentor chorused.

"Because once a portion of light gets sucked into the crystal," Avner began, "the only way to get the light back out is to enlist the aid of someone of pure light."

"That's the phrase you mentioned," Mentor said and Daniel nodded.

"Does that mean the Embodied One?" Daniel pressed.

Avner stared across the room as long lost memories started coming back. "Nay, a Way Shower, but one of the purest light. In the case of my brother, he was only retrieved with the help of my firstborn. And, though a mist clouds my vision, I recall we lost him forever in the effort."

A chill ran down Daniel's spine. "How was he lost?" he asked in all but a whisper.

"My brother had to empty all of his light into the crystal and my son became light. The light so flooded the crystal that it burst thereby freeing my brother's light to return to him. But we never saw my son again," Avner explained.

Daniel staggered at the news. Part of him was trapped in one of those crystals and only a Way Shower could free him. But the cost was too great, and he knew the Way Shower who would be determined to try.

"*Ellen must never know*," he thought desperately. "*She must never know*."

CHAPTER 12

Ellen only half listened to the Wizard and the Priest as they talked about the University. Her gut was in knots, and she knew the person in trouble was Daniel. Yet, after everything they'd been through, he wouldn't say what was wrong. A foreboding crept over her she couldn't shake. Suddenly, a stinging sensation scalded her hand. She leapt out of her chair and stared at the table where her mug lay on its side, steaming hot tea running in rivulets over the table.

Shaking her smarting hand, Ellen scrambled to the sink and ran cold water over the burn. The brothers watched, concern etching their faces. Finally, she grabbed the dish towel, returned to her seat, and mopped up the mess.

"You haven't really been here all day," the Priest noticed quietly.

"You're worried," Wizard stated as fact.

"True and true," Ellen admitted glumly.

"It's Daniel," the Wizard postulated.

She nodded. "I wanted to take a break this night, but he was insistent on coming. Said he needed better understanding of something that's been bothering him."

"But he hasn't said what?" the Priest asked.

Ellen shook her head. "Yet, when I tap into him, my stomach knots up."

The brothers shook their heads.

"You guys don't have something we could use to see what's happening to him, do you?" she asked. "A crystal ball? Scrying mirror?"

They shook their heads again.

"Our spheres are only to communicate between ourselves over long distances," the Priest explained.

"Like Tolkien's palantirs," Ellen commented.

"Do you know him?" the Wizard asked excitedly.

"Afraid not," Ellen replied. "He's been dead awhile."

"What a pity," the Wizard said sadly. "I was hoping to go to University and meet the chap."

"I took a literature course comparing works by Tolkien and C. S. Lewis," she offered hopefully.

"Sounds fascinating but...not the same," the Wizard replied.

"And yes," the Priest added. "We based the concept for the spheres on Tolkien's palantirs."

"No scrying mirrors?" Ellen persisted.

The Wizard studied her carefully. "Ellen, we're concerned, too. But Daniel has every right to his privacy. Even if I could vision with a scrying mirror, I wouldn't."

"Meaning you have one," she charged.

"Meaning, don't go looking for it," the Wizard said sternly.

Ellen sighed heavily, tears wetting her lashes.

"Have you dowsed?" the Priest asked.

Ellen grimaced and shook her head. "No, I've just been stewing."

"Well, get out the pendulum," the Wizard urged.

Obediently, she reached into her pocket and pulled out the obsidian fob. The brothers silently watched as she mutely asked questions and the pendulum gave its answers. At last, she dropped it onto the table.

"Well?" the Priest asked.

"Whatever it is, it's serious," Ellen said. "Seems to be something we've never encountered before."

"At least it's not Minions, Marauders or the Sultan," the Priest said with relief.

The Wizard patted her hand. "You'll figure it out."

Ellen looked glumly at the table and fingered the chain on the pendulum. "I hope so."

"Come," the Priest said rising. "Let's visit the Temple. I sense it has been far too long since you entered the Flames."

Ellen took a deep breath and nodded. "That does sound promising."

They rose, went up to the top of the Tower, and brought the Vortex up around them within the chalk circle. In no time they had traversed the

Desert to the City and sank into the Temple. When the Priest released the Vortex, Ellen was standing but a few feet from the Flames. Without hesitation, she walked forward and stepped through the bright wall.

Inside was a quiet place of solitude. Here, in the center of an oval of flames, worry, fear, even pain was often burned away leaving nothing but deep peace and contentment. Ellen took slow, deep breaths glad for such a place. As the Flames worked their magic, she remembered the day Michael had taken Daniel into the Flames while she and the Priest waited outside listening to the bellows of a forge and the ring of a hammer on metal. Daniel's heaven-made sword had been broken by Marauders, and Michael taught him how to reforge it. She smiled recalling his achievement and how proud he had been of his new skill.

Finally, she moved toward the back wall of flames and stepped out into the cool dark of the Temple. She turned and studied it.

"What I want to know is how you'll ever get the Flames and the Vortex to the coast so Way Showers can still pass those challenges," she commented thoughtfully.

"We're thinking of visiting the Great Red Dragon," the Wizard said, his eye twinkling.

"Do I sense another adventure coming up?" Ellen asked.

"We're considering it," the Priest replied.

"Good, I highly recommend it," Ellen told them.

"What I said," the Wizard added with a meaningful glance at his brother.

"Well, whatever," the Priest replied. "I have to get in food."

"And I'm not allowed in the City," Ellen reminded him.

"I'll go," the Wizard offered.

"I'll hold down the fort, er, Temple," Ellen promised.

Once the Temple doors closed on the brothers with a resounding clang, Ellen hurried past the side curtains, through the Priest's quarters and out the side door into the garden beyond. She hurried to the Priest's visioning pool, knelt beside it and picked up the bowl of petals. She hesitated for a moment then cast them upon the water. She held her intent to see what was happening to Daniel and soon the water cleared.

Unlike the fluid scenes she had always seen of herself at home in the past, she instead saw hazy snapshots of an antiquated study, a book that spat sparkles and Daniel's face drained of color. The scenes shifted to the Lands Below with the countryside passing swiftly by. Suddenly, the movement halted and over a rise she saw a Valley filled with endless caves. Something about seeing all those blank openings staring sightlessly at her gave Ellen the chills. The scene started to move in closer and one cave in particular seemed to stand out, but before she could see more, she heard the brothers' voices.

Quickly, Ellen reached forward and ran her hand over the water. The scenes disappeared with the ripples on the pool's surface. She jumped up and went inside to help. As she stocked the Priest's larder shelves, a ray of hope shined in her heart. There was a place and presumably a Book about that place. All she had to do was find the one and read the other. She'd be able to figure out what to do then.

Daniel was quieter than usual when he came to retrieve her. Ellen slipped her arms around his neck and felt his arms tremble as he held her. She buried her face against his shoulder, closed her eyes and drank in the perfume of his skin, the silkiness of his hair brushing her cheek and listened to the wind ruffle his feathers. Somehow, each detail, each nuance that was Daniel felt incredibly, achingly important in that moment.

Once home, he seemed to disappear, only showing up the moment Ellen started the car to go to the gym and run errands. That evening when she climbed into bed, a weight caused the bed next to her to sink down, and he finally faded into view. Ellen didn't even ask, just took his hand and let him guide her over the Bridge of Dreams. He left her with the brothers once again and winged his way to the Great Above.

Daniel flew aimlessly for a while until he spotted a familiar sight. His parents' home was directly below him and, in the far corner of the yard, the tree swing he and Ori had played on caught his attention. It was nothing special; just a slab of wood hung from a thick, sturdy branch by rope, but it suddenly felt to him like the safest place he'd ever known.

He glided down and landed in the yard staring at the swing. In his mind, he remembered Ori pushing him and how he had begged to go higher. Ori's wings were already developed enough to carry him on short flights, but Daniel's had been too small yet. He smiled to himself and almost thought he heard a sweet, childish laugh. Hope had loved that swing, though he'd been careful not to push her too high since, as a Way Shower, she didn't have wings to help her land gently.

Now, Daniel approached the swing, stepped through and sat down. He didn't swing, merely sat in the one place he had enjoyed the most as a child. Taking a deep gasping breath, he realized he would lose his light and these memories with it. Joy, happiness, love, all of the emotions that fed his light would eventually be gone and he would be but a shell. Almost, he considered telling Ellen. He knew that if anyone could find the way to restore him, she could.

But in a flash he was again kneeling on the beach after she had finished the Water Challenge and was holding her lifeless body in his arms. He had screamed until he was hoarse, had cried till he was dehydrated and ultimately had begrudgingly walked her into the Light before her time.

Daniel's chest heaved. "I can't do it again," he moaned fisting his hand. "Not yet. Not till it's her time."

He heard the soft rustle of grass behind him to the left and slowly turned his head. His mother was coming toward him from the house and she was glowing. Daniel smiled. It meant she carried a new angelic child.

"Why don't you come into the house?" she suggested as she neared.

Daniel shook his head. "I-I've got a tough decision to make. I just wanted a space where I could think."

She moved around and knelt on the grass before him. "Is this about Ellen?"

"A little or a lot," he replied, "and me. I-I think...I don't know," he said shaking his head.

His mother held his hands in hers. "Son, you have achieved things beyond what we imagined possible. You have more heart and depth and grit and determination in you than most. But," she paused, "you've developed the qualities as you worked with Ellen. You two are in symbiosis. You cannot separate her without losing bits of yourself."

Daniel swallowed hard.

"You will find a way through this challenge," his mother assured him. "Follow your heart, even if it leads you or another into danger. You will rise above it."

He helped her to her feet and squeezed her hand. She quietly returned to the house. Daniel rose to take off. As he did, something slowly separated from him and stayed behind. He turned to look and saw a bubble. Looking closely, he saw the images that had played through his mind of happy memories. He frowned with curiosity then turned and leapt skywards. He had one more place to go and one more person to see before he put his plan into action.

First, he landed in the Cloister Walk beside the Banqueting Hall and quietly slipped in through the oak door. In the cool darkness, Daniel went to his Choice Board and arranged the tokens on it. Finally, he pressed them down into their slots thereby activating them. As he left, a dark gray mist enveloped the board. He paid no attention to it.

Heading toward the front of the building, Daniel followed the road down along the cliff. When he neared the Tudor house that once belonged to Henry, The Way Shower Specialist's, Daniel stopped, sat on the stone fence and called to Oriel. He made the tone urgent, even desperate. On the battle field far away, Oriel heard his brother's call and slipped away from the others. His loyalty was always to his little brother.

Oriel came out on the road and spotted Daniel. He hurried toward him as Daniel looked up. Sitting beside his brother, Oriel's face was grave.

"You sent a distress signal. What is wrong?" he asked.

Daniel took a long, shaky breath. "Ori...I'm in trouble, and you're the only one I can trust with the full truth."

Oriel's face darkened with concern. "Go on."

"Ori, you have to promise you will not breathe a word of what I say to anyone," Daniel insisted.

Ori sputtered. "But Daniel, Ellen will want to know."

Daniel grabbed Oriel's arm forcefully. "She-must-never-know, Ori. Never! Understand?"

"Dani, what is wrong?" Oriel demanded becoming quite alarmed.

Daniel dropped his brother's arm and stared out over the cliff. "Do you remember a story about the Valley of a Thousand Caves?"

Oriel frowned for a moment then slowly nodded. "Isn't there some cave there with man eating crystals?"

"Light, Ori. They suck your light from you." Daniel's shoulders slumped forward.

Oriel studied him carefully, shock slowly registering on his face. "You found the Valley!"

"Worse, Ori. Much worse. I found the cave and the crystals and some of my light got sucked into one."

Oriel's face drained of color. "How do you get it back out?" he wanted to know immediately.

"I got Avner to read the Book of Lore. He wrote it in First Language."

Oriel's eyebrows raised.

"Apparently, I have to dump the rest of my light into the crystal and a Way Shower of pure light can shatter it and release my light," Daniel explained.

"Well, Ellen can...."

"There's more! This happened to one of the first Archangels. Avner's first Way Shower child was the one to free him."

"Then there's hope," Oriel said.

"The Way Shower was lost in the process," Daniel replied.

Oriel blew out a long breath. "Wow, not good."

"That's why Ellen cannot know," Daniel insisted.

"You can't keep something like that to yourself. Besides she'll figure out something's wrong," Oriel told him.

"Maybe, but the less she knows, the better," Daniel replied.

"But what will you do without your light?" Oriel asked.

"Become a shell," Daniel replied morosely.

"You'll need light from somewhere if you're no longer generating your own," Oriel proposed.

"But from where?"

Oriel thought for a moment. "The battlefield," he said quietly. "That's all I do all day is channel the One's Light."

Daniel's face brightened. "I could take up my orders to join Michael. He said they were available whenever I wanted them."

"Who would guard Ellen?" Oriel wanted to know. "You can't leave her with just anybody."

"Avner," Daniel proposed. "He's her angelic father, so there's a connection already established. And he's the first, the strongest. "

Oriel nodded. "That could work, but Daniel, this is going to be real hard on her."

Daniel nodded grimacing. "I know, but...what else is there for me to do? I can't let her sacrifice herself for me."

"And she would," Oriel agreed.

"Please, Oriel. Keep her safe for me," Daniel pleaded.

"I will do the best I can, brother. I just don't think much is going to mend her broken heart once you leave her."

"It's the best I know to do," Daniel replied running his hand through his hair.

Oriel placed a hand on Daniel's shoulder and gave it a squeeze. "I will keep your secret, brother. I promise."

Daniel sighed with relief. "Thanks."

CHAPTER 13

If Daniel had been quiet when he retrieved Ellen the night before, he was mute and pale this night. She sensed him slipping away from her, vanishing before her eyes. Her chest ached and her heart beat a rough staccato. Ellen tried to look at him, but he averted his eyes. The best she could do was fight back the flood that threatened to loose itself from her eyes.

Ellen finally did cry in the shower that morning at home. She looked wherever she went in the house, but Daniel remained invisible. Even when she went to the store, all she could see of him was a transparent outline. She was quiet that evening and grateful that Robert had class prep for the next day and midterm exams to grade. He disappeared into the office and never noticed when she went to bed an hour early.

When she crawled in, Daniel appeared in the doorway. He gazed at her for a few minutes then slowly made his way across the room and knelt at her side of the bed. He took her hand and pressed his lips to it.

"I know I've been absent lately," he began, his voice breaking. "You've been caught up in the excitement of helping the brothers create their University, and I wanted to let you have your freedom and independence in my world."

"And here I thought I just didn't want you to feel bored," Ellen quipped trying to lighten the mood.

The corners of his mouth turned up slightly and he cupped his hand over hers.

"W-would you mind not visiting the brothers tonight?" Daniel asked.

Ellen tilted her head to one side. "What do you propose?"

Daniel looked down and swallowed hard. "I...was thinking...maybe we could spend time together...at our home," he suggested hopefully, looking up through his glistening, golden lashes.

Ellen's mind raced. "*He has never spoken of our home there when we're here before*," she thought.

Butterflies churned in her stomach, but she nodded. "I'd really like that. It feels like forever since we've had some time together, alone."

Daniel smiled, relief flooding him. "*Just this one night*," he thought. "*I can give her all I've got left of me. Something to sustain her through what's to come.*"

With that he rose, sat on the edge of her bed and hummed her tune till she fell asleep. He eased her into the Between Worlds, watching with a warm glow as she cared for their son. Almost imperceptibly, Daniel left behind a baseball-sized bubble. If a viewer had looked closely, the scene of mother and son was captured inside.

When he and Ellen got to the Bridge and paused for the Dolphins to scan them, Daniel gazed around at the amazing piece of construction.

"Remember building this?" he asked.

Ellen nodded. "I think up until that point in time, none of us Way Showers really knew what we could do by ourselves let alone when we combined our gifts."

"Seriously, that's a concept to explore in the human realm," Daniel pointed out.

Ellen considered the suggestion thoughtfully. "That would be a great idea. But how do I find anyone besides Robert?" she wondered aloud.

"How did you meet him?" Daniel asked.

"An online dating site," Ellen replied with a groan. "Not like I'm going to use that method to find others."

"Maybe not," Daniel admitted. "But there may be other ways to use your gadgets to find others like you."

"I'll have to keep that in mind," Ellen said as the Dolphins let them go.

Lagging just a little behind her, Daniel again placed a bubble with all his memories of the Bridge being built at that point. He quickly caught up and, on the other side, he took her into his arms for the traverse into the Facility. Once there, he stopped before the crystal capsule she had laid in while Raphael had programmed the equipment. His own crystal column stood just a few feet away.

"Remember when Raphael told me I was pregnant with Nathan?" Ellen asked with a glow.

Daniel's heart swelled with joy. He remembered that moment as if it were happening in the now. Again, when they left, a bubble with a memory remained behind.

They walked outside into the bright sunlight, and he opened his arms to her. "Ready?"

Ellen smiled broadly and entered his embrace. He opened the silver doorway and flew straight through with her in his arms. A moment later, they stepped out onto the road, walked a few paces and turned onto the dirt road that ran past their slate home. Rather than turn in, Daniel continued leading her on toward the pond but turned off onto the trail into the woods. The entered under the canopy of the leafy trees, the scent of moist soil and moss filling the air. Their footsteps crunched the fallen leaves under foot as they followed the trail.

A hike?" Ellen asked brightly.

Daniel smiled. "It's been a long time since we've been in these woods."

She took his arm and hugged it. "We used to explore this whole place. Every day felt like an adventure...a safe one," she added. "No Marauders or Sultans or Ice Queens."

He leaned down and kissed the top of her head, the scent of her hair filling his nostrils. He swallowed hard, tears welling in his eyes.

"Oh, the bridge!" Ellen cried taking his hand and eagerly pulling him forward.

Daniel happily followed, every step bittersweet. She dragged him into the center of the rustic wooden bridge then propped her arms on the rails and peered over into the quietly pool below.

"They're still here!" she said excitedly, pointing to the large gold, red and white Koi who surfaced beneath them with mild pops as they opened and closed their mouths in search of food.

Daniel leaned over the rail next to her and helped her count.

"Where's the big one?" she asked searching.

He stood up and took a step back so he could watch her. He snorted softly and shook his head. Images of her as a child readily sprang to mind.

"*So little about her has changed,*" he thought. "*Still as inquisitive and adventurous as ever.*"

"Here he comes!" Ellen exclaimed.

Daniel checked and, sure enough, a three foot long Koi swam lazily out from under the bridge.

"I should have stopped at the house first for some bread," she complained. "They're really expecting something."

Daniel nodded and prodded her off the bridge to the trail on the other side. Behind them on the railing balanced a bubble of memories.

They meandered through the woods coming out up the hill near the fence around the farm. They followed it till they found where the big, brown-eyed, black and white cows were grazing. One in particular noticed their arrival, paused in mid-chew and ambled over. Daniel reached over the fence to pet her nose and face while Ellen grabbed handfuls of the tall grass near their feet. She held it out to the cow who took it, shook her head and mooed.

Ellen's eyes glittered. "Do you remember all the times we brought Hope up here?"

Daniel nodded. "She loved the cows."

"But this one was her favorite. It was the last cow she petted before we took her to your parents, and I woke from the coma," Ellen told him. "It was so hard to leave her behind."

He gave her shoulders a squeeze. "Parting, even for the best of reasons, is always hard," he said huskily.

She nodded her agreement and turned to head down the hill toward the pond. Daniel paused a moment before following. Left behind was another glistening bubble.

When they neared the edge of the pond where the great, old Willow had fallen out into the water, Daniel hopped up onto the trunk and nimbly ran its length to the farthest end. He stood looking at his reflection in the water. The log rocked and the surface of the pond rippled as Ellen crawled up onto the end near the roots.

"I came out here after you changed me back from being a Minion," he told her.

"Wanting to make sure you were really an angel again?" she asked.

Daniel shook his head. "No, the Embodied One said I was created to be multi-dimensional, and I wanted to see how I looked in the other dimensions."

"And?" Ellen prompted.

"It's how I found the part of me that was in the same dimension as your uterus so we could conceive Nathan," he replied.

She cautiously edged out toward him. He stretched out his hand, she grabbed it, and he steadied her till she was beside him.

"Can I see?" Ellen asked.

"Sure," Daniel replied nodding.

He closed his eyes and, as Ellen watched the pond, the image changed. It took him a couple of tries but she was suddenly staring down at a blue and silver striped cat that walked upright on humanish legs.

"Wow! I'm glad Nathan takes after you more," she exclaimed.

"This image is me," Daniel asserted. "Just not the me here."

He made one more change and Ellen gasped. There in the water was the image of the Minion he had once been.

"How can that be?" she wanted to know.

Daniel let the image go. "Raphael once told me that, in order for the Ice Queen to turn me into a Minion, that part of me had to exist in some other dimension. Since she couldn't create something of her own, she had to find something already in existence and twist it to suit her purpose."

Ellen nodded. "I guess that makes sense."

He knelt down for a closer look at the water then stood and grabbed her around the waist to fly her back to shore. He set her safely on the ground and they continued on, a bubble bobbing on the surface of the pond at the edge of the log.

Daniel took her hand and they meandered along the pond till they came to the orchard. They picked their way through as he held aside branches for Ellen. Without warning, he came to a halt as he gazed at one tree in particular.

"I will never forget this tree, this place," he whispered. "My first time."

Ellen slipped her arms around his waist and hugged him.

"You teased me," he recalled huskily, "but you also made it so special."

She smiled up at him. Daniel gazed down at her drinking in the glint of the sun off her red blonde hair and the glow of her skin. He bent nearer, pressed his lips to hers and kissed her hungrily. Pulling her closer, Daniel cupped the back of her head, his fingers tangled in her long hair. Ellen murmured into his mouth, greedy for more of him.

"I think," he said in between kisses, "we should...go back to the house."

"I so agree," Ellen replied.

He reached up into the tree to pick a couple of apples, handed her one then scooped her up in his arms and took to the air. Hanging on the branch in place of the apples was another bubble.

Daniel landed on the porch and led the way inside. He took in his surroundings as if seeing it for the first time. With a deep sigh, he led Ellen upstairs to their bedroom. She glanced into the bathroom, spotted the soaking tub and made her way to its side. She knelt, rested her arms on the edge, and lay her head on her arms. Daniel removed his shield and sword in the bedroom then joined her.

"So many memories here," she murmured.

"Hope's birth in this tub will forever remain my favorite," he said in a low, melodic tone.

As he spoke, the corner of the room brightened as his joy burst from him like radiant sunshine.

"I even hold the memories dear of when we shared our individual struggles," Ellen told him. "To know I could trust you with my deepest pain and that you would make it all right for me, then to do the same for you...." She sighed.

Turning, she looked up at him. "Do you remember Hunter's cabin?"

"When you wondered if I was appearing male for your benefit?" he asked.

Ellen nodded. "Do you remember what you told me?"

Daniel swallowed hard. "About deep love?"

Ellen nodded again. "That night when I told you what happened when I crossed into the Light and you told me how you ended up being turned into a Minion...that night, I finally knew what you meant by deep love."

He looked down nodding.

Ellen reached up and touched his cheek with her fingertips. "That night...I knew...if it were possible to take on your pain for you, I would gladly do it. I finally understood what drove you to give up your immortality with but the hope of regaining it IF I could discover myself."

Daniel looked up through his eyelashes. A moment of breathtaking silence passed between them. Even their breath seemed to hang in mid-air.

"Sacred space," Ellen whispered.

He nodded.

In moments, it passed and he gently pulled her to her feet. With an arm around her shoulders, he guided her back to the bedroom. In the tub, a large bubble with a glow in the middle nestled in the center. Daniel hastily kicked off his boots near the bed then pulled her into his arms and
102

pressed himself close.

"If I had the capacity to place value on things," he murmured, "next to the One, I value you most. I never knew how much I would change and grow when I became your Guardian. I had no idea how deeply I was capable of loving. Were I able to die, I would gladly die for you."

Ellen gazed up at him searching his eyes. "But Daniel, that's how I feel about you as well. I would sacrifice myself for you in a heartbeat."

He ran this thumb along her bottom lip to the corner. "You must never do that, you know."

"What? Sacrifice myself for you?"

He nodded.

"Why is this a one-way street?" Ellen wanted to know.

"Because, you were created with a destiny to help your kind grow and transform," Daniel explained. "I was created to guard your life. Yours is the broader purpose and there are others depending upon you."

Ellen closed her eyes and leaned her forehead against his chest. "It doesn't matter. I would do it anyway."

"I know," he whispered, his lips brushing the top of her head. "*All the more reason to hold to my plan*," he thought sadly, "*if nothing more than to protect her from her own good heart.*"

At that moment, the setting sun sent a last bright ray shining through the balcony door. Ellen turned her head to look. Pulling away, she led him onto the drying balcony off the bedroom.

"I remember one very wet, bedraggled looking angel," she said with a smirk.

"Ye-es," Daniel replied. "My first and last shower."

Ellen laughed then turned serious. She slid her arms around him. "I also remember the night when you recalled I needed to touch your wings in order for me to get pregnant."

At the very mention of his wings, Daniel's mouth went dry and heat burned a path straight down to his groin. He breathed heavily and began caressing Ellen's back and sides.

"I do remember," he agreed.

"Sort of wish we could do that again," she murmured, her hot breath fanning his chest.

"Something close sounds good to me," Daniel replied taking her jaw in his hands and kissing her hard.

He continued down her chin and neck to the hollow between her collar bones.

"Come," he said hoarsely leading her back inside. "I need to

103

demonstrate my love."

With that, Ellen pulled her shirt off over her head and removed her bra while he slid out of his pants. At the sight of her breasts, his nostrils flared. Daniel drew her back to him, cupped his hand over her breast and pressed his lips to hers. She moaned into his mouth. Working his way down, he bent his head to suckle her nipple and she cried out.

Pulling away, Ellen kicked off her shoes, ripped off her jeans and backed onto the bed. Daniel quickly crawled on stalking her almost like a cat. He ran his tongue and lips down the length of her body then stopped on the way up at the "V" between her legs. Ellen gasped and cried out.

Knowing her readiness, Daniel lay over her gently sliding himself inside. Slowly, he pushed in and pulled nearly all the way out. He watched her grimace and pant, but pushed back in again when she reached for him. With rhythmic thrusts, he listened to her moans. It was her night for pleasure.

Then, an idea struck him. "Stroke my wings," he murmured in her ear.

"A-are you sure?" Ellen asked.

"Touch them...feel them," Daniel insisted.

Hesitantly, Ellen reached up and felt the swan-soft feathers. Daniel sucked in a quick breath of air.

"More," he begged thrusting faster.

Ellen began stroking his wings, now lightly caressing them, now almost massaging the strong muscles that moved them. Daniel grunted, a hot passion swirling in his stomach. He continued until he felt the angelic spark moving within him. Concentrating, he brought the passion and the spark together in his abdomen. Suddenly, he felt the need for release.

"Don't...stop," he groaned, his thrusting taking on a pounding urgency.

Ellen tugged at individual feathers, and grasped handfuls as he lay fully over her elevating her hips till he felt the eruption and roared. Daniel felt the singular electric sensation as the angelic spark left him and entered her. Satisfied that it was now safe-guarded within her, he collapsed off to one side, pulled her close and wrapped himself around her in deep sleep.

CHAPTER 14

Throughout the night, Daniel periodically dozed and wakened. Sometimes he lay soaking in the feeling of Ellen's warm body tucked into his arms. At other times, he couldn't resist slipping inside her to experience the marvelous sense of joining and oneness. When the golden fingers of dawn crept across the morning sky, he rose, dressed and went downstairs to fix her breakfast.

Ellen blinked open sleepy eyes at the smell of coffee and bacon. Daniel smiled at her and set a tray of food down on the nightstand beside the bed.

"Mm, breakfast in bed," Ellen murmured sipping the hot coffee. "Been a long time since someone's given me such a nice wake up call."

Daniel grabbed a plum from the tray and took a bite. While he didn't need food, he had discovered a fondness for the taste of plums and peaches and often ate one while keeping Ellen company during meals.

After breakfast, she took a hot shower and dressed at a leisurely pace. She came downstairs to find Daniel waiting for her by the front door.

"Time to go back?" she asked.

"In a little," he replied, his voice tense. "I'd like to sit on the porch swing for a bit."

She studied his face, instantly perceiving a change in his demeanor. "Is something wrong?" she asked worriedly. "Everything was so pleasant yesterday and last night."

Daniel didn't respond. Instead, he led her outside, sat her on the swing and knelt before her. He took a couple of deep breaths and struggled to master his emotions. Finally, he looked her in the eye and held her gaze.

"Ellen, you know there's some kind of trouble," he began. "I'd be foolish to assume your sensitive nature has missed that."

She nodded. "But, we've always managed to muddle through trouble and come out on the other side," she reminded him. "Seems to be what we do best."

He nodded. "You are a courageous trooper, that's for sure."

"Then, why are you so upset?" Ellen wanted to know.

Daniel grimaced. "This trouble may be bigger than me.

Her eyes widened.

"I'm not omnipotent," he told her quietly.

"Well...no...that's true," she conceded. "It just feels like it at times."

He took her hands in his, and his voice took on an urgency. "Ellen, listen to me. Hear the meaning of my words," he said in a commanding voice.

Ellen quieted and studied his face intently.

"No matter what you see or hear from me or anyone else in the near future, I-love-you," he stated slowly and clearly. "No one can ever destroy that. Do you understand me? No one."

Ellen nodded slowly.

"I do not know what the future holds, but no matter how near or far I am, I-will-always keep you in my heart," Daniel assured her.

Tears trickled down her cheeks. "I don't understand, Daniel."

He cupped her cheek in his hand. "Hear me with your heart, dear one. It is where I will always reside."

Then he kissed her, his tears mingling with hers. Once he mastered himself again, Daniel wiped the tears from her cheek, rose and took her hand.

"Come. We should go back now," he announced.

Ellen felt like a small child as she stood next to him holding his hand. The world suddenly no longer felt safe and friendly. She could almost feel a nip in the air. Daniel opened the silver door, and they crossed through into the Great Above.

"Is it morning back home?" she asked.

"Not yet. Would you like to visit the brothers?" he asked.

"I think so," Ellen replied. "*Anything to shake this horrible foreboding*," she thought.

Daniel scooped her up and flew her to the Lands Below. He arrived at the Wizard's Tower and landed by the front door. He knocked and they heard the kitchen chairs scrape on the floor before the door swung open. Ellen smiled tightly and entered taking a seat at the table with the Priest and Simon.

Daniel grabbed the Wizard's arm and pulled him outside. "I've seen your looks," he hissed.

The Wizard nodded. "You haven't been yourself."

Daniel glanced at the ground and took a deep breath. "Wizard, you've been Ellen's protector here," he said looking back up. "Whatever happens to me, don't let her collapse into herself. Draw her out. Be her protector still."

"But...where will you be?" the Wizard asked.

Without replying, Daniel leapt into the air, spiraled up and winked out. The Wizard shook his head and muttered under his breath as he went back inside and closed the door. Simon was animatedly describing the quantum computer to Ellen while the Priest held his aching head.

"Can I show you what it can do?" Simon begged.

Ellen nodded. "Now would probably be a very good time," she told him rising to follow him into the basement.

"Coming?" Simon asked the brothers.

"Have a headache," the Priest moaned.

"We'll wait for the translation," the Wizard replied sitting down by his brother.

Simon hurried after Ellen, happy to have a willing audience.

When Simon's and Ellen's voices had died out and the Wizard was certain she was out of earshot, he pulled his brother close. "Something's afoot," he told the Priest.

"You mean, with Daniel?" his brother asked.

The Wizard nodded. "He told me not to let her collapse into herself, to draw her out."

The Priest looked up, his headache forgotten. "What do you suppose is going on?"

The Wizard shook his head. "I don't know, but whatever it is, it's big."

Daniel came out on the ledge in front of the cave entrance. He paced for a while bracing himself for what was to come. Finally, he clenched his fists, turned himself toward the empty maw and marched through the tunnel to the Crystal Chamber beyond. He found the crystal

107

that already contained pieces of his light.

With a pale countenance and shaking hands, he reached out, touched the quartz spires that stuck out from the center and felt a jolt like lightning go through his system. He screamed as the light was forcefully sucked from his body until he dropped into a heap on the ground, an empty shell.

A very radiant Daniel sat on the hard floor of a peach-colored, crystal prison. Slowly, he crawled to his feet and stood with his hands on his hips surveying the entire structure. It almost appeared to be glass except for the thickness of the walls and the folds and nodes throughout them. Near one of the nodes, he noticed a crack. Daniel took a step forward to examine it. Hopeful, he unsheathed his sword, channeled the Light and aimed directly for the crack. The Light shot from the tip of his sword, hit the crack and not only ricocheted off to bounce around the interior, but healed the crack in the wall as well. Having ducked as balls of Light zinged about, Daniel hesitantly rose to his feet. He stretched out his hand toward the crack to check. Sure enough, the surface where the crack had been was now smooth and shiny.

He sheathed his sword. "Light only reinforces this crystal," he thought. "Am I in the Prison of Light? I don't recall having done anything worthy of imprisonment."

Flustered, he checked the walls carefully for the viewing panel built into every Light Chamber in the Prison of Light. There were no viewing panels. Flummoxed, he sat on the floor to think.

"*One, Ellen must be in trouble*," he thought. "*Two, something with an intimate knowledge of the Light put me in here.*"

His mind flew to Avner, the first Archangel created and the first who turned to the Darkness. While he had repented his deeds and had sought redemption, the Embodied One had placed him at Michael's side on probationary status. Yet, while Daniel considered his range of knowledge, his heart was unconvinced that the elder angel would do anything of this sort.

"Three, I have to find a way to get out of here," he said aloud, rising to his feet.

He walked to the nearest crystal wall, placed his hands against it and tested his Immortal Strength against it. Not only did the wall not budge, but he found himself tiring...a blatant impossibility given what he had been created to be. Frowning, Daniel ceased his efforts to break the walls with Light and strength, and tried reversing the direction of the flow of energy. Power rushed back up through his arms stopping when he had reabsorbed what he had discharged.

With that exercise, Daniel was officially worried as he paced about his crystal prison. "I'm in a crystal prison that reflects the Light, absorbs my power and...somehow...I do not have my full complement of Immortal Strength."

He stopped pacing, put one hand on his hip while he ran the other through his long, golden blond hair. He shook his head, perplexed. "I'm stumped," he muttered. "I don't know where I am, who could have done this or how to get back to Ellen."

He spun around, momentarily catching a glimpse of a large face peering at him from outside. He stepped back from the wall and stared up at the face. There was something oddly familiar about it in spite of the distortions of the crystal. Suddenly, he rushed at the wall and started pounding.

"Help me!" Daniel cried. "Get me out of here!"

The face remained stoically emotionless as it continued to observe him, then it pulled back and disappeared.

"No!" Daniel yelled. "You've got to help me!"

Finally, he slumped to the floor in defeat. He was a prisoner of a crystal in a land of giants. Nothing was making sense and his concern for Ellen was mounting by the second.

In the Lands Below, Ellen finally climbed out of the basement. She was just headed to rejoin the brothers in the kitchen when they all heard a loud knock at the door. All three jumped and looked at each other. Seconds later, the knock resounded through the small house and Tower. Reluctantly, the Wizard rose and headed toward the door. He opened the top half and gazed out on an almost gray-hued Daniel.

"I've come for Ellen," he stated flatly.

"She's here. Come in," the Wizard offered.

Though he opened the door, Daniel remained standing stiffly outside. The Wizard looked back at Ellen who stared at this new Daniel uncertainly.

"It is time to leave," Daniel said turning dispassionate eyes on her.

Ellen moved to join him.

The Wizard stopped her for a moment. "Are you sure?"

She nodded. "I'll be ok."

She went to Daniel who awkwardly picked her up and before the brothers could utter another word, he was gone.

"Whoa!" the Priest exclaimed. "That is just not right."

Daniel came out in the Great Above and headed straight for the Great Halls and the Throne room. Ellen remained rooted to where she was.

"Aren't we going to the Facility so you can take me back?" she called after him.

"The Embodied One wants to see us," he replied still walking.

Growing more uneasy by the moment, Ellen hurried to follow him. They entered and went straight down to the front where the Embodied One awaited them.

"What exactly is this about?" the Embodied One asked. "You insisted the need was urgent."

"I thought you said he called us?" Ellen charged.

Daniel knelt. "I have come to announce I can no longer be Ellen's Guardian. I wish to take up my assignment with Michael and another Guardian be placed with her."

Ellen's mouth fell open and her head spun. "Daniel?" she whispered. "You can't mean this?"

"You were assigned to Ellen for a lifetime," the Embodied One reminded him.

"And I earned Choice in service to her," Daniel reminded him. "This is my choice." His voice was flat and devoid of emotion.

"This is true," the Embodied One acknowledged reluctantly.

Ellen's mind reeled and she nearly dropped to the ground. "After everything we've been through together," she murmured.

Daniel glanced at her over his shoulder. "Precisely."

Tears brimmed her lashes and streamed down her cheeks. "What did I do, Daniel? I'm sorry whatever it was. Please, give me the chance to make it right."

He shook his head and turned away. "It was nothing that could have been done any other way and...nothing can make it right."

Ellen sank to her knees and sobbed into her hands.

The Embodied One looked at her with pity then considered the Guardian before him. "If this is truly what you wish, Daniel...." he began.

"It is," Daniel snapped, rising and squaring his shoulders.

"Very well," the Embodied One said reluctantly.

In a moment, two more Archangels appeared in the Throne room. One was Michael, amazing to behold as his radiant brilliance bathed the room vying with the Light on the Throne. Youngest brother to Avner, he was the trusted leader of the Embodied One's forces. The other Archangel was Avner, himself, the first Archangel the Embodied One created and the strongest of them all.

In the way of things, the blend of Archangel and human female was required to produce a Way Shower. As such, Avner was also Ellen's angelic father. He went to her immediately, lifted her up and cradled her against him as she wrapped her arms around his neck and cried on his shoulder.

"Avner, I am appointing you as Ellen's new Guardian," the Embodied One quietly announced. "As such, you will need your sword back."

A sword of light appeared in the air between them. Avner reached out, grasped its hilt and drew it to himself.

"Take her back," the Embodied One instructed softly. "Take her back and keep her safe as only a father can."

Avner bowed his head solemnly, held her close and spiraled out of the Great Halls.

The Embodied One turned to Daniel. "I cannot read your heart, but I sense great pain," he said at last. "I do not understand what has driven you to this point, but I honor your decision."

Daniel stared straight ahead, unmoving."

"He is yours," the Embodied One told Michael.

Michael put his hand to his temple, issued Daniel a mental command, and the latter spiraled away to join up with Michael's forces.

"Sire," Michael said bowing on one knee. "Is this wise?"

"Wisdom did not guide Daniel's choice," the Embodied One agreed. "But until we can discover the cause for the sudden chill that has frozen his heart, we will never comprehend his choice."

Michael nodded and rose.

"Keep him close, Michael," the Embodied One requested. "Test him, challenge him and see if you can learn what troubles him."

Michael nodded. "My very thoughts exactly."

"If it be possible...if you find a way...bring him back to himself. He is pure love; his light has dimmed. Return him to radiance," the Embodied One requested.

"As you ask," Michael replied.

He unfurled his great wings and spiraled up and out, following his descendent to the battlefield.

CHAPTER 15

When Michael rejoined his men at the parade grounds where they awaited new battle orders, he stood on a high stand and surveyed their ranks. The post at his side was vacant having most recently been filled by Avner who now guarded Ellen. Michael felt his absence as a sharp pang.

His thoughts drifted to Avner, once his elder brother, first in everything. Michael had been the youngest of the original twelve Archangels. Avner had been close to the Embodied One, their sire, and had learned much from him. In turn he had treated his younger brothers more like sons, especially the youngest. He had taught him all the Embodied One showed him and had shepherded them well.

When the Embodied One had requested Avner's service as a liaison between himself and the Sultan, the One of Darkness, Avner had acquitted himself well. However, his naivety and curiosity had been his ruin. The Sultan had preyed on his insatiable desire to learn and grow, and Avner had fallen victim to the Sultan's wiles. He gave the Dark One his heart, immediately becoming a prisoner in his own body.

Trapped inside his immortal flesh, Avner had been forced to watch himself do and say things that warped his brothers' minds and turned them to the Dark as well, all but one. Avner's love for Michael had been so great, he had reversed the Sultan's tricks in order to spare Michael at great personal risk to himself.

Though the other brothers remained in the Prison of Light, still loyal to the Sultan, Avner had found the strength to repent his deeds, reach out to his daughter, Ellen, and seek redemption. Ellen had risen to the challenge, retrieving his heart from beneath a lake where the Dark One had hidden it. As she had with Daniel, she successfully transformed Avner from High Minion back to an angel.

Michael missed his elder brother whom the Embodied One had ordered to retrain at his side. Avner had accepted the order with graciousness and had carried out his duties with humility.

"*But he is perfect for Ellen now*," Michael thought.

He drew his attention back to the milling troops, his eyes falling on Daniel. A chill trickled down his spine. While the other battle angels talked and laughed amiably amongst themselves while awaiting orders, Daniel stood ramrod straight, eyes focused on some distant point, one hand grasping the hilt of his sword.

Michael sucked in air through his teeth. "He has dimmed his light purposely!" he breathed. "What could possibly have happened?"

Michael shook his head, concern gripping his heart for his descendant, for Daniel was in his lineage. He would do his best to learn his protege's secret. With that, Michael put his hand to his forehead and called to Daniel. Down below, Daniel slowly turned and looked up.

"*To my side, Daniel*," Michael said inwardly.

In a blur of light, Daniel appeared beside him.

"You have Avner's place," Michael said.

Daniel took up his former stance at Michael's side.

Orders came through buzzing in Michael's head like an angry swarm of hornets. He lifted his trumpet to his lips and blew a loud blast. Down below, his men snapped to attention. Another barrier between the divine and human realms was destined for destruction. It was up to them to assail it from their side hoping someone from the human side could break free from the mass lethargy and help them take it down.

Michael blew several short blasts. With what sounded like a clap of thunder, his men unfurled their great wings. Two blasts more and they leapt into the air spiraling off to do battle, Light-sword style.

Meanwhile, Avner took Ellen home and sat beside her all day while she cried inconsolably. His frustration grew as he realized how immaterial he was in her world without exerting great amounts of energy. She roused herself enough to dress and prepare dinner for Robert. She hid her sadness from him the best that she could. But every night she sobbed into her pillow crying herself to sleep.

Avner did the best he could to console her, but only Daniel knew her personal song, the one he had sung to her ever since her conception.

113

Daniel was the one trained to produce the comforting vibration that soothed her soul; Avner had no such training. Avner was out of his element and at a total loss unless something undesirable on the light-spectrum came to harass her; that he was trained to take care of.

Several weeks went by, and Ellen was in bed preparing for sleep one night. She snapped off her bedside lamp only to turn and see a sheen of light off to her left.

"Avner, what's that?" she asked and he faded into view.

He looked towards the light unalarmed. "You seem to have visitors."

As Ellen watched Nariel, the Wizard and the Priest came into view. Though not sharply defined, they were still quite recognizable.

"Ellen!" Nariel exclaimed rushing to embrace her. "Are you all right? We've been worried."

Ellen found herself surprisingly relieved and happy to see her friends. "I'm better than I was," she told them.

"We came to get you," the Wizard announced.

"Get me?" Ellen asked blinking.

"We have a surprise for you," the Priest replied.

"But you have to come with us to see it," the Wizard said.

Though her heart still ached, Ellen had to wonder what surprise the brothers could possibly have that was important enough for them to come get her.

"I brought something to help you drift right off to sleep," Nariel told her.

"*Where were you last night?*" Ellen wondered inwardly.

"Will you come?" the Priest asked hopefully.

Ellen took a deep breath and nodded. "For you guys, I'd do about anything," she told them.

Nariel untied a small sack from her belt. "I'm going to sprinkle this around you, and you'll be asleep in no time," she assured Ellen.

True to her word, Ellen's head barely hit the pillow and she was out. Before Nariel could take back the sack, Avner put his hand on her arm.

"Any chance I could keep that?" he asked. "I'm fairly useless at calming her or helping her sleep."

Nariel relinquished the bag. "I'll let you have this one, but I suggest that you drop off Ellen and pay a visit to Mentor."

Avner pocketed the sack and nodded. A bit awkwardly, he shifted Ellen into the Between Worlds. As they approached Nathan's guard post,
114

she hung back.

"What's wrong?" Avner asked.

"He's going to want to know where his father is," Ellen replied.

"Tell him the truth," Avner suggested.

"He's not going to understand," she fretted. "Heck, I don't understand."

Avner placed his hand on her shoulder willing his strength into her being. She straightened her shoulders and put one foot in front of the other until she was finally inside.

Nathan turned, spotted her and hurried to greet her. He stopped when he saw Avner and emitted a low growl.

"Who is this?" he demanded.

"This is Avner, my father," Ellen replied then looked to the angel. "This is Nathan, the child I was pregnant with...."

"When you retrieved my heart," Avner breathed.

"Where is father?" Nathan wanted to know.

"He has taken up a position with Michael and is on the battlefield," Ellen explained.

"He's your Guardian."

"Was," she replied softly.

Nathan tilted his head blinking his big amber cat's eyes. "I do not understand."

Ellen shook her head and covered her mouth. "Neither do I."

As tears threatened to spill over her lashes, Nathan wrapped her in his arms and purred. She quickly calmed in his embrace.

"*Oh to be a cat,*" Avner thought. "*Wish I could learn to purr.*"

"It will be all right, mother," Nathan told her stroking her hair. "You have your father. It will be all right."

Ellen nodded against his chest then reached up and gave his cheek a kiss. "Thank you."

She pulled away and headed through the back door toward the Bridge of Dreams. In no time, she and Avner had traversed into the Facility and he had whisked her down to Wizard's Tower.

"You know how to locate her?" the Wizard asked when Avner dropped her at his door.

"Yes."

"Good. We won't be here when you get back," the Wizard informed him.

Avner merely nodded before leaping into the air.

"So where will I be?" Ellen asked having overheard.

"Just come with us," the Priest said taking her arm and ushering her toward the Tower stairs.

Good-naturedly, Ellen went along. When they got into the Wizard's study at the top of the Tower, the Priest wasted no time gathering them inside the chalk circle and bringing up the Vortex. They took off at an amazing speed, and Ellen found her heart racing as she watched the countryside speed by below her.

Before long, the coast and an arm of the forest came into view. But Ellen gasped as they came over a rise and the promontory became visible. There, standing amidst the rocky crags, rose a granite castle complete with a seaward facing tower glistening in the morning sun. The Priest set them down in front of the outer wall gates, and Ellen stared in awe.

"You did it!" she exclaimed. "You built the University!"

"The outside at least," the Priest replied.

"The inside will take some more work," the Wizard agreed, "but it's a start."

"A start?" Ellen asked passing the gates and walking under the raised portcullis. "This is fantastic! You've got to show me the whole place."

The Priest looked at the Wizard who winked knowingly then followed as Ellen started darting in and out of doorways and climbing up and down stairs. At last she stood at the window of what would become the Wizard's new study at the top of the tower and breathed in the sea air. She turned toward the brothers, her cheeks pink and her eyes sparkling.

"I don't know how you did it," she said, "but this place is fantastic."

"We had help," the Wizard admitted.

"Lots of it," the Priest affirmed. "All the Way Showers."

"Even Simon," the Wizard told her. "He's already got his computer lab set up in the dungeon."

"Well, I have to hand it to you gents," Ellen said linking arms with them. "This even looks better than what you put on paper."

The Priest beamed.

"Figure out how to move the Flames and Vortex from the temple?" she asked.

"Still working on it," the Priest replied.

"But we've got ideas," the Wizard assured her.

"Lots of them," the Priest groaned.

"One or two might actually work," the Wizard said as they headed toward the stairs to go back down.

"Well, this was certainly worth crossing the Bridge to get me for," Ellen said as they walked across the broad plank floor of the Great Hall below.

Inwardly, the brothers sighed with relief.

When the trio strolled through the outer wall, Avner was waiting for Ellen.

"Time?" she asked.

"Almost," he replied.

The Wizard took her arm. "The castle isn't the only thing to see."

"Yes," the Priest hurriedly agreed. "You've **got** to come back."

Ellen eyed them curiously. "What else have you boys cooked up?"

"Oh, a little something in the woods," the Priest replied.

"And more in the cave below," the Wizard added wagging his bushy eyebrows.

Ellen chuckled and sighed with relief. "You two know my weakness." She smiled. "And I will come back."

The brothers beamed.

She studied them more seriously for a moment. "I'm just curious...."

"As always," they chorused.

Ellen feigned a pout. "No, seriously," she began again. "It dawned on me that I don't know your real names, though I guess by your accents you come from Britain."

The Priest and the Wizard looked at each other and shuffled their feet self-consciously.

"We don't remember," the Priest finally admitted.

"Your names?" Ellen asked frowning.

The Wizard nodded.

She stepped closer to them. "Try to remember, and here's a little incentive." She kissed them each on the cheek.

With that, Ellen went to Avner, and he whisked her away. They came out in front of the Great Halls and she looked at him questioningly.

"The Embodied One wants to see you," he explained.

Ellen studied the entrance to the Throne Room.

"Not there," Avner corrected. "He wants to see you in the Banqueting Hall."

A dozen thoughts raced through her brain and Ellen took off running for the Cloister Walk. She ducked through the heavy oak door that led into the Banqueting Hall and headed straight for the wall that ran parallel to the Cloister Walk. Hers and Daniel's Choice Boards stood there, though something strange was there as well. She slowed and approached cautiously, barely acknowledging the Embodied One who stood nearby.

While her board remained clear and visible, Daniel's was shrouded in an impenetrable, dark cloud. The entire board was completely occluded. Ellen glanced at the Embodied One seeking answers.

"Even I cannot see past this dense fog," he told her.

Ellen returned her attention toward the cloud. "Why do you think he did it?" she asked cautiously creeping toward the fog.

"I cannot say," the Embodied One replied. "I have literally been unable to see through the darkness shrouding the board. That alone has given me cause for concern because it should be impossible to hide anything from me."

"Do you sense evil?" Avner's voice rang out from behind Ellen.

The Embodied One shook his head but gestured for Avner to check for himself.

Avner moved forward pushing Ellen behind him. He stretched out his hand to touch the fog watching it disappear inside. After a few minutes of sampling, he withdrew his hand.

"I sense no evil, Sire," he said.

Ellen let out a sigh of relief. "Then he hasn't gone over to the One of Darkness."

"Yet, how could he have created this impenetrable screen without having done so?" Avner wondered.

"I do not know," the Embodied One replied. "What I do know is that by every report I receive from Michael, Daniel fights entirely for our side. He is ever in the thickest fray, always seeking to absorb and channel the most Light."

Tears welled in Ellen's eyes. "Then he's still good," she murmured. "His heart is still good."

"So it would seem," the Embodied One agreed.

Ellen crept forward and cautiously stretched out her hand feeling the edges of the cloud. Strangely, it chilled her heart but not her hand.

"Odd," she muttered.

When she tried to press her hand in further, she met with firm resistance. She felt no pain or electrical charge, just the distinct pressure back against her hand that matched her own forward momentum. The harder she pushed, the harder the cloud pushed back. Ellen finally withdrew her hand. The Embodied One waited expectantly.

"This definitely wasn't devised by Darkness," she announced.

118

"Then what?" the Embodied One pressed.

Ellen shook her head in amazement. "It's a mirror. The more intently you stare at it and probe it, the more of yourself you see. Because you're confused by its presence and nature, the cloud gains density and darkness. Until we can understand Daniel's reason for placing it there, a dark cloud is all we'll see."

"Ingenious!" Avner breathed.

"It really is," Ellen replied.

"Would the options on your Choice Board suggest a meaning for his?" the Embodied One wondered.

Ellen turned to hers and studied it. She shook her head. "None of mine makes sense. Receive light...enter light...dragons...book...find Daniel...reunite Daniel."

"We know where he is," Avner said frowning. "He's with Michael on the battlefield."

"And something like that on my Choice Board only creates more confusion, which is reflected in that cloud," Ellen said noting its hue had darkened.

"We are obviously not going to solve this mystery right now," the Embodied One acknowledged.

"And I need to return Ellen," Avner added.

The Embodied One nodded, Avner scooped her up, and they were gone in a flash.

CHAPTER 16

Though Ellen had intended to return to the brothers soon, sad news prevented that from happening. One of her closest aunts, elderly and in a nursing home with Alzheimer's, died just hours after her husband one sunny Sunday afternoon. With the funeral in Florida, a different sort of trip was required, one by plane. On the way down, Ellen distracted herself with magazines she'd picked up at the news stands in the airport. The funeral itself was short and sweet since almost all of the relatives were either already dead or too elderly to travel. On the flight home from Tampa, Ellen tried to console herself with the fact they had both been nearly ninety and in poor health. However, an uneasy feeling inside her, like someone had ripped away a safety net, prevailed.

She stared out the windows at the clouds below and thought of her own frail, elderly mother. *"She could easily be next,"* Ellen fretted.

By the time the plane's wheels touched the tarmac in the Northeast, a week had gone by. She gratefully fell into Robert's arms when he greeted her at the airport, gathered her things and went home. It didn't surprise her, though, that the brothers showed up that evening as she was crawling into bed.

"We were a little wo-....concerned," the Wizard said suddenly holding is ankle while his brother feigned a look of innocence.

"We thought maybe you'd forgotten," the Priest lied.

Ellen shook her head. "I had a sudden death in the family and had to go to Florida for the double funeral of my aunt and uncle," she explained.

120

"Oh," the Wizard said.

"Then...maybe this isn't the time," the Priest suggested turning to go.

"No, no. I'll come," Ellen assured them. "This would be the perfect distraction."

Avner sprinkled some of Nariel's sleep herbs and tried the vibrations that Mentor had taught him. Whichever worked, Ellen was asleep in minutes, and he was just as happy. There were aspects to the human interface that he was certain would never come easily to him.

Once Ellen was in the Between Worlds, she joined the brothers and they all went through Nathan's station and over the Bridge together. Before long, they had all returned to the castle by the sea. Avner stayed with Ellen this time.

As she and the brothers walked the parapet, her friends wore excited grins. In fact, as Ellen studied them, she was certain they looked years younger, less gray and more lean.

"So what's up?" she asked at last.

"You told us to try to remember our names," the Wizard reminded her.

Ellen nodded. "That I did. And...?"

"Well, we had help from one of Henry's ledgers," the Priest admitted and the Wizard slapped his head. "Ow! What's that for?"

"Sharing our secrets," the Wizard sniffed.

"Guys, I don't care how you discovered your names," Ellen replied. "I just wanted to know what they are."

"Edward," the Priest said.

"Alexander," the Wizard told her.

"A king and an emperor?" Ellen asked.

They nodded.

"Edward and Alexander," she said letting the feel of the names sink in. "I like them."

The brothers held their cheeks at the ready. When Ellen looked perplexed, the Wizard tapped his cheek. She blushed and leaned in to give each one a kiss. They looked quite pleased.

"So, does hearing and saying your names bring up any memories?" she asked.

The Wizard nodded. "I remember spending a lot of time in our father's library."

"We...didn't get along well with other kids," the Priest hesitantly explained.

"But you got along with each other," Ellen surmised.

They looked at each other.

"Well, not really that either," the Priest replied.

"At least not indoors," the Wizard said. "Outside the house, we always had each others' back."

The Priest nodded.

"Is it because you were different and intelligent and the other kids really felt intimidated by that?" Ellen wondered.

"Probably," the Priest said mournfully.

"Look, I know that the past wasn't the greatest," Ellen began. "I think every Way Shower is going to have had this experience."

"Even you?" the Wizard asked frowning.

"Oh, yes. I had a bully for every grade I was in," Ellen assured them. "However, you've so separated yourselves from who you really are, that you may be missing aspects that are very important to your being here," she said gesturing to the castle.

"So, what should we do?" the Priest asked.

"Instead of just being known by your titles, why not combine your titles with your names?" she offered. "You be Priest Edward and you be Wizard Alexander. Maybe in the process, you'll remember the aspects of yourselves that you need while maintaining your link to here."

"Think it will make us younger?" Priest Edward asked.

"From what I see, just learning your names already has. Now, what's in the woods?" Ellen wanted to know.

Priest Edward brought up the Vortex and soon set them down outside the wood. As soon as they hit the now well-marked road leading into the forest, Ellen noticed the distinct difference. Places had been cleared to grow shade-loving herbs and flowers. A small path wound past tall trees with house-sized trunks. Before long, they came upon a fallen log out of which a whole living and research facility had been hewed.

"We can hold meditation classes in the woods," Priest Edward told her.

"And we can learn what the herbs are for and how they're used," the Wizard added.

Ellen nodded. "I like this, too."

"Next week, Betsy and Toby are sailing up the coast. He thinks he can use the cove as a harbor for his ship, and she can run an Inn for Way Showers who are preparing to take up the Water Challenge."

"Fabulous!" Ellen exclaimed. "I love how all of you are working together and beginning to band together."

122

Meanwhile, Daniel stood on the battlefield surveying the enormous tear in the barrier that he and Michael's men had created. It was a good sized divide that weakened the structure considerably. Their greatest hope was that a Way Shower in the human reality would discover the opening and would help to tear it down from that side. At the thought of a Way Shower, Ellen's face came to mind. Though stoic and seemingly unmovable, Daniel felt a pang at the thought of her image.

Suddenly, he and Michael heard noise coming from the human side.

"Go, see what it is," Michael commanded and Daniel obediently leapt into the air to survey the scene.

Unfortunately, as he neared the tear, it became clear that Minions from the other side were facilitating repairs to it. Daniel watched them work for a little too long, got a little too close. One of them spotted him and, before he could slip away, sent a blast of Dark Energy knifing through him. Gritting his teeth against the pain, Daniel limped back to Michael, one wing badly injured.

"Minions...at the tear," he gasped out.

Michael blew his horn and his men leapt to the attack. Soon other battle angels were down and healing angels were carrying them off the field of battle and spiriting them away to the Great Above to be tended by Raphael. Daniel watched them go, desperately wishing he could be one of them.

"Can't let Raphael see me," he thought gasping as the pain took away his breath. *"He'd know."*

Through the agony, he knew of only one other person capable of healing him. With a grunt of pain, he opened his wings and spiraled out.

As Ellen entered her bedroom that night, Daniel suddenly fell through the ceiling and landed on her bed. She jumped back, startled, then stared at the wound across the join in his back.

"My lord, how did you make it here?" she asked hurrying forward.

Daniel gritted his teeth and moaned. "Help me," he pleaded. "Heal me."

A cool chill trickled down Ellen's spine. He had abandoned her and her heart still hurt.

"Why not Raphael?" she asked. "He's trained to deal with battle wounds."

Daniel grabbed her wrist and wouldn't let go. "Only...you. Heal...

123

me," he gasped out.

Ellen furrowed her brow. "*Something's going on,*" she thought uneasily.

Still, she couldn't stand to see him in such pain. She might feel hurt over what he did, but underneath it all, Ellen still loved him dearly. With a sigh, she moved closer and began laying her hands on different places while dropping into her heart space. As she watched, the wounds on his back closed, and Daniel finally lay limp and sweating against the sheets.

"You're pretty weak," she observed. "I don't think you should move for a while. " Ellen paused a moment desperately wanting to bite her tongue. "I think...you'd better stay the night." There she'd said it. "In my world recuperation often takes a little while."

He nodded his assent, gingerly hauled himself up onto a pillow and collapsed in exhaustion.

Avner faded into view, saw Daniel and gave Ellen a questioning look. She walked out into the family room and talked quietly.

"He showed up injured," she related. "But he wouldn't go to Raphael."

"Now, why wouldn't he go to Raphael?" Avner wondered.

Ellen shook her head. "Something's going on. First he cloaks his Choice Board so we don't know what his plans are. Then he refuses to go to Raphael for healing and comes to me instead. He's hiding something."

"Something he was certain you didn't have the capacity to discover, but he knew Raphael would find as soon as he went to work on him," Avner surmised.

Ellen nodded. "That's my guess. Avner, before he chose to go with Michael, he told me there was trouble, that he was in trouble."

"That is apparent."

"Why wouldn't he want me to know what it is?" she asked. "He said this trouble might even be bigger than him."

Avner's eyes widened. "That is very serious."

"Yet, for all intents and purposes, he's not in league with the One of Darkness. What could possibly harm him that isn't Darkness?" Ellen wondered.

Avner grew quiet as he tried to stretch his mind back through all his time. He was coming up empty only something niggled at the back of his brain, just out of reach. He shook his head.

"I feel like I should know," Avner replied. "But I just can't bring it to mind."

124

Ellen folded her arms across her as she headed back into the bedroom. "Well, if it comes to you, please let me know."

She stood observing Daniel as he slept, a pang stabbing her chest. She missed him so much. Seeing him, even in this condition, was almost too much. But as she edged closer, Ellen noticed the differences. She stroked his once golden hair now more a silver hue. She caressed his once radiant face that had taken on a pallor. Ellen touched his once shiny chest shield now dimmed and in shadow. She frowned at each discovery.

Finally, she went around to the other side of the bed, crawled in and turned off the light. "Whatever is wrong, Daniel," she whispered reaching out and squeezing his hand. "I will find out what it is. And I will find a way to restore you."

With that, she lay awake long into the night.

Apparently, Ellen drifted off to sleep at some point because when she opened her eyes the next morning, Daniel was gone. She sighed heavily and felt the bed where he had been. There was nothing in his spot to even suggest he had been there. With a heavy heart, she crawled out of bed and headed upstairs to cook breakfast.

In the Crystal, Daniel thought back in his mind to anything that might be helpful. He recalled standing on the log stretched into the pond and watching his reflection in the pond's surface. It was right after Ellen had changed him back from being a Minion and after Raphael had told him all angels were multi-dimensional. He had been curious to know "who" all he really was. He'd watched with no great curiosity as he saw all different views of himself, one of which had been a blue/silver feline, the powerful component the Embodied One had brought closer to the surface to give him his enormous Archangelic strength. Some aspects of himself had been the various guises he'd worn while in Ellen's world in order to become sufficiently corporeal when she'd been in trouble and needed him to be material.

Wearing a pensive frown, Daniel shifted between dimensional aspects. With each shift, he tried passing his hand through the wall of his crystal prison. He sampled the forms closest to his own, touched the wall and was hurtled back to the floor. Shaking his head and pulling himself to his feet, he shifted to forms ranging further and further away from his true nature. Different beasts, even monsters and little-by-little, the crystal felt less solid. Finally, he was down to his final choice.

"*Minion*," he thought shuddering. "*Only thing I've got left.*"

Daniel's mind immediately relived his torment in the Ice Queen's Minion's Lair when he had gone to rescue his brother, Oriel. Instead, Daniel had been captured and transformed into a mutated Minion and had been forced to fight his brother over and over again.

If it hadn't been for Ellen, the two brothers might still be there going through round after round of endless, pointless battles. She had alerted Michael, braved the Minion's Lair alone, stood between him and Oriel and had given him her living, beating heart, which had blocked the Leader's iron control. When Michael and his men followed freeing them, it had been Ellen, with Raphael's help, who had transformed him back to his Archangelic self. He shuddered at the thought of taking on that dimensional form again, even though he knew that in the context of the Minion's Lair, it had been warped and subverted for other purposes.

"*Still...if it will get me out of here,*" he thought.

Very carefully, Daniel allowed the change. He watched in the side of the crystal. At least what he saw mirrored there wasn't half-Minion, half melted angel like it had been when he'd languished in the Minion's Lair. Instead, the being staring back at him was symmetrical with batlike, leathery wings, shortened stature of body, bent legs and a horned, beaked head. He reached up and touched his face, tried out the leathery wings and moved about.

"*Not bad,*" he thought. "*I have total control this time.*"

Once again, Daniel tested the crystal's wall. The hairs on his arm stood on end as his hand slipped all the way through. Conserving his energy, he pulled his hand back and thought for a moment.

"*How can I let Ellen know this is me?*" he wondered studying his ugly reflection.

As he observed his image carefully, he suddenly honed in on the small, red eyes. "*Hmm,*" he thought. "*What if I could shift just enough so my blue eyes remained?*" he wondered.

Carefully, Daniel shifted just enough so that crystal clear blue eyes peered back at him. Taking a deep breath, he tested the wall again. When his hand went all the way through, he continued pushing the rest of the way.

"*Here goes nothing,*" he thought as his bat-winged form stepped out into the Crystal Cave.

He gazed around him then focused on what was important, that place deep within his heart where he knew Ellen resided. His form might have been altered, but he could still feel her and quickly got a fix on her. In an instant, he winked out guided by her unique signature alone. He
126

popped up in her room in the dark. Listening, he heard water running in the bathroom and knew she would soon enter. The moment of truth was at hand.

"*Will she recognize me?*" he wondered. "*And if she doesn't, will I still be able to get through to her?*"

The water stopped running and a minute later, Ellen turned on the light and stepped into the bedroom. She jumped back as soon as she spotted the dark, winged figure in the corner by her bed. Avner's wings snapped to attention, his hand grabbed the hilt of his sword, and he had it half out of its sheath before Ellen stayed him.

"That's a Minion," Avner announced.

"Trust me," Ellen said. "I know a Minion when I see one."

She continued to study the figure noticing its wholeness. "This one is a pure form from the actual Minion Dimension," she finally said. "It's not one the Dark One has mutated from something else."

Avner did not remove his hand from his sword but kept it at the ready.

Ellen carefully moved forward and slowly reached out to touch the leathery wings. She ran her fingertips up over the wings to the shoulders, up the neck and cupped both sides of the ugly face in her hands.

Daniel stood as still as he could barely daring to breathe while she touched him. He willed her to look him in the eyes, to notice his eyes, to look at him and see who he really was.

"This is all Minion," Ellen said again. "I don't sense an intent to harm me."

"Who sent you?" Avner demanded.

Ellen's eyes roamed over its body eventually trailing back upwards to its face. For a moment, she felt a tingle down her spine then she noticed the anomaly. She stared into its eyes then froze in place.

"Avner," she said slowly, her gaze never leaving those blue eyes. "What color are a Minion's eyes?"

"Red," he stated emphatically.

Ellen stared hard into those eyes reading the intelligence and familiarity behind them. Suddenly, she threw her arms around the Minion and held him close.

"Daniel...Oh my God, Daniel!" she cried. "What's happened? What on Earth is going on?"

Daniel could only make some guttural noises in reply but finally managed to croak out, "Trapped. Find me."

With a frown, Avner mentally contacted Michael who assured him that the angelic Daniel was standing right beside him.

"He's with Michael," he reported.

Ellen shook her head. "Only part of him is there," she insisted. "Some part of him is not with his battle self."

Daniel nodded.

She studied him. "You and your battle self are split?"

He nodded again.

"You're trapped?"

Daniel nodded but felt himself weakening. With the last of his energy he whispered, "Find...me," and faded from view.

CHAPTER 17

Ellen stared at the spot in the bedroom where the Minion had stood just moments before. She finally sat hard on the edge of the bed. She kept shaking her head, almost unable to comprehend recent experiences. At last, she turned and sat cross-legged on the bed holding her head in her hands. Avner remained motionless while he observed her bewilderment.

"Avner?"

"Mm-hm."

Ellen looked up. "How is it that one night I have Daniel with a battle wound literally drop in, and the next night I have a Minion show up claiming to be him trapped somewhere?"

Avner shook his head. "I have no answers."

"The Embodied One?" she queried.

He nodded. "I should think so."

"Then let's go."

After Ellen climbed in and turned off the light, Avner again lulled her to sleep and eased her into the Between Worlds. Ellen eagerly approached Nathan's guard station. As soon as she saw him, she opened her mouth.

"Nathan, has your father been through here recently?"

He turned and blinked. "No."

"Did a Minion come through here tonight?"

Again, "No."

Ellen ran her hand through her hair while Nathan approached wearing a pensive frown.

"I do not understand your questions, mother," he said.

"It's crazy. The night before last he literally fell out of the sky onto my bed with a battle wound," Ellen explained. "And tonight he appeared as a Minion claiming to be trapped."

Nathan gave a low growl. "How did he get past me?"

Ellen turned to Avner with a questioning glance.

"It is possible he slipped through in some other manner," Avner proposed.

"But I see all dimensions," Nathan protested. "I should at least have sensed my own blood."

Ellen gave him a reassuring hug. "It's ok. Something very strange is afoot. We're just going to have to figure it out."

"I will be more vigilant," Nathan told her.

"Vigilance alone may not detect this," Avner cautioned.

Ellen hurried across the Bridge and through the Facility. Avner wasted no time in popping her straight into the the Throne Room where the Embodied One was already waiting. As quickly as she could, she described the two recent experiences with Daniel. The Embodied One frowned deeply.

"I do not know what to make of this," the Embodied One said. "Michael constantly assures me that Daniel is at his side."

"Could he be two places at once?" Ellen wondered.

Avner's eyes narrowed. "Is that possible?"

"Well, technically yes," the Embodied One conceded. "But the how and why elude me."

Ellen finally spoke up. "Daniel told me he was in some kind of trouble that was bigger than him," she confessed.

The Embodied One fixed an intense gaze on her. "When?"

"The night before he asked to fight with Michael," she told him.

"Why didn't he come to me?" the Embodied One wondered. "Why didn't he tell me?"

Ellen shook her head. "I don't know...only...."

"Yes?"

"When I told him I'd happily sacrifice myself for him, he told me I should never do that," Ellen replied. "He seemed really afraid of that."

"So he hid his Choice Board to keep us from knowing what was happening," Avner postulated, "kept silent about the trouble and refused to tell either of you its nature."

A chill trickled down Ellen's spine. "Wherever he's trapped, only a Way Shower can find him."

"And you may be the only Way Shower with the capacity," the Embodied One surmised.

"Only to seek him would endanger you," Avner told Ellen.

"And he knew I would take that risk if I knew what was wrong," Ellen concluded.

A heavy silence filled the room.

"What now?" Avner asked.

"I want to talk to him...go to the battlefield," Ellen said.

"Michael reports that Daniel talks to no one," the Embodied One said.

"Let me try," she pleaded.

He nodded. "Take her, Avner. But keep her well back from the fray and protect her at all costs."

Avner bowed his head. "Yes, Sire."

Drawing his sword to have at the ready, Avner grasped Ellen firmly in his other arm and spiraled out of the Great Halls. The traverse was longer as they moved through a gray and purple sky scape. Before long, the image of angels and Minions in full battle engagement came into view. Beyond them Ellen could see the sparking tear in a huge barrier.

Avner landed on a hilltop well back from the fighting and shielded Ellen with his wings. She peered around his wings and scanned the fighting wondering how to find Daniel in the midst of the throng. Suddenly, a great column of pure light streaked toward one lone angel who stood in the midst of an angry swarm of Minions. The light connected with him and instantly radiated out from his upraised sword.

Ellen gasped. "Daniel!"

In awe, she and Avner watched as Daniel single-handedly flattened group after group of Minions. However, the pair on the hilltop were too intent in watching his prowess. Without warning, they heard a screech overhead, and Avner raised his sword.

Having sensed the presence of a Way Shower, Minions had left the main fight and were flying toward the beleaguered father and daughter. The sky was thick with leathery wings, and their harsh cries filled the air like thunder. A splash of white streaked toward them and Oriel landed nearby.

"Back-to-back," he called to Avner.

The two battle angels instantly shielded Ellen between their wings, each facing out to deal with the incoming enemy.

"There's too many of them!" Ellen cried.

The men didn't reply as they channeled the light through their swords cutting down as many Minions as they could. Yet, on the horde came swooping and diving at the huddled group menacing them on every side.

Though terrified, Ellen sank her awareness down into the ground and drew its strength up into her back. She placed one hand on the join of each angel, channeling the grounded energy into them.

Suddenly, Oriel cried out. Ellen glanced up, spotted a gash across the back of his shoulders and immediately placed a hand on either side of the cut. The wound closed and healed in seconds. Avner took a gash to the head, and she shifted her attention to him. Yet, in spite of being defended by two of the strongest Archangels, Ellen knew they couldn't hold out much longer.

"More incoming!" Oriel groaned.

Ellen peeked out between their wings and saw that the sky overhead was black with Minions.

"We'll never make it," she moaned.

"Don't give up yet," Avner urged. "Michael just got my message."

Oriel ducked, just missing getting stabbed, but his chest was bleeding.

"Just...keep us...going," he said through clenched teeth. "Only have to hold on...a little longer."

Suddenly, two bright stars appeared in the sky hurtling toward them. Minions tumbled from the sky in their wake. Ellen stared with her mouth agape as Michael and Daniel, brilliant as two suns, landed with heavy thuds beside them and held their swords aloft creating a shield of light. Oriel rose to his feet to join them while Avner hovered over Ellen keeping her safe.

The three radiant Archangels suddenly did something Ellen could barely describe. For a moment they seemed to suck their light inwards. Their bodies hummed like powerful generators and the ground around them trembled.

"Wait...." Michael ordered. "Wait...."

Minions swarmed over the ground coming closer with every second. It seemed like the small group was doomed. Ellen clung in fear to Avner closing her eyes and bracing for the worst.

"A-a-and...now!" Michael exclaimed.

With the force of an erupting volcano, the three Archangels suddenly loosed their light aiming it through their swords and cutting down the oncoming throng. The noise of the energy release was akin to the roar of a rocket lifting a space shuttle off the launch pad. Ellen clamped her hands over her ears fearing she'd go deaf. Without warning, all went quiet. Hesitantly, she raised her head.

The ground around them for yards was littered with flattened Minions while those still standing fled. But there was no escape for Michael's army awaited them and mowed them down as they ran. Avner rose and helped Ellen to her feet.

"Wow! That was close!" she exclaimed.

Michael turned and glared at her. "What are you doing here?" he demanded.

Ellen blinked at his anger. "I got permission from the Embodied One," she replied.

"He let you come here?" Michael asked incredulously.

She nodded.

Michael grumbled and turned to survey the battlefield. "We're rather busy right now."

"I can see," Ellen remarked. "How come there are so many Minions still active? I thought the Sultan directed them and he's been imprisoned."

Michael shook his head. "Minions in their pure form are a simple species," he explained. "Their purpose seems to be to build and maintain barriers. When not immediately directed by a more intelligent organizer, they will swarm barriers indiscriminately and keep building and strengthening them."

"So they don't care which ones they are...good or bad...old or new?" Ellen asked. "They just work?"

Michael nodded. "Now, why are you here on the battlefield? Why did the Embodied One allow this?"

"I wanted to talk to Daniel."

"He talks to no one," he said quietly.

"I know," Ellen replied. "But I have to try."

Michael nodded and began sending orders to his troops.

Ellen turned and looked at Daniel. He stood a ways apart from them, his sword sheathed, hands on his hips, and his hair tossed on a light breeze. His face was expressionless and his body unnaturally bright. She didn't know what to make of him, but he was the only one who knew what was wrong.

"Daniel," she called.

He did not acknowledge her.

"Won't you tell me what is wrong?" she asked slowly approaching him.

Still motionless.

"Can you explain why one night you came to me injured and the next night you came to me as a Minion claiming to be trapped?" she tried again stopping a yard away.

This time Daniel slowly turned his head and stared at her. His gaze sent chills down her spine.

"Did you split yourself, Daniel?" she pressed. "The Minion told me to find him."

Suddenly, Daniel's face contorted with rage. He rushed at Ellen roaring "No!" and shoved her to the ground. Without pausing, he leapt into the air and took to the sky.

Avner stepped forward, leant Ellen his hand and helped her up. Michael turned to follow Daniel.

"I will reprimand him," he asserted.

"No," Ellen said firmly, dusting herself off. "That was a message. I hit upon something...something that scared him enough to snap out of his trance and act."

Michael studied her. "Then what was he trying to say?"

"I'm on a hot track," Ellen relied. "Part of him is trapped, and he's afraid I'll find him."

"But why?" Avner wondered.

"That...is what I need to find out," Ellen replied. "I need to visit the University."

Avner opened his arms to her.

"Somewhere, somehow there's an answer to this, and I plan to find it."

With that he held her close and spiraled off the battlefield.

In no time, they had reached the coast and landed in the castle courtyard. Though empty, Ellen sensed someone was in residence. Without hesitation, she ran across the courtyard toward an oaken door, pushed it open and followed the trail of torches into the dungeon. Simon sat in the lab working on a gadget.

"Just the person I wanted to see!" she exclaimed bursting in the door.

He jumped and spun around sighing with relief when he spotted her. "What do you need me for?" he asked going back to his gadget.

"All the data from the old computer is on the quantum computer, right?" she asked drawing up a seat.

"Yes," Simon responded cautiously.

"Good. I need help accessing it," Ellen told him.

"It's over there," he replied nodding to his right.

"It will take too long for me to play with it," Ellen complained.

Simon shrugged. "And I'm busy."

Ellen blew her breath out in a huff. "I don't have time for your stubborn arrogance."

She put one hand on his shoulder and quickly sifted for a more useful parallel. She felt one solidify in her hand, drew it back towards Simon and set it on his head. She watched as small shudders moved down through his body. At last he stopped working.

"What is so important?" he asked annoyed.

"I want to know if there is any data on anyone splitting themselves in two in the past," Ellen requested.

Simon rose, went to the computer and put on an unusual grid-like helmet. "Speed of thought," he said noticing her questioning look.

With a swipe of his finger to unlock the computer, he mentally posed the question. In less than 30 seconds, the computer returned the answer.

"An Archangel generations ago lost his light to a crystal," Ellen read aloud peering over Simon's shoulder.

"He became a shell," Avner said, his voice booming through the dungeon.

Ellen snapped her head up. "You've seen this before?"

He shook his head. "Not like this. When my brother was lost, he collapsed to the floor his body but a hull."

"Says here," Simon added, "that he lost his light to some crystal in the...."

"Valley of a Thousand Caves," Avner finished.

"Then that's where I've got to go," Ellen declared jumping up.

"Um...you might want to rethink that," Simon told her.

Ellen turned her head. "Why?"

"Because my first Way Shower child found my brother's light but was lost when he returned it to him," Avner replied quietly.

Ellen staggered back."By lost, do you mean...dead?"

Avner shook his head. "We never knew. He simply vanished."

She grabbed a chair and collapsed into the seat. "So that's why he refused to tell anyone what was wrong," she breathed.

"Who?" Simon asked.

"Daniel," Avner replied.

"He knew I'd be the only one with the capacity to find him and...."

"You'd be lost in the process if you tried to rescue him," Avner said.

Ellen's head reeled, but Simon bent closer to the computer screen.

"Maybe not," he said. "There's something here about some ancient book in a Dragon's Lair."

Ellen raised her head. "Of course! We might not know where that Way Shower disappeared to, but the Great Dragon keeps track of all lives. He'd have to know." She jumped up and looked hopefully to Avner. "We have to go there."

"Go where?" Wizard Alexander's voice echoed from the stairs.

"The Dragon's Island," Ellen replied happy to see her friend.

"Edward and I were just talking about making a visit," Alexander replied.

"I've got to come too," Ellen insisted.

"Tomorrow," Avner told her. "Your time this night is up."

"I'm coming with you," Ellen insisted. "Don't go to the island without me."

With that, Avner picked her up and whisked her back home.

CHAPTER 18

Ellen's hope had sprung wings with the mention of the Dragon's Island. She remembered her past visits there. The first time she had gone there through the Wizard's back door and had been required to rewrite her life story. As the Great Red Dragon had put it, she had referenced her life so that it either read as a tragedy or some opera directed by another. Ellen had sat with a quill and ink and scratched out an authentic life story in which she owned both her sorrows and her triumphs. The Great Red Dragon had taken his good old time reading it, but in the end, he had pronounced it authentic and that Way Shower challenge had been met.

The second time she visited had been a little more thrilling. The Ice Queen had chased her through the caverns and had tried to turn her to ice when she went to open the back door. With Daniel's help, she escaped out onto the ledge overlooking a deep gorge. The Ice Queen hadn't been so easily deterred, however, and had attacked her knocking them both off the ledge. As they fell, the Ice Queen had whistled for her dragon. But Ellen now wore the Star Pendant and the dragon ignored the Ice Queen, flying to her instead.

What followed was a wild ride for Ellen as she clutched the dragon's neck until Daniel was able to hop on behind her and send the dragon winging for home. Ellen remembered the brightly colored parrots and chattering monkeys as they flew through the jungle on the island. Once inside the Dragon's Lair, she had removed the drug from the dragon's system that had given the Ice Queen control. Then she healed him and returned him whole to his grandfather.

The thought of returning to see the Great Red Dragon boosted her mood in a way nothing had for a long time. She even went out swing dancing with Robert that evening, which made him thrilled. They danced to great blues music and she chatted with acquaintances she hadn't seen in over a year. When they finally got home, they crawled into their separate beds after a sweet good night. Ellen had just turned off her light when Avner sat on the edge of the bed beside her.

"Are you ready?" he asked in his deep voice.

"Mm, yes," Ellen replied. "And after that workout tonight, I doubt it will take much to get me to sleep."

Avner agreed but still spread a little of Nariel's herbs around Ellen. Before she knew it, she was approaching Nathan's station.

She bit her lower lip and stared at the door. "Do you think I should tell him?" she asked.

"He is a young man tasked with an important job," Avner reminded her. "You do not know what he has already faced in his life."

"True," Ellen conceded ruefully, realizing how much of her son's younger years she had completely missed out on.

With a sigh, she moved forward and entered the station. Nathan was instantly on the alert when he heard the door whoosh open, but as soon as he saw his mother, he relaxed. He hurried to greet her and wrap her in a warm embrace.

"Have you heard anything about father?" he asked immediately.

Ellen nodded and looked down. "He's in quite a bit of trouble. And I may be the only one able to find and help him."

Nathan frowned.

"But if she does, your mother may be lost," Avner interjected quietly.

Nathan's eyes narrowed and his frown deepened. "Mother may be lost helping father? But father's already lost?"

Ellen looked up. "Something like that," she admitted. "Though there's a ray of hope to be found in a book the Great Red Dragon has in his possession."

Nathan snorted with a little hiss. "What can paper tell you?"

"Where to find the very first Way Shower," Ellen replied. "If he still lives, he's performed the same task I'm facing. I can learn what I must do."

"And what went wrong," Avner added.

Nathan looked from one to the other. Suddenly, he started pacing like a caged animal. "I should be the one to help father," he insisted with a

138

growl. "You should not put your life on the line."

Ellen reached out, caught his arm and stopped him. "Our responsibilities are what they are. The fact I haven't had any nasty surprises by dark figures threatening me in the night tells me you're doing a very good job."

Nathan paused and blinked thoughtfully.

"Honey, what you do here," Ellen said gesturing to the station, "keeps me safe at home."

His eyebrows raised. "Then, that is good. I protect my mother."

"And a whole lot of other people," Ellen assured him kissing his cheek.

She and Avner left directly and before long came out at the Castle by the Sea. Edward and Alexander were waiting for her. As she approached them through the gate, Ellen did a double take. Gone were the streaks of gray and the gaunt cheekbones.

"You gents look like maybe you're 30...if," she remarked.

"It's all this sea air," Alexander said.

"Hmph," Ellen snorted. "I'd say the sea has little to do with it."

"Are you ready to go?" Edward asked.

"Absolutely!"

The brothers turned her around, and they headed back out toward the cliff. They began descending the stairs cut into the cliff face, and Ellen spotted a ship anchored in the cover.

"Are Toby and Betsy here?" she asked.

"Been here a couple of weeks," Alexander informed her.

"He brought in some men who are building a pier," Edward explained. "Until then, we'll have to row out to the ship."

"Won't sailing to Dragon's Island take a long time?" Ellen asked.

Edward shook his head. "He's only going to take us far enough for us to manage the rest of the way by the Vortex."

Ellen knit her brow. "It has a range?"

"I would say so!" Alexander exclaimed. "Wouldn't want to ditch in the middle of the ocean, would you?"

"I never would have expected to," Ellen replied honestly.

Before long, they walked across the beach to where Toby's first mate waited with a small boat. They clambered in, he shoved the boat into the waves then took up the oars and rowed them out to Toby's ship. They pulled up alongside it and, while the brothers climbed the netting to the deck, Avner picked up Ellen and flew her up. As the brothers were helped over the rails, a bell sounded and the anchor was raised.

"Raise the mainsail," came the cry.

Ellen glanced up to see Toby standing on the bridge manning the helm. She hurried up the steep, narrow steps and soon gave him a hug.

"Got the big fella with ya," he remarked eyeing Avner.

She nodded. "Daniel's in a bit of trouble," she whispered. "We're looking for a way to help him out."

"To Dragon's Isle it be," he said loudly and soon the ship was plowing through the waves, the bow dipping then rising according to the rhythm of the seas.

"Betsy on the ship?" Ellen asked.

"No. She went back to Sea Town to get linens an' things," Toby replied.

"Darn. I was hoping to talk to her," Ellen said. "Well, tell her I said hello."

""Will do," Toby assured her and applied his attention to piloting his vessel.

The Sea Gulls flew overhead calling to one another and periodically dove into the waves only to come up moments later with fish. Eventually, the brothers made it up to the bridge and took a keen interest in surveying the horizon. Around mid-afternoon, Edward gave the signal and Toby furled the sails.

"Good luck," Toby told her as Ellen stepped into the Wizard's chalk circle.

She nodded then became lost to sight as the Priest brought the Vortex up around them and it lifted off the deck. Before they knew it, they were flying over the waves toward a tiny dot on the horizon. Priest continually checked his pendulum, while the Wizard and Ellen helped maintain the integrity of the Vortex. As the island drew closer, Ellen spotted the lone mountain that housed the Dragon's Lair.

"Straight up this slope to the ledge up there," she told Edward.

He nodded and navigated to a perfect touchdown just outside the entrance to the cave. They headed inside as soon as the Vortex sank into the ledge.

The walk was farther than Ellen remembered. *"Then again,"* she thought. *"Last time I was on the back of a runaway dragon."*

Soon, though, they spotted a warm glow and made their way toward it. In minutes, they entered the main chamber, stopped and stared. The two dragons sat amidst piles of books and scrolls, their tails wrapped tightly about the piles to keep them from sliding away. Books were stacked in nearly every nook and cranny and large urns were stuffed to

140

over flowing with scrolls.

"How will we ever find the books in this mess?" Edward wondered.

Alexander chuckled. "Looks like my bedroom at home."

"Ha! Looks like your study in the old Tower," Edward guffawed.

"I'm cleaning it," Alexander protested.

"You mean, you're moving it," Edward challenged.

Ellen ignored them and moved forward with Avner. They didn't get far before the Great Red Dragon let a breath of steam curl from his nostrils, stopped reading mid-sentence and turned his head toward them. Sniffing the air, he disentangled himself from his books and lowered his great red head toward them.

"Who's here?" he asked in a booming bass voice that echoed around the cavern.

The younger, green-colored dragon also stopped his reading and turned his attention toward them.

"Could it be?" he wondered aloud.

"Be who?" the Great Red Dragon asked.

"Why, I do think so, Grandfather," the Green Dragon said lowering his head for a closer look. "This is the woman who freed me from the Ice Queen."

"It's good to see you again," Ellen said, "particularly since you appear to have recovered so well."

The Great Red Dragon murmured deep in his throat. "Recovered indeed! You brought him back from the brink of death. I owe you a debt of gratitude."

"Could I ask a favor of you then?" Ellen requested. "For me and my friends."

The Great Red Dragon's forehead furrowed. "Possibly. What is this favor?"

"We seek two scrolls and a book," Ellen said. "Edward and Alexander would like to read the scrolls of their lives to help them remember who they've been."

As she spoke, the Green Dragon was already moving amongst the stacks and urns. He found one large gray urn, picked it up, dumped the scrolls into his hand and carefully picked out two with his claws.

"The other is the life of my first son," Avner announced. "He was the very first Way Shower. He disappeared after helping one of my brothers and was never seen again."

The Great Red Dragon blinked his heavy eyelids.

"Apparently, he disappeared after helping my father," Ellen said gesturing toward Avner, "retrieve the Light of one of his brothers from a crystal in a cave. But once the Light was restored, the Way Shower disappeared."

The Great Red Dragon studied Avner very carefully with a piercing gaze.

"We believe this...separation of body and Light...has happened again," Ellen explained carefully.

"To whom?" the Great Red Dragon demanded.

"To Daniel my...."

"The angel who sent me home!" the Green Dragon exclaimed.

"Is this true?" the Great Red Dragon roared.

Ellen nodded. "I'm just trying to find a way to find this cave and restore his Light. I thought if I could find information about the first Way Shower, I'd learn what has to be done now."

The Green Dragon neatly plucked an ancient book off a shelf with its claws and lowered it down to Ellen.

"His name is William," the Great Red Dragon said.

"You said is," Avner noted immediately. "Does this mean he yet lives?"

The Great Red Dragon pulled away. "Yes. He chose to hide himself. Perhaps you have an inkling why?"

Avner hung his head. "I do but things and my loyalty have changed."

Ellen turned and studied him. "What do you mean?"

Avner took a deep breath. "The original experiment was undertaken at the Dark One's suggestion."

"Before or after you'd given him your heart?" she pressed.

"Before," Avner assured her. "Harmless experimenting...or so I thought. And thus was I slowly ensnared."

Ellen glanced up reading a measure of uneasiness in the Great Red Dragon. She looked back to Avner. On the surface, he looked as he had since she had transformed him from Minion back to angel. Still, "*Can't be too cautious*," she thought.

"I'm sorry, Avner. I need to know your allegiance, and I can't trust words alone," she said.

He nodded, his countenance sorrowful. "I understand."

"Please kneel," she requested.

Avner knelt on one knee before her. Ellen placed one hand on his head and the other on his heart. She closed her eyes, slipped back into
142

herself and dropped into her heart space. She sought out the resonance for his motives traveling along his ancient timeline. In the past, she felt his insatiable curiosity, a trait she shared. In the present, she sensed regret and remorse. She allowed herself to rise to full awareness and let him go.

"I'm satisfied," Ellen told him.

Avner rose but said nothing.

The Green Dragon carefully plucked Ellen off the floor and sat her in a high chair before a book stand. Ellen placed the book on the stand and opened it. She scanned the pages flipping them quickly until she came to the place where William faced the crystal in the cave. She stopped for a moment and gazed at the hand drawn image of him in the upper left corner of the page.

"My brother," she whispered gently running her fingers over the picture.

With a deep breath, Ellen began to read. William had emptied himself of all his light pouring it into the crystal. In the end, the crystal burst when it could hold no more light. He had reabsorbed all the light that was not the angel's. But he had been unable to control the light or contain it. It had obliterated his form and he had fled the cave.

Ellen read the last piece about his fleeing the cave. She turned toward Avner. "Why would William feel he had to flee?" she asked point blank.

Avner hung his head. "We were doing experiments with capturing Light. That was how my brother ended up inside the crystal."

"And William was afraid you'd capture him as well," she surmised.

Avner nodded. "However, the results of the experiment so frightened me that I hid all knowledge of the Valley of a Thousand Caves and of the Crystal Cave. Though I wrote about them in the book Mentor has, I never gave any indication to their whereabouts and to this day, no longer recall."

Ellen took a deep breath. "So, Daniel just managed to stumble upon this Valley and this cave?"

"It would appear to be so," Avner replied. "He did try to read the book at Mentor's and even asked me to come read it since I'd written the passage in First Language."

"And you didn't ask him why?" Ellen demanded.

"I did," Avner responded. "He said he'd remembered a tale and tried to describe it to you, but couldn't remember."

Ellen sighed. "He did mention it, he just didn't say why it was important."

She returned to the book hoping to find information of William's present whereabouts. Flipping a couple of pages, she suddenly got excited. "Hey! He's still alive!"

Avner looked up hopefully.

"He lives in a darkened land full of flame and lava," Ellen continued.

"Volcanoes," Alexander suggested. "Some place where the play of light and shadow might give him a semblance of form."

Ellen looked up at Avner. "I've got to get there. I must find him."

He hung his head. "I fear he will not show himself if I accompany you," he said. "He may not trust me."

"Apparently, he may have a good reason not to," Ellen shot back.

"I will take you," the Green Dragon offered.

"Grandson," the Great Red Dragon growled.

The Green Dragon turned toward his elder. "They saved my life, this woman and her Guardian. How can I not repay this debt?"

The Great Red Dragon considered this for a moment then slowly nodded. "You may go, grandson. With my blessing."

He turned his great head toward Ellen. "See to it he returns in one piece," he charged.

"You have my word," she told him.

Ellen turned toward Edward and Alexander. "Are you guys coming or staying here?"

"Staying," they chorused.

Ellen smiled and nodded. She looked up at the Green Dragon. "Looks like it's just you and me.   Ready?"

The Green Dragon slowly lowered his body to the ground. Avner helped her climb onto the dragon's back.

"I promise a smoother ride this time," he said, a puff of steam exited his nostrils.

"Just don't take out any more bridges," Ellen joked.

"Understood."

With that, he rose to his full height, leapt into the air and took off back through the tunnel toward open air. In minutes they soared over the jungle and out over the sea.

CHAPTER 19

The Green Dragon soared over the waves quickly putting Dragon Island behind them.

"Do you have any idea where a cluster of volcanoes might be?" Ellen yelled against the wind.

"Yes," the Dragon replied. "The Ice Queen had me go there often as if seeking something. 'Tis dry and arid land, black and cracked. Dust and sulfur, hardened rock. Yet near the peak a caldera lies. Red is its surface where hot rock flies."

"Sounds like what we're looking for," Ellen agreed. "And I'll bet William was who she was searching for."

The Green Dragon banked sharply to its left and flew fast with great strokes of its long, leathery wings. They wove in and out of clouds till finally Ellen could just see the sparkle of waves and a chain of islands below. The Green Dragon craned his long neck to see them then dove for the largest island in the chain. He circled the mountain giving Ellen an excellent view of the caldera and a river of lava that ran down the mountainside oozing into the ocean with a hiss of steam.

He swooped down the mountain slope and landed near the shore. Lying flat for her sake, he waited while Ellen slid off.

"I shall wait on that near island," he told her gesturing with his wing toward a speck to their left.

"Because William is likely to have seen you before as well and won't approach," Ellen surmised.

The Green Dragon blinked his reply.

"Was there anywhere here where you ever felt he might be?" she wondered.

"There are places up the slope where I remember seeing movement," the Green Dragon told her.

"But you never told the Ice Queen?" Ellen asked incredulously.

"She never asked," he replied and leapt into the sky.

Ellen shook her head as she watched him go. Never mind how she would tell him she was ready to go back. That would figure itself out.

"Just how does one find someone who wants to remain hidden?" she wondered.

Shielding her eyes with her hand, Ellen scanned the barren, almost lunar landscape. A gust of wind brought an acidic, sulfurous odor to her nostrils. She covered her face with her other hand.

"*Man, that stuff stinks and it hurts the lungs,*" she thought.

With no plan, but certain the coast was empty, Ellen began making her way over the jagged, crumbly rocks. She wound her way toward the river of lava, watching for a while as it dropped into the sea. Then she climbed up along the lava flow headed for the top of the mountain. She had to stop to rest a few times and began to wonder why she'd failed to bring a water skin with her. Eventually, she crested a ridge of lava rock and found herself on more even ground.

There seemed to be the semblance of a path here, part of which veered off toward the caldera. She crept to its edge gazing out over the barren landscape towards various holes in the basin that opened to reveal molten lava near the surface. Clouds of sulfurous smoke bent away toward the upper end of the island taking the horrid odor with it.

Suddenly, Ellen felt the creepy sensation of someone watching her and fought the urge to whip around to see who was there. If it was William, she didn't want to do anything to spook him.

Ever so slowly, Ellen rotated till she was nearly facing the direction where she felt eyes watching her. She slowly raised her hands overhead.

"William," she called. "If that's you I feel, I am seeking you."

Ellen felt the intelligence withdraw a ways.

"I'm not here to harm you or capture you," she called again.

She waited but did not feel the intelligence press closer.

"William, I'm your sister," she called at last. "I'm Ellen. I-I just want to know that you're all right."

Now, she could sense those eyes again boring holes in her skull. The sensation of that intelligence coming closer was palpable. She turned her head slightly to the left and caught sight of a beam of light dancing

146

between two mounds of lava.

Her breath caught in her throat. "William?" she whispered.

"How do I know you're my sister?" a voice asked.

Ellen licked her lips. Good question.

"I'm a Way Shower," she replied. "Next to the last child Avner begot."

"Avner!" the voice exclaimed derisively. "I denounce him as father."

Ellen frowned and slowly put her arms down. "Why?"

"He would have imprisoned me had I not fled," the voice responded.

Ellen sighed sadly. "I suspected as much."

"He never had enough, never knew enough. He always wanted more," the voice replied.

"You...sound pretty bitter," Ellen remarked.

"Wouldn't you be if you had to flee your own father and hide for the rest of your life?" came the retort.

"Perhaps," she whispered.

"Why do you seek me?" the voice demanded.

"Honestly? I need your help," Ellen told him.

"For what?"

"I need you to tell me what you did to get Avner's brother out of that crystal," Ellen told him.

"Why?"

"William, my Guardian's light is stuck in one of those crystals. Please, William. I've got to get him out," Ellen implored.

Silence hung on the air for a while. "Avner didn't put you up to this, did he?"

Ellen shook her head. "No. In fact, he wouldn't even come with me. He knew you'd distrust him."

"He's right," the voice replied.

Ellen saw the light beam move back and forth as if someone were pacing.

"It's too risky," the voice said at last. "You'll become like me."

"I want to learn from what you did," Ellen replied. "Maybe there's some way to modify the procedure, make it safer."

"Perhaps," the voice said. "It was only an experiment."

"Then...you'll help me?" Ellen asked hopefully. "You'll tell me?"

"There is an overhang of lava nearby. Meet me there," the voice replied and the light zipped away.

Ellen leapt up and headed in the direction the light had taken. Soon, she spotted the overhang as well as a small pool of water along with some dusty, leggy plants that clung to a rock. She ducked under the overhang and stepped into the interior. Toward the back of the scalloped shell of hardened lava, she saw the form of a man. He flickered like the shadow cast by a flame.

"It was the only way to make myself at all visible or even really see you clearly," William said. "I knew there were others besides me. I just never got to meet them."

"I only met one other in Avner's lineage," Ellen admitted.

"Who?"

"The Ice Queen," Ellen told him.

"So, how do I know you aren't like them?" William asked shrinking into a corner.

Ellen sat down on the ground, crossed her legs and rested her hands on her knees palms up. "Come, see for yourself. I know you know how to sense evil. If you find any in me, I will leave and never return."

She waited quietly barely daring to breathe. Slowly, the flickering shadow crept toward her. It passed its hand over her, and the hairs on her arms stood on end. Finally, she felt pressure on the top of her head and over her chest. She felt a consciousness search her, roaming through the open spaces of her heart and mind then gradually withdraw.

"You are as you say," he announced, his voice cracking with emotion. "How did you manage to stay pure?"

Ellen smiled wryly. "I've had a most extraordinary Guardian, William, but that won't be any more unless I can get his light out of that crystal and restore him.

William squatted beside her. "Your light is strong," he said at last, "but not yet strong enough for this task."

"Then what do I do?" she implored.

"I stayed with a group of monks in a Monastery high in the mountains," William told her. "They had ways of opening themselves so they could see and experience the full spectrum of light," he told her.

"Do you think they would help me?" Ellen wondered.

"If you tell them you're my sister and that I sent you, I think so," he replied.

He rose and Ellen uncrossed her legs and stood beside him. Tears stung her eyes.

"To think I have a brother and I've found you, but I can't even give you a hug," she mourned.

148

"To think I have a sister who cared enough to fine me," William replied.

"Did you lose your form altogether?" Ellen wondered.

"Yes, I can't get it back."

Ellen's mind raced instantly flying to images of Visionary and Weaver. She shook her head. "That may not be entirely true," she told him. "I know other Way Showers, different lineages. They might actually be able to help."

"Give me a body again?" He snorted softly. "I doubt it."

Ellen smiled. "You have no idea what they can do or what any Way Shower can do."

She felt an inner tug.

"I think I have to go now," Ellen announced.

"Will you come back?" William asked wistfully.

"I promise and when I do, I'll bring a couple of friends with me," she assured him.

With a wave, Ellen ducked out from under the overhang and clambered up the hill. She turned back and saw him standing just inside the shadows. He waved and she blew him a kiss.

"*Time to go*," she thought and right on cue a huge shadow swept over the landscape.

Looking up, she spotted the Green Dragon. Minutes later, she was on his back headed for the Dragon's Lair, Avner and home.

The next day when Ellen got up, she got around sooner than usual and reached for a quarter Ativan. Avner watched her swallow the partial pill, tilted his head to one side and frowned. She caught his look.

"Just something for panic attacks," she told him.

"What is that?" Avner wondered.

"Panic attacks?"

He nodded.

"It's when my anxiety gets so high, I can't function and it won't turn off on its own," Ellen explained.

Avner glanced about them with concern. "Are you under attack? Are you expecting an attack?"

Ellen shook her head. "Medical tests. After spending eleven hours in the Emergency room two years ago after the attack, most things medical make me freeze."

Avner still didn't look as if he understood, but Ellen ignored him. It was a simple ultrasound. "*Just for baseline measurements*," her doctor had said. Ellen knew it was no big deal, but it didn't quiet her heart rate or blood pressure.

A quick drive down the road to the medical center, some basic indignities later, and she was headed back home. She was more interested in preparations for Thanksgiving. This year her friend, Katrina, was joining her and Robert. Katrinas' family was all on the west coast and she rarely got to see them. Actually, even Ellen hadn't gotten to see much of her lately since work at the credit union had become chaotic with system changes.

Ellen smiled to herself as she drove. Katrina was so much fun and so loving and supportive. They shared a lot of craziness between them. "*Actually*," Ellen thought biting her lower lip, "*we share way more than just craziness.*"

Truth was, Ellen had quit listing similar life experiences the two women had in common when she hit five dozen. Still they continued, like last Halloween when they'd both worn costumes with wings, even though neither had told the other. And Katrina had had a peculiar reaction to reading Ellen's novelization, Way Shower.

"It was as if she knew those experiences in a much more personal way," Ellen breathed.

A chill of excitement skipped down her back.

"*Is it possible that I've found another Way Sho*wer?" she wondered. "*A sister?*"

They had always joked that they were twins. Could there be more to it than that?

Unfortunately, Ellen didn't have time to press the issue. As it was the next week was a bustle between Roberts' class and workshop schedule at the University, and Ellen had to focus on editing his new textbook, which was due to the publisher before the end of the year. She had been postponing a trip across the Bridge till she could devote time to it.

Then one morning, her doctor's office called and Ellen made the drive out. The test results had come back with anomalies. There was no knowing exactly what might be wrong without exploratory surgery. However, local gynecologists were booked and many weren't taking new patients. She might have a two or three month wait to get seen. The doctor gave her a prescription for a progesterone that was at a chemotoxic dose, and Ellen drove home in shock.

Still she was determined to have Thanksgiving as planned and kept moving forward with preparations. However, she had never been known for having a good relationship with medication. As this one built up in her system, she became a walking zombie, unable to think or function. A call to her doctor got the dose halved, but it only halved the severity of the side effects.

But Thanksgiving finally came, Katrina arrived and laughter filled the air along with the odor of pies and turkey. They stayed at the table laughing and talking long after they'd finished eating. Late into the early evening, Katrina finally left. She had no sooner pulled out of the driveway when Ellen's cell phone rang. Robert grabbed it off the kitchen counter and answered. A moment later he brought it to Ellen.

She held it to her ear. "Hello?"

"Ellen, this is Zane. I have some bad news," her stepbrother said.

"Oh? What happened?" Ellen asked instantly alert.

"I'm at Robert Morris Hospital. I went to pick up mom and dad for Thanksgiving. Mom suddenly collapsed as I was helping her down the stairs. The doctor here thinks she had a heart attack. It all happened so fast, I couldn't call earlier. The doctor just pronounced her dead," came the reply.

Ellen's face went pale and Robert reached for her hand, a worried frown etched on his brow. "Are they going to do an autopsy?" she asked.

"Dad doesn't want one," Zane replied, "and the doctor thinks there's enough evidence of a heart attack to be conclusive."

"Well, at her age, he's probably right," Ellen concurred.

"I'll keep you posted as to funeral arrangements," Zane continued then hung up.

Ellen sat in solitary contemplation for the rest of the evening. Both Robert's and her mothers had died that year; his early in the year and now her mom. Then there had been the deaths of her aunt and uncle. And she had the results of the ultrasound to worry about. She went to bed that night too numb to think or feel.

CHAPTER 20

That night Avner sat at Ellen's bedside, a confused expression on his face.

She glanced up at him. "What?"

"I do not understand," he replied.

"Being upset at my mother's death?" she asked.

"No. I understand loss from having thought I lost William," he told her.

"The test results?"

He nodded. "They aren't life threatening."

"If it's cancer...." Ellen began.

Avner narrowed his eyes and scanned her body from head to foot. "I detect an anomaly in the pattern of your light, but nothing that will kill you."

Ellen studied him uncertainly. "How can you be sure?"

"I am practiced in the art of creating death-inducing disease," he admitted ruefully.

"And this isn't it?" she challenged.

"Not that I can see although I can take you to Raphael," Avner offered.

Ellen opened a prescription bottle on her nightstand, dumped out a pill, grabbed the accompanying glass of water and swallowed the pill.

"I think that for now, I'd rather find that Monastery," she replied. "I feel pressed for time."

"As you wish," Avner said taking out the small bag of Nariel's slumber herbs.

As before, Ellen dropped off to sleep and Avner helped her cross over. She paid Nathan a quick visit then pressed on. Once they traversed into the Facility, they faced a dilemma.

"Do you know where this Monastery is that William told me about?" Ellen asked.

Avner shook his head. "It must have been built during my time... elsewhere."

Ellen patted his arm reassuringly. "Well, let's see if Henry ever put the location on his Universe," she said heading out into the yard surrounding the Facility.

Avner picked her up and flew her straight down to the Great Halls, depositing her on her feet just outside the thick oak door. He opened it and Ellen slipped inside. She ran across the Banqueting Hall to a door in the far right corner along the back wall. Once inside, she lit lanterns, headed for the control mechanism and turned it on.

"I only sort of know how this works," she told Avner. "I wish Wizard were here. He's the real genius with this gadget."

"I believe he is still on Dragon's Island with his brother," Avner responded after a moment.

"Figures. All those books and scrolls. We may never get him out of there," Ellen quipped.

She pulled out her pendulum and started testing locations on the Universe. One finally lit up in a remote area.

"That's a ways away," she remarked.

Avner frowned as he studied the location. "Monastery of Light," he breathed. Clearing his throat, he said, "I think you might be better served if the Green Dragon took you there."

"Why?"

"At those altitudes ice formation could be a problem for the wings," he explained.

Ellen eyed him dubiously.

"*With that much light, the temptation would be too great,*" he thought inwardly.

Ellen stared off into space thinking about all the times she'd flown with Daniel. She remembered when the Ice Queen had tried encasing him in ice. Even once Ellen had freed him using the Temple Flames and he'd gone to fly them out of the cavern, they'd still barely made it. And when he had finally set them down on the mountainside, he'd shivered hard till she dug out a wool blanket from their knapsack and wrapped it around him.

"*I guess his reluctance could be legitimate*," she reasoned. But William's distrust of Avner was fresh in her mind. Ellen took a deep breath and shook off the uneasy feeling. With Daniel split in two and in trouble, she had no choice but to accept Avner's aid and his word.

"Ok," she sighed. "How do I get to Dragon Island?"

"Vortex or my wings," Avner replied. "Your choice."

"Then I was right," Ellen said. "The Vortex doesn't have a limit."

"The only limit is your mind and what you believe to be true," Avner told her.

"Well, right now even here, my mind is struggling to focus because of those meds," Ellen admitted. "I think we'll use your wings."

"Scenic route or travel for speed?" Avner asked again taking Ellen into his arms.

"Speed, please."

With that, he spun out of the Universe room and, after a very short traverse, landed in the tunnel leading into the Dragon's Lair. The brothers saw them coming and quickly swarmed her.

"You wouldn't believe what we've remembered," Edward gushed.

"Right down to how we used to light candles without matches," Alexander said, "and electrical lights flickered whenever we walked into a room."

"Nothing electrical was ever safe with us," Edward said proudly.

Ellen chuckled. "Robert's a big one for blowing street lights, making lights flicker during boring meetings, and is great at turning on fluorescent lights that don't want to come on."

"Robert?" Alexander asked with an edge.

"My husband back home," Ellen explained.

He turned away so she couldn't see his burning face and crestfallen countenance.

"He's a Way Shower, too?" Edward asked distracting attention from his brother.

"Yes, though I don't think he knows it," Ellen replied watching Alexander out of the corner of her eyes. "He just knows he's different and that I encourage his difference."

"So, you came back here because...?" Alexander snipped.

"I found William," Ellen told them. "But he said that before I can tackle the crystal holding Daniel's light, I have to increase the purity of my own light. Something about a bunch of monks in a Monastery on some very high mountains."

154

"He's not taking you?" Alexander asked testily with a nod at Avner.

"I heard wings, high altitudes and frozen feathers," Ellen replied.

"Hmph! Didn't think any of that affected them," Alexander muttered to himself.

"Don't mind him," Edward told her quietly. "He's...had a bit of a crush on you."

Ellen glanced over at Alexander and grimaced. "Oh. I...just thought he was being nice."

"He was," Edward agreed. "About 10 times nicer than normal."

She raised her eyebrows and shook her head. "Can't do anything right now," she murmured, "but I will have to make that right."

Ellen worked her way toward the Dragons.

"You!" the Great Red Dragon grumbled.

"Yes, sir," she responded brightly. "Me."

"Well, did you find this brother of yours?" the Dragon asked coolly.

"I did, thanks to your grandson," Ellen replied. "I was wondering if I could borrow him to fly to the Monastery?"

The Green Dragon bent his neck bringing his head around. "I know of no Monastery," he said.

The Great Red Dragon sighed and put down his book. "I do and the Abbott is long overdue for a visit. Besides, I have a book he wanted. If you carry the book, I shall carry you," he assented.

"More than happy to help and grateful for the ride," Ellen told him.

She waited near Avner while the Green Dragon sought out the book in question. She turned toward him taking him a little to the side.

"Why does everyone think you're faking an iced wing problem?" she whispered. "Why does William not trust you? Is there something I should know?"

Avner looked down at his boots. "Though I am redeemed, there is within me a danger."

Ellen frowned. "What sort of danger?"

He shook his head vehemently. "It is one I fight every day. One that is beyond help."

Ellen reached up and pulled his head down close to hers hugging him and pressing her cheek against his. "Daniel said the same thing to me, but I don't believe either of you," she whispered. "You don't need to be omnipotent. You just have to stop boxing yourselves in and look for options. There's always another way, and I'm determined to find it...for both of you."

"Ellen, you have enough with rescuing Daniel," Avner admonished.

She kissed his cheek. "I have enough for ALL those I love."

At that moment, the Green Dragon cried, "Ah-ha!" from somewhere back in the cavern.

The Great Red Dragon raised his head, steam rising from his nostrils toward the ceiling. Then he lumbered toward Ellen. Avner helped her onto his back, and the Green Dragon crawled forward, the book between his claws. He plopped the blue leather-bound tome in Ellen's lap.

She read the title to herself. "The Book of Light and Shadow."

The Great Red Dragon lurched, and Ellen clutched the book with one hand and his neck with the other. As he crawled past the others, the Great Red Dragon gave Avner an intense perusal.

"Ice?" he grumbled in a low, sub-harmonic tone. "Or are you hiding something?"

"Probably a bit of both," Avner replied evasively.

"Ye-es, but how long will you hide it from her?" the Dragon challenged in his low rumble.

"As long as I have to in order to keep her safe," Avner replied earnestly. "She is my only thought right now."

The Great Red Dragon grumbled on as he left the Lair. At the ledge, he spread his great, leathery wings and dove head long off the cliff plunging down and down until the wind caught his wings, and he swooped up over the treetops and into the clear blue sky.

"Next stop, the Monastery," he announced and left the sea behind.

"Actually," Ellen interjected. "Perhaps you could just set me down outside."

"What for?" the Great Red Dragon mumbled.

"I want to see if Visionary and Weaver will help my brother, William," she replied.

"They're on the way," he told her.

"Then you'll stop?" Ellen asked.

"For a moment," he agreed. "My wings aren't what they used to be."

He soared inland sailing across the land and swooping over the foothills of the Great Mountains. For a brief moment, the clouds to their right parted and Ellen glimpsed a deep valley lined with caves. Her heart skipped a beat knowing Daniel's light was somewhere down there. Then the Great Red Dragon banked to the left, and the remaining clouds obscured her view.

"*I'm coming, Daniel,*" she thought. "*Just hold on.*"

Inside the crystal, Daniel heard her thoughts and his heart went out to her. "I know you'll find me," he whispered. "I know you will."

On the battlefield, a stoic Daniel heard her thoughts and stopped in mid-air. Fear for her gripped his heart, yet hope sparked anew. "*You won't listen to me,*" he thought. "*I will not be your bane.*"

Soon the Great Red Dragon dipped into a lush mountain valley. He headed straight for a stately home high up on the hillside that was reminiscent of a two-story Swiss chalet. He drew up and braked landing carefully beside the structure.

Weaver, who was outside stacking wood, spotted them, set down the logs and hurried over. He yelled for Visionary to come out onto the balcony along the front of the house.

"This is an honor," Weaver said bowing to the Great Red Dragon.

"Just for a moment of rest," he told him. "However, the one I bear has a request."

Weaver and Visionary looked up and Ellen waved.

"What a nice surprise!" Visionary exclaimed.

"I wish I could stay," Ellen yelled down. "But I'm headed to the Monastery. I was wondering if I could ask you for a favor?"

Weaver took his gloves off and put his hands on his hips. "Let's hear it and we'll see."

"Long story short," Ellen replied. "I've found the very first Way Shower still alive. Only he's nothing but light...no form. I was hoping you might be able to create something for him so he could join us," she said. "He's been alone for all this time."

Visionary put her hand to her mouth. "That's awful!"

"Where is he?" Weaver asked.

"On a volcanic island out past Dragon Island," she told them. "The Green Dragon knows the way."

Weaver looked up to Visionary. "What do you think?"

Her eyes were closed as she searched her heart. "After how we were able to bring life to the images of the dead," she said after a while, "surely we can do something for this poor living soul."

Weaver looked back up at Ellen. "Ok. We'll do it."

Ellen sighed with relief. "Oh, thank you. You have no idea how happy this makes me."

"You?" Weaver asked.

"Yes! He's my brother!" Ellen yelled back. "His name is William.

Tell him I sent you."

The latter part floated back to them on the wind as the Great Red Dragon leapt into the air.

"Now I feel so much better!" Ellen exclaimed.

"Why?" the Great Red Dragon wanted to know.

"Because my brother will be taken care of even when I can't be the one to do it," Ellen replied. "Maybe he'll even get to live amongst other Way Showers and not be alone anymore."

"Hmm," the Great Red Dragon rumbled deep in his throat. "That will be good."

With that, Ellen felt his great wing muscles in his back bunch and flex with greater intensity. Up ahead the high mountain peaks loomed cold and foreboding. The Great Red Dragon climbed higher and higher till a spark of light caught Ellen's attention.

"Is that it over there?" she asked pointing to their right.

The Great Red Dragon craned his head to look and banked sharply in that direction. Before long, they approached a multi-tiered, rock building that clung to a ledge on the side of a mountain. Brilliant light shone from the windows on the top tier. The Great Red Dragon headed for the courtyard on the lowest level. As he made his landing approach, monks with shaved heads scrambled back inside to make way for his mammoth bulk. With a thud that shook the foundations, he touched down, folded his wings, and stretched his neck to the ground so Ellen could slide off.

She stood in the courtyard gazing about, the frigid mountain wind cutting through her shirt and jeans. *"Should have brought a parka,"* she thought wondering what was to happen next.

CHAPTER 21

Ellen waited in the cold courtyard with the Great Red Dragon. As she shivered in the frigid wind, she glanced upwards and noticed that the bright glow had left the uppermost level of the monastery and seemed to be traveling down through the building. A few minutes later, the glow appeared at the door. When Ellen squinted hard, she could see the shape of a man within the glow.

The glowing man said something in a language she didn't understand and clapped his hands. Monks to either side of him scurried into the Monastery, reappearing moments later with a fur cape. They hurried to Ellen's side and draped it over her shoulders.

"Th-thank y-you," she said gratefully through chattering teeth as she drew the warm, heavy cape tightly around her and over her head.

"Abbott," said the Great Red Dragon. "My visit is long overdue."

The glowing man laughed heartily. "Each visit in its own time. Did you bring the book?"

"My rider carries it with her," the Great Red Dragon replied.

He tapped Ellen on the back with the tip of his wing, and she stumbled forward. Taking that as her cue, Ellen walked up to the Abbott and produced the blue, leather-bound tome from under the cloak. She handed it to him with a bow of her head.

The Abbott accepted the book but held her gaze in his own. "Have you read the book?" he asked after a time.

Ellen shook her head. "I'm just the carrier."

"If you cannot read it to us, then why have you come," the Abbott wanted to know.

"My brother, William, sent me," Ellen replied. "He thought you could help me learn how to retrieve an angel's light from a crystal."

The monks around the Abbott shrank back.

"Why do you seek this knowledge?" the Abbott asked warily. "It can easily lead to corruption. We only shared it with one other. William was the result."

"Avner," Ellen thought. *"He must have learned the secret from the Abbott and exploited it."*

Taking a deep, frosty breath Ellen said, "My Guardian's light is trapped in one of those crystals. He's split and, if I don't find the way to reunite his two halves soon, the opportunity to do so may be lost. William said my light was pure but not pure enough. He told me you could help me purify my light."

The Abbott studied her carefully for a while. "William is indeed a pure spirit," he said at last. "While I will test you as well, if he has already sanctioned your light, I will accept that."

"It's getting cold," the Great Red Dragon announced. "If you're happy there, I'm going to return to warmer climates."

The Abbott looked up smiling and waved. "Good to see you, my friend."

The Great Red Dragon nodded, slowly turned his great body in the confines of the courtyard and leapt into the air. As the monks escorted her inside, Ellen glanced back at the swiftly disappearing figure, a lump rising in her throat.

"What have I gotten myself into?" she worried silently as she followed the monks through the dimly lit Monastery halls. She hurried to catch up with the Abbott, for the way was clearest near his radiance.

At the chalet, Visionary and Weaver stood together outside their home. He brought the Vortex up around them, and they took off.

"Can you sense where the dragon took Ellen?" Weaver asked.

With her eyes closed, Visionary sampled the patterns around them. One lit up like a streamer of light, and she pointed in that direction.

"The path is there," she told him.

Guided only by her vision, Weaver took them over the mountains out beyond the plains and assailed the ocean passage. In good time, he spotted the volcanic island on the horizon and headed toward it.

"I sense Ellen was set down on the coast," Visionary said, "but she didn't stay there."

"Where did she go?" Weaver asked.

"Up to the caldera," Visionary said, her head raised toward the flattened peak.

Weaver slowly took the Vortex up the slope. At the top, he paused.

"She definitely stayed near the edge of the caldera for a while," Visionary said. "However, I pick up another pattern and a place where they both met."

She pointed and Weaver eased the Vortex over the ground. Suddenly, there was a bright flash of light and he threw his hands up to shield his eyes. The Vortex collapsed in an instant, and they tumbled to the black, rocky ground. Weaver scrambled to help Visionary to her feet.

"We mean no harm," he shouted. "You don't have to attack us."

"Behind that boulder," Visionary whispered and pointed.

"Listen, Ellen sent us. She thought we could help you," Weaver added.

There was a moment of silence then a glow came out from behind a rock.

"Oh my!" Visionary gasped. "He's nothing but light. Not even his soul crystal remains."

"You can see me?" William asked, astonished.

"She's the Visionary," Weaver responded. "She sees patterns of light."

"Then who are you?" William asked.

"I'm the Weaver," he replied. "I take the patterns Visionary sees and weave them into form."

"Then Ellen did send you," William said, relief in his voice. "Do you think you can help me?"

Weaver turned to Visionary.

"I don't know," she said quietly. "I...can't find form in any of these patterns of light."

"I have a place where I can be seen," William offered.

The glow began to move and the couple quickly followed. When it ducked beneath the overhang, they carefully followed. There, the shadow of William became clearer.

Visionary slowly approached him, her arms outstretched. William remained perfectly still as she felt along the edges of his shadow.

"Yes," she said slowly. "Yes, I sense form here. I can work with these patterns."

"Good," Weaver said joining her at William's side. "You feed me the patterns and let's weave our friend a form."

The couple began their work starting at his head. For a while streamers of light spiraled through the air, but gradually they wrapped around the shadow figure between them like long strips of luminous gauze. Slowly, a figure appeared with eyes, nose, mouth and ears. Soon arms, hands, legs and feet took shape. The torso grew and filled with brilliant light.

At last, they held hands around the form and set their intent. Tension filled the air until they felt a sudden snap. They let go and backed away revealing a man with deep auburn hair who stood a little under six feet tall. His face bore finely chiseled features. His eyes glowed. He brought his hands up turning them over and over. Finally, he pressed his fingertips to his cheeks and swallowed hard.

"You have given me form again," he said at last. "How can I ever repay you?"

"Don't thank us," Weaver said. "Thank Ellen. She came to get us."

"Yes, Ellen," William said slowly. "I never imagined a sister." Then he glanced around and frowned. "She isn't with you?"

"She was on her way to the Monastery," Weaver replied.

"Monastery," William said slowly. "Yes, she wanted to purify her light." All of a sudden his eyes blazed with light. "The crystal! No! I must stop her! You must get me off this island."

Visionary had already found an outcropping of rock to sit on, and Weaver sank down beside her.

"The work takes a lot of energy," he explained. "We will need to rest for a while before we can bring back the Vortex and traverse the waves and land."

William crumpled. "She will try it and be lost like I was," he mourned.

"We can do nothing more right now," Visionary told him.

"But as soon as we're able, we'll get you off this island," Weaver promised.

"That will have to be good enough," William replied.

He left the overhang, climbed to the tallest point on the island and stretched his vision across the sea. "What have I done?" he moaned. "I didn't know you'd take me seriously, Ellen."

William ran his hand over his face relishing in the ability to feel again. *"Ah, but sending your friends to save me,"* he thought. *"Now, I know the kind of person my sister truly is. And I can do no less for her. I will come, Ellen. I pray I am not too late."*

162

The Abbott led Ellen and his monks up through the levels of the Monastery to a room on the top floor. There, surrounded by butter candles, he took up the only seat on the far end. The monks positioned her before him while another laid the <u>Book of Light and Shadows</u> at his feet. The Abbott studied her for a long while.

"How is it," he finally said, "that you are a Way Shower of pure light, yet you cannot read the book?"

Ellen studied him as well. "You appear to be a Way Shower."

He nodded.

"Have you always lived in the Lands Below?" she asked.

"Where else is there to live?" he responded.

Ellen tilted her head to one side. "You don't know?"

The Abbott narrowed his eyes. "Know what?"

She took a deep breath. "A Way Shower is the product of an Archangel father and a human mother. Besides this realm, there is the human realm. That's where I come from."

The Abbott eyed her distrustfully. "Then how got you here!"

Ellen shifted, her legs stiffening after the ride on the Great Red Dragon's back. A monk suddenly set a low stool behind her, took her arm and sat her down. She yelped in surprise but quickly regained her composure.

"The first two times I entered this realm," she said, "I had to come very near death. After the last time, the Way Showers who had previously lived in the human world but died before their time joined together to create the Bridge of Dreams. Now my Guardian helps me cross over at night when I'm asleep."

The Abbott frowned. "You said your Guardian's light is trapped in a crystal. How came you here?"

"No Way Shower can survive the human realm without a Guardian," Ellen explained. "The Embodied One assigned someone else until I can get my true Guardian's light back."

"The Embodied One?" the Abbott asked skeptically.

"In person, in the Throne Room," she replied.

"Describe it," he challenged.

"The Throne Room?" Ellen asked blinking.

He nodded.

"You enter by ascending the broad marble stairs beyond the front gardens at the beginning of the Great Halls," she explained. "If the Wards have been told of your coming, you go inside to a cathedral-like room capable of holding thousands. Tall, white marble columns support a high, vaulted ceiling, and no light is needed because the Light on the Throne illuminates every nook and cranny."

At last the Abbott smiled and nodded. "You have been in the presence of the One."

"Yes, sir," Ellen responded.

"And yet, you cannot read the book," he murmured mystified.

"Can't you?" Ellen probed.

The Abbott slowly shook his head. "I was told that one would come who could read the book and would enlighten us with its words. The Great Red Dragon has refused me the book this many years. I thought, when I saw you riding his back and bearing the book, surely you were this one."

Ellen considered his words. "Could my having lived my whole life in the human realm have something to do with why I can't read it? William said I was of pure light, but it wasn't pure enough. What did he mean?"

The Abbott mulled the dilemma in silence. Finally, he rose from his seat, slowly made his way down two steps and shuffled across the floor to her. He put his hands on either side of her eyes and stared hard.

"Your light is hidden deep inside," he said at length. "We must cause it to shine forth."

Without warning, he took Ellen in a head lock, placed his fingers on the right side of her head above her ears and bored into her skull. Shocked and frightened, she screamed at the top of her lungs.

"Too much nonsense is stuffed in your head," the Abbott announced withdrawing his fingers with a pop.

Instead of blood, a greasy black oil oozed from her head. Ellen threw her hands up trying to push him away. Monks suddenly closed in around her and held her arms to her sides.

"What are you doing to me?" she demanded.

Rather than answer, the Abbott took his fingers and stabbed her right between the eyes. He dug into her forehead scooping out brown globs of material like a thick English pudding. As he pulled his fingers out, he cast the material into a wooden bowl a monk held. When he was done, the monk hastily took it to a fireplace and tossed the entire bowl into the flames.

Ellen could see nothing around her. The world spun like so many intersecting kaleidoscopes. Even when she closed her eyes, the kaleidoscopic vision whirled. A moment later, the Abbott touched her forehead and packed a soothing paste into the hole between her eyes. He molded a PlayDoh-like material over the exterior. When he removed his hand, everything to Ellen was light. Whether she opened her eyes and tried to see the room or closed her eyes against the glare, the world was nothing but the most brilliant light. Form completely slipped away.

She slumped in the monks' arms, and they laid her on the floor. She heard movement like a thousand rats scurrying away. Alone, with no one to care for or comfort her, Ellen lay in the light.

CHAPTER 22

How long Ellen lay in the sea of light, she didn't know. It could have been days, weeks, years or moments. All she knew was light and a singular spinning sensation that made her feel centered in a whirling gyroscope.

After a while, when some thought was possible, she flattened her hands and felt the slick hardness of wax-covered stone. Bringing her trembling hands upwards, she felt her face, her head, her forehead. Struggling, Ellen tried to push herself up, but with nothing except brilliant light for a reference, she immediately discovered there were no directionals. All space seemed to be one.

Her head spun in dizzying circles and her stomach lurched. Ellen dropped back to the only solid surface she could find and curled into a ball. She tried covering her eyes with her hands, but the brilliance never ceased.

"Please, put out the light," she moaned. ""Turn it off! Turn it off!"

But there were no answering sounds, no comforting words, only the crackle of logs in the fireplace and the howl of the wind outside. Ellen lay moaning with no rescue in sight, and if rescue didn't come soon, she would go utterly mad.

On the Volcanic Island, William had paced till he'd nearly driven Visionary and Weaver mad.

"She's in trouble," he fretted. "I feel her...my sister. She's in trouble."

Agreeing to try before they felt ready, Visionary and Weaver rose and brought up the Vortex. William put his hands on their backs and willed his strength and light into them. They crossed the ocean and rose into the mountains in record time.

"Just get me as close to the Monastery as you can," William told them. "Time is of the essence."

In the end, Visionary and Weaver managed to drop him off in the courtyard before spinning off toward home.

William gazed upwards at the formidable structure, the moon reflecting off its white-washed surface. Brilliant light shone from the top tier, usually an indication that the Abbott was in residence. Yet, when he tried the main doors, they were locked. In fact, all the levels on the way up were dark and the windows barren.

"Got to climb," he grunted as he leapt for a hand hold where a piece of stone stuck out from the side of the building.

William climbed up the outside of the Monastery part monkey, part mountain goat as it would seem and the conditions required. Twice the wind threatened to rip him from his hand hold, but he clung to the building with tenacity. Finally, he made the top tier, found a window, pulled himself over the sill and landed with a thud on the floor inside.

Immediately, he threw his hands up to shield his face as he looked toward the figure in the middle of the floor.

"That's not the Abbott!" he gasped crawling forward. Adjusting his vision to the light, he suddenly cried out. "Ellen! Ellen, is that you?"

"Please make the light go away," she moaned.

He hurried forward, picked her head up off the floor and cradled it in his lap. "Ellen. It's William. I'm here."

Ellen grasped his jacket and clung to him. "Nothing makes it go away. William, why is the light so bright?"

"That's a very good question," he replied.

Checking her head over, he noticed the marks on the side and forehead. "No," he groaned. "No, they didn't!"

He looked up past the light toward the entrance of the hall. "Abbott!" he yelled. "Get thee here, Abbott!"

They heard the scramble of footsteps and then monks with the Abbott behind them.

"What-did-you-do?" William demanded to know.

"Her head was too full of filters and information to allow free flow of light," the Abbott explained.

William shook his head. "Ellen isn't like us. She cannot shutter

167

this light at will. She has no control. Her mind, her sanity will be lost to this."

The Abbott seemed disconcerted. "She said you sent her here for us to help her purify her light."

"I did. I didn't know how serious she was about pursuing it," William replied cradling her head against his chest.

The Abbott shook his head. "I do not know what to do."

A cold chill flowed down William's back. "I only know of one person capable of giving her shade."

"Avner," Ellen whispered.

"Yes, though that name is hateful to me," William admitted.

"He is banned from our premises," the Abbott told them.

"My...Guardian," Ellen said.

"He's your Guardian?" William wondered. "How did that happen?"

"With Daniel split...only one who knows my signature," Ellen struggled to gasp out.

"Your father," William assumed.

She tried to nod and the room spun.

"You-have-no-choice," William told the Abbott. "Avner is her only hope. You must allow him in."

The Abbott backed away shaking his head.

"It will be her blood on your hands," William insisted.

The monks fled the room, and William sat on the cold floor cradling Ellen.

"I don't know how to find him," William said.

"Pendulum," Ellen whispered. "Right pocket."

He slipped his hand into her pocket and found the obsidian fob.

"Ellen," he said caressing her face. "I have to leave you. I've got to find Avner. Will you be all right?"

She clung to him a little longer. "Water?"

William glanced about the room, spotted a pitcher and a tin cup and stretched his hand toward it. He brought the items back to her side, poured the water into the cup and brought it to her lips. Ellen drank like someone parched in a desert.

"So thirsty," she whispered. "Desert had nothing on this."

William put her hands on the pitcher and the cup. "They're right there if you need them. I've got to go find Avner."

Ellen grabbed the two items, wrapped herself around them and crumpled back to the floor. William hugged her.

168

"I'll be back, Ellen. I promise I'll be back."

Ellen nodded slowly.

"Hang in there till I get back," he admonished.

"I'll try. Just get Avner," she pleaded.

"Leaving now."

Wasting no time, William dashed across the floor and made his way down through the tiers. As he approached the main door, monks withdrew the bolt and opened it wide. He rushed out into the courtyard.

"Let's see," he thought. "The Vortex felt...like so."

Slowly, the whirling wall of wind surged up around him.

"And Weaver used this to navigate," he muttered, awkwardly holding the pendulum in front of him.

The obsidian fob remained stationery and the Vortex didn't move.

"Come on," he urged. "I've got to find Avner."

With a sudden lurch, the Vortex rose off the courtyard base and began hurtling through the air. William bounced around in its center desperately trying to remain upright.

"How do they steer this thing?" he wondered.

As he asked, the Vortex evened out and took a smooth path through the mountains finally approaching the Valley of a Thousand Caves. It set down on the near side and gradually receded into the ground. Once it was gone, William pocketed Ellen's pendulum and scanned the hill around him. He spotted Avner sitting on an outcrop of rock staring at the valley below. Fisting his hands, William forced his feet to move. When he slipped on some loose shale causing pieces to tumble over the edge, Avner snapped his head up.

William stopped dead in his tracks and the two men stared at each other. Avner swallowed hard barely able to believe his eyes. William thought of his sister, took a deep breath and forced his feet forward.

Avner shook his head. "I thought you were lost...gone."

"No thanks to you," William spat, stopping a few feet away.

Avner turned back to the valley. "No, you are right. So much that has happened is 'no thanks to me'," he replied sadly.

"Look we don't have time," William insisted. "Ellen is at the Monastery. She needs your help."

"The Abbott has banned me," Avner replied.

"And I told him he had no choice but to let you in," William said.

Avner just shook his head.

"Are you going to abandon her the way you abandoned me?" William challenged.

169

Avner remained silent.

"For some reason, she believes in you," William cried. "God knows why since you sit there like the stony-hearted person you are. But-she-loves-you."

A shudder ran through Avner, and he slowly looked up.

"She-needs-you," William implored tears brimming his lashes. "Doesn't that mean anything to you?"

Avner seemed to suddenly come to some inner determination. He gave the Valley one more glance.

"My demise started with this Valley," he said quietly. "May this be the beginning of the end."

Rising to his feet, he approached William. "I will go, Abbott or no Abbott. I am not the person I once was. Will you fly with me or use the Vortex?"

As much as William cringed inside to think of flying with Avner, time was of the essence.

"With you," he murmured.

Avner wrapped him in strong arms, leapt skyward and spun out. Bypassing courtyards, barred doors and monks, Avner and William arrived in the top floor room where Ellen still huddled on the cold stone floor. Avner went to her at once scooping her up in his strong arms and holding her close.

"Avner?" she whispered.

"I'm here, child," he told her in low, soothing tones.

"Please make the light turn off," she begged.

"Very soon. I promise," he assured her.

Avner turned to William. "Find pillows, blankets, skins, anything I can lie her on in comfort."

William nodded and disappeared out the door. He reappeared minutes later with his arms laden and several monks following.

"Arrange them here before the Book," Avner instructed.

William and the monks made a bed of sorts and, once the monks had fled the room, Avner laid Ellen on it.

"Hold her head," he instructed.

William knelt down, once again took Ellen's head and cupped it in his hands. Avner opened the Book of Light and Shadow and began to read. Setting it down, he went to Ellen, gently turned her head to the left and cupped his hand over the hole above her right ear.

"For her, this area is what instructs her body as to where she ends and others begin. It tells her body where it is positioned in space," Avner told William as he worked. "We must return those capacities to her."

Avner's hand glowed and wisps of light gray smoke curled out from his fingertips. He carefully molded the wisps then blew them into the hole. As he and William watched, the hole completely closed up as if it had never been there.

Ellen sighed. "The dizziness stopped."

"Good," Avner told her, bringing her head around so he could examine her forehead.

He carefully removed the materials the Abbott had packed into that hole and she moaned.

"It will be better soon," Avner assured her.

He held his hand over her forehead and shook his head. "Not every filter is a hindrance," he told William. "Some create the different planes which, when they come together, allow your mind to perceive surfaces and objects. These are useful filters."

Again, wisps of gray curled out from his fingertips and he molded them then blew them into the hole. Gradually, the hole closed until it disappeared.

Ellen blinked and looked up. "I can see you!" she exclaimed.

She reached one hand up to touch Avner's cheek, the other to William's. "Thank you," she whispered. "Both of you."

CHAPTER 23

Avner took Ellen's hand and helped her sit up. William remained at her side. Ellen gazed about the room in wonder.

"I can see so much I could never see before," she marveled. "Is this what it's like for you?" she asked turning to William.

"Hard to say," he admitted looking into her glowing eyes. "Once I got my form back, my vision changed."

Ellen looked toward the book. "Can I read it?"

"You don't need to do this," William told her. "I had no idea how seriously you'd take everything."

Ellen smiled weakly and gave him a wink. "I'm serious...till I'm not."

Avner helped her up and let her lean on him. Ellen walked the few steps to where the book lay and dropped to her knees. She used both hands to open the cover then stared at the pages.

"Can you make it out?" Avner asked.

"I can see the light and follow that," Ellen told him, "but the shadows elude me."

Avner placed his hand on top of her head for a moment. Suddenly, she gasped in delight.

"Oh, goodness! It's so simple and it makes so much sense!" she exclaimed. "Have you read this, William?"

"Well...no," he admitted.

Ellen stretched her hand back to him. "You must read it," she insisted.

Their fingertips touched and Ellen pulled him closer. He knelt beside her peering over her shoulder.

"Just looks like a bunch of swirls," he complained.

Avner shifted his hand from Ellen's head to William's. The younger man stared hard at the pages until a look of wonder spread across his face.

"I should have read this Ages ago."

"The time wasn't right then," Avner said lifting his hand. "The time is right now."

Ellen closed the book and William helped her stand. They heard the shuffle of feet as the monks and the Abbott crept into the room. The Abbott looked toward them, the huge Archangel with his hands on the shoulders of Ellen and William, both of whose eyes glowed bright.

"The Book," the Abbott managed. "Could you read it?"

Ellen nodded. "It's so simple, Abbott. You will figure it out. It's just patterns of light and shadow that make up the world. Nothing more; nothing less."

With that, the monks gasped. All three beings became like wavering flames that slowly melted away.

With less fanfare than ever, Avner appeared on the walkways between the formal gardens in front of the Great Halls. Ellen gazed about taking things in anew.

"Is it time for me to go back?" she asked.

"Not yet," Avner assured her. "Would you be all right if I spent some time in the Meditation Gardens?"

"Go ahead. I'll be fine."

She and William watched him disappear in two strides. Ellen grabbed William's arm and led him to an alcove along the cliff wall. They knelt on the bench, leaned their arms on the wall and took in the breathtaking view of the Lands Below from their high perch.

"I don't get it," William said at last. "He's so different with you."

Ellen sat on the bench and drew her knees up to her chin. "You were his first."

"So?"

She chuckled. "You don't know about birth order," she told him. "See, in the human realm, I have a daughter. I was so young when I was pregnant with her that my doctor didn't think I'd know how to care for her. So every time I visited his office, he gave me a book list. I'd go to the library, get the books, read them and get a new book list the next time I saw my doctor."

William turned toward her. "Did it help?"

Ellen shook her head. "Not a wit. First time the nurses left me alone with her in the hospital and she needed her diaper changed, I didn't have a clue."

William frowned. "What did you do?"

Ellen looked down. "I pretended she was one of my baby dolls I'd gotten for my birthday as a child and tried to remember how the pretend diapers had gone on them."

His eyes opened wide. "Really?"

She nodded and looked up at him. "Children don't come with a set of instructions, William. The first is always the hardest because you haven't got a clue. You do your best and hope everything turns out all right in the end. And parents are usually harder on the first one. They expect a lot. By the time the second one comes along, they've figured out what really hadn't been good ideas the first time around and make changes."

William frowned. "Do you...do you think Avner just didn't know what to do with me?" he wondered.

Ellen stretched out her hand, took his and pulled him down onto the bench with her. "William, Avner was the first Archangel the Embodied One created. When he was thinking of things to try on the others, he always tried them out on Avner first. Avner probably didn't know any different and just did the same thing with you."

William went very still, his heart nearly stopping. "Avner...was an experiment?"

Ellen shrugged. "I guess...in a way."

"So, he just experimented on me until things went wrong," William whispered.

Suddenly, a spark zipped up Ellen's spine. She squeezed William's arm hard. "Say that again...louder."

He looked at her. "He experimented on me till something went wrong."

Ellen's mouth dropped open, a million puzzle pieces finally falling into place.

"What?" William asked seeing the look on her face.

"Oh my god, I know what happened," she breathed. "I know why Avner was the first to turn to the Darkness, why he needed to experiment. He wasn't curious. My god! He was desperate."

Suddenly, she bolted up and ran full tilt through the gardens.

174

William only hesitated a moment before he was close on her heels. They dashed down the Cloister Walk scanning each Meditation Garden as they went. Finally, Ellen spotted Avner's wings and the top of his head. They careened toward the garden only to skid to an abrupt halt just outside.

Inside the garden, Avner held his head in his hands, his shoulders shaking in sobs. Ellen looked up at William with a worried frown. He shook his head, equally clueless.

Quietly on tip toe, Ellen entered the garden and approached Avner. She reached his side and laid a hand on his shoulder. He jumped, startled by their sudden presence and hastily tried to dry his eyes.

"It's ok," she soothed. "I figured it out. I know."

"Know what?" Avner sniffed.

"I know why you turned originally and it had nothing to do with being overly inquisitive or hubris, did it?" she asked pointedly.

Avner took a shuddering breath and slowly shook his head.

"William got your brother's light back but was in trouble himself," Ellen said. "You took him to the Monastery because the monks studied light. When they gave you the Book to read, the Book that would allow you to reform him, you could only read the light, like I could until you helped me comprehend the shadows."

Avner's face contorted with anguish. He looked up at William. "But there was no one who had read both sides of the book."

"Only there was one who could help you comprehend the shadows," Ellen added.

"For a price," Avner whispered.

Ellen knelt and took his hands in hers. "For a horrible price. The Dark One would give you his knowledge of the shadows so you could read the book and reform William, IF you gave him your heart. If you turned to his service."

Avner nodded tears streaking down his cheeks. "I...tried....so hard," he gasped. "Tried...to find...some other way."

He broke down again in sobs that wracked his body and covered his face with his hands.

"And in the end, no price seemed too great if you could get William back," Ellen surmised.

Avner nodded though he didn't look up.

William's face was white as a sheet. "You did that...for me?"

Avner lifted his head, stared at William and grabbed his arm. "No sacrifice seemed too great if it gave me the hope of getting you back."

"And then the Darkness fell," Ellen murmured.

"And then the Darkness fell," Avner repeated with heavy sadness, "until you found my heart and returned it to me."

William wavered in place then sank to his knees. "All these years I've hated you. I thought you'd abandoned me...tossed me aside like a broken toy."

Avner shook his head vehemently.

Suddenly, William reached out and threw his arms around Avner's neck. "I never wanted to hate you. I just couldn't understand why you'd gone away and left me all alone."

Avner patted his back. "All that matters is that I have you back now."

Ellen smiled to see their reunion, but something still niggled at the back of her mind.

"This isn't everything, is it?" she asked quietly.

The men pulled apart and Avner shook his head.

"My brothers," he said.

"The ones still in the Prison of Light," Ellen surmised.

"They are in that state because of me and only I can free them," Avner replied fatalistically.

"Let's not go there yet," Ellen told him. "With a shift in perception, there's always another way."

Avner shook his head sadly. "In this case...I'm afraid not."

Ellen studied him, her eyes narrowing and flashing several times. Before he could shutter himself, she picked up something lying deep inside his mind, something dark with an oily sensation she had definitely come across before. Ellen didn't reach out to it, just sampled it around the edges before Avner's walls went up. Without words, she knew in the pit of her stomach what it was and what he was doing to shield those he loved from it.

"*That's a discussion for another day*," she thought rising to her feet.

"It really is time I get you back," Avner announced.

"Back?" William asked with a confused frown.

"I'm only here when I'm sleeping in the human world," Ellen explained.

"Then...what do I do?" William wondered. "Where do I go?"

A light flared behind him and softened. William turned to see another Archangel standing close by.

"This is Uriel," Avner said. "The Embodied One thought you might like some company and help adjusting to being with other Way

Showers."

"I've been assigned to be your Guardian Angel," Uriel explained.

"But, where will I go?" William fretted.

Ellen took his arm. "I've got two very good friends you ought to meet - the Priest and the Wizard," she told him. "They'll keep you busy."

Then looking at Uriel she added, "Take him to the Temple in Desert City. The Flames of Truth and Vortex of Power should be no big deal to him, but everybody has to start somewhere."

Uriel nodded his agreement.

Ellen slipped her arms around William for a good-bye hug.

"Will you come back?" he asked. "Can I visit you?"

"I'll be back though maybe not soon," Ellen replied as Avner picked her up. "Ask the brothers how to cross the Bridge," she said in an echo as Avner whisked her away.

William watched Avner scoop up Ellen, leap into the air and spiral out. He swallowed hard and reluctantly turned toward the angel beside him.

"Don't know why anyone thought I'd need a Guardian," he grumbled.

"This realm is far different from what you once knew," Uriel told him. "And as the Flame of God, I understand being the flames better than most."

William turned away and scanned the Meditation Garden. He longed for Ellen to come back. She felt like the piece he'd been missing all his life. And he was still reeling with shock at having learned the lengths his father had gone to in order to get him back.

"What a price to pay," he breathed shaking his head.

"Yes, it was," Uriel agreed. "And, when Ellen died upon returning his heart to him, Avner gave her his last mortal breath."

William glanced up at his Guardian. "He...became mortal?"

Uriel nodded. "For a time. Even before he totally came to his senses, he paid the ultimate price to save Ellen."

William shook his head, the overwhelm increasing. "He really loved us."

"More than you yet know," Uriel said cryptically.

William raised an eyebrow in question.

"Come," Uriel invited. "I like Ellen's suggestion. The Temple is a very good place to begin."

Reluctantly, William allowed Uriel to carry him. They flew up and over the Great Halls then swooped down over the cliff. The wind rushed through William's hair, and he couldn't help but be taken up with the scenery passing by below him. Soon, they glided out over the desolate Desert until William spotted an oasis and City walls. Beyond, a gold dome glinted in the harsh sunlight. Uriel flew straight toward the Dome and landed on the portico before the Temple.

Once the door swung open and William stepped into the cool, dark interior, he stared about him in amazement. "None of this was ever here before," he breathed.

"It was all created by the First Priest," a young man in priest's robes said as he entered from a darkened alcove. "I'm Priest Edward. I don't believe we've met."

William gave Edward a sidelong glance and continued studying the Temple. "Amazing!" he said. "Whoever built this Temple had a good understanding of Light and Shadows. They're blended together masterfully."

Edward frowned in confusion. "I'm sorry. I didn't get your name. Have we met before?"

William looked him over carefully. "No. Do you travel back and forth from the human world, too?"

"No, no. This is my home. Who do you know who does that?" Edward asked warily.

William spotted the Flames and moved toward them. "My sister."

"Ellen?" Edward asked. "You wouldn't be William, would you? She was frantic to get to an island to find you."

William stretched out his hand toward the Flames. "She did," he replied stepping within the wall of fire.

"*So much more comfortable than lava fires,*" he thought as he stood in the midst of the Flames. "*I feel Ellen's signature. She likes it in here.*" He smiled, glad to be following in her footsteps.

At last William walked out the other side. "She finds peace within the Flames," he commented.

The Priest nodded. "Most of us do."

Uriel gestured toward the Vortex, and William continued toward the whirling wall of wind.

"Few ever make it on their first try," Edward told him.

William wasn't listening. "Is this the same Vortex people travel in?" he asked looking back.

Edward nodded.

Again, William stretched out his hand, pushed on through and found himself in its center. Now he understood why he had struggled to control it. *"You need a sense of its foundation before you can manipulate and navigate with it,"* he breathed. He sensed Ellen within it as well, sensed her powerful mastery of this test. Before long, he came back out.

"Ellen didn't think I'd have any trouble with these," he told Edward. "Looks like she was right."

Priest Edward studied him. "So if the trials are no match for you, what can I do for you?"

"William has been alone a long time," Uriel spoke up. "He needs introductions to other Way Showers."

"Well," Edward said. "He's come to the right person. I was just about to head to the Tavern for dinner. You should join me and meet the Tavern Owner," he announced heading for the door.

Hesitantly, William followed him giving Uriel a backward glance. Uriel nodded encouragingly and William stepped back out into the merciless sunlight. Edward was past waiting and chatted non-stop as they threaded their way past town folk and entered the Tavern down the street.

The sights and sounds and smells overwhelmed William's senses, and he staggered about feeling shell-shocked. When they reached the bar, William stared at the Tavern Owner and narrowed his eyes.

"Don't I know you?" he demanded.

The Tavern Owner studied him while wiping down a tankard. "From a time before I was assigned to the human realm. Avner's boy, aren't you?"

For the first time that day, William drew himself to his full height and declared, "Yes. Yes I am."

Warmth trickled all down through him. He belonged to someone; a father who'd really wanted him. Life had definitely taken a turn for the better.

CHAPTER 24

When Ellen awoke the next morning, she looked around the bedroom half expecting the world to look different and to see William standing nearby. Neither was the case, which was disappointing. She turned toward the nightstand, saw the prescription bottle and reality came rushing back in slamming her in the face. A moment later, Robert entered with her cup of coffee. He slid into bed beside her and cradled her in his arms.

"How did you sleep?" he whispered so as not to disturb the dog yet.

"Fine."

"We can't stay in bed long," he added. "We need to leave early to make your mother's funeral."

More reality hurled toward her at light speed. This time the news was a kick in the gut.

"I think I forgot," Ellen admitted.

"Your mother's funeral?" Robert asked incredulously.

"With these meds," she responded, "I think I'm lucky to remember my own name."

He hugged her tighter till Boodles started whining in her crate. They waited to see how long she'd talk to them that morning. In minutes the Bichon's whine had changed to a trill.

"Guess it's time to get up," Ellen groaned.

Robert slipped out of bed, grabbed her coffee, came around to unlatch the crate door and set the mug on her nightstand. Ellen sat up to
180

take the hated medication and get ready for a most unpleasant day.

Thanks to the effects of the drug, her only uncle looked like he'd stepped off the deck of the Starship Enterprise. His son, looked like he had a bug-eyed grasshopper head and his daughter looked more like her dead mother. When someone asked where her own daughter was, Ellen's head spun. She couldn't remember if she told her or not but remembered a Facebook post from that morning saying her baby was running a fever.

"*That must be it*," Ellen thought. "*Calen must be sick.*"

Ellen looked toward the front of the church. She was glad the casket was closed. That had allowed her to line up pictures of her mother in far better years, and she preferred to remember her then. Plus, the flowers were beautiful and softened the scene. The service was blessedly short and she was glad to escape the church and head back home.

Thankfully, over the next couple of weeks her doctor found a drug she tolerated better, and she began to think and function better. Next came a specialist, whom she saw before Christmas and who hastily scheduled surgery for a few days after New Year's.

Ellen hadn't even considered a trip over the Bridge of Dreams until now. "*The way things are going*," she thought, "*I just need to stay present and focus on what's happening.*"

Still, it was a shock and brought a rush of emotion when she entered the hospital on the day of surgery. The surgical nurses all came over to her as she got close to the OR to introduce themselves. One in particular, a tall slender blond woman, leaned closer over the gurney, and Ellen caught the name on her tag.

"*Hope!*" she thought. "*She's here with me! My Hope!*"

The young woman smiled brightly at her and patted her shoulder reassuringly.

Encouraged and relieved, Ellen said good-bye to Robert and let the surgical team wheel her away.

It felt like she had just fallen asleep when she woke up in the recovery room. Hope was nowhere to be seen, which was a little disappointing. However, Ellen was more interested in how her body felt. Strangely, she felt a profound change she couldn't describe. She knew something was drastically different.

A few minutes later, the tall, dark-haired, middle aged woman who was her gynecologist breezed in for a quick chat. "You had a large polyp blocking most of your uterus and a smaller one behind it," Dr. Garfield told her. "Otherwise, everything else looked fine. And 99.9% of the time, polyps are benign, so you're probably good to go. We'll know for

181

sure after the pathology report comes back. Till then, I'll see you in four weeks."

With that Dr. Garfield shook Ellen's hand and left.

Relieved, Ellen went home with Robert at the end of the day. They stopped at their favorite KFC since she hadn't eaten anything since the night before.

"That's really good news that everything's fine," he said working on his grilled chicken.

"It's definitely a relief," Ellen said, though somewhere in the back of her mind something niggled at her brain as if warning her not to be too hasty. She pushed it aside choosing to focus on the good news, instead.

For the next week, Ellen took things easy and mostly slept. Avner didn't push her to cross the Bridge at night, and Robert picked up "finding" dinner by day. Toward the middle of week three, a physician's assistant from Dr. Garfield's office called.

"Dr. Garfield wanted us to move your appointment from next week to tomorrow, and we've made an appointment for you with a gynecologic oncology surgeon," the young woman announced.

Prickles erupted on Ellen's scalp and traveled throughout her body. "What is this about? Why the oncology surgeon?"

Suddenly, the woman on the other end became very flustered. "We got your pathology report back early, and Dr. Garfield wants to discuss it with you tomorrow."

The world came sharply into focus for Ellen. "I'm sure she does," she replied in a low growl.

Ellen hung up and called Robert at his University office.

"Bad news," she told him. "They got the path report back and I have to go in to see Dr. Garfield tomorrow."

"Why would they move your appointment up?" he wondered.

"Only one reason she'd want to see me sooner," Ellen replied, "and something her PA let slip confirms it. She wants me to see an oncology surgeon."

Robert was silent for a moment. "Cancer?"

"Only reason I know of to see an oncologist," Ellen replied and hung up.

The appointment the next day merely confirmed her suspicions.

"I'm sorry," Dr. Garfield said as she entered the exam room. "I had your file marked 'Do not tell patient over phone'. But apparently, she missed it."

"In all honesty," Ellen said. "The tip off was being called in a week early."

"The test results came back Stage I, slow growing cancer," Dr. Garfield explained. "I'm really sorry I gave you false hope. I've only seen two polyps in my whole career come back with cancer. The good news is that the cancer appeared to be completely contained within the larger polyp. But you'll need a hysterectomy at the least. We'll set up an appointment for you with the oncology surgeon we usually refer to."

"I think I'd like to get a second opinion as well," Ellen told her. "A couple of people have said good things about a center in New York."

"We can get your slides and records for you any time you need them," Dr. Garfield responded. "Just let me know where you want them sent."

Ellen and Robert drove home in shocked silence.

"Does any of this stop?" she whispered.

He sighed heavily suddenly sounding and feeling very old. "We've been through so much. First, the break in and attack, then your coma, the double pneumonia...."

"It feels like it's never ending, "Ellen agreed. "I don't know how much more I can take."

"Look, maybe I should cancel that out of town lecture week after next."

Ellen shook her head emphatically. "I'll probably need you to take time off work to take care of me later. You'd be better off working now when I can still be a bit independent."

"But I don't like the idea of leaving you," Robert countered reaching for her hand and squeezing it.

"I don't like the idea of the whole blessed thing," Ellen grumbled. "Let's just keep things as normal as possible until we can't anymore."

He squeezed her hand again. "All right. If you're sure."

"I'm sure."

While Ellen kept the appointment with Dr. Garfield's gynecological oncology surgeon, she was glad she had already decided to get a second opinion. The office itself was too busy with cancer patients being processed in assembly line fashion. Then neither the doctor nor his physician's assistant had made time to read important notes that Dr. Garfield had sent concerning residual effects from the home attack. In fact, in studying the team, the only one who seemed to have his act together was the resident who was shadowing the surgeon, and he couldn't say a word.

But more curious to Ellen was the fact that every time she did consider surgery with that office, she got the distinct sensation throughout her body that it would revolt. She couldn't put her finger on the exact origin of that sensation or even describe it. Ellen just knew down to her toes that to have surgery there would produce horrific results. She bailed on that office and never looked back.

True to her curious nature, Ellen got on Google to see what the most common recommendations were for her type of cancer. Mayo Clinic, Johns Hopkins, NIH, Memorial Sloan Kettering all said the same thing; partial hysterectomy. One clinic in Texas had its own way of dealing with cancer that didn't necessarily require surgery, but it would require her to be away from home for one to two months. Ellen shook her head at the thought. She couldn't bear to be away from Robert that long.

She finally stopped looking. The thought of cancer made her angry. Considering the long haul of surgery and recovery made her feel like never crawling out of bed again.

The day came for Robert to leave for his trip. He stood at the top of the stairs and looked at her, set his bag back down and wrapped his arms around her. "I don't want to leave you," he murmured.

"I don't want you to, either," Ellen confessed, "but one of us has to keep working."

He nodded against her head. "I love you," he said giving her a long kiss.

"I love you, too."

Ellen watched him get into his car from the kitchen window then the car backed down the driveway. The house felt completely empty without him, and she went downstairs to curl up with the dog while her heart felt forlorn.

That evening, after a quick chat with Robert, she climbed into bed. Spotting Avner by the door, she waved him over.

"Why is this happening?" Ellen asked.

Avner shook his head. "I don't think anyone quite understands the rhyme or reason...."

Ellen shook her head. "No. I mean why this? The Embodied One promised I wouldn't have to be on the brink of death again in order to enter your realm. Yet, this is a disease that could put me there. Why isn't he keeping his word?"

Avner considered this for a moment. "Maybe it's only the perception of such a serious threat."

"If I don't get that second opinion soon and have surgery, it's the most likely outcome," Ellen replied.

184

He nodded his understanding.

She was quiet for a moment. "Has anyone told Daniel?"

Avner froze. It was the one question he had been hoping she wouldn't ask. "Yes," he reluctantly replied.

"Any reaction?" Ellen asked.

"According to Michael, none," Avner reported.

Ellen knit her brows. "If I died, he'd have to come to walk me into the Light, right?"

Avner nodded.

"So, would it be just his shell or would his light be released to come, too?" she wondered.

Avner frowned but said nothing.

"If I died, would I be able to choose to live in the Lands Below?" Ellen asked.

"If you died before your time, yes," Avner replied.

"It doesn't feel like my time," she murmured and turned off the light.

The next day Ellen absent-mindedly walked through the house and gathered up prescription bottles. She crawled onto the king bed downstairs and dumped the bottles in the middle. Avner sat on the edge of the bed eyeing them suspiciously, a growing sense of alarm creeping up the back of his neck.

"What are these?" he asked.

Ellen sighed heavily. "Pain killers."

He frowned. "Are you in pain?"

She shook her head.

"Then why?" he wondered.

"If I took enough of these," Ellen said turning over a bottle, "I would go to sleep and never wake up."

Avner sucked in air through his teeth. "Suicide."

She nodded. "When I consider what I'm facing, it becomes a more attractive option every day."

Avner deepened himself calling density to his form as Ellen started to open a bottle. Suddenly, a large, very solid hand cupped hers and held it in place. Ellen gasped in shock and looked up.

"Why are you stopping me?" she moaned.

"You need another option," Avner replied.

"I'm out of other options," Ellen replied.

Avner shook his head, scooped up the bottles of pills and tossed them in the garbage.

"How do you know this isn't some trial thing I have to go through in order to grow?" Ellen asked petulantly remembering what Daniel had once told her about having to watch her go through difficulties rather than being able to intervene.

"I don't," Avner replied. "I wasn't trained. I'm here specifically to keep you alive."

Ellen sighed and fell back against the pillows.

"You need to see Raphael...tonight," Avner insisted forcefully.

Ellen sighed heavily. "Maybe you're right. Maybe there is some other way," she admitted. "I'm just getting so tired of having to look."

Avner nodded, his heart heavy. She was his daughter, and even he couldn't do anything for her. The sadness made his chest ache.

As soon as Ellen was asleep, he whisked her over the Bridge and straight to Raphael's Healing Facility. Raphael was waiting for them and ushered them into a private room. As soon as the door closed, Avner laid her on a bed and Raphael sat beside her.

"Avner says you were thinking of taking your human life," Raphael said quietly.

"It looked good for a while," Ellen admitted.

"Why?"

"I was given a serious diagnosis...cancer," Ellen replied. "They want to do surgery. Without it, it's likely to come back and kill me. I'm just so tired of going through these medical rounds."

Raphael nodded. "Let me scan you," he said, his eyes glowing. In response, his hands glowed, and he slowly swept them over her body.

"Yes, I detect where the cancer was," he finally told her. "Your body walled off the remaining scraps of energy your attacker forced upon you. Now that they're gone, there is no further danger."

"'Is that why I felt so different when I woke up in the recovery room?" Ellen wondered.

"I should say so," Raphael responded. "Your body was using a lot of energy to keep your attacker's energy at bay."

"Was that just human energy?" Avner asked, an uncomfortable feeling hitting the pit of his stomach.

Raphael passed his hand over Ellen's abdomen again. Frowning, he looked up and shook his head. "No. It was Minion."

Ellen gasped. "Robert did say he saw a monster when he was first attacked. He didn't realize it was a man till he was pinned on the floor later."

Avner held his head. "They are after you," he breathed.

"But isn't it all gone now?" Ellen asked.

"Yes, it is," Raphael assured her.

Avner breathed a sigh of relief. *"They've lost the tracking signal,"* he thought, *"and I'm shielding mine."*

"Then why do I still need surgery?" she wanted to know.

"I think it is time to speak with the Embodied One," Avner said. "There may be more going on than meets the eye."

"I concur," Raphael agreed. "There's too much happening that I can't explain."

Avner put his hand to his temple and closed his eyes in concentration for a moment. His actions were swift when he blinked them back open. He crossed the room to Ellen's bedside in one step, scooped her up and spiraled out.

CHAPTER 25

In seconds, Avner and Ellen appeared inside the Throne Room. Raphael popped in right behind them. Avner set Ellen on her feet and the trio walked toward the front. While the two angels knelt with heads bowed, Ellen first sought to shield her eyes as she normally would do. It slowly dawned on her that if she shifted her vision just enough, the glare no longer hurt her eyes.

She watched as filaments of shadow began forming within the Light of the One on the Throne. As they swirled together, a shape appeared in the midst of the Light. Before long it became a familiar figure who approached them.

"Wow!" Ellen breathed. "I actually saw Light and Shadow combine to create form."

The Embodied One smiled as he drew closer. "That is a rare event that few have ever witnessed."

"Thank you for the privilege," she told him.

Avner and Raphael rose.

"Now, what is the trouble?" the Embodied One asked.

As quickly as possible, Ellen explained her recent diagnosis and surgery. Raphael added his findings, particularly the disturbing fact that Ellen's former attacker had left some sort of marker in her.

"What is most disturbing," Avner said, "is that it may have allowed Minions to track her."

The Embodied One's face was grave. "Thank you, Raphael. I will take this from here."

188

Raphael bowed his head and left.

The Embodied One scanned her for a moment. "No, it is truly gone." He looked up at Avner.

"I was not aware of plans the One of Darkness had for her," he told them. "In truth, I had forgotten about my children."

"That attack happened way before the accident that put you in a coma," the Embodied One told Ellen. "But that accident may have been purposeful."

"You mean, you think a Minion was driving the car?" she asked in horror.

The Embodied One nodded.

She turned to Avner.

He nodded as well. "While I might have forgotten you as part of the Dark One's plan, he would never have forgotten and would have sought out your whereabouts."

"So, I've been vulnerable all this time," Ellen surmised.

"And may still be," the Embodied One said.

"Less so," Avner added. "Without that marker, they can no longer track her."

"Back to hit or miss?" Ellen asked.

"So it would seem," the Embodied One agreed.

"Then what now?" Ellen wondered.

The Embodied One looked up at Avner then to Ellen. "You need a fully trained Guardian Angel."

"But Daniel...."

"Is split," the Embodied One said. "Unless a way is found to restore him, you need another assigned."

"One split such as he was restored in the past," Avner reminded him.

"And you lost your son for all these Ages," the Embodied One reminded him. "We cannot afford to similarly lose Ellen. The stakes are too high."

"But I read the <u>Book of Light and Shadows</u>," Ellen protested.

The Embodied One shook his head. "That allows you to see and manipulate light and patterns of information," he told her. "The light within you is still but your own. You would be swallowed by that crystal and then both you and Daniel would be lost."

Ellen sighed and thought back to her Choice Board remembering the options. "My Choice Board said find Daniel, free Daniel and reunite Daniel," she said aloud. "Those options wouldn't be there if it weren't possible. I already know the approximate location. I just need to do the other two."

The Embodied One took a deep breath before turning to Avner. "Please step back so I may speak more privately."

Avner bowed his head and walked back nearly to the entrance.

"What good was it for me to read the book, if that won't help me free Daniel?" Ellen asked in a hoarse whisper.

When Avner was out of hearing, the Embodied One spoke very quietly. "There is a way, Ellen," he told her. " But it would require that you risk everything. Before you read the book, you could never have undertaken this feat. Now, you know what is within the Light and how the Shadows work. Now, you could do this."

Ellen frowned, a chill entering her spine. "What exactly do you mean?"

"Ellen, you are very resourceful," the Embodied One said. "You have managed to accomplish things few others would have dreamed of."

"But...?"

"This is one trial you cannot complete solely on your own, with your own power," he said laying his hand on her shoulder. "This crystal could easily absorb all your energy and consider it, as you would say, a snack."

Her heart dropped into the pit of her stomach. "Then there's nothing I can do?"

"No, there is one thing you can do," the Embodied One told her. "But it comes with a steep price."

The world around her went silent and her mouth went dry. "What?"

"You must give up forever who you've known yourself to be and join me in the Light," the Embodied One said. "Only in my Light can you accomplish this task and save Daniel. But...." he added holding up one finger, "you will never be the same again. It is an all-or-nothing proposition."

Ellen staggered back wishing Avner were there to catch her. "May I have some Time to think this through?"

"I insist," the Embodied One agreed. "Daniel needed as much as well."

Ellen's eyes widened. "Wh-when he gave up his immortality?"
The Embodied One nodded.

"That was an all-or-nothing deal, too, wasn't it?" she asked.

"Yes. And it was no easier for him than this is for you."

190

Ellen's heart pounded in her ears. "May I...may I see him again?"

"On the battlefield?" the Embodied One asked.

She nodded.

"That experiment did not go well last time," he reminded her.

"Maybe because I carried the marker, which is gone now," she said.

The Embodied One considered this for a moment then called, "Avner! To me!"

Avner was there in an instant.

"Ellen wishes to observe Daniel on the battlefield again," he told the angel.

"Sire, we were overwhelmed last time," Avner protested.

"She no longer carries the marker," the Embodied One said. "Without that, I believe you are safer."

Avner bowed his head. "As you wish."

He wrapped his arms around her, leapt into the air and spiraled out. Avner paused their journey in a between dimension.

"Ellen, this isn't wise," he said nervously.

"I have to, Avner. I have a life changing decision to make. I have to know it's the right thing to do," Ellen told him.

Avner sighed. "All right. But I'm keeping you farther back."

"As long as I can see Daniel," she told him.

He nodded and resumed their journey. He brought them out on a hill near the battlefield, but the fighting was a considerable distance away. Ellen strained to see who was who, but at this distance it was impossible.

"Avner, I can't see anything," she complained.

However, as she spoke two streaks of light headed toward them. Michael and Daniel soon landed nearby.

"Again?" Michael asked in frustration. "Do you have a death wish?"

"Lately," Ellen said approaching Daniel, "I have."

Michael was taken aback but Ellen ignored him. She studied Daniel's figure, his face, his cold, emotionless eyes. Her heart ached to see him like this. She wanted to slip her arms around him and bring the love back. But that was part of his light and it was gone. Instead, she adjusted her vision till she could actually see inside him. A roiling ball of light sat about waist high, but every moment that passed, it diminished slightly.

"Oh my," she breathed looking up at him. "That's why you asked to be on the battlefield. You don't have a personal source anymore.

You're borrowing from the Light, and it only lasts so long."

Gingerly, Ellen reached out and touched his arm. The skin felt like a thin layer of stone or porcelain. Her heart sank even further.

"I know I said I'd take on your pain for you," she whispered swallowing hard. "Really brave words till I'm face-to-face with that reality."

Ellen withdrew her hand and backed away. Daniel had never once acknowledged her presence. She headed back to Michael and Avner.

"He...can't survive much longer like that, can he?" she asked.

Michael stared at the ground. "I think not."

"What happens to an angel when his form is no more?" Ellen wondered.

"His light would return to the Light never to be seen again," Avner replied.

Ellen's breath caught in her throat. "Take me to the Lands Below, please," she requested.

Avner nodded, picked her up and whisked her away.

Michael stood watching Daniel. The truth was, he kept him at the front nearly constantly. His light dimmed too quickly these days.

Avner set Ellen down at the oasis outside Desert City.

"If you don't mind, I need to sort some things out," she told him.

"Just think of me when you're ready to return," he replied.

She nodded and watched him leave. She turned toward the fountain, splashed the cool water on her face and took a drink.

"Ellen!" she heard someone call.

Looking up, she spotted William just exiting the gate. He waved and jogged over. He picked her up giving her a bear hug then set her back down.

"I never thought you were coming back," he said.

Ellen headed for the shade of some palm trees and sat down. William joined her.

"It's been a little rough the last month or so," she said quietly. "My mother died then doctors diagnosed me with cancer."

"Cancer?" he asked. "The way you say that doesn't sound good."

"Usually it's not," she admitted. "Some people die of it. In my case, I'm pretty sure it's not what kills me."

William frowned in confusion.

"I had some Minion tracking device in me," Ellen explained in hushed tones.

His eyes widened.

"I had surgery and it's gone now."

"So, everything's fine, right?" he asked hopefully.

Ellen shook her head. "I need a full Guardian, one who's been trained. I either have to get Daniel back or have someone else assigned."

"So, you read the <u>Book of Light and Shadows</u>," William pointed out.

She shook her head. "It isn't enough. According to the Embodied One, I'd be a snack for that crystal...his words."

William let out a low whistle. "So what do you do?"

"Remember why Daniel has meant so much to me," she replied getting to her feet, "before my life changes forever."

The Vortex started coming up around her. William realized she was planning to leave.

"Not without me!" he yelled pushing off the ground and diving inside the whirlwind.

In an instant, the Vortex took off heading for the Dormant Volcano.

CHAPTER 26

As the Vortex lifted off the ground and headed into the Desert, Ellen was startled to find William inside it. The Vortex rocked a bit till she could get her equilibrium back.

"What are you doing here?" she demanded.

"You don't seem so good," William replied, unsteadily getting to his feet. "I thought I'd keep you company and make sure you're ok."

Ellen huffed and stared straight ahead. "I wanted to be alone. It's why I sent Avner back to the Great Above."

"I didn't know," William said. "But Ellen, you feel wrong...like the light is draining out of you."

Her features softened and she reached over to squeeze his hand. "I'm a bit depressed and a whole lot scared," she admitted. "I'm just trying to find my courage."

William put his arm across her shoulders and kissed her temple then watched to see where they were headed.

First stop, Ellen took them out into the Desert till there was nothing to see but sand for miles around. Once the Vortex receded, she walked a few paces and dropped to her knees. William squatted beside her.

"What's so special about the sand?" he asked.

"First place I met Daniel," Ellen replied, her voice sounding far away. "He was so battered, he could hardly open his eyes. His wings were torn."

The scene went through her mind like it was yesterday, seeing the torn wing feathers flapping in the hot desert breeze, his bloodied face and bruised chest in spite of his well-muscled physique.

William shook his head. "I don't understand. How could somebody beat up an Archangel?:

Tears trickled down her cheeks. "He had just given up his immortality. He fell out of the sky and Marauders attacked him. They even got his sword away from him and broke it."

Williams' face turned ashen.

"C'mon," she said rising and bringing up the Vortex.

William obeyed and they soon cut back across the Desert to the Dormant Volcano. Ellen seemed to search for a specific location before setting down. When the Vortex receded, they were in a fighting ring where dust devils sparred in wild spurts about the interior. Ellen shielded her eyes and looked up into the stands to where pins still anchored chains to one wall.

She swallowed hard. "The Marauders eventually captured us. They chained Daniel up there," she said pointing, "and threw me out here to fight. If I fought, I'd become a Marauder. Every time I refused, they hit Daniel harder. I was finally knocked out and we were dumped back into the cells to rot."

Ellen headed toward the side of the hill where a door hung off its hinges. William grabbed it and tore it down, and she led the way inside. It took a bit but she found their old cell. The doors stood wide open and the rocky cell was empty.

She stumbled toward the far corner, knelt and touched the ground then suddenly spotted a flicker of white. Examining the wall closer, Ellen carefully pulled a lone angel feather from a crack in the wall. William studied her with mixed emotions.

Ellen put the feather to her lips then suddenly broke down crying. "It's his feather," she sobbed. "His feather."

"Down here?" William asked in wonder.

She nodded, wiping her eyes with her fingers. "He was so bad, he had the real chance of dying. It's where I found out I could heal. I kept asking him, 'Why?' and he kept saying 'Whatever it takes'."

"Whatever it takes for what?" William asked.

"To learn who I was, to learn I could heal others, to learn how to heal myself."

William sat down hard. "Wow!"

Ellen looked up. "I know. He gave up his immortality and kept doing whatever it took for me to wake up, to find this side of me called a Way Shower I never knew existed."

"But why go back and remember all this?" William wanted to know.

"Because the Embodied One is offering me some opportunity to do the same for him," Ellen whispered. "I want to remember how it felt when he kept demonstrating deep love. I keep wondering if I can find that in me."

William stared at his sister in awe. "You've already done so much."

She trained intensely serious blue eyes on him. "It isn't enough if he's not restored and there's something I could have done about it."

"You can't be the only one who can help him," William pointed out. "Hey, I did it once before. Let me do this again."

"Way Showers can die in these lands," Ellen explained. "You have far less of your form than you might suppose."

William remained quiet but he watched how tenderly Ellen touched that angel feather. Gently, he reached out, took the feather, started braiding a section of her hair and wove the feather in with the braid. He pulled a thread from his shirt making sure the feather was securely anchored.

"Thank you," she whispered before standing and bringing up the Vortex.

She passed over Hunter's home too embarrassed to describe what happened there. She'd gotten her first lecture on deep love there, and her first kiss on the forehead.

"Want to see the Memorial Wall?" Ellen asked.

William nodded.

Ellen got the Vortex set again this time bringing them into the mountain pass. Once she'd set down, William stared in wonder at the hundreds of holographic heads that lined the wall.

"All Way Showers?" William asked.

She nodded. "All captives of the Ice Queen who died in the cavern," Ellen explained. "But I want to go up over there," she said pointing to the other side of the gap.

They worked their way across the frigid river that flowed through the mountain pass and climbed the rock wall on the other side till they reached the entrance on top. They entered the tunnel and Ellen followed her pendulum. It finally led them to a spiral staircase that wound down to a heavy, oak door. They pushed it open, Ellen grabbed and lit the remaining torch and they headed across the crumbly floor.

She held the torch up and slowly scanned the walls. Rotting

wooden shelves lined the walls from floor to ceiling, but not an angel or mythical creature remained to testify to the Ice Queen's purpose for their destruction. Encased in her special ice, she had drained each one of their light until they had crumpled into dust and had blown away.

"Out this way," Ellen said heading for the far door. She pushed it open and edged out onto the ledge.

"How did an island get out there?" William wondered.

"It was connected by a land bridge once," Ellen explained.

"So, what was he...like chained to the rock?" William asked.

"He was in the process of being frozen in the ice the Ice Queen used for draining the light as her power source," Ellen replied. "I got here and almost couldn't help him. I was so afraid of heights, I almost couldn't cross over. But it was Daniel and he was in desperate straits."

"And you found the courage," William assumed.

Ellen nodded.

"C'mon, let's get out of here," William suggested. "I think you need some sunshine again."

The Vortex was rising even before he stopped speaking. She took them out over the island then shot straight up and out the air vent at the top. They came out on the mountainside and found a flat rock on which to sun themselves.

"His wings had only started working again," Ellen reminisced. "It took everything he had to get us out of there. He sat here for a long time afterwards just shaking."

"So when did he get his immortality back?" William asked. "Assuming he did get it back."

Ellen went very still and pale. A breeze swept up the mountainside tossing her hair and spinning Daniel's feather.

"One of the challenges I went through to find a way to heal myself was to split into clones and go to the same location in three time periods," she said quietly. "The first two were no big deal. The third was the real test."

William frowned as he listened.

"Daniel was held in stasis on an island. Between my platform and his island was a dark abyss," she told him. "I had to use the pendulum to find the invisible path to free him."

"And...?"

"The Sultan was there when I completed the challenge," Ellen told him. "He dumped Daniel down into his Lava Pit and I followed." A lump rose in her throat. "The Sultan wanted me, but Daniel took my place."

"With the Sultan?" William asked incredulously.

Ellen nodded. "He knew I was the only one who could find him... and I did. The Priest and the Wizard had already headed to the Throne Room about Daniel's imprisonment. I went back for Daniel. Only he was being tortured...so I sent the Sultan to the Throne Room in a fireball."

"Big mistake," William commented.

"Well, first I had to heal Daniel and he was so broken, I never thought that would happen," Ellen related. "Then we went to the Throne Room, trapped the Sultan and hauled him back to the Pit under the Dome."

Williams' eyes grew wide. "You did all that?"

Ellen nodded. "I did all that with barely a second thought."

He frowned. "Then what's the problem now?"

Ellen sighed and stood up. "Back then, I felt invincible, and Daniel and I did everything together...mostly. And in the human realm, things were always in stasis until a miracle made everything better, and they kept happening."

"But now?"

"Now...I feel more alone than I ever have," Ellen confessed. "Daniel's split and his time is running out. And on the human end, I'm not in too great shape. I'm terrified in a way I've never felt before."

She started crunching through the icy snow cover down toward a lower altitude. William watched for a minute or two pondering everything she'd told him. At last, he got up and followed her. He caught up to her as they entered a pine forest. The thick bed of needles swallowed up all sound including their footsteps.

William finally stopped her and turned her toward him. He put his hands on her shoulders. "Ellen, I don't know what it's like to go through all that. What I do know is that you have to be the bravest person I've ever known."

She returned his gaze. "There's two kinds of courage, William. There's the courage you feel in the moment a catastrophe happens. Then there's the courage you have to dig up day-after-day to put one foot in front of the other toward something that scares you to death. I'm really good at the former and lousy at the latter. I've developed really excellent avoidance skills. Daniel excels at both."

"Look, whatever he does, Ellen, he does knowing he can't die," William told her.

"He gave up his immortality for a while," she reminded him.

"And he knew if the worst happened, he would be reabsorbed into the Light he was created from and channeled every day," William added.

198

"His demise was not a total unknown. He has perfect comfort in the Light. My guess is he was far more afraid for you if the challenges proved to be too much than he was for himself."

Ellen staggered back and sat down hard on a log. "He wasn't afraid to die," she whispered in awe.

William shook his head kneeling before her.

"I...I walked into the Light before my time," she told him. "I sacrificed my still beating heart and was sent back just my soul crystal."

"You reformed yourself."

She nodded. "Earth challenge. Not many have a need to undertake it."

"So, you've been on the other side. Why be afraid?" William asked.

"Because all I remember is intense, sharp pain," Ellen whispered. "And if I go through with this surgery in the human world, it's just the promise of more pain for months. William," she said her lower lip quivering, "I'm terrified of pain."

He reached out, put his arms around her and rocked her. In moments, Ellen's body shook with sobs.

"How can I get past this terror?" she cried. "It feels like it will consume me. It drains all my energy and nerve. What I know I want to do, I can't do."

William continued to rock her, all words of wisdom fleeing his thoughts. How do you encourage someone to undertake their greatest fear?

"Look," he said pushing her back a little so he could capture her gaze. "There is no one who can tell you to do this."

She nodded.

"And you can't do this for him or anyone else," William warned her. "If you do, you'll regret the decision and will resent him forever."

Ellen took a deep breath and nodded again.

"If you do this," William continued, "you do this because you feel the pull in here," he said pointing his finger at her chest. "The decision doesn't come from here," he added tapping the side of his head.

She nodded again. "You're right. I've been trying to think myself into this decision, but I've got to feel my way through."

William clapped her on the shoulder and helped her up.

"One more stop," Ellen announced. "Time to visit the brothers and check out the Forest."

With that, she brought the Vortex up around them and took off for the coast. William watched the changing scenery with great interest. If he'd ever seen these lands before, he'd forgotten them long ago. Before long, they came up over a rise and saw the Castle on the coast.

"The brothers' University," Ellen announced.

"Brothers?" he asked.

"Priest and Wizard," Ellen explained. "Fraternal twins."

"I know Edward," William said.

"Well, get ready for Wizard Alexander," she told him.

At that moment, an explosion rocked the Sea Facing Tower and smoke belched from the windows high up.

"What was that?" William cried as the Vortex wobbled.

"That...would be Alexander's latest experiment," Ellen chuckled.

"Good Lord!" William exclaimed.

"Yes, rather," Ellen replied setting the Vortex down in the midst of the courtyard.

She headed straight toward the main building with William following.

"Ellen!" came the cry from off to their left.

She stopped in her tracks and turned to see Edward dashing toward them from the stately chapel that had been built for his use. She was really pleased to see that youth had returned to him.

"Seems like you've found yourself again," she commented when she gave him a hug.

"Alex, too," Edward said and greeted William.

They got half way across the Great Hall floor when Alexander came dashing down the stairs.

"I spotted incoming from my tower window and forgot the experiment," Alexander said hurrying over, picking Ellen up and spinning her around.

She laughed and gave his cheek a kiss.

William watched all of their interactions. It was obvious how much Edward and Alexander cared for his sister, and how thoroughly she cared for them in return. But the biggest difference was in her energy. Whereas before she'd appeared to be so depleted and lifeless, in their presence her vitality shone.

The small group all sat down at a long table, and Ellen filled them in on the details as quickly as possible. The brothers were quite silent when she finished.

Alexander shook his head. "Don't have a courage potion for you."

"Didn't know you did potions," Ellen teased.

"He didn't," Edward said. "Seriously, I have no clue how to help you."

"I was thinking the use of your Forest Meditation Glen might be nice," Ellen remarked.

"Any time," the brothers chorused.

At that moment, Simon pushed open the Dungeon door and headed toward them. "I have this idea how I can bring others with me to this place," he announced abruptly.

Ellen narrowed her eyes. "What exactly do you mean, Simon?" she asked, her voice low in her throat, almost menacing.

Chills raced down William's spine, and he suddenly realized that in her own right, his sister was a force to be reckoned with.

Simon dropped onto a bench across from them and held out a schematic. "If I build this machine on the human side, I can bring anyone through, not just Way Showers."

Ellen's arm snaked out and she clamped her hand around Simon's wrist. "If you bring the average person here, they will either die or go insane, Simon. There is a reason even Way Showers have to undergo certain challenges. They need to expand their capacities to meet the rigors of this world."

Simon sneered. "I've done that Flame thing, and I'm just fine." He struggled to pull his arm back.

"You've barely left your basement hole," Ellen retorted. "You don't actually know what's out there."

"You're just jealous of what I can do," Simon yelled finally wrenching his arm free. He got up and stalked back to the Dungeon.

"He's trouble," William said in a low voice.

Ellen stared at the Dungeon door. "He's coming up on a challenge that may just be bigger than he can chew."

"So what do we do?" Edward asked.

"Leave him to it," Ellen replied rising. "He's one person who refuses to learn from others. He'll have to experience this for himself."

"But what if he drags some poor innocent here with him?" Alexander fretted.

"We'll have to deal with that when it happens," Ellen replied. "For now, have a heart and show William around. I, for one, am headed to the Forest."

Ellen turned and strode toward the door.

"Where can I find a woman like that?" Alexander breathed.

"She's out of your league," Edward quipped.

Ellen stopped in her tracks, spun around and stalked right back to the brothers. She grabbed each one by the robes, pushed them back into a thick support column and growled.

"Listen here, gents. You're out of no one's league. You're in a league of your own," she snarled.

The brothers' eyes grew wide and they held their breath.

"Now," Ellen said backing down. "Don't ever let me hear those horrid words pass your lips again."

"Ye-yes, ma'am," they stuttered.

Ellen released them, turned around and headed back toward the door. As she passed William, she gave him a sly smile and a wink.

"*Why that vixen,*" he thought grinning in amusement.

Ellen wasted no time getting into the Forest. While she spotted the brothers' Meditation Glen, she looked for the mammoth tree she had encountered on her first visit. As soon as she spotted it, she hurried forward, put her back to its trunk and leaned fully against it. Closing her eyes, she breathed deeply and all the tension left her body. After a time, her eyes suddenly popped back open and she knew.

CHAPTER 27

Ellen headed back to the Castle. Avner met her at the gate. She waved to the brothers and William.

"Time to go back," Avner announced.

"I have to make one stop first," she told him.

"Where to?" he asked picking her up.

"The Great Halls," she replied. "I have a decision to finalize."

Avner nodded, leapt skyward and winked out. Moments later, they appeared near the Cloister Walk. Ellen hurried to the side door and slipped into the Banqueting Hall. She went straight for her Choice Board but stopped for a moment to observe the cloud around Daniel's.

Narrowing her eyes and shifting her focus, Ellen gazed gently at the dark mass. Gradually, she saw strands of shadow that pulled apart. With a little more time, she might have been able to unravel the whole mess. As it was, she got one quick glimpse of his board.

"'Return to Ellen'," she read gasping. "Then he does believe it's possible."

Fortified by that small nugget of hope, Ellen turned her attention to her own Board. She took a deep breath and blew it out hard. While she studied her options with deep concentration, she absent-mindedly fingered the feather William had woven into her hair.

"Ok. Here's the list," she said aloud. "Find Daniel, surgery, free Daniel, wild card, reunite Daniel, wild card." Ellen's eyebrows raised. "Two wild cards! Wow!"

"Challenge of a lifetime," a deep voice resonated from behind her.

She turned to see the Embodied One. "I know. William told me I have to make the decision for myself, selfish as it sounds. Truth is, I'm not ready to die, and I'm not ready for Daniel to return to the Light. I don't think he is either," she added with a nod toward his board.

The Embodied One nodded in agreement, and Ellen turned her attention back to the Board, lined up her choices the way they felt for her then locked them into place. She was trembling when she pivoted back towards him.

"Ok," she said in a shaky voice. "I'm ready."

The Embodied One stretched out his hand to her, and the next thing she knew, she was in the Throne Room.

"There is a reason you must go through with the surgery," the Embodied One told her. "When you were near death before, you were almost fully here. You could act in and on this environment almost as well as a denizen of this realm. I have noticed, however, that when you cross the Bridge of Dreams, more of you remains at home."

Ellen considered this news. "But if I were under anesthesia, I would exist here more like I did when I was close to death."

He nodded.

"That's probably the one piece of this whole deal that frightens me the most," Ellen admitted.

"I know," he said kindly, "and I can only lend you the strength to get through it."

"Raphael doesn't have something that could block the pain?" Ellen asked wishfully.

"Not and still leave you capable of achieving success," the Embodied One replied.

Ellen swallowed hard. "Then that's how it has to be," she said quietly.

"What you do need to do is create a support network on the human side like you've created here," the Embodied One instructed.

Ellen snorted softly. "Easier said than done."

"Not really," he countered. "You may have been hurt in the past by people you called friends, but you have people close by and afar who actually desire to support you. By giving in to your fear of rejection, you deny them the opportunity to create a space of intimacy for themselves."

Ellen blinked. "I deprive them of something?"

"Every time you withdraw yourself."

"But how will I know who the right people are?" Ellen fretted.

"You won't," the Embodied One told her. "Some will come and

help then leave. Others will develop a deep bond with you and will stay. Open your heart. Have no expectations. Be surprised."

Ellen took a deep breath. "This seems to be the 'Face Your Fears' trial. Any more?"

The Embodied One smiled. "Maybe. I understand humans are very afraid of losing their sense of individuality."

"I guess so," Ellen replied.

"I'm asking you to do just that," the Embodied One said. "You cannot restore Daniel with just your light, and I cannot give you mine for this purpose. You must lay your trust on me and become my Light."

Ellen's heart raced fast and thudded hard in her chest. "H-how?"

"By merging with my Light, letting go of all form and thought and just be," the Embodied One replied.

"William said Daniel was never afraid of dying," Ellen mused. "For him it would just have been a matter of...."

"Going home," the Embodied One finished. "My children are at home in my Light."

"Are you asking me to become one of your children?" Ellen wondered.

The Embodied One laughed. "You already are; you just haven't known it. I'm asking you to embrace the Light, own it, be it, rely on it and not yourself. Then you will become like Daniel, confident that you can never fail when you reside in me."

Ellen shook her head. "Humans always want to be powerful, but this isn't about power, is it?"

The Embodied One shook his head. "And yet, if you rely on my Light and not your own, you will be more powerful than you could have dreamed in ways you couldn't imagine."

"This kind of sounds like way back when Daniel told me to stop referencing my life according to teachers and authorities, and own what I was capable of doing on my own terms," Ellen said.

"Only what you're capable of in your own power cannot compare to what you're capable of when you become my Light and rely on it."

Ellen squared her shoulders and put her hands on her hips. "At the moment, I only want to be powerful enough to find and restore Daniel. Anything else is icing on the cake."

"Then it is time, my child," the Embodied One said, his form becoming diffuse. "Just allow the process. Do not resist. I guarantee you no pain."

Ellen let her arms drop to her sides and closed her eyes. The room brightened till she could see the Light with her eyes closed. Gradually, she felt her own edges becoming diffuse, and the Light was now inside. Before she knew it, there was no inside or outside, just a sense of being. And then....

Ellen woke with a start and sat straight up in bed. She brought her hands up in front of her face then ran them over her body. She touched her hair, disappointed that Daniel's feather hadn't 'traveled.'

"Did that really even happen?" she wondered lying back in bed.

She lay there till Boodles picked up on her wakefulness and started to stir. Ellen got up and started her morning dog routine.

Later, after getting showered and dressed, she sat at the computer and scanned through Facebook. "*What the heck*," she thought and began to type her status about the upcoming surgery.

A "friend's" status caught her eye. She'd never met Kyle. "*Actually, I've only met a couple dozen of these people that call me friends*," Ellen mused.

Kyle had studied the same modality she had, but had since branched out to something else. Maybe it was her curiosity since Kyle and his wife lived in Australia, and that was exotic. But she clicked on his page and read his biography then a description of the work he was doing now. Something about it tugged at her heart. Before she knew what she was doing, she'd bought and downloaded his e-book and had paid for a Process.

Next, she remembered that her west coast friend, Bev, had studied meridian tapping with a particular teacher whom she admired. Ellen had been one of Bev's 'guinea pigs' when she was getting certified, and she liked this version of tapping to ease anxiety and fear. Now, Ellen figured she needed help on the purely human level to work her way past this terror. A few emails later, and she had a Skype appointment with the Master Teacher.

She paused for a while to check on how that felt. "*I think I need someone I can connect with face-to-face*," she thought and Katrina's face automatically popped into her mind. She emailed her and a mutual friend, Danielle, affectionately known as Danni. Within the week, she found time to have lunch with both of them.

Robert came home, talked with his Department Chair and put his college on notice he would be on caretaker duty for a while. They drove down to New York City for an initial appointment with Dr. Gilman. They both liked her, but Ellen still held out the hope that a less radical surgery could be performed. It was quite a blow to hear Dr. Gilman voice that the only option was a radical hysterectomy.

Back home, Ellen was surprised at the outpouring of love and support she got on a daily basis from her Facebook friends. In fact, their energy was so palpable, she could feel their prayers, well wishes and energy modalities buoying her up.

She went through the Process with Kyle, surprised by how potent reading words out loud could feel. Something was definitely changing inside her. But what intrigued her most were the words that kept repeating through her head. "I will follow the bright and shining path of the Creator." Like a song stuck on mental replay, those words would not leave her day or night. She said them over and over finding strength and a sense of calm from them.

Another trip down to the City for pre-op testing, and then it was time to take the dog to the boarding kennel. She and Robert would be staying in the City for a week.

"I think I may very well never want to see this City again," she told Robert as the car service took them from the airport long-term parking down to their mid-town hotel.

They were arriving a little over a day early. Ellen would be on a liquid fast all Sunday, and fasting plus road trip was more a recipe for disaster. She and Robert got their room with a kitchen, unpacked then headed out to the market just a block-and-a-half away. They picked up what she would need and food for Robert and hunkered down in the room.

Sunday dragged until the evening came when she downed some prophylactic medication to prevent allergic reactions during surgery. As daylight waned the terror grew so overwhelming, Ellen looked up the hospital's number.

"I don't think I can do this," Ellen told Robert. "I think they already got all of it. I've spent the last three years trying to rebuild my health over and over again. I just don't know if I can choose to trash my health."

Robert met her gaze. "I'll support whatever decision you make," he told her evenly.

She took a deep breath and sighed. "You haven't said anything to me about how you feel. I need to hear what this surgery means to you."

Robert sat quietly for a moment. "I haven't said anything about it because it's your body and only you can make this decision. It is a huge surgery, and if you didn't want to go through with it, I'd understand."

"But what does this mean to you?" Ellen insisted moving closer to him.

"I know all the data on this cancer," Robert replied. "I know that without this surgery, it's very likely to return."

"No, Robert. What does this mean for you?"

He took her hands in his. "If you have this surgery, it means I get to keep you with me for a while longer. And I sure want you in my life as long as I can have you there," he finally confessed.

"Wow!" Ellen breathed. "Why didn't you say that before now?"

"Because I didn't want you to feel any more pressure than you already were," he told her.

Ellen wrapped her arms around him and held on tight. "Right now, I can't do this for me. I really needed to hear what it meant to you. I'll go ahead with the surgery for you."

She didn't sleep much that night and morning came way too early. They packed up her things, got a cab downstairs and headed for the hospital. She checked in and went to a prep room. All her vitals were taken and information checked and double checked. At last, an OR nurse established an IV and gave her medicine to relax.

Ellen reached up to hug Robert.

"I'll be here waiting for you when you wake up," he promised.

With that, the nurses wheeled her away.

CHAPTER 28

Once in the OR, the nurses helped Ellen off the gurney. A kind case worker came over and introduced herself.

"Wendy," she said gesturing toward a nurse in the back, "told me about the attack you survived three years ago. I have days when I can hardly get out of bed. I can't believe you went through that and still you come in here. Gives me a whole new perspective."

Ellen didn't quite know what to say.

The case worker introduced her to everyone in the room who waved at her.

"*Not like I'll ever remember them*" Ellen thought.

When all the names had been called and Hope's wasn't on the roster, Ellen felt disappointed. If there was one surgery where her presence would have been reassuring, this was the one.

"The anesthesiology nurses are getting an air blanket set up," the case worker told her. "That will help to keep your body warm during surgery, because otherwise the OR is kept quite cool."

While they untangled the clear plastic sheet with holes in it, Ellen scanned the room. What really grabbed her attention was the robot they were setting up and the control console against the wall.

"The whole surgery is done laparoscopically," the case working explained. "Once the incisions are made, the nurses will slip the robotic arms inside and Dr. Gilman will maneuver them from the console. It's really cool," she gushed. "What you see on the screen makes everything look like it's right in front of your face."

"*I'd rather be on the console end of this thing playing,*" Ellen thought groggily.

The anesthesiologist motioned for her to come over. Butterflies erupted en masse in her stomach. Yet, Ellen knew a lot of her friends were praying that minute. Some had even promised to 'be with her.'

As Ellen lay down on the table, suddenly she saw people come into focus around her. There was her favorite artist who did her book covers, Kai, and his girlfriend. There was a husband and wife couple that she and Robert enjoyed when they attended seminars together. There was Katrina as live as day. Ellen gazed about her in awe.

Plus, Avner and Nariel stood nearby. Even Oriel came into view.

"For my brother," he whispered in her ear. "He'd want to be here."

The anesthesiology nurses slipped a cap over her head then the anesthesiologist put a clear mask over her face.

"Breathe deeply," she told Ellen. "I promise I'll keep you breathing."

Ellen took one breath then another. Usually, she'd already be out by now. She felt a little panicky. The next breath she took a deep, hard pull of gas then....

Ellen found herself standing on the rise overlooking the Castle. Avner stood beside her.

"How'd I get here?" she asked disconcerted.

"Not by the Bridge of Dreams," he replied.

Her head spun a little. "I think I need to get my bearings," Ellen said.

She took a step and nearly fell. Avner caught her and carried her to the Castle. He swooped over the courtyard and entered the Great Hall. Edward, Alexander and William were gathered at the long table looking somber. Simon sat across from them with his head on the table.

Avner sat her in an armchair nearby and put a stool under her feet. William came straight over.

"You don't look so hot," he remarked.

Ellen glanced up at him. "You do realize you say that at least once every time I come here? You're going to give me a complex."

"Yeah, but you don't," he insisted. "You look a little green."

"I just went into surgery. They're probably trying to get me fully knocked out and stabilized," she explained.

"So, you're going to do it then?" Alexander asked coming over. "You're going to go after Daniel?"

She nodded then held her head. "Just as soon as my head stops spinning."

At that moment, Ellen noticed Simon. In particular, she observed he was not his usual callous, arrogant self. Instead, he was moaning and white as a sheet.

"Since it's not Halloween, so no ghosts allowed, what's up with him?" she asked.

Edward and Alexander just backed away and William wasn't saying a word. All of a sudden, Ellen got a cold chill down her back.

"No! You didn't!" Ellen groaned trying to stand up.

William grabbed her arm to steady her and helped her to the table. She dropped onto the bench across from Simon.

"Your experiment?"

He nodded without looking up.

"Who?" she asked.

He shook his head.

"You don't know?"

He shook it again.

"You won't tell?"

He froze.

"Susannah," she breathed remembering their conversation in the computer lab eons ago.

He took a shuddering breath and nodded.

"Where-is-she?" Ellen demanded.

"I don't know," came the muffled reply.

"Sit up, Simon," she commanded.

When he didn't move, his Guardian stepped forward, yanked him up and held him there. Simon's eyes darted wildly about.

"Simon, this girl's life depends upon what you tell me," Ellen insisted. "What did you do?"

Simon balked. Ellen sifted through parallels. One locked into place and his face became calmer.

"I-I hooked us up to this machine, like in Inception...I-I told her we could double dream," he stuttered.

"Are you a chemist?" Ellen asked quietly.

"No, see I got this formula off the Internet," he replied. "I've tried it dozens of times before. Never had a problem."

"Then what?" Ellen probed.

"I-I...told her we had to hold hands so we wouldn't get s-separated," Simon confessed.

"Yet you landed...here?"

He nodded.

"And she landed where?"

"I don't know."

"Did she come through at all?" Ellen wondered.

Simon nodded. "They dowsed. Said she did."

Ellen glanced over and Alexander had his pendulum swinging. "Give him a pendulum."

Edward pulled one from his pocket and put it on the table in front of Simon. He pushed it away. Ellen picked it up, forced his hand open and dropped it into his palm.

"You need to learn to use this and fast," she hissed. Looking up at his Guardian, she added, "Force him if you need to."

Simon looked alarmed. "I-I didn't think he could do anything like that."

"This is an emergency," Ellen told him bluntly. "Maybe these guys will help you, maybe they won't," she said nodding toward the brothers. "I've come here during major surgery because it's my one shot to rescue someone I care very much about. I miss this chance, and it's over."

She pushed off from the table and stood on steady legs. "Nothing like a shot of adrenalin to set things right."

"Uh...we were planning to come with you," Alexander said.

Edward nodded.

"Then come," Ellen invited.

"But what about him...and the girl?" Edward asked.

Ellen sighed. "Guys, remember when I said he refuses to learn from others and has to have the experience for himself?"

They nodded.

"This is that," she said.

"But that girl didn't ask for this," Alexander protested.

"Should she suffer because of that idiot?" Edward asked.

Ellen narrowed her eyes, turned toward Simon and stared at his fear-stricken orbs. "What do you think, Simon? Should Susannah suffer because you wouldn't listen to the voices of experience?"

"B-but it worked for me," he sputtered.

"Does she have any medical conditions?" Ellen asked.

"I-I think she's diabetic," he replied.

Ellen got a sinking feeling in the pit of her stomach. "Simon, diabetes changes how people metabolize drugs."

His eyes widened in panic. "Oh my God! I didn't know. I so

didn't know."

Ellen sighed. "You really are that desperate for someone to like you."

He blushed bright red, his Adam's apple working furiously.

She shook her head. "This is your challenge, Simon," she said quietly. "It's your time to be the hero, understand?"

He nodded slowly.

Ellen turned to the brothers. "I can't tell you what decision to make," she told them. "But this is like Fire, Wind and Water. No one steps into the Fire for you. No one can hold your power in the center of the Wind for you. And no one can swim the Water challenge for you."

"Speaking of Water, we passed," Edward announced proudly.

Alexander whacked him on the shoulder. "Not now, you idiot!"

Ellen chuckled then she out-right laughed. "With everything so serious, right now is perfect timing." She gave the brothers each a hug. "Congratulations!"

"You never hug me," a timid voice said.

Ellen turned her head to see Simon staring forlornly at her.

"After the way you act?" Alexander charged.

"Yeah, you try everyone's patience," Edward added.

But Ellen quietly made her way to Simon's side of the table, leaned over and wrapped her arms around his boney shoulders.

"I have faith," she whispered, "that if you follow your heart and not your head, you'll do fine and so will Susannah."

She gave him an extra squeeze then straightened up.

"Well, guys, if we're going, we've got to head out soon," she announced.

William was already hauling packs in from the kitchen. They heard heavy, booted feet land in the courtyard then the crunch of gravel. The light from the doorway was momentarily obscured as Oriel, Uriel and Chanochiel, the Educated one of God, entered.

"We're going by Angel?" Ellen quipped.

"We decided after I realized even I don't remember the Valley's location that this was the better method of travel," William told her.

"Sounds good. Any heavy coats in these packs?" Ellen asked.

"Why?" Edward asked.

"Because on my way to the Monastery, I think I might have spotted the Valley through the clouds," Ellen announced.

"Well, that narrows down the terrain considerably," Alexander said heaving a sigh of relief.

Avner motioned to Ellen and took her aside. "I will not allow my brothers to enter that Valley. It's too dangerous for them."

Ellen nodded in agreement. "Quite frankly, once we find the cave, I don't want you going in."

"We'll see," he replied cryptically. "What about the other Way Showers?"

She shook her head. "They can stay outside the Valley with their Guardians."

"Not me," William declared having eavesdropped.

Avner and Ellen turned stern countenances on him. "Especially you!" they chorused.

He held his hands up and backed away.

Edward and Alexander came huffing out of a storage room and threw several fur coats on the table.

"I think these will be warm enough," Alexander puffed.

Ellen tried to lift one. "Yes, but can we still walk?"

Edward and William laughed.

"Ok guys. Off we go," Ellen insisted slinging her pack over her shoulder and carrying the coat outside.

Once they were gathered in the courtyard, the Guardians picked up their charges and took off headed inland toward higher elevation.

Simon stood in the doorway to the Great Hall watching them go. "They were serious," he squeaked.

Aloniel, Simon's stolid oak-tree Guardian, nodded. "Today you either grow up and take responsibility for your actions, or someone dies."

Simon looked up at him. "Susannah?"

His Guardian nodded.

Simon went back inside. There on the bench was a pack and lying on the table was a coat. A note on top said, "Good luck. Holler if you get stuck. -A"

He stared at the note then slowly set it down. Suddenly, Simon scooped up the pack and coat, spun around and headed for the door.

"Will you take me?" he asked his Guardian.

Aloniel shook his head. "Not till you attempt the Vortex."

Simon's shoulders drooped and he trudged in the direction of the chapel. "Better late than never."

CHAPTER 29

Snow blew hard obscuring the surroundings. The wind howled about the mountain and drifts were building fast. A lone, mousey blond woman in her mid-twenties lay on the ground, her eyelashes dusted with white frost. Without warning, a figure, cast dark gray by the storm, came into view. It scrambled over the uneven ground searching here and there.

"Susannah!" a woman called. "Susannah! Can you hear me? Are you all right?"

The blonde blinked her eyes open knocking snow off her lashes. She squinted up into the whirling white, her breath sending out puffs of steam.

"Susannah!" the voice called again.

"Here," the blonde whispered.

The dark figure stopped abruptly. "Keep talking," the figure urged.

"I'm here," Susannah said, her voice stronger. "Over here!"

Before long, the figure came into view, an angel with snow crusted wings. She spotted Susannah in the snow and hurried forward. She dropped to her knees in the snow beside Susannah and started brushing the the white flakes off the freezing woman. Susannah tried to sit up, and the angel quickly wrapped her arm behind her shoulders to support her.

"Wh-where am I-I?" Susannah asked, her teeth beginning to chatter.

The angel stopped and stared. "You can see me? Hear me? Feel me?"

Susannah looked up at the woman with beautiful, wavy, golden hair. "Of course. Why not?"

The angel put her arms around Susannah and chafed her shoulders to warm her up. "Because in the human world, you cannot."

"Which means?" Susannah asked attempting to crawl to her feet.

The angel helped her stand and shielded her the best she could with her wings. The angel looked about them, concern growing on her face.

"Which means...you're in my world only...that's impossible," the angel breathed.

Susannah wrapped her arms about herself. Dressed in capris, a short sleeved button down shirt and dressy flip flops, she was in imminent danger of frost bite.

"I have to get you out of here," the angel insisted. "There must be a cave or an overhang somewhere."

"Wh-who are y-you?" Susannah asked leaning against her.

"I'm Levana, you're Guardian Angel, and I've got to find you some shelter."

The angel wore a brightly woven cloak over her main clothes. She quickly unfastened the pin that held it and wrapped the cloak about Susannah's shoulders.

"I'm going to look for shelter," Levana told Susannah. "Just huddle for a moment. I won't be long."

Susannah sank back to the ground and tucked her feet inside the cloak. She desperately tried to remember how she'd gotten there. The image of a lanky, geeky guy at work came to mind. He'd fumbled all over the place when he'd come to fix her computer. She'd smiled at him, and his clumsiness had gone to new levels. Still, there was something wistful about him, and she'd found herself making up excuses to go talk to him in IT.

She had taken him out for coffee to thank him for fixing her computer. He had talked non-stop about quantum computing, and it had been way over her head. But when Susannah mentioned the movie, Inception, that she had watched with her father on her last visit home, Simon had become keenly interested.

Suddenly, he started dropping by her desk every day telling her factoids about the movie and possible science behind it. She hadn't wanted to be mean, but after her boss complained about a drop in her productivity, Susannah had been forced to tell Simon to stop coming by.

She didn't hear from him or see him again for a month and when she glimpsed him in passing, he looked so dejected. Then one afternoon, she'd found a note on her desk when she came back from lunch.

216

"Meet me at the coffee shop," was all it had said, but it was in Simon's handwriting.

When Susannah had arrived, he was already there sitting in a corner. She threaded her way through the tables and patrons, and he held up a cup of coffee in shaking hands. She'd had to grab it quickly before he dropped it. She took a sip.

"Exactly how I like it!" she exclaimed, impressed that he'd remembered.

He'd given her a shy smile. Then he had launched into some idea about double-dreaming and Inception. He knew how it could be done.

"I've got the whole set up," he'd gushed. "It'll be just like the movie. Will you try it will me?"

While Susannah had been fairly certain Inception was a nice fantasy played well by Leonardo Di Caprio and company, Simon was actually asking her home. She couldn't possibly say no.

And that was how she'd ended up hooked up to a machine that looked exactly like the one in the movie.

"Um, you really believe this is safe?" she asked as she sat down in a lounger, and he tipped it back so she'd be comfortable.

"I've tried it a dozen times now on myself. It's perfectly safe," he assured her.

"How long will we be out for?" Susannah asked. "I need to eat a snack in a little while."

Simon turned a dial as he strapped himself in. "Just five minutes. That's all we need to prove it works."

Susannah breathed a sigh of relief. "Ok. As long as I can eat in 30 minutes, I won't go hypoglycemic."

Simon had gone to hit the button, paused and reached out to her. "We have to hold hands," he'd said. "That way we're sure to arrive together."

Susannah had smiled at the obvious ploy and had taken his hand. He hit the button, and the next thing she'd known was snow, and Simon was no where around.

She heard footsteps and peeked out from under the cloak. Levana scrambled back to her side, put her arms around her and helped her up.

"I found a deep overhang," Levana told her. "Not a cave, which would have been ideal, but a lot better than out here."

Susannah gratefully hobbled along with her Guardian. Before long, they spotted the overhang and Susannah ducked under.

"Get way into the back," Levana instructed. "I'm going to block up the entrance with snow for more protection from the wind."

Susannah nodded and crawled all the way in till her back hit the mountain. She rewrapped Levana's cloak around her and shivered. Levana tossed armloads of snow at the entrance, patted it into a wall and went back for more. Finally, satisfied they were sufficiently protected, she slid under the overhang.

"How are you doing?" she asked crawling closer to Susannah.

"I can't feel my toes," the young woman replied.

Levana moved down to her feet and began massaging them.

"How long do you think it will be before Simon's machine takes me back?" Susannah asked.

"He apparently didn't watch the movie," Levana replied.

"What do you mean?" Susannah asked, suddenly worried.

"In the movie there was always someone back on the other side to provide the 'kick'," Levana reminded her.

Dread washed over her. "You mean...I'm stuck here?" Susannah cried.

"Only until help arrives," Levana replied.

"But how long will that take?" Susannah fretted.

"Hours, maybe days," Levana estimated.

"But I'm diabetic," Susannah protested. "I took my insulin thinking I was going to eat. You've got to get me out of here."

Levana froze inside. As a normal human, Susannah's physical health issues followed her into this realm. She was not designed for the angelic realm because she was not a product of a human/angel union. She was designed to walk straight into the Light or linger on an in-between plane if for some reason she could not cross immediately.

"I'll call for help," Levana said going deep within herself. She sent a May Day message to the Great Above hoping someone would hear and come in time.

Simon reluctantly entered Priest Edward's new chapel at the Castle. Priest and Wizard, for they wouldn't allow him to use their names, had figured out how to transfer the Flames and the Vortex from the Desert City Temple to the Castle Chapel. He stared at the Flames.

"Step into them," Aloniel instructed.

"I can't do it."

"You did it before," Aloniel reminded him.

"She was here," Simon replied.

"Ellen didn't step into them for you. You stepped in alone,"

Aloniel said.

"She did something to them," Simon said suspiciously.

"They are older than all of you," Aloniel told him. "No mere Way Shower has the ability to alter them."

"Not even...Ellen?" Simon asked.

"Not even Ellen," Aloniel assured him.

Simon dropped his pack and coat on the floor and slowly approached the Flames. Reaching out, his hand touched the Flames, and he again marveled at his warm, unsinged flesh. Taking a deep breath, he stepped inside and entered the most soothing space he'd ever experienced.

It suddenly dawned on him that he was always holding on tight, keeping thick walls raised between himself and others. He had long ago stopped trying to make friends. He was too awkward; he didn't understand emotions; social rules escaped him. And then he met Susannah.

Her face floated in front of him and he stared at it dreamily. Without warning, gusts of snow swirled around it, obscuring her from view. Simon reached out to bring her back and broke the back wall of the Flames. The image vanished instantly and he pushed his way out of the Flames.

"I saw her!" he cried, shaking.

"Where? Did you see where?" Aloniel asked.

Simon shook his head. "There was too much snow."

"Snow?" Aloniel pressed.

"Yes, like a blizzard," Simon replied. "Wait! Does that mean something?"

Aloniel's eyes glittered. "She must be in the mountains. That's the only place you're going to find a blizzard."

Simon reached for his pack and coat. Aloniel stepped between him and the items blocking his way.

"Dude, I gotta get going," Simon protested.

"Not until you attempt the Vortex. You may not be able to survive without being able to call on it," Aloniel told him.

Simon's shoulders slumped and his head hung forward. "It's too powerful for me," he complained. "I'm just a wimp."

"The act doesn't work here," Aloniel said turning him around. "People let you get away with it in the human realm because if they don't, you become too obnoxious to tolerate. That doesn't work here. I have an endless supply of energy straight from the One of Light. You cannot begin to wear me down." The Archangel folded his arms across his chest for added emphasis.

Simon looked up, saw Aloniel's countenance and slowly turned around. Inside, a tremendous battle raged. No one had ever backed him down before. He took pride in winning every battle of wills and forcing others to cave. He glanced back over his shoulder; Aloniel's face was radiating intense light.

Simon swallowed hard. He'd lost a battle. In stunned silence, he reluctantly shuffled his feet toward the Vortex. He remembered his previous attempt and how hard the stone floor had been when the Vortex had hurled him back.

"I can't do this," he cried.

"Fear won't work either," Aloniel said firmly.

"But it will fling me across the room," Simon whined.

"And I'll be here to pick you up off the floor," Aloniel assured him.

Simon looked back. "I hate you!" he spat.

Aloniel neither blinked nor flinched. "I don't really care," he told Simon. "I was assigned to you for life. I take my marching orders from the One, not from you."

"I really have to do this?" Simon grumbled.

"Yes," Aloniel's voice rang out echoing throughout the Chapel.

"Ok, you don't have to shout," Simon retorted and turned again to face the Vortex.

He closed his eyes, swallowed hard and started to walk forward.

"*Follow your heart, not your head*," he heard Ellen's whispered voice.

"Be the hero," he whispered. "Be the hero."

Suddenly, a surge of energy hit him. "Be the hero!" he cried and lunged forward.

One moment he was outside the wall of wind, the next moment he was inside. Simon stared all about him, first in fear then in awe.

"I did it," he breathed then shouted, "I did it!"

The party of four Way Showers and their Guardians flew through the foothills toward the main pass into the higher mountain ranges.

"Where did you see it?" William yelled.

"The Great Red Dragon was flying up toward the Monastery," Ellen yelled back. "There was cloud cover off to our right, but the clouds parted briefly. That's where I think I saw it."

"Did you stay flying straight?" Avner asked.

"No, the Great Red Dragon banked to the left and the clouds hid

220

the valley again," she replied.

He furrowed his brow pensively. "I have an idea where that may be," he said.

Avner banked to the right and began weaving toward the pass. The others followed him. As they neared the pass, snowflakes began falling in earnest. The higher they went in elevation, the more the wind picked up. The angels were tossed about by the sharp blasts of frigid air.

Avner halted mid-air. "We have to fall back," he said. "Too risky. Our charges will become sick and freeze."

Ellen peered through the blinding storm, her heart lurching. She needed time and this blizzard was slowing her down.

"I agree," Oriel said. "Let's find shelter and keep them safe and warm."

With her spirits sinking, Ellen let Avner fly her away from danger. They returned to the pass, found a fallen tree and made a large lean-to from it. Alexander had a fire started in no time. Ellen sat off by herself staring numbly ahead.

Avner crawled over to her. "I know your concern," he told her, "but the Embodied One is slowing time in your world."

She smiled tensely. "This thing could go on for days," she remarked.

Avner peeked out the air vent. "I think not. It's too early in the season for a prolonged blizzard."

"I hope you're right, Avner," she said.

Ellen ate with the others but said little. She turned in early but lay awake worrying.

"*How much Light can you be?*" she heard the the Embodied One ask.

Ellen frowned. "What do you mean?" she asked.

"*You have need for speed,*" he replied. "*How much of my Light can you be right now?*"

The question seemed odd, yet at the same moment, she got the image of an old-fashioned lantern with a metal windscreen wrapped around her chest. She mentally pulled the windscreen back and more light shone out. With that, she fell asleep.

CHAPTER 30

Ellen felt the ground rocking as she slowly worked her way out of a dream and to a semi-wakeful state. She blinked her eyes open to find Avner shaking her.

"Hm?" she asked groggily.

"Snow stopped," he told her.

Ellen slowly sat up. "How about the wind?"

He shook his head. "Still pretty gusty. Edward will get sick."

"I won't be far behind him," she admitted. "What do we do? We can't stay here."

"We're working on that," Avner replied backing up and crawling outside.

Still groggy, Ellen crept toward the others. Alexander had the fire stoked and William was preparing breakfast. He smiled at her and handed her a tin mug of coffee. Ellen wrapped her hands around it for warmth, inhaled deeply of its aroma and finally took a sip. They ate quickly and were packing up when their Guardians called them out.

When Ellen stepped out into the frosty air, she pulled her coat tighter around her, grateful for its warmth.

"We found some lengths of rope in your packs," Avner said. "We're going to form a chain. One Guardian will advance in front to clear a path and his charge will follow. To make certain we can't get blown off the trail, we'll rope ourselves together for safety."

They all lined up and roped in. Avner fought his urge to go first and protect the others. As Ellen's Guardian, she was his first priority and he stuck to that.

"I'm a better choice," Uriel told him. He pulled his sword from its sheath. "Flame on," he commanded. Instantly, the blade turned to tongues of flame.

"Just be careful not to create mud that could freeze," Avner cautioned. "Someone could take a bad fall."

William came directly behind Uriel, then Chanochiel and Alexander. Avner and Ellen followed them with Oriel and Edward bringing up the rear.

Uriel ended up sheathing his sword and using his great bulk to plow a path through the snow drifts while William trampled the snow hard underfoot. The path was widened and hardened by each team in succession. To Ellen it was such slow progress. Yet, at least they were moving in the right direction.

Inside the Vortex, Simon studied the walls. "Now, how did they make this thing move?" he wondered.

He slipped his hand into his pocket, felt the pendulum and pulled it out. He scoffed inwardly at the magical contrivance, held it by one end and twirled it about. Immediately, the Vortex shook and weaved.

"Whoa!" he exclaimed promptly dropping the pendulum.

Simon got on his hands and knees and began crawling around inside the Vortex. His foot hit something kicking it outside the Vortex. The next thing he knew, the Vortex sent him hurtling through the air into the Chapel. Aloniel caught him before he could hit the floor. He stood Simon on his feet, slapped the pendulum back into his hand and shoved him back inside the Vortex.

Simon tried over and over again to use the pendulum to control the Vortex. Each time he got hurled out, and each time Aloniel sent him right back in. One time Aloniel made him try using the pendulum outside the Vortex. He eventually had to put his hand over Simon's and gift him some sense of control.

Finally, Simon lurched back inside the Vortex, sweaty and exhausted. Again he heard Ellen's voice tell him to "follow your heart, not your head." He shook his head wondering how that was done. Suddenly, Susannah's face popped into his mind.

"Where are you?" he wondered.

As he said that, the Vortex began to spin faster but with an even balance. It slowly lifted off the ground.

"My things!" Simon yelled. "Get my things!"

A moment later, Aloniel hopped inside with Simon's pack and coat. "Where to?"

"I don't know," Simon replied. "It didn't start to move till I wondered where Susannah was."

"Aha!" Aloniel said. "Finally, a thought in that skull about someone other than yourself."

Simon glowered.

"Ask the pendulum to show you where Susannah is," Aloniel instructed.

"Where's Susannah?" Simon asked out loud, feeling foolish.

The fob immediately swung in a specific direction.

"Tell the Vortex to follow the pendulum," Aloniel instructed.

"I don't hear anybody else talk to their pendulums," Simon pouted.

"That's because they figured it out without help and internalized it," Aloniel replied. "Stop stalling."

Simon huffed but dutifully stared at his pendulum. "Vortex follow the pendulum. Pendulum go straight to Susannah."

And with that, they were off. The Vortex passed through the Chapel walls and headed for the mountains. Simon gazed at the land zipping below them.

"Tree," Aloniel mentioned. "Tree!" he said a little louder. "TREE!" he yelled.

Simon snapped his head up in time to say, "Miss the tree."

The Vortex handily skirted the tree while jostling them around and continued on.

"Wow!" Simon breathed. "I can actually do stuff here."

"I think that's what Ellen has been trying to tell you for a while," Aloniel remarked.

Simon ignored him. They were entering the foothills of the mountains and, for the first time in his life, he had a purpose. He had to rescue someone, someone he wished liked him.

In no time, the Vortex reached the pass and headed toward higher elevation. A gust of wind threw them sideways.

"Stabilize this thing!" Aloniel yelled.

"How?" Simon asked desperately.

"I don't know," Aloniel replied, "but if you can't, you need to set it down."

"I've got to find Susannah," Simon insisted.

"It won't do her any good if we get blown out of the sky," Aloniel pointed out.

Simon ignored him and kept thinking about nothing except getting to Susannah. Gusts of wind blew the Vortex sideways. The going was getting rougher.

"Be the hero, be the hero," he chanted.

"Set-this-thing-down," Aloniel insisted.

"I've got to be the hero," Simon replied.

"Even heroes listen to reason," Aloniel retorted.

Suddenly, a gale-force wind caught the Vortex and carried it sideways careening towards the side of a mountain. Simon threw his hands up to shield his face. When impact became obvious, Aloniel grabbed him around the waist, yanked him out of the Vortex and stuttered to the ground. They tumbled end-over-end landing upside down at the base of a tall pine.

Aloniel righted himself and popped his head up out of the snow bank. Looking around, he didn't see Simon, so he felt in the snow till his fingers touched a leg. He grabbed hold and yanked him up and out. He set the sputtering Simon right side up on his feet. Simon tottered about for a moment as he regained his equilibrium then he glanced around.

Miraculously, the pendulum had wound its way around his finger. But the pack and coat were gone.

"I'm through," he sniffed. "I failed."

"You still have the pendulum and two feet," Aloniel said. "Let's go!"

"But I'll freeze," Simon protested.

"Not likely if you keep moving," Aloniel pointed out. "But if you don't find Susannah, she could die."

"Don't you know where she is?" Simon asked.

"Simon, I'm not omniscient. I only have a homing signal for you because you're my Charge," Aloniel told him.

Simon blinked snow out of his eyes and stared in shock. "This is really up to me?"

"Yes, now grab hold of my belt and dowse," Aloniel ordered.

Simon grabbed the back of Aloniel's belt with one hand and sent the pendulum spinning with the other. "We should head towards two o'clock," he yelled.

Without another word, Aloniel hurled himself into the snowbank pushing the drifts aside with his body and arms. Slowly, the pair moved out and crept across the snow-veiled terrain. Periodically, Simon yelled out course corrections as they inched along. From high above where two angels hovered watching, the pair looked like insects amidst the white.

"Shouldn't we help them?" the first angel asked. "Levana called for help."

The second angel shook his head. "The One says to wait."

"They look like they'll never make it," the first angel remarked.

"The One say 'wait and see'," the second angel said.

And so, they hovered watching and waiting.

In under the overhang, Susannah's condition was deteriorating. The snow and wind continued throughout the night with no let up. Levana cradled the young woman in her arms, sang her birth song and wrapped her wings about her. But Susannah was gradually losing it, first becoming irritable and angry. Now, she was just very quiet and in and out of consciousness.

"Please, hear me," Levana whispered. "If help doesn't come soon, Susannah will not make it, and this is not where she dies."

Far into the night the Guardian kept watch. At first light of dawn, the snow stopped swirling and the wind's howl was more hushed. Gaining hope, Levana ripped a strip off her bright cloak. She crawled outside, yanked a snow laden branch off a sapling then tied the strip of cloth to the branch. She planted the branch near the entrance to the overhang and scanned their surroundings.

Finally, certain she'd done all she could, Levana crept back inside the overhang and once more cradled her charge in her arms. She closed her eyes, sang her charge's song and thought of days long ago.

Around noon, Ellen's team had climbed well up into the mountainous terrain. They paused to catch their breath, and she brought out her pendulum.

"Monastery is that way," she announced pointing up to the left.

"That means the Valley's over this way somewhere," William added.

Edward and Alexander were heatedly discussing something just out of earshot. Finally, they seemed to come to some decision and headed back toward the rest of the group.

"Edward thinks we should split up," Alexander said.

Ellen frowned. "What's up?"

Edward shook his head. "I'm worried about that girl. She hasn't been found yet." He let his pendulum swing so Ellen could see.

Ellen pulled hers out and began her own queries.

"Is Susannah safe?"

"Yes," it swung.

"Has she been rescued?"

"No."

"So, she made it to a safe spot out of the weather, but Simon hasn't found her," William surmised.

"Has Simon headed out to find her?" Ellen asked.

The pendulum returned a "Yes."

"Is he close?"

"No."

She frowned. "Is he in trouble?"

"Yes."

"Is he at least trying?" she wondered in exasperation.

The pendulum swung a big "Yes."

"Well, good for him," she remarked.

"Look, we know you aren't going to let us go into the Valley with you," Alexander said.

Ellen grimaced and looked down.

"We think we'd be more useful if we tried to find them and help out," Edward added.

Ellen nodded. "You two are old hands at this. I don't have to worry about you."

"And you've got the best with you," Alexander replied nodding to William, Avner and Uriel.

"Ok, guys. Time to split up," Ellen agreed. "Just be careful."

The brothers each gave her a hug.

"Thanks for not thinking we were ditching you," Edward whispered.

"No way. If I got in trouble, you'd be back here in a heartbeat," Ellen said with confidence.

With that, the brothers hoisted their packs, took a pendulum reading and headed off in a new direction with their Guardians. Ellen was sad to see them go.

"They'll be all right," William said coming up and putting his arm around her shoulders.

She nodded. "I know."

Turning, Ellen trudged back to Avner and Uriel.

"Eat a bite," Avner encouraged. "Then we'll head out again."

Ellen dug into her pack and pulled out nuts and jerky. She ate them, took a swig from her water skin and slung her pack back on her shoulders.

"Wind has died down more," Uriel noticed.

Avner checked out the skies. "Flying would save time."

Ellen was already at his side. "I'm all for it."

"Great," Avner said and scooped her up.

Uriel got ready with William and they took to the air.

"Let's see," Ellen said trying to remember, "the Great Red Dragon flew through there," she said pointing to a crack in the cliff wall.

Following her directions, Uriel and Avner flew through as well.

"I was looking off to the right," she said squinting at the seemingly endless cloud cover, "and for a moment, the clouds parted."

As she watched, thin strips of clouds seemed to pull apart revealing a deep Valley with what looked like hundreds of blank eyes staring back.

"It's there!" she yelled excitedly. "I just saw it!"

Avner banked sharply with Uriel following. Before they knew it, they sailed through the damp, chilly clouds and came out into the clear on the other side. Down below stretched a deep valley with steep sides that were riddled with caves. Avner and Uriel landed on the ridge along the top.

"Is this it?" Ellen asked Avner, holding her breath.

He and William edged forward gazing in the Valley, distant memories returning to each in a flash.

Avner nodded. "This is it."

Ellen crept to the edge. "The Valley of a Thousand Caves," she breathed, but her heart sank. "There are too many," she fretted. "How will I ever find the right one?"

"Wish I could tell you I remember the way," William said.

"Or me," Avner added.

Ellen shook her head. "No, this is my challenge. It's up to me to figure out...though any suggestions are welcome."

"Well, we need to establish business first," Avner said. "You," he said pointing to Uriel and William, "are not going down there. I've already seen what those crystals can do. Not taking any chances."

"Besides which," Ellen added, "if something happens to us, we'll need back up."

William nodded. "Still hard for me to let you go down there."

"I'll be fine," Ellen assured him.

"How do you want to attack it?" Avner asked near at hand.

Ellen scanned the Valley. "Get me down in closer."

Avner obliged by scooping her up, spreading his wings, and gliding in a descending spiral to the Valley floor. From there, Ellen shielded her eyes with her hand and scanned the walls. She let her eyes narrow, tried sifting the light and shadow and eventually gave a heavy sigh.

"Nothing?" Avner asked.

"Nothing," she replied dejectedly.

He walked up to some of the lower cave entrances peering inside each and hoping for clues.

"Follow the bright and shining path of the Creator," Ellen thought. *"What does that really mean?"*

Ellen continued to stare at the Valley as if expecting something to magically appear. Suddenly, she noticed a sparkle at a cave entrance. She jogged over. "Avner, I've found the way."

He hurried to her side. "Where?"

Ellen pointed. "Sparkles! Do you see the sparkles?"

Avner adjusted his vision and sure enough he saw them. "That's it!"

"My bread crumbs," Ellen breathed and dashed into the cave.

CHAPTER 31

Simon was soaked through by daybreak, but they had made decent progress. While the snow had finally stopped falling, the continual wind sliced through his thin clothes like a knife.

"*What I wouldn't give for that coat,*" he thought.

They were trudging through a valley when he suddenly called out, "Stop!"

"What now?" Aloniel asked.

"The pendulum is pointing back. We must have gone right past her," Simon replied.

They turned and scanned their surroundings.

"It says over there," Simon announced watching the pendulum swing and pointing. He looked up and squinted hard. "Just looks like endless snow."

Aloniel was also studying the terrain, and he saw movement on the breeze. He put his hand on Simon's head, turned it slightly and made a subtle adjustment to his vision.

"Hey! What's that flapping?" Simon asked.

"Not a bird," Aloniel replied.

"Got to find her," Simon declared and tried to run.

Instead, he fell face first into a snow drift. Aloniel hauled him out, set him on his feet and shook his head as he studied him.

"For all the smarts you have, some days you make me wonder." Simon glared at him.

"Grab my belt and let's go," Aloniel instructed.

Reluctantly, Simon grasped his belt again, and Aloniel plowed through the snow. They found the strip of cloth attached to the branch.

"They've been here, all right," Aloniel confirmed. "This is a piece of Susannah's Guardian cloak."

"Wonder where they went?" Simon asked turning in a circle and looking up at the trees.

"Well, they didn't fly," Aloniel said. "Maybe they found a cave or an overhang."

Simon frowned.

"On the mountainside," Aloniel added in exasperation turning Simon around. "You do know what a cave is, right?"

"Seen pictures."

Aloniel let his foot slip and kicked a hole in the wall of snow blocking the entrance to the overhang. Simon was still looking up the mountain slopes.

"They would have been blown off the slopes last night," Aloniel remarked. "Might want to look lower."

"Oh, right," Simon said finally shifting his gaze.

Three times he swung his eyes past the hole without seeing it. Aloniel rolled his eyes.

"*Levana,*" he communicated inwardly. "*We're right outside, but he has to be the one to find her. Any chance you can get her to call out?*"

"*She's not doing well,*" Levana's voice rang in his head. "*But I'll see what I can do.*"

Inside the cave, Levana put her hand over Susannah's chest and shared her energy with her. Susannah blinked her eyes open.

"Wh-where am I?" she murmured groggily.

"In the overhang," Levana replied. "Remember the storm?"

Susannah's eyes grew wide and she tried to sit up. Suddenly, a shadow blocked the light coming through the snow wall. As she listened, she heard muffled voices.

"Hey!" she called. "I'm here! I'm in here! Hey! Help! Get me out of here!"

Outside, Simon suddenly heard a noise. "What's that?"

Aloniel squatted down. "Sounds like a voice."

Simon dropped to his knees and listened. "Susannah?"

"Help!"

"Oh my God, she's buried!" Simon shrieked and began frantically

231

clawing at the snow.

Before long he had a hole then more. He kept digging further in till he spotted an arm and a leg.

"Susannah, I'm coming," he yelled pushing his way into the space carved into the mountain."

He finally spotted Susannah, crawled over to her and took her in his arms.

"We're going to get you out of here. I promise," he said rocking her.

"Simon...I'm too weak," Susannah whispered.

"What's wrong?"

"I need to eat...blood sugar's too low," Susannah replied, her eyes closing and her head becoming a heavy weight on his arm.

"Susannah!" he called. "Susannah, don't die."

Tears streamed down his cheeks as he looked up at Aloniel, who peered under the overhang. "What do I do?"

"Didn't the brothers leave you a note?" his Guardian asked.

Simon nodded. "But how do I call them?"

"How did you control the Vortex?" Aloniel pressed.

"Pendulum," he replied quickly feeling around and finding the fob. He closed his eyes and let it swing.

"Priest, Wizard, help!" was all he managed.

Not far away Edward's pendulum started swinging furiously. He grabbed Alexander's arm.

"Look!"

Alexander studied it for a moment. "He's calling us. No time to lose now."

As if on cue, Oriel and Chanochiel scooped them up and took off. Edward focused hard on the pendulum not his queasy stomach. They entered a snow covered valley and kept to the area where valley floor met mountainside.

"There!" Alexander shouted. "Down there!"

Oriel and Chanochiel banked a hard left. They soon landed beside Aloniel and Levana.

"They're in there," Aloniel said pointing.

Alexander took off his pack, pushed it in ahead of him and squeezed under the overhang.

"Wizard, thank God," Simon squeaked.

"Is she dead?" Alexander asked.

232

Simon felt her carotid artery then shook his head no. "Low blood sugar. She's diabetic. She needs to eat."

"Aha!" Alexander exclaimed. "She needs some sugar."

He opened his pack, rummaged around till his hand touched a small bag, then he pulled it out. He untied the ribbon around it. Taking out one soft candy, he held it up.

"Open her mouth," he instructed.

Simon awkwardly pried Susannah's lips and teeth apart.

Alexander bit off the top of the candy, turned it upside down and dumped the contents onto her tongue.

"What is it?" Simon wanted to know.

"Gummies with pure honey centers," Alexander replied. "Gift from Betsy."

The two men sat beside Susannah holding their breath. She swallowed once, began slowly licking the honey off her lips then groggily blinked her eyes open. Alexander dipped his hand into his bag and drew out a second candy.

"Have another," he offered placing it in her hand.

She accepted it gratefully, dropped it into her mouth and leaned back in Simon's arms while she chewed.

"Thank you," she managed to whisper.

"We've got to get you out of here," Alexander insisted. "Visionary and Weaver's house isn't far. You'll be ok there."

"Who are they?" Simon demanded.

"More Way Showers," Alexander replied.

He tied his pack tight and pushed it out topside. Edward grabbed it and set it aside. Next, he took Susannah's head and shoulders.

"Grab her legs," he instructed and Simon put his hands under her thighs.

Together, they shifted her toward the opening and pushed her into fresh air. Hands above ground caught her and pulled her out. Alexander came next then Simon. Edward had already pulled blankets from their packs. Levana was wrapping one around Susannah. Edward draped the other around Simon's shoulders.

"C'mon, the house is just a little further," Alexander urged.

Aloniel shook his head. "There are two angels waiting overhead to assist. Susannah must go straight to the Great Above. Raphael is waiting to receive her."

"Who's he?" Simon asked.

"Archangel in charge of healing," Levana replied. "If anyone can pull her out of this, he can."

She held Susannah close and leapt into the sky. A moment later, those on the ground watched as two larger angels joined her, and a moment later they all sped away.

"I want to go, too," Simon said.

"You need to warm up," Aloniel admonished.

"When my mom was in the hospital, they let me visit but they didn't let me stay," he replied. "The night I went home instead of sneaking back in was the night mom died. I want to stay with Susannah."

Aloniel looked to the others.

Edward and Alexander nodded.

"Let him go," Edward said.

"We'll be up at the Chalet warming up if anyone needs us."

Oriel and Chanochiel picked up their charges and headed off.

"Now? Please?" Simon asked.

"You said please," Aloniel remarked in amazement.

"Please take me to Susannah," Simon begged.

Aloniel took him into his arms, leapt skywards and winked out.

In the Valley of a Thousand Caves, Ellen soon discovered that the entire place was riddled with a complex network of tunnels and chambers. Without the sparkles to guide them, she and Avner would have been utterly lost.

Just when it seemed the sun was sinking lower on the horizon every time they exited a cave, Ellen glanced up and spotted an entrance that looked different from the others. It had a ledge outside, and the sparkles on it lit up the dusky gloaming. She pointed it out to Avner.

"Someone paced on that ledge," Avner remarked studying it.

"It was Daniel," Ellen insisted, her excitement growing. "I can feel it...feel him. Fly me up there."

Without hesitation, Avner wrapped an arm around her and headed for the ledge. They landed just outside the tunnel entrance, and Ellen took her pendulum in hand.

"He **was** here!" she exclaimed, her eyes literally lighting up. "This has to be it. The Crystal Cavern."

A sinking feeling in the pit of his stomach told Avner she was right.

"Look, I meant it when I said don't come in with me," Ellen said firmly.

Unbeknownst to her, he was fighting his own internal battle. Avner turned away and listened as her footsteps receded into the tunnel. He breathed heavily both fearing the den inside and fearing for her safety. He clenched and unclenched his fists.

"I lost one," he moaned. "I can't bear to watch another be destroyed."

Meanwhile, Ellen walked down the tunnel, her eyes lighting the way. As she went, though, the light in the tunnel got brighter and brighter. She came around a corner and faced a well lit opening. Ellen crept forward, peered inside and gasped. The chamber was huge and the walls, ceiling and floors were all covered by crystals of all shapes, sizes and colors. The largest crystals were rounded and peach colored, but no matter. They all glowed.

Ellen staggered and leaned against the wall. "I'll never find him in that place," she worried. "It's so vast and there are so many crystals. How can I possibly find the right one?"

Ellen closed her eyes and dug down deep. Somewhere, she and Daniel still had to have a connection. In her mind's eye, she saw the blue-eyed Minion who had come to her bedroom begging her to free him. This place was his prison. She brought to mind her most recent visit to the battlefield. Ellen could still feel the delicate, brittle skin under her fingertips.

"Not much time left," she thought.

Taking a deep breath, she opened her eyes and stood up. Stepping just inside the Crystal Cavern, she first tried adjusting her eyes to see shadows in the glow. When that didn't work, she looked for sparkles, but everything glittered brightly already.

On a hunch, Ellen took a couple of steps forward and scanned the ground. She noticed broken and crushed crystals on the ground and knelt down to get a closer look.

"Footsteps!" she breathed, her heart pounding.

With hope growing, she slowly pressed forward constantly watching for more broken crystals. Deep into the cavern, she suddenly found a spot that looked like someone had sat down hard. Lifting her eyes, Ellen scanned the nearby area. *Maybe he can hear me,* she thought.

"Daniel!" she called. "Daniel! Are you in here? Can you hear me? Help me find you!"

Inside his crystal prison where he had huddled on the floor to conserve energy, Daniel thought he heard a noise, like the crunch of footsteps on brittle crystal. He picked up his head listening ever more carefully. The crunching sound was growing louder and drawing closer.

Suddenly, he heard someone yell. He was certain of it. Daniel unwound himself, got up on his knees and waited, eyes closed, willing himself to hear.

"There!" He heard it again. There were definitely words, but the crystal distorted them. He pushed to his feet and looked up through the crystal.

"*Someone is there*," he thought, his heart pounding.

"Help! Let me out!" he yelled at the top of his lungs.

He stopped and listened.

"*Maybe, if it's Ellen, I can connect with her*," he hoped.

Dropping deep into his heart space, he sought that place that could connect with her. "*Ellen!*" he called via their link. "*Hear me!*"

In the cavern, Ellen suddenly felt the hairs at the nape of her neck prickle. She spun around certain that someone was watching her. Seeing no one, she suddenly stared at the orbed peach crystals directly before her. The prickly sensation intensified.

Crouching down, she studied each crystal carefully. Ellen had just begun shaking her head in disappointment when, suddenly, she spotted movement. Ellen got closer and looked harder. All of a suddenly, she raised her hand to her mouth as tears squeezed out the corners of her eyes.

"Daniel," she whispered. Then as adrenalin shot through her, "Daniel! I'll get you out!"

Ellen scrambled back to her feet and started to unshutter the Light when a sudden flurry of wings and a thud behind her made her jump.

"No!" came a loud roar.

She turned in time to see battle Daniel lunge for her. Ellen leapt out of the way only now, he stood between her and the crystal that imprisoned his light.

CHAPTER 32

Aloniel took Simon straight to Raphael's Healing Facility. As soon as they set down, Simon was in motion.

"Where's Susannah?" he demanded of everyone he passed.

Two large healers exited a room. Simon ran into them and struggled when they tried to detain him.

"Where is she?" Where's Susannah?" he cried hoarsely.

Suddenly, a tall Archangel wearing an emerald green tunic over brown pants stood beside him. Simon felt a hand on his back then he sank limply forward into the angels' arms.

"Take him next door," Raphael, the angel in green, instructed.

The two angels carried Simon away and lay him in a bed.

Moments later, he blinked his eyes open and frantically searched the room. "Susannah!" he yelled.

Raphael entered. "Be still, Simon," he commanded.

"But...."

"These are Halls of Healing. Peace will prevail," Raphael told him.

"But Susannah," Simon persisted, albeit quietly. "Please, sir. Where is she?"

Raphael raised his hand toward the far wall. Like turning up a dimmer switch, the wall gradually became transparent.

Simon struggled to sit up. Spotting her lying on the sheets in a similar bed, he swallowed hard. "Is she...will she be all right?"

Raphael sat on a chair beside his bed and gently pushed Simon back against the pillow. "Her well being is determined by how quickly we get you fit enough to cross the Bridge," the healer said passing his hand over Simon's body.

Instantly, a pair of healers brought in a warming lamp. Another pulled the sheets back and slathered a warming gel on Simon's feet. He felt himself slipping and fought to stay awake.

"Susannah will need emergency services as soon as you come to," Raphael's voice said as if from far away. Something squishy was placed in his hand. "Go quickly, now."

With a start, Simon opened his eyes and gazed around his apartment. The line from his Inception machine was still on his wrist. He tore it off, looked over at the lounger and scrambled to his feet.

"Susannah!" he called, desperately ripping the line off her as well. "Susannah, wake up!"

Suddenly, he looked down at his hand to see one of Alexander's gummies in his palm. He stared at it long and hard before moving into action. Simon tipped back Susannah's head, opened her mouth, bit the top off the candy and poured its contents into her mouth. He waited but she wasn't coming around.

Terrified, he ran to the kitchen, frantically fumbled through take out order bags, found some packets of maple syrup and duck sauce and hurried back to her side. He bit them open and poured them into her mouth. When she still didn't respond, he squeezed his eyes tightly closed, pulled at his hair and rocked.

"C'mon," he urged. "C'mon."

Suddenly, she started coughing and he raced to sit her up. She blinked her eyes open but closed them quickly.

Grabbing his cell phone, Simon dialed 911. While he spoke to the dispatcher, he quickly gathered up his Inception machine, took it out to the porch and smashed it, then bagged up any tubes or vials. By the time the EMT's arrived, it was merely the scene of a diabetic who hadn't eaten on time.

With fear clutching his heart, Simon watched the ambulance pull away. He went back inside the house, sat in his mother's old chair and rocked.

A week later, there was a knock at the door. Simon left his computer to answer it.

"You Simon?" a graying, middle-aged man asked.

"Y-yes."

"I'm Susannah's father," the man said. "I'm taking her home. Any man who would keep a diabetic from eating so he could watch a movie is self-centered and dangerous...to-my-daughter. You stay away from her. Do you hear me?" the man yelled in Simon's face.

Simon nodded, backed up and started to shut the door. Through the slit, he watched the older man get into an older model Oldsmobile. In the passenger seat, he spotted Susannah.

Simon closed the door all the way, sat down and let tears flow down his cheeks. "She's ok," he whispered.

After an hour or so, he went to a drawer in the kitchen, pulled out a key, headed for a metal filing cabinet in the dining room and inserted the key into the top drawer. With trembling hands, he reached in, grabbed a two inch thick file, pulled it out and took it to the dining room table. He carefully opened it and read the top page of the file.

"Simon Littlefield
Age 10
Diagnosis: DSM-IV 299.80   Asperger's Syndrome

Simon has an IQ of 185 per WISC and is especially talented in computers and physics. However, he has no sense of the emotional life of those around him. He is manipulative and hard to handle (note: possible ODD).

Father died of a heart attack two years ago when trying to restrain Simon during an aggressive outburst.

Mother is alive but in poor health. She does not have the physical strength to adequately manage Simon.

Suggested placing Simon in a home for children with autism spectrum disorders. Mother refused and I won't push. After so recently losing her husband, losing her son could worsen her health."

Simon dropped the file, closed his eyes and shook as tears streamed down his face. "I killed them," he whispered. "I'm the reason they're dead."

"*You're the reason your mother lived another 14 years*," Aloniel's voice resounded in his head.

"How?" Simon asked aloud. "How?"

"*You gave her purpose*," Aloniel responded. "*You were what she got up for every day*."

"Then why-did-she-die?" Simon raged, his face reddening.

"*Simon, it was her time. She died because it was her time,*" Aloniel replied. "*Nothing more and nothing less.*"

Simon took in great gulps of air. "Then I didn't kill her?"

"*No, Simon,*" Aloniel assured him. "*You didn't kill her.*"

"But...I nearly killed Susannah," Simon said.

"No, Simon," Aloniel replied. "You actually saved Susannah's life."

Simon quieted as he thought about this. "I didn't know what she meant by needing to eat," he said at last.

"*And she hadn't been careful herself about checking her blood sugar level and taking her insulin,*" Aloniel confided. "*Here's a secret. Mum's the word.*"

Simon nodded.

"*This brush with death is what finally makes her be consistent in taking care of her diabetes. You've saved Susannah's future, Simon,*" Aloniel told him.

Simon calmed and centered. Finally, he looked at the doctor's name and number on the file. He went to his computer, looked him up, found an address and grabbed his keys. An hour later, he knocked on the door of a Colonial brick home, the thick file tucked under his arm.

An elderly gentleman answered.

"Dr. Gerard?" Simon asked.

"Yes, but I'm retired now," the elder man said.

"You diagnosed me with Aspergers," Simon said shoving the file toward him. "I wasn't ready to play nice with others then, but I want to learn the rules now. Please," he added quietly.

The elderly man studied the young man's ashen face. "You're serious about this?"

"Yes, sir. I want to learn how to be human," Simon told him emphatically.

Dr. Gerard backed up and ushered Simon inside. The door closed on a beautiful sunny day.

One day as Susannah was returning from a coffee break, she spotted a note with distinctive handwriting on her desk. She picked it up ready to toss it in the trash until she caught one word, "Please." Susannah opened it and read the note. Nervously, she put it in her purse and tried to forget about it for the rest of the day.

When five o'clock came, she powered down her computer, locked her desk and grabbed her purse. The note fell to the floor. She picked it up, stuffed it inside and hurried from the building.

In her head, she was directing her feet towards her car. But the next thing she knew, she was staring at the sign for the coffee shop. Shaking her head, Susannah pushed open the door and stepped inside. There, in the back corner, sat Simon. He looked up, tried to smile and held up a coffee.

Smiling in spite of herself, Susannah threaded her way back to the table and sat down. She took the coffee Simon offered, took a sip and relaxed.

"Just the way I like it," she said.

"Thank you for coming," Simon told her. "I-I want to apologize for that stupid experiment. I nearly got you killed."

Susannah snorted and shook her head. "It wasn't you, Simon," she assured him. "I wasn't paying attention to my blood sugars. It wasn't the first time something like that happened."

"No?" Simon asked, his eyebrows rising in surprise.

"*Told ya*," Aloniel whispered in his ear.

"Just the scariest," she admitted. "It's changed how I deal with my diabetes now. I monitor myself like I should."

"Oh. Good," Simon said. "So, I was wondering...if...maybe you'd go out with me."

"Like on a date?" Susannah asked.

Simon nodded. "I was thinking dinner. I-I like this place...I mean, restaurant of your choice."

Susannah studied him and broke out into a smile. "I'd like that. When?"

"Now. We're both here, we've finished work for the day. It's time to eat," Simon rattled off mechanically.

Susannah smiled broadly. "It's a deal."

They rose together and walked out the door heading down the street. Simon bit his tongue hard and listened while Susannah talked about her life.

In the Crystal Cavern, Ellen stared hard at the angel blocking her way.

"Daniel, step aside," she insisted.

"No!" he roared.

"You sound like the Hulk," she quipped wondering what to do.

He growled.

"Definitely the Hulk," Ellen said.

As she studied him, she noticed thin segments of light shining in jagged strips across his body. She narrowed her eyes slowly realizing they were cracks letting out what precious Light he had managed to store.

"Daniel," Ellen said quietly while trying to move into a better position. "You have to let me help you."

He kept side-stepping always making sure to block her. "No!"

"Your light is leaking," Ellen continued, trying to find a way to dodge past him. "You haven't much time left. Let me help you."

He shook his head. "No!"

"Daniel, please," she begged. "Don't do this to me. Don't make me watch you fall."

He wavered for a moment. In that split second, they heard the quick beat of wings and Avner swept Daniel off his feet. Daniel wrestled with the elder angel, desperately trying to break free.

"Go!" Avner grunted. "Hurry!"

Ellen scrambled over to the crystal holding Daniel's light. She dropped down, saw the light shield opening and prepared to grasp the Crystal.

"*Don't be light*," came a familiar voice. "*Be me!*"

Suddenly, Ellen was snapped back to the Throne Room, back to the moment when she had dissolved into the Light and she and the One became one. In the Cavern, the Light grew and grew and grew. Avner watched her disappear into the Light, not even a filament of her pattern remaining.

The crystal in which Daniel's light was held prisoner began to hum, the pitch increasing up the octaves till it was ear splitting. Inside the crystal, Daniel covered his ears with his hands and writhed on the ground. Outside in the cavern, other crystals had picked up the resonance and were also humming.

Avner couldn't stand it anymore. He let go of Battle Daniel and covered his ears. Battle Daniel watched the glow increase to white hot. Suddenly, he screamed "No!" and hurtled forward.

Avner watched as if in slow motion. First, Daniel's crystal broke then all the others capable of harvesting light shattered. As Battle Daniel flew straight at Ellen, his fragile skin could no longer hold and the gaps letting out the light grew bigger. Simultaneously, Daniel's light stretched up from the crystal and moved toward her. Both parts of Daniel converged within her light and were gone.

Avner grabbed the hair on the crown of his head in horror. "*Gone!*" he thought. "No! No! Not gone!" he roared.

242

Yet, even as he grieved, hope flickered. In the midst of the white hot light, he saw wisps of shadows, strips of dark against the Light. They separated into two ovals and pulled away from each other. As they did, form took shape before his very eyes. He saw the smaller and the taller.

"Ellen," Avner whispered. "Pull out of it, Ellen."

He stared, willing her to leave the Light. Very slowly, the smaller image began to back away. It was imperceptible at first, but soon Avner became confident of its progress.

"Come on, Ellen," he urged. "You can do this."

Without warning, he heard a shout and saw a familiar figure run toward the white hot Light. Before Avner could stop him, William charged into the Light, grabbed the smaller form and hauled it out backwards. He and Ellen fell back against the floor, whole and unharmed.

They all watched as the Light began to swirl as if being sucked into the taller form like water down a drain. As it did, the form grew denser, more solid. Without warning, the light blinked out and Daniel stood on wobbly legs. Ellen dashed forward catching him before he tumbled and slowly lowering him to the ground.

"You're back," she whispered. "You're finally back."

But Daniel looked at her with eyes that neither comprehended her speech nor recognized her.

"Daniel?" she asked frowning. "Daniel?"

He stared straight ahead.

She looked up to Avner. "Did your brother act like this when he came back?"

Avner knelt beside her on one knee and studied Daniel. "No. He knew us, was grateful to be back."

Ellen swallowed hard. "Does this mean not all of him came back?

Avner stood. "To Raphael...immediately."

"I'll stay near the entrance to the cave," William said. "Just take him to the healers."

Uriel scooped up Ellen and Avner cradled Daniel. "For your sake and the sake of my daughter's heart, Raphael had better be able to make you whole," he said and spiraled up and out.

CHAPTER 33

Ellen came out in the Healing Center with Uriel, who immediately left and returned with William. Avner was already there laying Daniel on the very bed he had once occupied. Raphael was at the bedside in an instant. Oriel and Chanochiel appeared with the brothers.

While the others clustered in the hall around the doorway, Ellen and Oriel entered and went straight to Daniel's bedside. She broke away from Oriel, knelt beside the bed and took Daniel's hand.

"What's wrong with him?" Ellen asked looking to Raphael.

The Healing angel slowly and methodically inspected every inch of Daniel's body. Finally, he turned to her.

"His form is solid and thorough," he stated, "and his Light is very strong."

"Then why doesn't he know me?" Ellen pressed.

"Or any of us?" Oriel added.

"It would seem," Raphael began, choosing his words carefully, "that some of his Light was lost."

Ellen's veins turned to ice. "Wh-what do you mean?"

Raphael looked to Ellen and Oriel. "His memories did not return with him. He is...a blank slate."

Ellen turned to Oriel whose face was a grimace of grief. "What does that mean, Oriel? What does that mean for him?"

His shoulders heaved for a moment before he mastered himself. "We'll have to take him to the Embodied One," Oriel replied, "but...."

"But what?" Ellen asked, afraid she already knew.

Oriel shook his head. "He will most likely return to the Light from whence he came."

Ellen shook her head in disbelief. "No," she whispered. "It can't be! I freed his light. It can't be!"

Avner suddenly put his hand on her back as he knelt beside her. "His form had gaping cracks by the time he entered the Light," he told her quietly.

She glanced over her shoulder at him, then looked to Oriel and up at Raphael.

"*All the memories we made together*," she thought. "*They're all lost.*"

"I'll take him to the Throne Room," Oriel said.

"Wait!" Ellen cried.

"I cannot, Ellen," Oriel said gently. "I must take him."

"I'm coming, too, then," she declared.

"That is unprecedented," Raphael huffed.

Ellen pushed herself to her feet, tears trickling down her cheeks. "Isn't that what I'm best known for?" she declared bravely.

Avner patted her back. "I'll take you."

Ellen stepped back to let Oriel near Daniel's side. With uncharacteristic tenderness, he gathered up his younger brother and hugged him to himself. Avner went to gather up Ellen when Hope and Abiriel appeared in the room. Abiriel, Daniel and Oriel's youngest brother, looked at the empty bed, his face pale.

"I'm sorry," Ellen said. "Oriel just took him and I'm going, too."

Hope leaned in close and whispered in her mother's ear. "Not all memories reside in the Light. Some are held in places."

Ellen frowned but had no time to question. Avner whisked her straight to the Throne Room faster than he'd ever flown before. They appeared as Oriel was laying Daniel before the One.

"*Not in Light but in places*," Ellen thought as she raced toward the Throne. All of a sudden, it hit her and she knew the answer.

"Please," she called. "Please wait!"

The Light on the Throne had already begun to expand its glow, and Oriel was backing away. Instead, Ellen flung herself forward and threw her body over Daniel's. The Light halted, retreated and the Embodied One hurried down the steps.

"What are you doing?" he demanded. "Do not stand in the way of this process."

Ellen closed her eyes and shook her head. "His memories aren't gone," she declared in a tremulous voice. "I can find them."

"What do you mean?" the Embodied One asked in a low voice.

"Not all memories are Light," she said quoting Hope. "Sometimes places hold memories. If I can just find the places where those memories are stored, I can help him."

The Embodied One was silent for a while as he considered her words. "And where would you seek those memories?" he asked.

Ellen looked up. "Our home. The one you created for us."

The Embodied One contemplated the possibility. "What do you propose?" he asked at last.

"Let me take him to our home," she requested. "Let me find his memories. If I fail, we'll return and he can rejoin the Light. Just...please... give me the chance to try."

The Embodied One's face softened. "Very well. But when you hear me call you back, you must come."

Ellen nodded.

The Embodied One bent over Daniel, took his hand and raised him up.

"If it be possible, Ellen," he said opening the silver door, "restore him."

Ellen took Daniel's hand and led him to the door. "Thank you," she said glancing back over her shoulder.

As she pushed through the door with Daniel, her Choice Board came to mind. *"Restore him,"* she thought. *"That's on my Choice Board and there are Wild Cards."*

Her heart beat faster as hope's flame rekindled in her heart. They stepped out onto the lane above their home and started walking. Once they turned onto the dirt road that ran past it, Ellen almost stepped onto their walk but stopped.

"Last time we were here, he had a purpose," she thought. *"We weren't just reminiscing."*

Ellen looked up at him, put her arm around his waist and guided him further down the dirt road. Where the forest trail turned off, she led him onto the narrow track.

"Remember when we were here before?" she asked hoping to spark some recollection. "You took me on this lovely hike through the woods."

They kept going until she spotted the bridge, and Ellen hurried forward. Scraps of bread sat ready for her, and she started tossing them to the Koi in the water below. She tried to get Daniel to cast some bread, but he stumbled backwards, his elbow hitting the top of the rail hard. Ellen heard a pop and turned to see Daniel's eyes flutter.

"What just happened here?" she wondered checking the area

around him.

Daniel ignored her for the Koi, which he was now thoroughly engaged in. Ellen frowned pensively as she watched him.

"*Something really important just happened here*," she mused.

Wanting to move on, she pulled him off the bridge and along the path till they wound their way up to the farmer's fence. She looked very carefully till she found the exact place they had stood before. Her favorite black-and-white spotted cow ambled toward them. Ellen picked some tall grass and handed it to Daniel. He stumbled as he stretched forward. Again, she heard a pop and looked around. No matter, he was now actively engaged in feeding and petting the cow.

"He left something behind," she breathed, her excitement growing. "He may not know me, but he now remembers those Koi and that cow."

With growing hope, Ellen dragged Daniel away from the farm and pointed him in the direction of the pond. When they got near the fallen tree, she helped him climb onto it and awkwardly followed. They inched out on the trunk as it bobbed in the water until they reached the very end.

"Do you member looking at what you are in all those dimensions?" she asked.

Daniel stared at the water.

"Maybe if we get closer," Ellen suggested kneeling.

He got down, too, and kept his hands on his knees. Ellen went to drape her hand in the water and hit something smooth and springy. Surprised, she looked over the log and spotted a clear bubble with images in it.

"*Images!*" she thought excitedly. "*Memories!*"

She took Daniel's hand, wrestling with him for a moment, and finally convinced him to reach his hand down towards the water. It hit the bubble and Ellen heard a pop. Daniel blinked then stared at himself in the pond's surface as thousands of images flashed past at lightning speed.

When he stood up again, his body had more tone and he walked with greater confidence. Ellen led him off the log and headed for the orchard. She looked around with a perplexed frown wondering where he might have hidden memories then suddenly remembered the apples he'd picked but they never ate. Ellen looked up into the tree and spotted a bubble.

"Daniel," she called. "Would you pick me an apple? The one right up there," she instructed pointing.

Though he moved like an automaton, it was clear he understood her request. He rigidly moved his arm, reached up and knocked into the bubble that was located just before Ellen's desired apple. His eyelids fluttered quickly as images and emotions flooded him. He retrieved his hand, turned toward Ellen and studied her, recognition growing on his face.

"Daniel? Do you know me?" she asked taking his hand.

He nodded very slowly.

Elated, she tugged him forward. "I bet you left some memories at the house," she said trying to hurry him up the road.

They reached the slate house, she led him inside then stood looking around. *"Not down here,"* she thought shaking her head.

Ellen quickly maneuvered him to the staircase and helped him up. They stopped by the bed. She tilted her head sideways studying his sword and chest shield.

"I bet you'd be more comfortable right now with those off," she murmured.

She reached out, unbuckled his sword belt and eased it to the floor then looked at his shield. Ellen put her hands on the sides of the shield but couldn't figure out how to remove it.

"What do you do to pop this thing off?" she asked him.

The words seemed to register with him but it took him a few moments before he suddenly moved muscles in his chest. The shield came off into Ellen's hands and she nearly dropped it.

"Whoa! That thing is heavy!" she exclaimed lowering it to the floor and sliding it out of the way.

Glancing around, Ellen spotted the bathroom and the soaking tub inside. *"Yes,"* she thought. *"He had to leave something there."*

She led him into the bathroom towards the tub. She spotted a sparkle inside it and hurried forward. Dropping to her knees beside the tub, she turned back and held out her hand for him. His steps were stiff but he reached her side and dropped heavily to his knees. He spotted the large bubble inside the tub and stretched his arm toward it. It burst in an explosion of light and baby's laughter. A tear slid from the corner of his eye. He turned to look at Ellen.

"Our daughter, Hope...that baby...she gave me the clues to your memory," she told him.

Daniel tried to smile.

She cupped his cheek in her hand and smoothed away the tear with her thumb. Reaching up, Ellen kissed his cheek then got to her feet and pulled him up beside her. She drew him back out into the bedroom but, though she scanned the bed, she found no signs of a bubble. So, Ellen led

248

him out onto the balcony. Sure enough, over by the rails set for wings, there was a bubble. Daniel saw it and headed over unbidden. He touched the bubble, felt a zap of lightning streak through him and shuddered, his wings trembling.

He turned and Ellen swallowed hard. His interest was quite obvious and made her mouth go quite dry. She took Daniel's hand and led him back inside. As they approached the bed, she stopped and looked up at him. He seemed to be waiting, expectantly.

"You can understand me, right?" Ellen asked.

Daniel nodded.

"But you can't speak yet?"

He slowly shook his head .

"Where could that part of your memory be hidden?" she wondered.

"*Inside,*" his voice said in her mind.

She studied his face pensively. Robotically, he attempted to kiss her and nearly knocked her over. A light dawned in Ellen's eyes.

"You stored something...in me?" she asked.

He started breathing harder though he didn't move.

Ellen swallowed hard and thought back to the last time they were there. Daniel had insisted on making love to her; sweet, gentle, passionate love. Suddenly, her eyes grew large.

"*He had me stroke his wings!*" she thought.

Wings amongst his kind were never touched except between the pairs who were committed to producing children. It had been by touching his wings that he had been able to impregnate her.

"*But I didn't get pregnant,*" Ellen thought, "*because I can't in this dimension any more, and he didn't shift to another dimension. What was he doing?*"

With a tingle dancing up her spine, Ellen moved closer to him. "*I have to find out.*"

She kissed his chest and took his hands placing them on her hips. Looking up into his eyes, Ellen slowly unbuttoned her blouse shrugging it off when the last button popped.   She undid her bra and dropped it to the floor.

"This is what you want?" she asked in a whisper. "This is what you need?"

Daniel's lips parted though he made no sound.

Ellen slipped her arms around him pressing her breasts against his abdomen. He slid his arms around her, awkwardly holding her. His hard length pulsed against her tummy, and she was instantly wet.

She pulled back enough to run her tongue over his chest and swirl it around his nipples. Daniel gasped. Ellen pushed away, unbuckled his belt, undid his pants and pushed them down. She wet her bottom lip with her tongue at the sight of his erection.

Getting Daniel's boots off was a struggle, but as soon as she'd tossed them aside, she shed her pants and shoes, backed onto the bed, took his hand and pulled him after her. Daniel's motions were clumsy but his intent was clear. Once she lay back, he dropped over top of her.

Ellen took his length in her hand, rubbed it then positioned him between her legs. He shook with the effort to get his body to obey his desires. Ellen grasped his hips and pulled him into her. He slowly pulled out, and she helped him enter again.

Daniel began to thrust in earnest. It was all Ellen could do not to go wild. She had dreamed of this moment for months now. All she wanted was to have him back.

He grunted with effort rasping out, "Ellen."

"Daniel! You said my name!" she exclaimed, elated.

He panted with the struggle. "Wings," he exhaled.

She blinked. "Wings?"

Then it hit her; his wings were the key. Gently, she reached up and caressed the swan soft feathers. They had always drawn and intrigued her.

"More," he insisted, thrusting harder.

She gasped at the heat and friction and grasped the tops of his wings. With long, firm strokes she massaged his wings and his ardor grew.

Without warning, Ellen felt a strange sensation in her chest. Prickles and heat began pulsing over her heart.

"*I'm not having a heart attack, am I?*" she worried.

But the sensation eased downward into her abdomen. Suddenly, a rounded bump appeared under the surface of her skin and began to move around her abdomen. Ellen's eyes widened in terror.

"Daniel, what's happening?"

He held her arms down, continued thrusting until her body shuddered. At that moment, he took a huge breath and the object in her stomach was sucked out of her and into him.

Ellen lay on her back hardly daring to believe what she'd just felt. When she looked up, Daniel was panting hard with his head down, his long hair draped over her chest. After a moment, he started breathing more normally, and when he raised his head, his eyes sparkled.

She put her hands on either side of his face. "Daniel?"

He leaned forward sampling her lips and wrapping his arms around her. "I'm home."

Ellen started to cry. She hugged him close, tears of joy spilling down her cheeks and wetting the pillows.

"Oh, God, Daniel. You had me so worried," she murmured.

He pressed his cheek against hers mingling their tears. "I know. I am sorry."

"What just happened?" she asked.

He pushed up to look in her eyes. "When we were here before, I jettisoned my angelic spark into you. I knew you would keep it safe for me."

Ellen's eyes widened and she gave a soft gasp.

"And now, you have just returned it," Daniel told her.

"So...you're back to normal?" she asked barely daring to breathe. "Back to being you?"

He nodded and sampled her lips. As if to prove it, his erection pulsed inside her. "Let me show you just how much," Daniel whispered bending down and tasting the sweetness of her breasts and nipples.

Ellen grasped the sheets and arched her back. "I want all the proof you can give me."

Daniel chuckled low in his throat. "My pleasure."

With that, he surrounded her with his arms, lifted her hips off the bed and ground against her till she begged; begged for him, for his manhood deep inside her, for her release. And he gave it to her over and over again.

CHAPTER 34

Daniel and Ellen curled around each other and slept soundly. When a rooster crowed nearby, Ellen opened her eyes. She was surprised to see one of the farmer's birds on their balcony rail. Daniel lifted his head to see as it crowed again.

She sat up and watched as he slid from the bed and headed for the balcony door. Was it her imagination, or had he bulked up even more?

"*Nice view*," she thought catching her bottom lip with her teeth as she watched his taut bottom disappear out the door.

A minute later there was a squawk and the flap of wings, and their early morning alarm clock took off.

"You didn't hurt him, did you?" Ellen asked slipping into a bathrobe as she headed his way.

Daniel gazed at the rising sun and breathed deeply. "I didn't hurt him...just sent him home where he would be more appreciated."

Ellen ducked under a wing and leaned against his side with her arms around him. He slipped an arm around her shoulders.

"Every day on the battlefield, I thought of you," he said quietly.

"I missed you, too, but...why didn't the part of you on the battlefield want me to find you?"

Daniel pulled her close. "I had Avner read the Book of Lore. I read what happened to his first Way Shower child."

"William," she told him.

He glanced down at her. "He was lost in the attempt to restore Avner's brother."

"He was found...by me...and the Green Dragon," Ellen informed him.

"And he's all right?" Daniel asked.

"You can meet him when we return and see for yourself," Ellen replied.

"I was so afraid for you if you tried," he admitted.

She chuckled. "I know. You shoved me down on the battlefield."

His eyes widened in horror. "Ellen, I'm so sorry."

She shook her head. "You were communicating and gave me the key to where you were by warning me away from it."

"Still, Ellen, I would never hurt you," he protested.

She hugged him. "If you had wanted to hurt me, more than just my pride would have been bruised. You were as 'gentle' as you were able to be."

"I'm glad to know I showed some restraint," he said.

Ellen caught the glint of sun off the pond.

"Do you remember coming to our rescue?" she asked.

He frowned. "When?"

"When I insisted Avner take me to the battlefield so I could talk to you. We were swarmed by Minions and even with Oriel's help, we were going under fast," she told him.

"What did I do?" Daniel wanted to know, his brow knit pensively.

"You and Michael came streaking across the sky like two stars. You two stood by us and let out some shock wave that flattened half the Minions," Ellen explained. "The rest fled."

Daniel was quiet for a while. "There were so many battles," he breathed. "They've become a blur."

"Why?" Ellen asked.

"Why did I fight?" he asked.

She nodded.

"Oriel gave me the idea," he confessed. "He was the only person who knew my plans, and I swore him to secrecy."

"Did it have something to do with the light?" Ellen asked.

Daniel nodded. "Without my own light, I would have crumpled and returned to the One. But as long as I was channeling the Light, I had a chance."

"For?"

He smiled down at her and kissed her forehead. "For you to find my light and reunite me with it."

Ellen shook her head. "You're too complex," she chuckled. "You wanted me to find your light and stay away from it at the same time."

He put his hand under her chin and tilted her face up toward him. "You never like to be told no."

"That was all on purpose?" she cried.

Daniel shook his head and kissed her. "Not intentionally. It just worked out well."

He gave her another kiss and let her go.

"Trying your wings?" she asked as he gave them a couple of test flaps.

In response, Daniel leapt into the air and took off. Ellen watched him soar through the air and bank around the pond. He turned back toward the house, swooped in low and literally plucked Ellen off the porch.

"Whoa!" she yelled laughing.

The smile on his face was all she needed to see. Joy radiated from his being.

She took a deep breath and let it out. *"Time to go back."*

Daniel banked around toward the house again, brought himself up and neatly landed on the porch. They entered the bedroom and went about the business of getting dressed.

"You ready?" Ellen asked. "The Embodied One hasn't called yet."

"Yes," Daniel said strapping on his sword and lifting his chest shield into place. "I am ready."

He took her in his arms, opened the silver door and flew through. They came out in the formal gardens in front of the Great Halls and found Oriel, Abiriel and their parents waiting quietly. When they spotted him, they hurried over for a joyful reunion.

"Brother, I really thought I'd seen the last of you," Oriel said hugging him.

"Sorry, guess I gave a scare all the way around," Daniel apologized.

He turned to his parents hugging them then went to Abiriel, who was still wide-eyed over recent events. Daniel put his hand on his younger brother's shoulder and held his gaze.

"Not every Guardian goes through the things I have," Daniel told him. "But if you do, do not give fear place."

Abiriel nodded and hugged him.

The party made their way toward the Throne Room.

"He will still need to be tested," Zelig said quietly.

Ellen glanced back at him. "What tests?"

"You will see shortly," Zelig replied.

Butterflies began a tap dance in her stomach as they ascended the stairs and went inside. Down near the Light, Raphael, Michael and Mentor were already waiting with the Embodied One.

Ellen frowned.

When they reached the front, Daniel knelt before the Embodied One. The Embodied One placed his hand on Daniel's head searching him.

"Rise."

Daniel stood with his head bowed.

"You feel whole to me, Daniel," the Embodied One said. "How do you feel?"

"Myself again, Sire," Daniel replied.

The Embodied One turned his head toward Ellen and spoke so that only she heard, "*Well done.*"

To Daniel he said, "I will not give my final word until you have been tested."

Ellen frowned again but Daniel nodded his acceptance.

"Raphael will re-examine you for physical soundness and fullness of Light," the Embodied One continued. "Michael will test your battle and flight skills, and Mentor will determine your continued fitness as a Guardian."

Daniel looked sideways towards Ellen and shot her a look of encouragement.

"Until you have been deemed fit in these three areas, Avner will continue to guard Ellen," the Embodied One added.

Avner appeared in the Throne Room beside her.

"Come," said Raphael. "I am confident of my assessment."

Daniel turned, gave Ellen one last look then disappeared with Raphael. The others had already headed for the door, but Ellen remained in place.

"This is necessary," the Embodied One said quietly.

She nodded. "If he were in our military or secret service and had been severely injured, his fitness would be tested before he could return to active duty."

"Then you understand," the Embodied One said.

"I get it," Ellen replied. "I just don't like it."

Avner put his arm around her shoulders and led her outside. Daniel's family was still waiting.

"It is no sorrow to return to the Light," Zelig said as she approached his father and mother.

His mother, Aviva, gave her partner a frown of reprimand, moved forward and took Ellen's hand. "Even so, we are grateful that you restored his light and have returned him to us."

Ellen tried to smile. "I guess I'd feel better if he didn't have these tests to go through."

"He'll pass," Oriel stated firmly.

"I hope so," she sighed.

"Ellen," he said commandingly, and she looked up at him in response. "Since the Minion's Lair, I've learned more about Daniel than I ever thought possible. I know his mind. I know his feel. He-will-make-it," he stated emphatically.

Ellen smiled and gave Oriel a hug. "Thanks. I'll borrow your confidence."

"I have to get back to Hope," Abiriel announced.

"Tell her thanks for the tip," Ellen said. "It was the key."

Abiriel smiled, leapt skywards and spun out.

"We will take our leave as well," Zelig said.

"And I'm due back on the battlefield," Oriel said. "And Ellen... thanks."

She watched them all head off leaving her standing with Avner in the midst of the gardens.

"Do you want to go home?" he asked.

Ellen shook her head. "My guess is that I'm still in surgery. I think I'd like to miss that."

"Somewhere else?" Avner asked.

Ellen slowly turned in a circle as she gazed at the world around her. "I'm lost."

"How about the brothers," Avner suggested.

Ellen considered it. "I guess so. It's the one place where I always know I'm welcome."

In the Healing Facility, Raphael placed Daniel in a crystal chamber where sophisticated technology scanned every particle of his being. Though Daniel looked calm as he watched Raphael work, inside a small seed of concern registered. When the chamber finally opened and he could step out, Daniel looked to his friend questioningly.

Raphael studied the information passing on the holographic screen before him. Finally, he turned it off with a flick of his hand and stepped away.

"So...?" Daniel asked.

"No anomalies," was all Raphael would say.

"And that's good?" Daniel pressed.

Raphael grimaced briefly. "I can't disclose the results, Daniel. Let's just say, there aren't a lot of changes from last time."

A knot tightened in Daniel's stomach. He had no memory of last time.

"I'm sending you on to Michael," Raphael declared. "He's waiting at the Academy."

Daniel nodded and took off. He wasted no time in arriving at the aerial arena. Michael studied him as he landed.

"I need you to remove your shield and sword," Michael directed.

With a frown of confusion, Daniel complied.

Handing him training weapons and shield, Michael faced him. "Graduation drill," he barked. "Take your post."

Daniel blinked. *"Graduation?"* he thought leaping skyward and zipping toward a high platform. *"That feels like eons ago."*

He held his equipment at the ready and faced Michael on the opposing platform.

"It's a test of memory," Daniel realized, sucking air in through his teeth. *"He already knows I can fight."*

Behind his eyes, a stream of memory modules rushed past as Daniel sifted them for memories of his graduation day.

"Begin!" Michael ordered.

A shot came zipping at Daniel, and he just managed to dodge out of the way. Suddenly, he heard Michael's voice in his head as memories stacked up that were pertinent.

"The object of Graduation drill is to disarm your opponent by firing two shots or less."

At lightning speed, Daniel saw his entire strategy from years ago play out in his mind. Before Michael could fire again, he took off.

"The way to win," Daniel thought, *"is mental blocking and inter-dimensional hops."*

He instantly shuttered his mind and began disappearing and reappearing randomly around the arena. Michael knew Daniel's battle strategies well and was ready for him. The drill appeared ready to become a stalemate when suddenly Michael felt a tap on the back. He spun around to face Daniel's weapon at his throat.

"Score," Daniel announced.

"Win," Michael conceded. "Best three out of four rounds."

Daniel returned to his stand and awaited the opening command.

He won the next round, too, but it was obvious that Michael knew his moves too well.

"*Time to shift it up*," he thought.

"Begin!" Michael ordered.

Daniel began his normal pattern just barely staying ahead of Michael. Then suddenly he disappeared for an extended period. Michael rotated on his stand waiting for the internal signal that Daniel was about to pop through. For a moment, he thought he felt it, but didn't see him no matter where he looked. A puzzled frown crossed his face.

"Daniel, it's against the rules to hide inter-dimensionally," he yelled.

Suddenly, the platform rocked and Daniel sprang up from underneath landing directly in front of Michael with his weapon again raised.

"Score," he declared.

Michael threw his hands up and shook his head. "Win. That does it, Daniel. Gather your things and go see Mentor."

Daniel glided back to the ground, replaced his chest shield and strapped on his sword. Michael landed beside him. He started to open his mouth then closed it.

"I know," Daniel said nodding. "You can't give me the results."

Michael shook his head. "Only thing I have to say is I'm glad you're on our side."

He clapped Daniel on the shoulder and sent him on his way.

CHAPTER 35

Daniel flew up the hill to the familiar stucco, two story building and landed on the balcony. The doors were wide open; Mentor was expecting him. Daniel took a deep breath and entered. This school had always felt like home to him. His feet felt the worn plank floorboards through his boots and knew their way without direction. Mentor waited up ahead watching him closely. Daniel stopped when he reached his side.

Mentor studied Daniel's face and eyes carefully. He raised his hand and held it over Daniel's heart assessing its strengths and weaknesses. He nodded to himself and turned toward his ancient desk in the corner.

"Do you remember the simulator?" Mentor asked.

Daniel's mind flashed back to earlier times. "Yes."

"Let us go there," Mentor said.

He led Daniel through an arch to their right and over the edge of the hall to the floor below. Angels of all descriptions used the open space in the center of the building to traverse up and down the levels.

Mentor and Daniel headed toward a set of plain double doors and entered the room beyond. They waited quietly as a trainer and student completed a simulation. When they finished and had left, Mentor brought a bar down across the door. He turned back toward Daniel.

"Let me show you the child's purpose and timeline," Mentor said opening a screen between his hands.

Daniel watched a little blue-eyed, curly haired boy be born and his life play out to the end.

"Now, you will enter the simulation ring," Mentor instructed. "For every action and non-action, you must justify your decision based on the child's projected life purpose."

Daniel nodded his understanding, walked forward into the center of a circle built into the floor and turned to face Mentor.

The older angel gazed at him with compassion then announced, "Begin."

Immediately, Daniel was in the midst of the child's world, inside his home where the sun shone outdoors and chaos reigned within. Daniel estimated the child to be about seven and instantly knew that his name was Barry.

The little boy walked up the driveway to the front door wearing a back pack. He turned the knob and entered the house with his head down. Daniel was instantly alert.

"*He's afraid to be home*," Daniel thought.

Barry went to head upstairs to his bedroom but his father came into the room.

"Backpack," the man ordered.

Barry stood still on the stairs. Daniel put his hand on the child's back sending his strength into him.

"Stop," Mentor called. "Reason?"

The scene paused and Daniel stood upright. "The child's demeanor shows fear. The father's voice and stance suggest threat. There is an experience coming that the child is dreading. I'm offering him the strength to face it," Daniel replied.

Mentor nodded. "Continue."

The scene continued as Barry slowly turned around and descended to the living room. His father ripped the backpack off his shoulders, yanked on the zipper then upended the contents onto the floor. He picked through it till he found a note.

"Mrs. Johnson again," the father said in a mocking, sing-songy voice. "Teacher's pet. Gotta stay after school again."

The father grabbed Barry's arm and thrust his face into the child's. "What was it this time?"

"Nothing," Barry mumbled.

Daniel watched very carefully. As he shifted his vision to assess emotional stability he picked up two very important cues.

"Stop," he called.

"Assess," Mentor directed.

"This father is drunk and physically abusive. This is one of hundreds of times he has attacked this child," Daniel related.

Mentor nodded. "Go on."

"In assessing emotional levels and self-control, it is clear that with his present level of alcohol consumption and emotional state, he will either maim or kill Barry during this event," Daniel explained.

"Corrective action?" Mentor requested.

"Unsuspecting stranger at the door catching the father in action and calling the police," Daniel said. "Or father suffering sudden medical emergency requiring hospitalization."

"Which would you choose given his life purpose?" Mentor asked.

Daniel mentally scanned Barry's lifeline in his mind. "Stranger takes action," he replied.

"Justify."

"As an adult, Barry becomes a priest who protects children from abuse even when it means confronting superiors," Daniel said. "He must have an earlier life event that gives him faith in the power of the stronger to protect the weak."

"And why not the father with a medical emergency?" Mentor asked.

"Were that scenario to play out, Barry would carry the belief that he had 'magically' caused his father's ill health. He would hold himself responsible and unconsciously seek out life experiences to punish himself for causing his father's problem," Daniel delineated. "He would never become a priest and very well might also become an alcoholic thus passing the problem and purpose to yet another generation."

While Mentor's face remained a neutral mask, his eyes twinkled. "Thank you," he said. "You may go."

Daniel nodded, stepped outside the circle and waited at the door for Mentor to remove the bar.

"Raphael, Michael and I must confer before we give our recommendation," Mentor told him. "You have Time. Return to the Throne Room when you are called."

Daniel nodded in acknowledgement, exited the simulator room and left. He went back toward the Great Hall and entered the Banqueting Hall. Removing the cloud of shadows from his Choice Board, he stared at the options he had chosen. The very last one was "Continue as Ellen's Guardian." It was still locked in place and still lit up.

"*Wonder if it still holds with all that's happened*?" he mused.

Avner took Ellen straight to the Castle. The brothers immediately welcomed her, as she knew they would. Even Simon was there and came out of the dungeon to join them. She filled them in on returning Daniel's memories, minus a detail or two, and told them about the testing he was undergoing.

"He'll do fine," Alexander assured her.

"It's got to be just a formality," Edward added.

"Do they do formalities like that around here?" Ellen wanted to know.

The brothers looked at each other then down.

"Thought not," she said with a heavy sigh.

"I...agree with Wizard," Simon said quietly.

Ellen glanced up at him.

"I have been reading the angelic annals," he said. "I have read Daniel's story. Given what he has already accomplished, the probabilities are high with extreme confidence that he will succeed at this, too."

Ellen smiled. "For once, Simon, your statistics give me hope."

"Yes, ma'am," he said nodding in deference.

She raised an eyebrow in query and glanced at the brothers. They shrugged their shoulders helplessly.

Suddenly, Ellen looked around the room. "Did anybody see where Avner went?"

The three men shook their heads.

"Excuse me," she said rising and heading out the door.

The courtyard was empty as she jogged across it. Not sensing Avner within the Castle walls, Ellen went through the gate and stood on the road outside. To her right, she could see the new pier and activity around Toby's ship. To the left, a breeze rustled her hair. Something felt foreboding and for a moment, a dark figure seemed to rise up near the Forest.

With a worried frown, Ellen took off toward the Forest. Closing in, she suddenly heard a voice and ducked behind a tree on the hill. She edged around the trunk and peered out over the meadow before the Forest. A large, Minion-like figure stood in the midst of the meadow.

"You are mine," it raged. "You have always been mine."

It instantly shifted back to Avner. "I have my heart back, and my heart was given to the One of Light long ago. I have my son back. I am no longer yours."

The Minion figure rose up out of Avner's body. "Your brothers," it roared. "Would you abandon them, too?"

It shrank back down to the one figure of Avner now down on one knee. "What must I do to save them?" he asked.

And the Minion returned. "A trade. Your light for your brothers' freedom."

When the Minion shrank, Avner was now down on both knees. "And my children?"

The Minion rose up. "Your knowledge of the Light for their lives."

Ellen watched as Avner returned gasping. As he went to open his mouth, she darted out from behind the tree screaming, "No!"

The Minion looked up at her opening its mouth to roar, but Avner's visage battled with its. In the end Avner won. He stood upright staring at Ellen with little red eyes. He closed them and when they opened again, his clear blue eyes had returned.

"We should return," he said hoarsely.

Ellen nodded.

He grabbed her, leapt into the sky and rushed toward the Great Above. Landing in the formal gardens, he set her down and started toward the Meditation Gardens.

"Avner," Ellen called.

He stopped.

"Whatever he wants, don't do it," she urged. "It's a trap."

"It's my only choice," he retorted.

"There have to be others," she replied. "Give me a chance to find them."

"I'm running out of time," Avner said disappearing as he walked away.

"Ellen!" she heard a familiar voice call.

Ellen turned around to see Nariel gliding toward her. Nariel landed nearby. The two women hugged.

"The Facility is all abuzz with the news," Nariel told her.

"Look, Nariel, I don't want to be rude, and I know you're busy, but is there anyone around here who could help me get a message to the Wizard and the Priest?" Ellen asked.

"Well, you'd want Gabriel and his messengers," Nariel replied.

"How do I get a hold of him?" Ellen asked eagerly.

"I'll let him know you need a messenger," Nariel told her. "Where will you be?"

"Henry's old home," Ellen told her. "And thanks."

While Nariel went her way, Ellen took off down the road at a jog. She reached Henry's old Tudor-style house, reached under the doormat for the key, opened the door and hurried inside. She flew through the dining room, took a right into the library and frantically began scanning the shelves. Finding a book that piqued her interest, she pulled it off the shelf then sat at Henry's old desk.

Ellen opened the book, squinted to read the handwriting with its artistic flourish but found what she sought. Quickly, she opened Henry's parchment box and pulled out a sheet of paper. She opened the inkwell, picked up the quill and dipped it into the ink. She started scratching out a frantic message to the brothers and had just signed and sealed the message when she heard a knock at the door.

Ellen picked up the letter, left the library and opened to the door to find a tall angel with wavy golden hair and a large, open bag filled with scrolls and letters slung across his torso.

"I'm Gabriel," he said by way of introduction. "Nariel said you're looking for a messenger."

Ellen nodded while mentally tallying the number of documents he was carrying. "I am but I guess I should have been more specific. This," she said waving the letter, "is urgent...emergency type urgent."

"No problem. Where to?" Gabriel asked.

"Wizard and Priest at their University," Ellen replied.

He took it from her fingers. "First stop priority," he said turning.

"Oh and...can you wait for the reply?" she asked nervously.

"Return message also urgent?" Gabriel asked.

"Yes," she squeaked timidly.

"Done," and he disappeared in a blur of light headed over the cliff and toward the sea.

Ellen paced inside Henry's old house for a while then went outside and sat on the wall along the cliff. Before long, she noticed a streak of light heading toward her and stood up hopefully. In moments, Gabriel stood beside her. He reached into his bag and pulled out a return letter.

"Thank you so much," she breathed. "What do I owe you?"

Gabriel looked at her strangely. "Nothing. This is my job. Now, if I were you, I'd head back toward the Great Halls. I carry messages, not passengers."

Ellen didn't wait to see him leave. She locked Henry's house, tucked the key under the doormat and opened the message to read as she walked. She devoured each word carefully, shouted "Woo-hoo!" at the end, then ran the rest of the way to the Great Halls.

Though she was panting when she got there, she didn't stop. She ran up the stairs, slowed to pass the Wards at the door then hurried through the Throne Room toward the front. Again Michael, Raphael, and Mentor were already waiting beside the Embodied One. She glanced around and spotted Daniel just coming through the door. He acknowledged her as he approached but looked nervous.

Daniel headed straight towards the Embodied One and knelt before him.

"Rise."

Daniel stood with his head bowed.

"Let's hear the reports," the Embodied One said.

Raphael took a step forward. "I have thoroughly scanned every particle of his being," he said. "Physically he is 100%. The only change was to his light."

Daniel swallowed hard.

"Whereas before it was complete minus his memories, it is now whole including his memories," Raphael announced.

Ellen let out a sigh of relief, but Daniel waited motionless.

Raphael stepped back and Michael came forward. "I put him through the Graduation Drill," he opened. "Not only did he execute every move he made in his prior Graduation Drill perfectly, but in two subsequent drills, he bested me as well. I thought after all this time fighting beside him, I knew every move he had." Michael shook his head. "Fat chance. Daniel's more than battle ready."

Daniel had expected that. *"What else could Michael say when I beat him three times in a row?"*

His heart thudded in his chest as Mentor came forward.

"Daniel has always been one of my prized students," he began. "He has always assessed situations well and considered how best to aid his charge, but...." Mentor said pausing, "what he demonstrated in the simulator today showed an advanced ability to project consequences of his own actions on behalf of a charge as they apply toward the charge's life purpose. If anything, Daniel should take over teaching for me, and I should retire."

Daniel heaved a huge sigh of relief.

"Then is your assessment of Daniel in agreement with his return to full active duty?" the Embodied One asked.

"It is," Raphael, Michael and Mentor chorused.

"Daniel, welcome back," the Embodied One said. "Please resume your duties as Ellen's Guardian."

Ellen let out a warhoop, leapt at Daniel and threw her arms around his neck. "We did it!" she exclaimed.

Mentor smiled warmly enjoying the opportunity to savor his

265

favorite student's success.

Suddenly, Ellen let Daniel go, grabbed his hand and turned to leave. "Thank you, sir," she called over her shoulder to the Embodied One. "Gotta go."

"What are you doing?" Daniel hissed.

"Avner's in trouble and I've got the cavalry coming," she replied heading out the door. "Let's just hope we're not too late."

CHAPTER 36

"Where are they?" Daniel asked Ellen as they jogged down the Great Hall's stairs. "Who's coming? And what is going on?"

Ellen stopped at the foot of the stairs and looked up at him. She shook her head. "There's so much that's happened," she told him. "There's no time to fill you in."

"Let me tap your memories," Daniel suggested reaching toward her forehead.

Ellen ducked and shook her head.

"Ellen!" he exclaimed. "Why not?"

She cringed. "There are some things I'm not ready to share."

"Ellen," he insisted. "No secrets. We've never had secrets. What are you hiding?"

A most pained expression crossed her face. "Please, Daniel. Not now. Avner's in too much danger. We have to act fast."

Daniel's eyes narrowed as he studied her. "What-did-you-do?"

Ellen grew quiet. "Whatever it takes."

A cold chill trickled down his spine.

"Ellen! Daniel!" Alexander yelled from the corner of the building near the Cloister Walk.

Ellen snapped her head around, spotted the posse and took off toward them. Daniel followed more slowly, still trying to puzzle out her cryptic remark.

"Where is he?" Edward asked.

"He loves the farthest Meditation Garden," Ellen replied.

"It was built after he turned," Uriel reported.

"After he left for the Dark One?" Alexander asked.

"Yes."

"Aha," Ellen breathed. "That's why he stays there. The Dark One would have markers for every place except there. When Avner's in that garden, the Dark One can't trace him."

"Wait! What do you mean the Dark One?" Daniel demanded.

Oriel moved to his side, put Daniel's hand on his forehead and instantly shared recent events with him. Daniel broke the connection and turned to Ellen.

"He'll betray us all!"

She shook her head. "No! I watched him fight the Dark One. Besides, considering how long he's either been fighting beside Michael or guarding me? No way. It's because he learned to shield himself so thoroughly in the first place that he could reach out to me without alerting the Dark One."

"But it doesn't sound like you totally freed him," Chanochiel reasoned.

"I think he has some sort of tracker," Ellen replied. "I caught a glimpse of it once when I searched his mind. He shuttered it off fast. But he knows that I know."

"So, what's the plan?" William asked.

"He said he was running out of time, and he's looking to save his brothers," Ellen informed them. "If we move now, he may still be in the Meditation Garden."

Without hesitating, the Guardians lifted their charges and flew down the Cloister Walk. Unbeknownst to them, Avner glanced up at that moment, spotted Ellen and, with deep sorrow in his heart, disappeared.

The group landed in the center of the Meditation Garden and spent several minutes searching. Ellen went to the bench where she had often seen him sit alone. A small stack of acorns were piled on the seat. On top lay a single pink dogwood flower.

"He fed squirrels," William said coming up behind her.

"And this?" Ellen asked picking up the flower.

"Your favorite when you were little so father told me," William replied.

"Then he was just here," Ellen said glancing about.

"Looks that way," Edward agreed hurrying over.

"But why would he evade us?" William asked.

"To protect you guys is my guess," Alexander said.

Ellen thought back to the battle of wills she had watched. Suddenly, she gasped. "He's going to turn himself over to the Dark One to free his brothers."

The others looked at her in horror.

"The Throne Room," Edward and Alexander chorused.

"Hurry!" Ellen urged.

The Guardians picked up their charges and whisked them away.

As soon as Avner spotted Ellen with Daniel headed his way, he knew she was intent on finding an alternative plan. He'd tried that before without success. With his heart heavy, he lay down the things that always kept him company in the garden, the one place he hadn't known from before and where the Dark One couldn't find him.

Instead of looking up, he faded and space-shifted into the Throne Room. He headed toward the front and dropped to his knee. The Embodied One hurried down the steps toward him.

"Rise Avner," he instructed. "What is this urgency?"

Avner unbuckled his sword and held it out to the Embodied One then lay it on the floor. He popped off his chest shield and lay that before him also.

"I thought when Ellen returned my heart that I was free," he said in a low voice. "I thought once my children were safe, I was free." Tears streaked his cheeks. "The Dark One has hooks where nobody would expect to find them. I am sorry, Sire. It has been such an honor to serve you again."

At that moment, Ellen and company careened into the Throne Room. They ran toward the front and were halfway to Avner when they skidded to a halt. His body began vibrating and, without warning, was yanked backwards and disappeared. A collective gasp went up.

"What has happened in my own Throne Room?" the Embodied One demanded.

"Sir, I could explain but it would take too long and time is of the essence," Ellen said.

He waved her forward, placed his hand on her forehead and accessed her memories.

"The Dark One has been spying all this time?" he fumed.

"No sir," Ellen assured him. "I've seen what's there, and I've experienced the barriers Avner erected. He did everything he could to protect us and you. It's why he spent so much time in the back garden.

He couldn't be tracked there."

"But he's lost to us now," the Embodied One said slowly.

"No he's not," Edward cried.

"We've got a plan," Alexander declared.

"And technology," Simon added.

The Embodied One scanned the group. "Way Showers rescuing angels?"

"Come now, there's precedent for that," Ellen pointed out.

He studied her and smiled. "Yes, there is. All right. If you can rescue him and protect the secrets of the Light, go."

With no time to spare, Ellen rejoined the others. The Way Showers made a tight circle, and their Guardians huddled close in behind them creating a barrier with their wings. Edward and Alexander brought up a large Vortex to contain them all. Once it was stabilized, Ellen pulled out her pendulum, took William's hand and, together, they searched for Avner's signature.

"Got it!" she breathed.

The Vortex whirled faster and slowly lifted off. The Guardians placed a hand against their charge's back lending them strength and the Vortex shot off.

Avner arrived at the Dark One's throne already on bended knee. A roiling black cloud emanated from the Throne of Shadows. Within it, two bright red eyes pierced the Darkness that crept into corners and obscured the view of the Throne Room at every turn.

"I always knew you would return to me," the Dark One gloated sending chains lashing out from the Dark Cloud to ensnare Avner's wrists.

"My brothers," Avner demanded.

The One of Darkness waved its hand of dark mist. In the Prison of Light in the Great Above, ten Minions suddenly dropped to the floor of their cells writhing as horns receded, wings shifted and bodies transformed. They sat up feeling their skin and hair, and checking out white feathered wings.

In the Throne of Shadows, the One of Darkness hissed and steam curled out toward Avner, "They are free."

Avner sighed with relief.

"Now...our other deal," the One of Darkness said. "The secrets of the Light for your children's safety."

Avner went cold, the life draining from him. He saw William's and Ellen's faces in his mind, heard her laugh, thought of their camaraderie.

270

"I'm waiting," the One of Darkness insisted impatiently.

"Forgive me," Avner whispered, a lone tear trickling down his cheek. He looked up at the Dark One and shook his head. "I will not betray my Creator."

Before the One of Darkness could send his whip lashing out, Avner sucked his awareness deep into his being, retrieved his light and threw up impregnable walls. All that was left for the world to see was a babbling idiot on the floor.

Enraged, the One of Darkness lashed out again and again, the dark whip coiling about Avner's body. But Avner's awareness was no more. Furious, he paused and stared at his nemesis.

"You must weaken and I have all eternity to wait," he howled, drew back his arm to lash out again and froze.

Out of nowhere, a swirling Vortex popped into the throne room and hovered over Avner. It slowly lowered until it set down around him.

"How much time have we got, Simon?" Ellen asked.

Simon slipped a small holographic projector under Avner while monitoring a large, wrist watch like device on his arm. "I've temporarily slipped this piece of reality out of the time stream," he explained. "It will only last as long as its power module holds."

"Ok then," Ellen replied. "Simon, you monitor the time and be ready with the hologram."

He nodded.

"Edward, Alexander, be prepared to haul us out fast."

"Right," they chorused taking up positions behind Avner with their pendulums out.

Ellen took William's hand and positioned them in front of Avner.

"What are we going to do?" William asked.

"The Dark One wants the secrets of the Light," Ellen replied slyly. "So we're going to give it to him."

William's jaw dropped.

She turned to Daniel. "You know that cloud thing you put over your Choice Board?"

He nodded.

"Can you do one to reflect light?" Ellen asked.

A slow smile spread across his face. "That I can."

"Ok. Aloniel, Chanochiel, when that cloud goes up, and William and I expose our light, cut Avner's chains," Ellen instructed. "Then everyone get ready to move."

Everyone tensed.

"Ok Daniel, now," Ellen said quietly.

He stood in front of her and William and slowly wove a cloud of shadows that reflected the light. When he was finished, he stepped behind them. William and Ellen looked at each other, squeezed each others' hands and closed their eyes. Gradually, their inner radiance grew until their skin emitted light.

"Five seconds power remaining," Simon called.

The radiance before Avner grew until it became blinding.

Daniel glanced back over his shoulder. "Now!"

Aloniel and Chanochiel raised their swords overhead, drew upon their inner well of immortal strength and brought the heaven-forged blades crashing down upon the chains. There was a deafening metallic clang and the chains snapped apart in slow motion.

"Releasing time continuum...now," Simon announced.

The Dark One stared and let his whip fall from his hand. A huge ball of the purest Light emanated from Avner completely obscuring him from view.

"Ha! Weakling!" he exclaimed in delight. "I knew you would not resist me."

The Dark One rose off his throne and slowly crept toward the Light. In it he saw filaments of reflective shadow. He tilted his head this way and that.

"What is this?" he growled.

He reached out his hand and grasped a filament. Yanking it out of the Light, he took another and another and another. Gradually, the Light dimmed and he saw Avner behind it. In a rage the Dark One lunged through the Light prepared to strangle Avner, only he fell right through the angel. At first, shock registered on his misshapen face. Then he spotted a small, black box and picked it up turning it over and over in his hand. Suddenly, his face hideously contorted in violent rage as he crushed the box letting its dust slip between his fingers.

"I freed your brothers!" the Dark One howled. "You-owe-me!"

"Set a course for the Bridge of Dreams," Edward yelled.

"Visionary and Weaver are waiting for us there," Alexander said.

The Vortex swept out of the Dark Lands and over the countryside. It lifted up toward the Great Above.

"We don't have time for a gentle transition," Ellen shouted.

The Guardians all grabbed their charges, braced themselves and, as soon as the Vortex hit the Facility, yanked the entire Vortex through the portal. Edward and Alexander set them down in the center of the Bridge between the Great Dolphins. Hope, Abiriel and Nathan waited on the side closest to human reality.

Ellen looked around.

"We made the circle like you described it," Weaver said.

"It's perfect," Ellen replied. "How's the triangle coming?"

Oriel and Chanochiel were hovering over the abyss holding Edward and Alexander.

"Just about done," Alexander reported.

"Have you ever done anything like this before?" William asked.

"On a much smaller scale," Ellen replied. "And it never included angels and representations of darkness." She looked over at Simon. "Are you ready with that containment field?"

He glanced up and nodded.

Ellen took a deep breath. "Ok everybody. Get ready. This could be a bumpy ride."

CHAPTER 37

Ellen positioned herself near Avner's head. William held him upright because all tone had left his body.

"He's really in deep," William noticed as Avner's eyes rolled back in his head and his tongue lolled out the side of his mouth.

Ellen touched Avner's head. "That's ok. I'll find him."

She shifted herself internally several times until she was able to find the areas where his awareness had previously been. Recorded memories crowded around shouting and talking. Ellen pushed past them and kept tacking. Suddenly, she noticed a few sparkles. Edging closer, she smiled.

"Breadcrumbs!"

Following the trail Avner had left for her, she reached a thick dark wall so dense there was no way in or out. Ellen considered it for a while.

"*Wonder if this is like the mirrored cloud Daniel created?*" she thought. "*The harder I try to get through it, the more solid and impenetrable it becomes.*"

As an experiment, Ellen pressed her hand against it. The dark wall hurled her back.

"Wow!" she exclaimed slowly approaching it again. "What would let me in?"

Ellen closed her eyes and began to hum. "*Hm,*" the thought hit her. "*How would it react to light?*"

She stood before the wall and opened the shutter. Light poured out bathing the dark wall in a warm glow. She let herself breathe and be light. Slowly, she eased forward and was rewarded when the wall let her through.

Inside the den behind it, nothing much resided. Yet, Ellen spotted two sets of eyes; one small and red, the other one sad and blue.

"Avner!" she called softly. "If you hear and understand me, blink."

The blue eyes blinked.

"Are you trapped?"

They blinked again.

"Do you still have control of the barrier?"

They blinked one more time.

Not wanting to give their plans away, Ellen backed out and eased from his mind. She blinked her own eyes then looked around, the others finally registering.

"Did you find him?" William asked.

She nodded. "There's a minor Minion keeping him trapped."

"The tracker we're after?" William wondered.

"I think so."

"Do we still dare do this?" Visionary asked.

"We don't have a choice," Ellen replied bringing out her pendulum. "Ok, one Vortex as Minion vacuum cleaner coming up."

Ellen closed her eyes, let the pendulum swing and brought up a narrow funnel of howling wind containing a lightning storm within.

"Here we go," she announced directing it over to Avner and up onto the top of his head.

"Go!" she commanded.

The churning funnel entered the top of Avner's skull. As it did he started foaming at the mouth and shaking his head.

"It's not anchored there," William told her.

Ellen directed the funnel down through Avner's body. He spasmed and shook in response. When the funnel finally reached the soles of his feet, they heard a snap on one side and a ping on the other.

"Ok, that released it," William announced.

"Containment field," Ellen barked.

Simon crept to the edge of the Bridge, set down a glowing box, backed up and hit a button he carried in his hand. Vortexes on different axes erupted out of it.

"Ok, ejecting it now," Ellen declared bringing the funnel up out of Avner's head.

A pale Minion started writhing out of Avner's head. It screeched and stretched like rubber as its head and torso were pulled free but its feet were obviously anchored internally.

Ellen turned her head towards Hope and Nathan. "Any chance one of you could hold this Vortex while I try to release this thing internally?"

Abiriel instantly grabbed Hope and positioned her off the edge of the Bridge. In seconds, Ellen felt the Vortex yank away from her.

"Got it!" Hope called.

"Nathan, can you tell if this thing is anchored in more than one dimension?" Ellen asked.

Nathan moved closer and walked around the exterior of the circle. "You cannot free it, mother," he told her. "You do not exist in enough dimensions."

"Thanks," she told him. "Great," she muttered to herself.

"What now?" William asked.

Daniel touched her shoulder. "Michael taught me something that might work."

"Go for it," Ellen encouraged.

"You and William will have to move back," he told her.

Ellen nodded and moved toward the railing of the Bridge to help Hope with the funnel. William carefully lay Avner down and went to the edge of the circle without stepping over it.

Daniel took out his sword, held it before him, closed his eyes and shifted through dimensions. As he did, his sword gradually altered until it was a black handled, long, slender blade. Daniel opened his eyes, stood with his legs apart, knees slightly bent, the sword held horizontally before him and his shield hand held fingers pointing up and palm out.

In a flash, he raised his sword slicing through Avner in varying dimensional levels. The Minion howled and screamed. Nathan stood by carefully monitoring Daniel's progress.

"One more, father," he called.

Daniel spun around and ran the blade from the top of Avner's head all the way down through his body. The Minion zipped free of Avner.

"Into the triangle," Ellen yelled to Hope.

The two women shifted the funnel until the Minion was directly over the triangle. They dropped their arms and it plummeted into the holder.

"What's the safest dimension in which to contain it?" Ellen asked glancing over at Nathan.

"Limbo," he replied.

"Got that, boys?" Ellen asked.

Edward and Alexander gave her a thumbs up. As their pendulums swung, the triangle began to vibrate. Suddenly, the Minion seemed first to be nearly ejected out of the triangle then rapidly sucked back in. The triangle folded in on itself and winked out. The vast chamber was instantly silent.

Ellen hurried to Avner and dropped on her knees beside him. "He's pretty bad," she said dropping into her heart space and working to stabilize him.

Oriel and Chanochiel flew Edward and Alexander back onto the Bridge. Hope and Nathan crowded around as well.

Visionary edged closer to the circle. "We'll go alert Raphael," she told Ellen.

"Thanks."

Visionary and Weaver left with their Guardians. Moments later, Raphael and several healers appeared. Ellen moved out of the way and let him through. Raphael quickly scanned Avner.

"Get him to the Healing Facility, now," he barked to his healers.

The men quickly bent over Avner, hoisted him onto their shoulders and carried him away.

"Will he be all right?" William asked.

"That thing ripped up a good bit of territory inside him," Raphael replied.

Ellen bit her lip nervously. "Maybe we shouldn't have done that."

"And left him with the Dark One for eternity?" William exclaimed.

Raphael put his hand on her shoulder. "There was no way to extract that thing gently."

"Does it mean we and the secrets are safe now?" Ellen pressed.

Raphael nodded. "And the Dark One can no longer track him."

William and Ellen let out a collective sigh of relief.

Raphael turned and quickly disappeared.

Ellen looked up at Daniel. "Will you take me to the Healing Facility?" she asked.

"We're all going, "Edward declared.

Nathan came forward and took Ellen's arm. "Please, let me know how he's doing," he requested. "I cannot leave my post."

Ellen hugged him. "Definitely."

Nathan looked at Daniel blinking his amber cat's eyes. "Will you teach me that sword trick?" he asked.

Daniel nodded. "One of these days."

Hope came over with Abiriel. "How did you know I could hold the funnel, mother?"

Ellen looked at her and frowned. "Guess I assumed. You are my daughter after all."

"Yeah, well. I'd never tried anything like that before," Hope confessed.

"Nothing like on-the-job training," Ellen remarked.

"Ready?" Daniel asked.

"Yes."

Ellen put her arms around his neck and they joined the other Way Shower/Guardian pairs in a mass exodus. They all landed in the hall of the Healing Facility. William and Ellen went in watching as Raphael worked on Avner. They held their breath in anxious silence until Avner gave a cough and slowly opened his eyes. Raphael continued working on him then finally rose and approached the siblings.

"I have done what I can for now," he announced. "He needs rest."

"He needs Light," a deep voice from behind them announced.

They all turned to see the Embodied One standing behind them. They moved aside to let him through. He knelt beside the bed.

"Avner!" he called.

Avner opened his eyes and looked up. "Sire."

"Avner, my son, well done," the Embodied One said.

Avner smiled then coughed. "I could not betray you...or the Light."

"My faithful one, welcome home," the Embodied One said warmly.

Suddenly, ten angels faded into view in an arc around his bed. Avner looked up and smiled with tears glistening in his eyes.

"Brothers," he whispered.

"They were saved because of you," the Embodied One told him.

Avner spotted Ellen and William and began to cry. They knelt on the other side of the bed.

"We're here," William said.

"We're safe," Ellen assured him.

He reached a hand up to them. "I would not...give up...the secrets," he whispered. "You...will never...be safe."

"You can't protect us, father," William told him.

"And we would never have wanted you to betray the One," Ellen added. "We're proud of you."

Avner took her hand and kissed it, tears wetting his lashes.

The Embodied One looked at Ellen. "You always believed in the good in his heart."

278

She nodded.

"Was he good because you believed?" the Embodied One asked. "Or was he as good as you believed?"

"Frankly," Ellen replied, "it doesn't matter if in the end he's known as being good."

The Embodied One nodded. "Stand back," he requested.

William helped Ellen up, and they backed away. The Embodied One placed one hand on Avner's head, the other on his heart. He hummed low and let his radiance grow. After a few minutes, he stopped and took Avner's hand.

"Rise, son," he invited.

Avner threw off the covers, swung his legs out of bed and stood up. Those in attendance and in the hall outside cheered. William and Ellen hurried around the bed and embraced him. Avner put his hands on their heads then wrapped an arm around each.

"Avner, I'm afraid you and your brothers may not be safe for a while," the Embodied One said.

Avner looked up. "If we stay near the Light?"

"That is one possibility, but you are also worn from your struggles," the Embodied One added.

"Then what?" Avner asked. "Return to the Light?"

The Embodied One shook his head. "I have prepared a place for you. Rest. Speak to your brothers. Teach them well so they can freely return to my path. After an Age, you will return to my service."

Avner bowed his head. "We are grateful." He hugged William and Ellen and let them go.

The Embodied One drew a vertical line in the air and a slice of bright light shone out.

"Go and rest," the Embodied One invited.

Avner went to his brothers and ushered each one through the door. At last, it was his turn to go. He embraced William and Ellen separately, holding them close, content in their presence. Then he released them, stepped through the door and was gone.

The Embodied One raised his hands, his eyes scanning the Way Showers. "With me," he said.

They all blinked and found themselves in the Throne Room with their Guardians.

"I have much gratitude to share," the Embodied One declared. "I never quite dreamed what Way Showers could accomplish when working in cooperation."

They murmured amongst themselves.

"I don't think any of us dreamed it, either," Visionary admitted.

"If only this cooperation would transmit to the human realm," the Embodied One remarked.

"We have to find each other there first," Ellen said.

A curious look crossed Simon's face but he said nothing.

"Well, my father and I are pleased with our creations," the Embodied One said warmly. "We love surprises, and you haven't let us down."

CHAPTER 38

The Way Showers and their Guardians filed out of the Throne Room, down the stairs and into the gardens beyond. Visionary and Weaver were the first to say good-bye and leave for their mountain home.

Simon shifted his feet nervously until Ellen looked his way. He cleared his throat.

"I...um...have to thank you," he told her.

"For what?" Ellen asked.

"For telling me to 'be the hero' and for leaving me on my own," Simon replied.

"You came through," she said.

"Did you know I would?" he wondered.

She tilted her head to one side and studied him. "Yes, somewhere inside I think I did. I think you were tired of manipulating people. I think you wanted people to like you, but to break the walls you'd put up, it would take an all or nothing struggle."

Simon nodded.

"How's Susannah?"

He smiled shyly. "We're dating."

"Good," Ellen said hugging him. "Good for you."

He waved good-bye to the others and left with Aloniel for the Facility.

The brothers were next, eager for their hugs. Ellen held Alexander a little longer and whispered in his ear.

"You do realize that if I weren't married and didn't have the relationship with Daniel that I do, I would have been very interested in you," she told him.

Alexander blushed bright red. "Just come back soon," he replied huskily.

The brothers brought up the Vortex and took off.

William looked forlornly at Ellen. "Father is on a much needed break, and I take it you're headed back?"

"Very soon," Ellen confirmed. "I will really need to return soon."

He nodded and looked at the ground. "I miss you when you're gone," he told her. "You're like this piece of myself I never knew existed yet longed for."

Ellen slipped her arms around him. "Ever since I was a little girl, I longed for a brother. After my human father died, my mother remarried and for all sorts of reasons, it was a very bad fit with my stepbrothers. Finding you makes me feel like I'd love to stay here permanently... almost."

"I sometimes wish I could...end up in the human world," William told her.

"There's never a guarantee we'd find each other," Ellen warned him.

"You...don't know Simon in the human world?" William asked incredulously.

"I wouldn't even know where to begin looking," Ellen confessed.

He gave her one last squeeze. "I'll miss you till you come back."

She kissed his cheek. "Me, too."

Ellen watched as Uriel spirited him away.

Daniel observed her quietly. "Ready to return?"

Ellen shook her head. "I still owe you an explanation. Can we go to our home for a little while?"

He nodded and opened the silver door. They crossed through and slowly walked down the road. Ellen's feet dragged as she ascended the front steps. She let Daniel open the door and even carry her upstairs. She wandered out onto the balcony and stared out over the pond. Daniel waited silently beside her.

"I-I had cancer," she told him at last.

His eyes widened.

"Stage I, slow growing," Ellen continued. "I thought the hysteroscopy got it all. I felt so different when I woke up."

"Wh-where was I?" Daniel wondered.

Ellen glanced back at him. "Split."

282

He swallowed hard. "I'm so sorry."

She patted his arm and turned back to look at the pond. "The Great Red Dragon took me to the Monastery so I could purify my light and learn to read the <u>Book of Light and Shadows</u>. I hoped it would tell me how to save you."

"Did it?"

Ellen snorted. "After what the Abbott did to me, William and Avner had to come rescue me. I wasn't saving anybody after that adventure."

Daniel frowned. "Then how?"

She leaned against the rail. "The Embodied One offered me an option...one that would work only, I'd have to be as fully here as I was the times I nearly died."

"But he promised you wouldn't have to come close to death again in order to cross over," Daniel protested. "That's why you built the Bridge of Dreams."

"And I'm not near death," Ellen assured him.

"Then...how?"

She sighed heavily. "I was told by a specialist that I needed a radical hysterectomy to ensure the cancer would never come back. The Embodied One said I would be in the perfect state while under anesthesia to rescue you."

"Wait!" Daniel said placing his hand on her shoulder and turning her around. "Are you saying, you're in surgery now?"

"I'm not sure exactly where I'm at," Ellen confessed. "Avner wouldn't let me look, and I had to agree he was probably right."

Daniel studied her face, his own registering bewilderment. "But... why?"

Ellen pursed her lips. "On one hand, I wasn't ready to die. And on the other hand, I wasn't ready for you to return to the Light. It was the most difficult, most terrifying decision I've ever made, but I remembered all the times you'd taken those beatings for me and still told me 'Whatever it takes'," she reminded him.

"I thought that phrase sounded familiar, but Ellen, Dear One, you were never meant to reciprocate that for me. I should not have been some benchmark for your actions," Daniel chided gently.

She rubbed his arm as she gazed up at him. "Wasn't it? Aren't you the one who taught me about deep love? About giving all?"

Daniel's Adam's apple worked furiously but he had no words with which to respond.

Ellen fisted her hand and tapped his chest shield. "Still, it came right down to the night before surgery. I almost canceled. I was ready to call the hospital. I was so frightened."

He frowned. "What stopped you?"

"Robert," she confessed. "Up till then he hadn't said a word about how the surgery would affect him, but I wanted to know. It turned out that it meant the world to him, meant he had greater certainty of keeping me with him longer. "

Daniel smiled in spite of himself. "So, you had another reason to do what it takes."

Ellen nodded. "The two people I love most in my life. One I could have let down and at least you had resources. I would have regretted that later, I'm sure, but it was an option. But I couldn't let down Robert. Since the attack, we've clung to each other. He needed me; wanted me. I-I had no choice."

Daniel ran his hand through his hair. "So, you'll be coming out of anesthesia in a while."

"And I'll be in pain."

He wrapped his arms around her. "I'll be there with you every minute. I'll do anything I can do to soothe you or ease your pain."

Ellen started crying. "I know."

"I'll help you make it," he promised. "I just can't believe what you risked to help me and to be with Robert."

She smiled tightly. "Daniel?"

"Mm-hm."

"Would you make love to me one last time. I feel like everything that makes me feel feminine is being stolen from me. Please, I want one more time to feel like a woman," Ellen told him.

Daniel scooped her up in his arms and carried her inside to the bedroom. After setting Ellen on the bed, he doffed his sword, shield and boots and slid his pants off after. Ellen unbuttoned her blouse, unfastened her bra, and he watched her nipples harden in the cool air.

He moved toward her, taking her in his arms and holding her close. "Whatever you want," he whispered kissing the top of her head. "You are my only focus."

"Soft, slow, close, tender," she murmured softly. "Those are the things that make me feel most loved and feminine."

Daniel lifted her head with a finger under her chin and pressed his lips to hers. "You are most loved."

He nudged Ellen back onto the bed crawling in beside her and

284

gently trailing his fingertips over her chest, down between her breasts and fluttering them over her stomach. Daniel unfastened her pants, unzipped them and tugged them off along with her shoes.

Then, starting with her toes, he trailed kisses up her feet, ankles and legs till he reached her belly once more. He rubbed and caressed every inch of her body. Daniel took his time, watched her face, listened to her moans and held her close. As her body responded to him, he slipped his hand between her legs and felt her heat and wetness.

Wrapping his arms around her, Daniel shifted into position between her legs. As he slid inside Ellen's silken heat, he kissed her neck up to her jaw then molded his lips over hers and stole her breath away.

Moving slowly and deliberately, focusing on her pleasure, he suddenly thought of his wings. He pulsed inside her and licked his suddenly dry lips.

"I can give her that," he thought. *"One last time. It has always given her joy."*

Daniel kissed her again and looked into Ellen's eyes. "Touch my wings. Caress them."

She frowned, puzzled.

"It is your joy," he told her. "Take that joy."

Ellen placed her fingertips on either side of his mouth and kissed him in return. He moved aside and she crawled out from under him. He lay on his stomach awaiting her sensual touch.

Ellen trailed her fingertips down the join between his wings, and he shivered. She leaned over kissing, licking and mouthing his sensitive flesh. He gasped. She pressed her face to the base of his wings stroking outwards with her fingers. He moaned and fought to maintain control. After a while, she massaged down his back to his taut buttocks and kneaded them listening to his groans.

Unable to contain himself any longer, Daniel rose up, wrapped his arms around her and plunged himself into her welcoming heat as he lay her back on the bed.

"Keep touching my wings," he instructed.

Ellen didn't understand why but didn't have to be told twice. As she once more stroked the swan soft feathers, Daniel felt the angelic spark come together inside him. In moments he shared it with her.

They collapsed together, Daniel rolling off to one side and curling himself around her with his arms, legs and wings. He lay for a while listening to Ellen's slow, rhythmic breathing.

"Better take her back now," he thought after a while.

He vibrated on her frequency sending her into a deep, deep sleep. When Daniel was certain she wouldn't awaken, he eased out of bed and dressed. Then he wrapped a blanket around her and headed for the Bridge of Dreams.

Ellen heard hushed noises around her. No one talking, just the slight movements of someone shuffling papers. The next thing that hit was the pain, and it was a lot worse than she'd expected. She'd had open abdominal surgery in her twenties and a laparoscopic surgery after. Since the hysterectomy was being done laparoscopically by a robot, she had hoped for a pain level somewhere in between. But as she took a breath, pain stabbed her from her navel all the way down.

"Wake up, Ellen," Daniel whispered in her ear. "You need to wake up and ask for a pain killer."

Ellen forced her eyes open, the room appearing as a blurry haze. She closed them again.

"Come on, you can do this," Daniel urged.

She opened her eyes again, this time spotting a nurse off to her right who was quietly doing paperwork.

"Could I have a pain killer?" Ellen whispered.

The nurse immediately looked up, rose and got a syringe, which she injected into a port in Ellen's IV line.

"Thanks," Ellen said weakly.

"Would you like something to drink?" the nurse asked.

"Yes, please."

The nurse left and quickly returned with a cup of ice water and a straw. She gave it to Ellen who gratefully drank.

Several minutes went by as she lay there, then Ellen heard Robert's voice. She opened her eyes as he entered the room and tried to smile.

"How are you doing?" he asked, his face looking tired and worn.

"I made it," she whispered.

Another nurse ushered him back out and attendants came to wheel her to her room. By the time she got there, Ellen needed more pain meds. Soon after she was settled, a nurse brought Robert in. He tucked her belongings into her locker.

"How long was I in surgery?" Ellen asked.

"A long time," Robert replied. "Four-and-a-half hours."

"Oh my God," Ellen responded. "I had no idea it would take that long."

"When the surgeon called me in to tell me how the surgery went, she said you'd wake up in the recovery room in an hour-and-a-half," Robert continued.

"How long was it really?" Ellen wanted to know."

"Three hours."

"Whoa! I was either under anesthesia or sleeping it off for nearly eight hours!" Ellen exclaimed.

"Yes, and I didn't dare leave your things all day to go get something to eat," Robert told her.

"My goodness. Go eat," Ellen insisted.

"I think I need to," he said rising. "I'll be back right after I get some food in me."

Ellen watched him leave and let her eyes wander around the hospital room that was every bit as pretty and well-appointed as an upscale hotel room.

"Guess I was really busy elsewhere," she mused.

Daniel cradled her, letting the heat from his body warm and comfort her. "You were. And you were marvelous. But listen to me."

"Mm-hm," she murmured groggily.

"You've done enough, ok? You rescued William, me and Avner. You made a hard choice to reassure Robert. You're done giving for the year," he insisted. "The rest of this year is about you. You need to rest, regain your strength and heal. I won't let you do anything more."

Ellen smiled. "From where I'm laying, that sounds pretty good to me."

CHAPTER 39

As the days turned into weeks, Ellen wished she had a magic wand to zap away the pain. It lessened ever so slowly but was quick to return if she did too much. Her two month check brought cause for celebration when the surgeon announced pathologists couldn't find a single cancer cell.

The next day, she and Robert boarded a plane for Cancun for a much needed rest. With a balcony on which to catch the warm ocean breezes, an infinity pool below for soaking and a beach for luxurious sunning, they both felt much of the tension of the last six months ease away. Every night they sat out on their balcony and watched the fake pirate ships from town sail by with their rigging lit up like Christmas trees advertising a party cruise.

Once they returned home and Ellen was more comfortable, she decided to cross the Bridge.

"You're sure you're up for this?" Daniel asked.

"I think so," Ellen replied. "I'm finally off the pain meds and sleeping through the night. I'd like a change of scenery besides the house, and this is the only way I'm going to get it."

"Ok," Daniel replied letting her settle into bed before singing her song and easing her into the Between Worlds.

They came out on the trail that approached Nathan's station. While Ellen gave him a hug and briefly chatted, something sparkled and caught Daniel's eye. He walked over, noticed a bubble and touched it. Immediately, there was a pop and Ellen turned toward him. He stood with his eyes fluttering and his face taking on a soft glow.

She moved toward him and touched his arm. "Did you leave memories here, too?"

He looked up slowly and smiled. With a deep breath, Daniel put his arm around her shoulders and approached Nathan. Their son blinked his amber cat's eyes.

"I am sorry I could not come to your aid," Nathan apologized quietly.

Daniel shook his head. "Don't be. You are exactly where you are supposed to be."

"To guard the passage between worlds," Nathan iterated.

"But, do you even have anyone besides Simon and me crossing?" Ellen wondered.

Nathan nodded.

"Have you actually picked up any dark hitch hikers?" Daniel probed.

"Yes. I have barred three travelers from crossing over because of what they carried within them," Nathan responded.

Ellen frowned, but Daniel took it in stride.

"This is exactly why we built this way station, why Nathan, who can see all the dimensions, is posted here, and why the Dolphins scan everyone. The possibility of minor Minions gaining entry was too great to ignore."

"Could there ever be a time when they tried to overpower him?" Ellen wanted to know.

"It is for that very reason that I wanted to learn your sword technique," Nathan added.

"Michael's," Daniel corrected, "but I can see what you're both saying."

He gently pushed Ellen back out of the way and studied Nathan. "You see all the dimensions, but can you shift your body into any others?"

Nathan blinked. "I have not tried."

Daniel nodded, turned Nathan around and put his hand on the center of his back. "I want you to shift your vision into another dimension. I will shift your body so you can feel what that's like."

Nathan nodded and focused.

"That's it," Daniel said in a low voice. "I see that. Now feel this."

Slowly, Nathan's body changed until he appeared in human form. Ellen walked around to see.

"Good job," Daniel commended. "Now try another."

Nathan continued to concentrate. The next shift gifted him with wings like his father.

Daniel let him feel that then let go of the shift, and Nathan returned to his silvery blue self.

"Those are dimensions you're familiar with," Daniel commented. "Try shifting into them on your own, then try to shift into unfamiliar dimensions," he recommended. "You need command over those shifts before you can work with the sword."

"Thank-you, father," Nathan said. "I will practice."

Daniel clapped him on the shoulder then he and Ellen left. When they got to the Bridge, they paused for the Dolphin scan.

"You know, if you left a bubble of memories back there, would you have left any elsewhere?" Ellen asked.

Daniel turned his head from side-to-side, spotted a bubble and headed straight for it as soon as the Dolphins released them.

"Not too many more," he said. "It is feeling fairly full in here."

Ellen appeared lost in thought then suddenly brightened. "We stopped near my capsule in the Facility."

Daniel nodded. "Let's go."

They went through the portal on the other side of the Bridge into the Facility and headed straight for her capsule. Sure enough, another bubble bobbed there. Daniel touched it and absorbed those memories as well.

He shook his head. "So much happened to us," he remarked.

Ellen pursed her lips. "But I don't remember us going anywhere else in the Lower World. You didn't leave memories there."

Daniel cupped her cheek and caressed his lower lip with his thumb. "Some memories, Ellen, serve a purpose. And when they've served their purpose, it's better to let them go and not constantly try to pick them back up."

She leaned into his hand. "I know I could sure use a case of selective amnesia for a few things," she agreed.

He let her go. "Where to?"

"Oh, the University," Ellen replied. "If I don't show up there, the brothers will never let me live it down."

Daniel chuckled, led her outside, picked her up and headed out. Just before he veered over the cliffs, a sparkle off to his right caught his attention. He made a mental note to come back.

When they reached the University, no one was in the Castle. Ellen dowsed locating activity down below, so Daniel flew her down to the pier to check things out. A small, bustling seaport village was now clinging to the rocky cliffs. Ellen spotted the Teacup and Bed sign that had been Betsy's Inn in the Sea Town south of there and hurried up the narrow, winding lane with Daniel following. As soon as she got to the door, Ellen knocked. After a few moments, the door open and Betsy peeked out.

"Ellen! Daniel!" she exclaimed throwing the door wide open and drawing them inside. "What a lovely surprise! You must have a cup of tea."

The pair entered, took a seat in the parlor and were soon sipping hot tea.

"So, are you and Toby staying up here permanently?" Ellen asked.

"We'll have to see," Betsy replied. "It all depends upon whether there are actually students or not."

"Then no one else has come through?" Daniel wondered.

"Oh, there is Simon," Betsy replied. "A bit odd, if I don't say. And there have been two young ladies and a gentleman."

Ellen's eyebrows raised. "Well, that's a start."

"Yes, but if you ask me, Wizard...I mean Alexander, is a bit disappointed," Betsy told her.

"Where is he anyway?" Ellen asked. "The Castle is empty."

"Oh, they're all down in the Sea Cave," Betsy told her. "Toby's helping too."

Daniel frowned. "What are they all doing there?"

"Hoping to create a staging ground for the Water Challenge, I think," Betsy said.

Ellen and Daniel stayed a little while longer then left and headed across the beach toward the large, dark opening in the cliff below the castle. As they neared, they could hear the low, echoing booms of the waves hitting the rocks and above that, the yells of men at work. Daniel picked her up and flew her inside. They landed on a wooden platform at the water's edge and watched the scene.

Edward and Alexander balanced what looked like a large glass bubble on a Vortex while Toby and his men manned the ropes attached to it from long boats in the water. They worked together to slowly lower the bell into the water and set it within a metal stabilizing ring. Once it clanged into place, Ellen was astonished to see the Undersea King and some of his people swim up inside it and secure the bubble in place.

Once done, the Sea People left, Toby and his men rowed out of the cave, and the brothers joined Ellen and Daniel on the platform. The brothers each gave her an enthusiastic hug.

"What do you think?" Edward asked surveying their efforts.

"I'm impressed," Ellen replied. "I can't believe you got the Undersea King to help."

"He's more amenable now that you removed the barrier," Alexander explained.

Ellen and Daniel both felt chills go down their spines. When Ellen had undertaken the Water Challenge, she had nearly made it to the end but the Water barrier the Ice Queen had put in place stopped her. Together, she and Daniel had broken through it, but she herself hadn't made it. Daniel had walked her into the Light, the most gut-wrenching moment of his very long life. But Hope's Angelic Spark had been waiting to send her back, though only her Soul Crystal had remained. Daniel had been captured and turned into a Minion against his will while Ellen had had to reform her body around her Soul Crystal before she could come to his aid.

"That's probably one of those memories you left behind," Ellen said mentally.

Daniel winced. *"I thought...hoped I had. But it echoes loudly in my spirit,"* he replied in kind.

"Want a ride in our elevator?" Edward asked heading towards a cast iron, gated contraption hanging from a thick cable that ran through a large hole that had been bored down through the rock.

Ellen looked it over dubiously. "Where does it go?"

"Straight up," Alexander replied.

"Can I just meet you up top?" she asked. "There's no floor on that thing. You can look straight down."

"And that bothers you?" Edward asked.

"And how," Ellen replied.

Edward and Alexander both stepped inside onto the iron grating. "You fly all over with angels, but our solidly constructed elevator bothers you."

"Uh-huh," she replied.

They shut the gate, threw the lever and the contraption started creaking upwards. Ellen shivered.

"Meet them up top?" Daniel asked.

"Oh yes," Ellen replied slipping her arms around his neck.

They flew out of the Sea Cave and up to the Castle. Daniel landed in front of the gate. Ellen spotted William heading toward them along the road from the Forest and waved. William spotted her, waved back and started jogging.

"I left a few more memories for myself at my parents' home,"

Daniel informed her. "Mind if I leave you and go retrieve them?"

Ellen shook her head. "No, go ahead. Just remember to come get me."

Daniel nodded and took off.

William reached her side a few minutes later and swept Ellen off her feet.

"Been down to see what the brothers are doing in the Sea Cave?" he asked.

"Just came from there," Ellen replied as they headed through the gatehouse. She spotted a door and a set of steps off to the left. "Does that lead to the Castle walls?"

William nodded.

"Want to?"

"Sure," he replied leading the way.

They climbed the narrow, smooth stone steps and came out on the wall walk in the bright sun. They ambled along the wall till Ellen found a spot with a good view of the sea.

"So, how long are you here for this time?" William asked leaning his arms on the parapet and staring out at the endless waves.

"Just till the night is over," Ellen replied.

He glanced over at her, looked back out to sea and nodded.

Ellen frowned. "What's wrong, William?"

He glanced down for a moment before turning toward her. "I just miss you...that's all."

Ellen studied him carefully. "I miss you, too, but...there's more."

William stood up fully and ran his hand through his hair. "I don't belong...anywhere," he told her. "All that time spent on that island so isolated and alone. I thought, if I could only be around others again, I'd be happy."

"But you're not," Ellen concluded.

He shook his head. "There's no place for me, no job for me to do, no person who makes being here feel worthwhile...."

"Avner's gone," she surmised.

"And no place feels like home," William admitted. "The only time I really feel content is when you're here."

"And I can only stay so long at a time," Ellen told him.

"It never seems like you come often enough," William complained.

"I know," she admitted. "After the surgery, the pain just didn't let me sleep soundly at night."

His face blanched. "I'm sorry. I forgot about that. How are you doing?"

"Better," Ellen told him, "but I've been told it could take a full year to completely heal."

William swallowed hard. "I wish I were there and could help you."

Ellen patted his arm.

He slid his arm around her shoulders, held her and leaned his chin on the top of her head. They stayed like that for a long while, brother and sister, staring out to sea.

In the Great Above, Daniel had returned to his parents' home. He set down near the tree swing, found the memory bubble he'd left and touched it. Several layers of children's laughter broke free and entered his heart. A moment later, he heard footsteps in the grass and slowly turned. His father approached with a smile on his face.

Daniel studied him. "Mother had the child."

Zelig's smile broadened. "Come...meet your new sister."

Daniel's heart leapt in anticipation as he followed his father back inside the house. His mother was in the sitting area, her wings neatly tucked into a chair while she rocked the cherub. Daniel knelt beside her, gently brushed his fingers over the baby's sweet face and let her grasp one of his fingers in her tiny fist.

"At least maybe one of my children will have a different path than that of Archangel," Zelig said hopefully. "I'd like to see them now and then."

"Oh Zelig," his mother chided. "We're proud of each one of our boys."

Zelig held Daniel's gaze. "That we are, Aviva. That we are."

Daniel stayed for a while longer till he felt his inner alarm go off. He took leave of his parents and sister, headed back to the Castle and retrieved Ellen. Once she was home, she spent a lot of time thinking. He watched and tried hard not to mentally pry, but one name kept registering. *"William."*

CHAPTER 40

Two weeks later, Robert had an overnight trip to lecture, and Ellen took the opportunity to cross the Bridge again. Daniel eased her to sleep and beyond, and they stopped at Nathan's station. He was particularly happy to see them.

"I've been practicing, father," he announced.

"Let's see," Daniel encouraged.

Nathan stood before them and slowly shifted through a long set of dimensional figures. Daniel nodded, his eyebrows raised in appreciation of his son's budding skill.

"Speed could be faster," he commented. "But the changes feel very solid."

Nathan squared his shoulder proudly.

Daniel gently moved Ellen back and drew his sword. He motioned for Nathan to do the same.

"All right. Take a solid stance," Daniel instructed setting his feet shoulder-width apart. "Grasp your sword and raise it up before you. And this time, instead of making the physical shift in your body, channel the shift out through your sword."

They worked together for several long minutes before both of their long swords narrowed into a darkened, slender, curved blade.

"Excellent," Daniel told him. "Now shift into another dimension. Hold that resonance, and channel that through the sword."

Again, father and son worked together side-by-side. At one point, Daniel put his hand on the back of Nathan's neck and helped him adjust.

But once he got it, his amber eyes shone.

"You've got the idea," Daniel told him. "Keep practicing. You will get it. Then just apply that to your sword training."

Ellen observed the two men quietly. For all the time Nathan hadn't spent with them while growing up, it was obvious he idolized his father.

As she and Daniel walked out the back door leading toward the Bridge, she took his arm as they walked.

"Nathan looks up to you so much," she told him.

"He is an honorable young man."

"Yes, but while you're working with him, you don't see his eyes," Ellen responded. "He hangs onto every word you say, every move you make. Your teaching him this sword technique means the world to him."

Daniel frowned. "I'm not sure I should inspire idolatry in him."

Ellen blew out a breath. "It's not like worshipping you," she tried to explain. "We were absent from his childhood, but he had to have heard stories. And now this great man, his father, thinks enough of him to teach him. He wants to live up to that."

Daniel nodded. "Like I look up to Michael."

"Exactly," she said finally moving on after the Dolphins finished their scan. "Which makes me think, when did Michael teach you that?"

"On the battlefield," Daniel replied emotionless. "Minions would be woven into the fabric of the barriers. He taught me to be his Pair, and we would cut the Minions out to weaken the barriers."

She nodded.

Once through the Facility and outside, Daniel looked to Ellen for direction. She held out the pendulum and looked perplexed.

"Looking for William?" he asked.

"Yes, but he's not with the brothers," Ellen replied.

"Where is he?" Daniel asked.

"He's up here...I think at Henry's," she said, a mystified look on her face.

"Let's go," Daniel said ready to fly her.

She looked up apologetically. "Do you mind if I go alone?"

"No, go ahead," Daniel replied watching her turn and head off along the road that ran along the cliff.

For once there were no pressing issues, no quests to undertake. He stood looking around then set off on his own allowing his feet to take him wherever they would.

Meanwhile, Ellen reached the old Elizabethan style home, noticed the door was ajar, pushed it open and tip-toed inside. She glanced around not noticing anything out of place.

"William?" she called and started edging forward.

In the library, William sat at Henry's old desk with a thick, black leather volume open to a page near the middle. He ran his finger along under the lines, scanning quickly before flipping to the next page. He heard a voice then the creak of a floorboard.

"William! There you are!" Ellen cried.

He nearly fell off his chair, hastily stuck a slender piece of white silk between the pages and snapped the book shut. He turned toward her and smiled.

Ellen hurried forward, gave him a hug and peered over his shoulder at the title of the book.

"Way Shower Lives," she read. "What's that about?"

"Seems Henry found a way to collect information about every Way Shower ever born," William told her. "He kept the information here."

"Probably used his Universe," Ellen murmured opening the book to the first page. "Hey, it's about you!"

"Don't read that, Ellen," he pleaded trying to take the book from her.

But Ellen had already picked up the book and headed for a nearby armchair. She sat down, swung her legs up and draped them over one chair arm. William held his head in his hands.

"Huh! You weren't just a tad arrogant, were you?" she asked still reading.

"Maybe," William muttered.

She winced. "Ooo! Fight! Really?" Ellen glanced up at him over the book.

He nodded, chagrined.

"Doesn't look like you and the Tavern Owner will ever be best of friends," she commented.

William pushed his chair back, scraping it along the floor, got up, took the book from her and closed it.

"Those weren't my better days," he admitted. "Just leave them be. I'm not that person anymore."

Ellen studied him closely. "Is that why you're having a hard time fitting in, finding your place?" she asked.

"Maybe." He set the book on the desk. "Plus, it seems that everyone except the monks have spent time in the human realm."

Ellen shook her head. "It's not all it's cracked up to be. Trust me,

William. If I didn't have Robert back home, I guarantee you I'd take up residence here."

"At least you have someone," he pointed out. "When you're not here, I have nobody."

"So who were you reading about?" Ellen asked curiously.

"Just...Way Showers...looking at where they've been...what they've done," he said evasively.

Ellen took a deep breath and sighed. "Ok. You're lonely and purposeless. I'm here. What do you want to do?'

William thought for a moment. "Take a walk," he suggested. "You can tell me what it's been like to live in the human world."

They got up and headed for the door. "Only if I can gloss over some of my more painful moments."

William frowned. "I guess, but save them for another time."

So the siblings strolled arm-in-arm along the road, Ellen telling stories from her childhood and life growing up; William hanging onto every detail.

As soon as Daniel took Ellen back at the end of her night, William called Uriel and headed for the University. He entered, crossed the gravel courtyard and made his way toward the Dungeon. As luck would have it, Simon was in.

"William, want to see my latest modifications to the system?" Simon asked as soon as he heard his footsteps on the cobbled floor.

William bit back what he was dying to ask and said, "Sure." Listening to Simon seemed to be the key to getting information later, he'd found.

"I discovered a way to entangle the quantum computer I'm building at home with this one here," Simon explained enthusiastically.

"So, what does that mean?" William asked, a tingle flying up his spine.

"It means that while I'm here, I can tap in there and access information from the human world," Simon replied.

William found a seat, drew it closer and looked at the screen. "Does this mean, if I had some information about Ellen, I might be able to locate her there?"

"What have you got?" Simon asked.

William started sharing some of what he'd read in Henry's book.

Simon entered the information and waited. Finally, he shook his head. "The search seems to go out into the human world, but it doesn't return a response here."

298

William hung his head.

"You need me to find her there?" Simon asked watching him closely.

"I'd like to know if it's possible," William replied.

Simon considered. "When I go back after this night, I'll start the search. If I find her, I'll let you know. Meanwhile, I'll have to work on the quantum entanglement."

William straightened up. "Thanks. I appreciate it."

Once Ellen and Daniel returned home, life went back to a routine until one afternoon she heard the doorbell ring. Thinking it might be the mail woman with a package, she hurried down the stairs, opened the door and stood staring in shock. On the other side of the screen stood a tall, lanky young man who looked vaguely familiar.

"I'm Simon," the young man announced. "I found you, Ellen."

She pressed her hand to her mouth and opened the door as if in a dream. "How in the world...?"

He smiled knowingly. "Priest and Wizard helped," Simon replied following her upstairs and out onto the deck.

Ellen got him some iced tea then sat out with him.

"They read through one of Henry's ledgers, which by the way, is now scanned into the quantum computer," Simon told her. "Found little bits of information. Robert's a professor at a university in the northeast. That at least narrowed down the territory I'd have to search. I didn't have to search the whole country."

"Internet searches did the rest," Ellen surmised.

He nodded. "I just wanted you to know, I'm real. I wanted to know it wasn't all a dream. We're...not alone."

Ellen smiled. "It feels so...strange to be able to talk with you here."

She jumped up, got a 3X5 card and wrote her phone number and email address on it. He took out a business card and handed it to her.

"Now...we can get a hold of each other," she mused staring at his card.

Simon got up to leave but paused as he was going out the front door. "Oh yes. Wizard says, 'Don't forget to visit. We have real students now'."

That night when Ellen crawled into bed, she made up her mind. "It's time I go back," she told Daniel. "If the brothers have real students coming, real Way Showers crossing over, I want to see."

He smiled and waited for her to get comfortable. Once she was tucked in, Daniel sat on the edge of her bed, sang her song and eased her into the Between Worlds. As they approached Nathan's sentry post, they could see him practicing with his sword through the clear door. They let the door slide open and waited till he acknowledged their presence.

"That looks pretty awesome," Ellen commented as they stepped inside.

Nathan blinked his amber cat's eyes. "Thank you." He looked to Daniel for confirmation.

"Let me see from the beginning," Daniel instructed.

Nathan began the routine all over again. Daniel watched carefully, shifting his vision between dimensions to perceive the changes. He nodded as he watched. "You're getting pretty good."

"Well, let's hope you never have to use this technique," Ellen said.

Nathan brought his sword down in front of him and shifted dimensions until he and the sword were completely in a common dimension. "I have already used it once."

Ellen frowned and Daniel looked concerned.

"What happened?" Daniel asked.

"A man tried to cross who was a Minion wearing a human suit," Nathan replied. "When I denied him passage, he attacked. I separated Minion from suit."

"But where did the Minion go?" Ellen wanted to know.

"When this station was devised," Nathan explained, "a device was included to remove the Minions."

"I guess the Embodied One knows where they go?" Ellen asked uncertainly.

Daniel nodded. "I would think, but it wouldn't hurt to ask." He looked up at Nathan. "Did you report the attack to the Embodied One?"

Nathan nodded. "Immediately."

"Was he concerned?" Daniel pressed.

"He seemed to have been expecting it," Nathan replied.

Ellen sighed. "I guess Avner was right. William and I will never be safe because the Dark One wants pay back."

"But I am on guard," Nathan said drawing himself up to his full height.

Ellen went over and gave him a hug. "And apparently, I have a lot to thank you for."

She gave him a kiss, and they left. Once outside the Facility,

300

Daniel flew her straight to the University.

They were surprised to find a couple dozen students crisscrossing the courtyard of the Castle. Ellen headed for the Chapel first, opened the door and entered. She and Daniel watched Edward carefully shepherd new arrivals into the Flames of Truth. He spotted her and hurried over.

"You really do have people here," Ellen said as she hugged him Edward beamed with pride.

Daniel and Ellen left and headed to Alexander's Sea Facing Tower. She heard his voice echoing down the spiral staircase and hurried up. Half-way up he had built a new room for his Universe. It was obvious from the updated control panel that Simon had helped with the install. At present, Alexander was busily sending a group of students through his back door. When they whooshed out, he hopped off his chair and headed over for a hug.

"You were such a Gandalf/old man sort when I first met you," Ellen remarked shaking her head in wonder. "But now, look at you! You're so energized and vibrant."

"I was going to be a Professor of Philosophy or Physics," he told her.

"And now, you are a professor," Ellen concurred.

She and Daniel retraced their steps down the stairs, and she checked in the Dungeon where Simon was working with a couple of computer technicians. He turned in his seat, spotted her and quickly finished. He walked over offering Ellen a shy smile.

"You still want a hug?" she asked gently.

He blushed and she gave him a quick squeeze.

"I wanted to warn you, William's not here," Simon told her.

"What do you mean 'he's not here'?" she asked concern edging her voice.

"He...felt out of place," Simon replied. "He had the Embodied One place him in the human world."

"As a baby?" Ellen asked.

Simon shook his head. "As an adult. He wanted to find you."

Ellen blanched. "But he has no skills. He has no idea what it's like. How will he survive?" she fretted.

"I gave him as much background before he left as I could," Simon told her.

"But, will the Embodied One even place him in the same time period as me?" she worried, turning to Daniel.

He shook his head. "I don't know but we can find out."

"Throne Room?" she asked.

He nodded and sent a message to the Great Above.

"Thanks for letting me know, Simon."

He nodded. "If I come across him over there, I'll send him your way."

She nodded.

"Ok, the Embodied One is waiting," Daniel told her.

"Let's go," Ellen said securing herself in his arms.

In a flash, they were standing in the Throne Room of the Great Above. Ellen hurried toward the Embodied One.

"Where did you send William?" she asked breathlessly. "What time period? What country?"

"He is where he asked to go," the Embodied One replied.

"In the human world with no prior reference for what that world is like as an adult," she charged.

"That was his desire," the Embodied One confirmed.

"But...how will he survive?" she pressed. "He has no vocational skills. No job, no money...he'll be homeless."

"Apparently, he has a strong faith that I will thoroughly support him on his quest in spite of what he seems to lack," the Embodied One replied evenly.

Ellen blinked hard looking like she'd just been slapped in the face.

"Ellen," the Embodied One said, "when Way Showers are born into the human world, they forget who they are and have to rediscover themselves. They also forget I promised to fully support their mission. With William entering the human world as an adult, he will remember who he is, what he's capable of, what his mission is and knows my support is ever present."

Ellen shrank and swallowed hard. "I may just become jealous," she said. "That sounds so...relaxing. No worries; just trust."

"We are looking to see how we can make it the same for those of you who were born there as well," the Embodied One explained.

"I think if he ever does find me, that will pretty much be my proof," Ellen remarked.

The Embodied One dismissed them, and Daniel took her home. For several days Ellen remained lost in thought.

"Are you worried about William?" Daniel asked.

"Not as much as I'm worried he'll show up on my doorstep and I'll have some explaining to do to Robert."

"Think it might be time to tell him?" Daniel prodded.

"Yeah, sooner rather than later, too," she replied.

That Sunday morning as Ellen and Robert sat on their deck watching the birds fly to and from the back yard feeders while they ate breakfast, Ellen finally mustered the courage to mention the topic.

"You know how you used to ask me where I went when I was in the coma and had pneumonia?" she asked.

Robert nodded.

"I wondered if you still wanted to know," she asked.

"Yes. I was just waiting for you to be ready to tell me," he responded.

Ellen took a deep breath. "I crossed over into the realm the angels live in," she began. "I found out there are people called Way Showers who have special capabilities because they're a cross between male Archangels and a human mother."

"And you're one of these Way Showers?" Robert wanted to know.

She nodded. "But so are you."

"Just what do Way Showers do?" he wanted to know.

"Well, in your case, you see patterns of information and figure out ways to perceive them differently," Ellen told him.

"And no one else does this?" he pressed.

"How many scientists have come up with some of the concepts you've developed lately?" she pointed out. "Didn't that one editor a couple of years ago tell you your paper was the most innovative in your area to come out in a decade?"

Robert considered this for a moment then slowly nodded. "So are there other Way Showers besides us?"

"There are some who permanently live in the angelic realm," Ellen explained. "They were badly injured here on Earth and were given the option to stay there instead."

"Are there any still on this side?" Robert wanted to know.

Ellen nodded. "In fact, one of the guys I'd met while in the angelic realm tracked me down here about a month ago. Kind of spooked us both out because we were forced to acknowledge we hadn't been dreaming."

Robert looked puzzled. "You talk as if you still go there."

Ellen nodded. "We all got together on that side and built the Bridge of Dreams so I wouldn't have to keep nearly dying to cross over and so others could find their way over."

"Bridge?" Robert queried curiously.

She nodded.

"That's interesting because a couple of times I had this dream that I was standing on this bridge looking up at these giant...."

"Dolphins?"

His eyes widened. "How did you know?"

"They're self-intelligent beings that scan everyone who comes and goes to make sure that no harmful elements of Darkness cross over," Ellen explained.

"Then...it wasn't a dream?"

Ellen shook her head.

"Wish I remembered more," he mused.

"When it's really important to you, you will," Ellen assured him.

CHAPTER 41

A man in his early forties road a bus north from Pennsylvania. He sat near the window, his shoulder length, wavy, auburn hair partly obscuring his face. He stared at the passing scenery without really seeing anything. The bus pulled into a small town on a long, narrow lake. He waited his turn at the stop then stepped out into the aisle and reached overhead for his duffel bag. He stepped outside into the hazy sunshine, scanned the area and finally headed toward the lake.

He walked across an overpass and found a black-topped trail that ran along the shore of the lake. People jogged past in gloves and hats. Dogs walked along sniffing here and there. The wind off the lake was cold, and he buttoned up his leather jacket and pulled on a knit hat.

He pulled out his wallet, opened it and counted the money he'd saved from his last job. Just before he closed his wallet, he stared at the picture on his driver's license.

"William de Foe," he muttered. "Hard to get used to seeing my face staring back at me."

He slid the wallet back into his pocket, his fingers touching his pendulum fob. He pulled it out and spent a few minutes with his back to the wind dowsing out his next move.

"Ok, credit union not bank," he said and pocketed the pendulum.

William redirected his footsteps back toward town. He crossed the busy, one way road that ran past a local market, spotted the sign for a credit union and felt the hairs at the nape of his neck stand on end. With a nod to himself, he entered and soon had opened a savings account.

On the way out the door, he spotted a woman in her forties, with blonde hair and a distinctive, personal style headed toward the employee entrance. Ellen's face flashed through his mind overlapping this woman's and he knew he had to act fast.

"Excuse me," he called. "Do you have a moment?"

The woman stopped, turned toward him and offered him a big smile. "How can I help you?"

"I...uh...just arrived in town," William began frantically wondering just what to say. "I've been searching for my sister. We were separated at birth."

"Twins?" the woman exclaimed.

William nodded.

The woman extended her hand. "I'm Katrina. I wish I could help you but I don't know of anyone who's missing a twin brother."

"Maybe you'd know where I could find a place to stay," William offered.

"Actually, I just may. Do you have something I could write on?" she asked.

William felt his pockets and pulled out a business card someone had given him. Katrina quickly jotted down a name and phone number on the back.

"This is my friend, Danni's, number," Katrina told him. "One of her tenants just broke his lease to move, and she's desperately looking for a new tenant so she can make her mortgage. Tell her I sent you."

William smiled. "Thank you. You've been a big help."

Katrina watched for a moment as he walked away. "*I'll help him find his sister,*" she thought, "*if he doesn't mind going to dinner first. He's hot. I've got to tell Ellen about this.*"

A few days later, William began his new job at the local university pushing his custodial cart through the halls and going office to office cleaning. He religiously read the name plate of each professor when he reached their door. He drew the business card from his pocket, checked the name, sighed and shoved it back in.

A couple of weeks later, he was moved to another set of buildings to work. Whereas the previous set of buildings had been older brick structures, the latest set were definitely newer. William continued his routine and worked his way from the lower floors to the top. He left the elevator, turned the corner then another and stopped his cart just a little past a lab door on his right. Pivoting toward the office door on his left,

306

he looked at the name plate and his heart nearly stopped. With his hand shaking, he retrieved the card from his pocket.

"Robert Pompea," he breathed.

William swallowed hard. How was he going to know if this was Ellen's husband? He knocked on the door then opened it. "Have any trash or recycling?" he called.

The middle-aged man at the desk turned toward him and smiled. "Hi! My trash is there," he said gesturing behind him, "and I just have a couple of more items for recycling."

Robert stood and rifled through piles of papers, grabbing a couple of handfuls. "You're new," he remarked, tossing the papers into the blue recycling bin.

"Yes, both to the area and to this building," William admitted as he walked in and picked up the two bins. He turned and spotted a picture of Robert and his wife hanging on the wall.

Robert noticed his gaze. "That's my wife, Ellen," he said proudly. "Picture's a little old. It's from our honeymoon, but it's my favorite."

William simply stared unable to take his eyes away.

"Is something wrong?" Robert asked.

William swallowed hard, set down the bins and drew his wallet from his back pocket. "I've been searching for my sister," he replied, his eyes never leaving the picture. "All I ever had was this photo of a little girl. I had an artist age her in a drawing."

With trembling hands, William pulled a folded piece of paper from his wallet, opened it and handed it to Robert. Robert took the paper and compared the drawing to Ellen's picture.

"It does look a lot like Ellen," he agreed handing the drawing back, "but she's never mentioned a missing brother."

William shook his head. "She probably never knew. I didn't know until my mother admitted to stealing me from the hospital when I was born. She gave me what little she could remember on her death bed, and I've been trying to find my sister ever since."

Robert sat in stunned silence. "Do you know where you were born?"

William took out a weathered birth certificate and handed it to him.

"Same hospital, same day, same year," Robert remarked. "That's a little too much sameness to be a coincidence."

William's heart started a rapid staccato. "You don't suppose your wife would be willing to meet me...just so we could see?"

"Do you have a phone number or email?" Robert asked. "I'll talk to her tonight and see what she says."

William quickly wrote down his information on the piece of paper Robert pushed toward him and spent the rest of that day and night on pins and needles, half-hoping and half-fearing he'd finally found Ellen.

The next morning after a fitful night's sleep, William received an email from Robert.

"My wife says she would be happy to meet you," Robert said. "Would you like to have dinner at our house tonight?"

With his heart in his throat, William typed and sent his reply. This day couldn't go fast enough and 6:30 pm couldn't come soon enough.

That evening at 6:15pm the doorbell rang. Boodles raced to the top of the stairs barking loudly. Ellen was in the kitchen checking meat under the broiler, so Robert hushed the dog and hurried down the stairs to open the front door.

"Are you nervous?" Katrina asked her as they worked in the kitchen.

"My hands are shaking so bad, I'm afraid I'm going to drop something," Ellen confessed.

They heard Robert open the door and say, "Hi. Come on in." He held out a bag of dog treats and shouted to be heard over the dog. "If you give one to Boodles, she'll calm down. It's how we let her know who's friend or foe."

Ellen and Katrina heard the treat bag rattle then the dog came trotting into the kitchen and crawled into her crate to chew.

William appeared at the top of the stairs.

"Ellen, Katrina, this is William," he announced.

William said "Hi," in a shy, quiet voice.

Ellen waved and turned back to the stove. Katrina turned toward the stairs and stopped dead in her tracks nearly dropping the pot she was carrying. Ellen glanced over at her.

"Hey, you're supposed to be keeping me grounded," Ellen teased. "What's up?"

"I know him," Katrina breathed. "He needed a place to stay when he got into town, and I sent him to Danni's. He's renting one of her units."

Ellen's eyes flew wide open. "You mean...he's the hunk you've been babbling about?"

Katrina nodded as William followed Robert into the dining room toward the platform rockers, and Boodles hastily left her crate to check them out...mainly for more treats.

308

"Oh my God!" Ellen exclaimed softly.

"Honey," Robert called. " William thinks he may be your brother."

Ellen set down the dish she had in her hands, stepped out of the kitchen into the dining room and never once took her eyes off William. The transition from the angelic realm to the human realm seemed to modify some features, but the familiarity was there.

"You two look a lot alike," Katrina said following her.

William handed Ellen the birth certificate and drawing. Ellen picked up her birth certificate off the stand and compared them.

"Ok, right down to the exact same time?" Ellen remarked. "My mother told me about the other babies being born that day, one before and one after. She said nothing about another one at the same time."

"According to the woman who raised me, your...our mother was given a heavy dose of ether," William explained.

"Yes," Ellen agreed. "She was. Mom said they put her into twilight sleep."

"So it was nothing for this woman to spirit away a twin without her knowing about it," William said.

Ellen turned to Katrina. "Is he for real?"

"Brigit says yes," Katrina replied.

Ellen shyly gave William a hug and whispered in his ear. "What are the real names of Priest and Wizard?"

"Edward and Alexander," he whispered back.

"Who is my Guardian Angel?" she persisted.

"Daniel and mine is Uriel," he responded without hesitation.

William reached into his inside jacket pocket and pulled out a long, white angel feather. He handed it to Ellen. "Do you remember this?"

Her jaw dropped as she gingerly took the feather clearly remembering when she had found it in the Marauder's prison cell, and William had braided it into her hair. Suddenly, Ellen clung to him.

"You're real! Oh my God, you're real!"

"And I found you," William replied holding her close.

When they finally pulled apart, Robert took William's jacket to hang in the hall closet, and Ellen introduced Katrina. He studied her closely as if he should know her. While Ellen returned to the kitchen for their meal, the two talked.

"I feel like I've met you," William said.

Katrina nodded. "You stopped me outside the credit union looking...."

"For my sister," he completed, recognition lighting his eyes. "And

I needed a place to stay, so you sent me to Danni. I have to thank you for that. Apparently, you were a life saver for both of us."

Ellen bustled in with the food, and the four of them were soon laughing and chattering away like old friends. When the evening wore on and it was time to go, Robert went to retrieve their coats.

"Can I use your phone?" William asked Ellen. "I don't have a car so I need to call a cab."

"Oh, don't do that," Katrina protested. "Danni's place is right on my way home. I can drop you off."

William looked at her shyly. "Are you sure you don't mind?"

"No, it's really on my way home," Katrina insisted.

"It is," Ellen asserted.

"Well, yes. A ride would be great," William agreed.

He took his jacket from Robert and helped Katrina on with hers. William turned to give Ellen a hug.

"I can see what you mean by 'human reality isn't all it's cracked up to be'," he told her.

"How so?"

"Part of me thinks, 'Of course I found Ellen. That's half my purpose for being here'," William confessed.

"And...?"

"There is this piece in the back of my mind that thinks this whole thing is just crazy," he admitted.

"Welcome to my world, brother," she said and gave him a kiss on the cheek.

Ellen reached for Katrina to give her a hug. "Now, don't stay out too late," she whispered.

Katrina giggled. "We'll see."

As William and Katrina headed down the stairs and out onto the front deck, Ellen heard Katrina ask, "So, is it too late to stop for a cup of coffee?"

Ellen was pretty sure William agreed only if he could buy. She shut the door behind them and smiled.

Ellen spent a lot of time in silent contemplation after turning off her light that evening.

"Does it make me an abject fool for spending so much of my life worrying that I won't have what I need or want?" she asked aloud.

Daniel sat on the edge of her bed. "No. You've had to discover who you are. And even with this evidence right in your face, you're still
310

going to revert to your habit of worry. But it's going to be harder and harder to stay there. You have too much physical proof otherwise now," he told her.

"This is scary, Daniel," Ellen whispered. "I can't go back to being small anymore, can I?"

"No," he replied. "No, you're two worlds have collided. You can never go back."

EPILOG

In the days that followed Ellen's reunion with William, he spent as much time as he could with her. Often he stayed for dinner and was relieved to find Robert welcoming of his presence. Now and then, Katrina joined them and laughter would fill the house.

"This is what I was missing all those years," he thought as he basked in the warmth of companionship.

More often than not, William left with Katrina, and Ellen watched as their friendship began to take a more romantic turn.

One Sunday afternoon, William sat in a maroon platform rocker in Ellen's dining room watching as she and Katrina hung lightweight objects from the ceiling fan. Robert stood nearby and led them in an exercise to see if they could get the objects to move from a distance. When a small, blue, stained glass angel began to visibly swing, Katrina let out a squeal of delight.

Without a second thought, William smiled warmly at her enthusiasm and listened as the women bantered back and forth. A moment later, Ellen glanced his way, caught his look of admiration as he watched Katrina and grinned inwardly.

In his chair, William pulled his pendulum out of his pocket and watched it swing. Ellen broke away from the game heading as if to go up the hall. Instead, she paused beside him, bent over and whispered in her ear.

"Checking out the future of your love life?" she teased.

William's face burned bright and he caught and pocketed the

312

pendulum.

Ellen pulled back a little noticing his discomfort. "Are you falling in love?"

"Maybe," he grumbled.

Ellen gave him a hug around the neck. "Good. You two would be happy together."

That night Ellen lay in bed thinking. She didn't even realize that she'd left the light on way past her bed time. Daniel noticed and eased onto the side of her bed.

"Worried about your brother and Katrina?" he asked.

Ellen jumped, startled. "Oh Lord! I was lost in thought."

"Not about William and Katrina?"

Ellen shook her head. "I was kind of hoping they'd get together," she admitted.

"Then what?" Daniel probed.

She took a deep breath and let it out slowly. "William being here in this reality...Simon finding me...I can't pretend all of those experiences in the Angelic realm were just dreams."

Daniel nodded.

"But instead of this knowledge making me feel better," Ellen continued, "I find myself plagued with questions...questions and no answers."

Daniel tilted his head. "Like what?"

"Why can I only become the Light in your world?" she began. "Why doesn't what I know there translate here? What really is my purpose? And in the midst of the big questions, the personal ones. How can I feel like a woman again? How can I feel strong and good about myself? The list feels endless," Ellen complained.

Daniel furrowed his brow. "I can't answer most of those."

"But I want answers, Daniel," she protested. "I need them. I don't even know my own body now. I don't know how to tell when it's comfortable or not. I look in the mirror and, between this pixie cut and the sudden weight gain, I don't know who that person is staring back at me. I feel lost!"

Daniel sighed. He knew it was all true. "Come. Let's cross the Bridge tonight," he suggested.

"Do you think the Embodied One would see me?" Ellen asked reaching over to turn off her light.

"I've already sent a message," he replied.

"Thanks," she said sinking under the covers and closing her eyes.

Before long, Daniel had eased her to sleep, into the Between Worlds and over the Bridge. When they left the Facility, Daniel paused.

"The Embodied One is attending another matter. He will call for us," he told her.

"I don't want to go far," Ellen said.

"Let's go to our home," he suggested.

She nodded and in no time they had stepped through the silver door and were walking down the dirt road.

"Want to sit by the pond?" Daniel offered.

Ellen nodded and let him lead her to a log on the bank. She sat down and he straddled it facing her. He moved closer so his knee touched her thigh. Ellen gazed out over the water watching a family of swans gracefully swim past.

"I may have a solution to some of the personal things that bother you," Daniel said quietly.

Ellen turned back to look at him. "Oh?"

"Remember the last time we were here?" he prompted.

"When we finally retrieved your memories," she said.

Daniel nodded. "I had you...," he took a deep breath as heat surged through him, "touch my wings."

Ellen reached up and kissed him. "I never forget those times."

He pursed his lips trying to rein in the desires that were quickly overtaking him. He nuzzled her cheek pressing his lips to her ear. "I cannot experience that without producing a spark and passing it to you."

Ellen sat very still thoroughly entranced by the warmth of his body so close, the press of his face to hers and the heat of his breath against her ear and neck. "Do you mean I have an angelic spark in me now?"

Daniel nodded against her, moved his head slightly and kissed her cheek. He kissed down her jaw line to her chin then sampled her lips.

"But...I can't have children in any dimension now," Ellen protested.

"The spark isn't for child making," he whispered kissing her neck.

Ellen leaned into his kisses, her head beginning to spin. "You are making it very hard to think," she murmured.

"So are you."

Ellen finally kissed him again and pulled back. "What do I do with this spark?"

Daniel took her hand and licked his lips. "This spark...inside you... is all angelic. It's eternal."

314

She nodded for him to continue.

"You can tap it, use it if you will."

Ellen frowned. "For what? How?"

He tenderly touched her cheek. "It is embryonic potential waiting to be guided by thought since there is no blueprint for a child within you."

"Like stem cells?"

Daniel took a moment to access what he had picked up of human science. He nodded. "Yes. But it is infinite and eternal."

"So I can keep using it over and over again?"

He nodded. "Say you wanted to grow your hair long again. You could direct those cells to rebuild your hair, make it grow faster."

Ellen considered this. "That would be nice. At least I'd look more like me. But what about more weighty issues?"

Daniel thought. "Well, say you wanted to feel more feminine to yourself. You could direct those cells to rebuild what the surgery took away."

Ellen's eyes widened. "Are you serious? Regrow organs?"

He nodded. "Or heal yourself. Since they are nothing but potential, there is no limit to what you can direct them to become."

"Just for myself?" Ellen asked, her eyes narrowed.

"They are within you and have no more purpose now except for what you give them," Daniel explained.

She nodded and opened her mouth to speak. Daniel held up one finger.

"Time?" she asked.

He nodded, stood and gave her a hand up. With one swift move, he opened the silver door and whisked them through into the Throne Room. They hurried down to the front where the Embodied One waited.

"You had questions for me?" he asked as they approached.

Ellen reached his side. "Dozens when I was back home."

"And now?"

Ellen ran her sweaty palms over her jeans. "There's so much I don't understand," she began. "I became Light here, became one with you. But at home, I almost can't remember what it feels like or access that state. Yet, it feels like I must."

The Embodied One nodded. "It is important but you won't experience it the same at home as you do here."

"Why not?" Ellen wanted to know.

"When you walked into the Light after the Water Challenge, did you see your father or did you feel his presence?" the Embodied One asked.

Ellen thought. "I felt him and understood his meaning without words."

The Embodied One nodded. "Had he been able to live here, you would have seen a recognizable physical form but it would have been different from the body they laid in a casket."

Ellen thought about Henry and how he had appeared. Given that his body had been going through torture when he chose to remain in the Angelic Realm, the difference made sense.

"Doesn't William look different in the human realm compared to how he appeared here?" Daniel prompted.

Ellen's eyes widened. "Now that you say that, yes. Both he and Simon look different in the human realm but recognizable. What I notice more is a familiar feel to them and their personality matches what I know."

The Embodied One nodded. "Each world creates an experience of its own."

"Kind of like watching me change as I access different dimensions only less drastic," Daniel added.

"So, what you're saying is that I just have to learn how becoming Light feels in the human realm," Ellen concluded.

"Exactly!" the Embodied One said.

"Then, am I supposed to be using it for myself or others?" Ellen wanted to know.

"Both," the Embodied One replied. "When you come up against a challenge, ask yourself how much of my Light you can be for that challenge. And then allow for change."

"This sounds too easy," Ellen remarked skeptically.

"It will become easier the more of yourself you become," Daniel said.

"Huh?"

"In the Monastery after the Abbott's treatment, how did you feel?" the Embodied One asked.

"Like I was sick and going crazy. There was so much Light, and I couldn't tell where I ended and anything else began," Ellen replied.

"In that moment, you were closer to your true self," the Embodied One explained. "The Abbott removed the filters that create separateness and a sense of physicality. In that environment, there were no markers for you to navigate, which is why you felt sick."

"But that's who I really am?"

"In that moment, you were more a being like your father is now," the Embodied One explained.

"And when I became your Light?" Ellen pressed.

"You embodied your father and all that is because that is who I truly am," the Embodied One replied.

Ellen rubbed her temples. "Somewhere inside, I feel like I get it."

Daniel rubbed her back reassuringly.

"Ok, another question," Ellen said.

The Embodied One nodded.

"How does all of this fit into my purpose? What is my purpose?" she asked.

The Embodied One looked to Daniel and nodded. Daniel turned her to face him.

"What are you always trying to do for yourself?" he asked.

"Get healthier, fix problems, feel better," Ellen listed.

"But do you do that by staying the same?" Daniel prompted.

"No. That would never work. I have to dig to find the space in me that needs to change so the other things can happen," Ellen replied.

"And what happens to people around you who come into contact with you?" Daniel urged.

Ellen thought for a moment. "Well, some of them have pretty big life changes, even if we weren't doing anything 'serious'."

"Robert not the least of these," Daniel pointed out.

Her brow furrowed as she turned toward the Embodied One. "So, am I some sort of change agent?"

"You are, at your core, transformative power. You transform yourself and when others get near you, they find themselves transforming as well. They cannot help it because of who you are," the Embodied One explained.

"So, you mean if I'm just a presence in someone's life, if they're around me long enough, they'll change?"

"Not even length of time. You comprehend time/space," Daniel pointed out. "If they need transformation, your presence can make it happen right away."

Ellen looked shell-shocked. "This is what people mean by being?"

Daniel and the Embodied One nodded.

"Sometimes being needs a mental intention first," Daniel said, "but there isn't much to do."

Ellen held her hand up. "This is going to take a little time to sink in and digest."

"Yet, if you allow yourself, you will find you already know this," the Embodied One replied. He slowly turned to Daniel. "I sense a question in your heart."

Daniel's face turned red, and he looked most uncomfortable.

"No question is a wrong question, Daniel," the Embodied One said kindly.

Daniel nodded and cleared his throat. "I-I've sensed that more of Ellen's learning experiences will be in the human realm from now on. I... uh...wondered...what now becomes of our...." Daniel's voice faltered.

The Embodied One smiled. "Daniel, you are her Guardian for life."

"Yes, but...."

"I think he means the relationship we have at the home you created for us," Ellen interjected quietly.

Daniel looked to her gratefully then down at his feet.

"Yours is a unique relationship yet not the only Guardian/charge symbiosis I'm investigating," the Embodied One admitted. "I have watched the resonance and coherence between the two of you increase. In turn, that seems to produce an even more strongly bonded partnership that allows for changes to grow and expand at exponential rates."

"So, what does that mean for us?" Ellen wanted to know.

"That you have my blessing until you walk into the Light for your long deserved rest," the Embodied One replied.

Daniel raised his head, took Ellen's hand and brought her hand to his lips. She slipped her arms around him and stood on tip toe to give him a kiss. The Embodied One observed quietly.

"So this is how the bond is strengthened...by this sharing of soul," he thought.

At last Ellen pulled back and Daniel wrapped his arm around her to lead her out of the Throne Room. They had only taken a few steps when she turned back.

"Why?" Ellen asked, her voice bright and clear against the silence.

The Embodied One, who had begun his return to the Light on the Throne, stopped and seemed to glide backwards. He paused and turned his head.

"I understand the accident, the pneumonia, even the cancer," Ellen said breaking way from Daniel and moving toward the Embodied One. "I needed to be able to experience this realm as fully as possible. But why the attack?"

"Ah," the Embodied One breathed.

"And if it was just an attack on me so a Minion could place a tracker, why was Robert involved?" Ellen pressed.

The Embodied One stood breathing silently for a moment. He finally put the palms of his hands together. When he gently eased them apart, a holographic medium stretched out into the room. Within the medium, Ellen saw people moving and between them semi-transparent barriers of all densities and colors.

"Do you see how many barriers have been built up in your time?" the Embodied One asked.

Ellen nodded as she stared pensively at the hologram.

"The more dense the barrier, the older it is and the more human thoughts have added their energy to its formation," he explained.

"These are what Michael's army assails," Daniel said quietly. "We do what we can from this side to weaken the barriers, but if no one or not enough people assail it from the human side, the Minions repair it, often weaving themselves into its structure, thus distorting the original message."

"It must be hard to dislodge humans from the barriers," Ellen surmised.

The Embodied One nodded.

"Is that the why?" Ellen asked looking up at him.

"Partly. It takes a huge experience to shake humans free of deeply engrained barriers," he admitted.

"But that's not all?" she pressed.

He shook his head. "To dissolve these barriers, it will take humans radiating Light. But you cannot fill a blocked vessel. The blocks must be broken free and removed in order to hold and radiate more Light."

"The deeper and more intense the darkness you experience, the greater amount of Light your physical body will allow you to hold and radiate," Daniel added.

Ellen stared at him. "You've known this?"

He nodded solemnly.

"In fact, you've even seen how much Light I will be capable of holding," she pressed.

Daniel nodded again.

"Th-that's why you had to stand back and allow things to happen to me," Ellen whispered in awe.

He looked down, swallowed hard and nodded.

"How did you manage?" she wondered, laying her hand on his arm.

Daniel raised his head and held her gaze. "Each time I witnessed your hardships, I held an image in my mind of what the outcome would be for you. Sometimes, I even projected it as a filter over what I saw happening to you. The goal...knowing where you were going...made most things bearable...just."

"So...did you ever see me getting to this point?" Ellen asked.

Daniel smiled and his face grew radiant. "Here and so much further. And I will be with you every step of the way."

To Ellen, it felt as if her heart might burst. Then the Embodied One dissolved into Light while Daniel and Ellen allowed themselves to slip away into its embrace.

Ellen awoke the next morning and glanced about her bedroom. She shook her head and blinked her eyes.

"*Was it all a dream?*" she wondered, throwing off the covers and crawling out of bed.

A flash of white caught her eye and she turned toward the wall above her bed. There, hanging from a peg was the white, angel feather William had given her.

Ellen smiled and headed upstairs.